the RAT CATCHER

the RAT CATCHER

HUGO AUGUST DETECTIVE SERIES, BOOK ONE

REBECCA BARRETT

WITCH CREEK

PUBLISHING

The Rat Catcher
Hugo August Detective Series, Book One

© 2023 Rebecca Barrett

Published by Witch Creek Publishing

The story, all names, characters, and incidents portrayed in this production are fictitious. No identification with actual persons (living or deceased), places, buildings, and products is intended or should be inferred.

Library of Congress Control Number: 2023909397

ISBN 979-8-9883075-0-1(Paperback)
ISBN 979-8-9883075-1-8 (eBook)

Stock image ID: D5BEC1 license from https://Alamy.com

Cover Design and Interior Formatting by Becky's Graphic Design®, LLC
www.BeckysGraphicDesign.com

Printed in the United States of America

For Leslie and Kathy

More than gems in my comb box shaped by the God of the Sea,
I prize you, my daughters . . .

One

Hugo rested his forearm along the top of the door as he stared into the open Frigidaire. The freezer box was thoroughly encased in frost and he tried to think what the frozen lump fused to the ice trays might be or when he might have placed it there. His gaze drifted down to the contents of the refrigerator shelves. Except for the ketchup and mayonnaise, the remaining items were just as iffy to identify. He reached in and grabbed a can of Budweiser. As he closed the door, he saw the box of Lucky Charms sitting on top of the refrigerator and grabbed it, too.

He turned up the volume of the radio as he settled into the over-stuffed, fading, wing-backed chair in the front room of the shotgun rental house he now called home.

Forney was calling the game. *"Coach Bryant is conferring with assistant coach Mal Moore. The kicker is warming up on the sidelines. It looks like they're going for the field goal. The Bear is trying to repeat his success of '65 with another national championship."*

Hugo popped the top on the can of beer.

Forney was giving the line-up for the kick when someone banged on the screen door. Hugo crossed the small room to look out into the bright afternoon light. Junior Knight stood on the other side of the screen, hands in the pockets of his trousers, and a cigarette dangling from his lips.

"What?" Hugo stared at him through the screen.

"Got a dead old lady over on Dauphin Street."

"Dead how?"

"Don't know. Heart attack, maybe."

"So? What's that got to do with me?"

"Old society dame, that's what."

"Can't they call her doctor?"

"He's at the game."

"Of course he is." Hugo sighed, set the nearly full can of beer on a small table by the door. "You might as well come on in while I get a shirt."

He went through to the middle room of the house that served as the bedroom. From the armoire he pulled a clean shirt off a hanger and slipped it on over his tee shirt. He snatched a tie off the back of a ladder-backed chair and knotted it loosely. It was Saturday for Christ's sake.

Junior stood over the old radio, his body listing slightly to the left, a satisfied look on his face. Hugo crossed the room toward the front door, scowling as he pulled on a sports coat. It looked like he would miss the rest of the game.

"Come on," Hugo growled as he hit the frame of the screen door with the palm of his hand sending it banging against the exterior wall. As he cleared the small front stoop in two long strides, a turquoise and white '56 Chevy burned rubber away from the curb at the next house over. Hugo glanced to his left.

Maurice stood on his front porch looking after the car as it sped away. He wore what appeared to Hugo to be a woman's floral print housecoat tied at the waist with a sash. It was way too short for his gangly frame. Maurice turned, glared at Hugo, and went back into his house, a mirror image of Hugo's own shotgun. The door slammed behind him.

Junior looked from the neighbor's front stoop to the Chevy disappearing two blocks away. "What's that all about?"

Hugo grunted. "Let's get this over with."

"How much you got on the game?" Junior trailed behind Hugo to the car.

"I don't bet when Bama plays."

"Superstitious, are you?"

Hugo ignored the question and slid onto the passenger seat of the city issued sedan.

Junior got in behind the wheel. "Shouldn't take long."

"Long enough." Hugo tried to tune the car radio to the station broadcasting the game but all he got was a lot of crackling static. With a sigh, he turned it off.

He hadn't had a free Saturday in the two months he'd been on the job. The chief had seen to it that he caught every crap call that came into the station. Well, he'd bear it. For now.

It was hot for early November and Hugo had on a lightweight wool sports coat. He adjusted the side vent of the Ford Fairlane then rested his elbow on top of the lowered window.

Junior pulled away from the curb and eased down the street.

Hugo glared at him. "You want to get the lead out?"

"She's not going anywhere. She's dead."

"Well, I'm not and I don't want to spend all Saturday afternoon sweating through my clothes just because the chief wants to pander to Old Mobile."

Junior cut his eyes at Hugo but said nothing.

⚜

THEY PULLED INTO a long driveway and rolled to a stop on the oyster shell parking bay in front of wide steps that led up to a front porch deeply shaded by a slate roof. Huge ferns hung from chains placed along the support beam, a few of their tendrils beginning to brown with the cool nights. The slate roof continued up to reveal two dormer windows.

All was quiet.

"Name?" Hugo sat staring up at the house.

"Camden."

"Huh." Hugo opened the door of the sedan and stood, taking in the meticulously kept lawn. Two other cars were parked side by side in the parking bay. The mailman's truck was out near the street.

Hugo let his gaze travel over the cream colored, Mercedes two-seater with the top down. Junior came around the hood of the police car and gave that low sissing whistle he made with a trick of his tongue against the back of his teeth.

Hugo grunted and gave the black Cadillac Coupe de Ville a glance as he started up the steps to the porch.

The front door of the house swung open and Bebe Prescott stepped onto the porch, an unlit cigarette between the fingers of one hand and a lighter in the other. She stopped at the sight of Hugo, the cigarette half-way to her lips. Her eyelids fluttered.

"What are you doing here?"

The unexpected sight of her left Hugo momentarily speechless. At some level he had known that sooner or later he would encounter her. He had thought he was prepared for that eventuality. He was anything but.

He touched the knot of his tie. "Someone called the police about a dead woman."

Bebe lowered her lashes, placed the cigarette between her lips, flicked the lighter into flame, and held it to the tip as she inhaled deeply.

Her long, blond hair was held back from her face by a wide, green band of cloth. The color matched the bold floral print of a short mini skirt. The burnt orange, sleeveless, turtleneck hugged her slender torso and small breasts. The picture was completed by a pair of saddle brown, calf-hugging boots. Hugo thought she hadn't changed much over the past five years.

"What happened?"

She exhaled a long plume of smoke and averted her gaze. "My Aunt Ruth. The mailman found her and called Daddy."

"Sorry." Hugo couldn't remember Bebe having an Aunt Ruth. "Where is she?"

Bebe looked up at him. "The attic."

"The attic?" Hugo frowned. "How did the mailman find her?"

"I don't know. You'll have to ask him. Or Daddy."

Junior moved past Hugo and Bebe Prescott. He opened the front door and arched his eyebrows as he glanced from Hugo to Bebe and back again.

Hugo lifted his chin in a gesture for Junior to go ahead. He watched through the doorway until Junior disappeared up the staircase leading to the second story landing before turning his full attention to Bebe.

"How've you been?"

"Great." Her eyes narrowed slightly. "How was Vietnam?"

He hesitated. "Hot. And humid."

"You must have felt right at home then." She flicked ash from her cigarette and looked away. "Turn left at the top of the stairs. You'll see the door to the attic."

The corner of Hugo's mouth twitched in a ghost of a smile. "Good to see you, Bebe." He entered the house and followed Junior's path up the stairs.

⚜

THE FIRST THING Hugo thought as he stepped through the door at the end of the landing was that he'd never seen such a clean, tidy attic. His second thought was that rictus hadn't done Ruth Camden any favors. The death grin had contorted her features into a fright mask.

Haywood Prescott stood to one side in the narrow space. Junior leaned over the body that sat upright in a rocker, her head thrown back, her body arched in extremis. Her hands gripped the arms of the chair with claw like fingers.

"Mr. Prescott," August said by way of greeting.

Prescott nodded. "Where's Chief Goode?"

"He couldn't be reached. Probably off fishing for flounder." Hugo hesitated. "I'm sure he'll regret it when he learns of your aunt's death."

Haywood Prescott narrowed his eyes and stared at Hugo.

The look from Bebe had amused him. This look did not. "The postman found her?"

Prescott didn't answer the question. Instead he said, "I know you. Hugo August."

"Mr. Prescott."

Hugo waited while Prescott studied him.

Finally, Prescott spoke. "Wayne called me. Lately, Ruth had taken to waiting for the mail. Her check came on the first, apparently, and she didn't like to leave it in the box."

"So, she didn't answer the door and the mailman decided to call you." Hugo, in his turn, studied Haywood Prescott. "Did he do that often?"

"Never." Prescott glanced at his aunt's body then quickly away. "You have to understand. Ruth is old. She'd recently started insisting that her check be placed in her hand."

"I see." Hugo paused. "Did he enter the house? Is that why he called?"

"No." Prescott rocked back slightly, his gaze on the rough boards of the attic ceiling, and sighed. He lowered his gaze to look Hugo in the eye. "She was difficult, okay? In fact, she could be a real bitch. She was upset that the check hadn't come the day before. It was already overdue, apparently. Wayne probably didn't want to be raked over the coals again so he called."

Hugo nodded. "Okay." He paused again. "The mailman had her check and when she didn't answer the door he called you."

Prescott nodded.

"And you came over and found her."

"No. It was Bebe."

Hugo lightly touched the knot of his tie. "I see." The silence stretched for several seconds. "So why did you call the police?"

"She's dead."

"I agree, Mr. Prescott, but as you say, she's old. It appears she might have had a heart attack. This is really a job for the coroner, at best."

"It just seems wrong somehow."

"Do you have reason to think it isn't a natural death? That someone harmed her?"

Prescott frowned. "Not really. I mean, she pissed off people on a regular basis. There were days I wanted to wring her neck but I can't think anyone would actually do anything to her."

The attic was cooler than the rest of the house, Hugo noted. "When did you last see her?"

"A week ago, maybe? Bebe dropped by yesterday, brought her some papers to sign. Said she found Ruth up here in the attic going through old trunks."

Junior, who had slipped back downstairs to call the mortuary, popped his head around the door and signaled Hugo with a jerk of his head. Hugo looked around the attic.

It was neat and tidy. A bookcase stood to the right of the chair that held Ruth Camden's body. Its shelves held a collection of books, photo albums, small boxes of various sizes and materials, a magnifying glass, and other odd bits. The lid was askew on one of the porcelain boxes.

"Why don't you go on downstairs and wait with Bebe. O'Sullivan's will be here in a few minutes."

"Doesn't her doctor have to pronounce her or something?"

"He's out of town. Probably at homecoming. I'll have Oscar Rhys run by the funeral home and sign the death certificate."

Haywood gave this course of action some thought. Finally, he nodded, turned to the door, and went downstairs.

Hugo strolled around the space to the degree that the slanting roofline would allow his six-foot height. He lifted the top of a cedar hope chest to reveal a layer of tissue paper covering a lacy dress. It looked as if it hadn't been disturbed in years. The smell of moth balls assaulted his senses when he opened the door of an armoire. Inside hung a row of garments, one of which appeared to be a military uniform. Some type small furry animal formed the collar of a woman's coat.

Hugo closed the armoire and returned to the body. He had seen death in many forms in Vietnam but not so much since joining the

Mobile Police force. Mainly he'd investigated the results of Saturday night knifings which were rarely fatal, domestic altercations in Birdville, even a protest against the razing of shotgun houses in his neighborhood that had resulted in a heavy equipment operator getting punched in the nose.

He could understand Prescott's feeling about his aunt's death. He felt a flush of anger at the thought that Bebe had been the one to walk in on this sight.

A bluish tinge had settled in Mrs. Camden's finger tips and earlobes. Hugo took one of the lobes between his finger and thumb and pressed. When he released it, the flesh was white but slowly returned to the bluish color. *Less than twelve hours*, he thought. *Give or take.*

He reached across the body and lifted the slightly askew lid on the small porcelain box. It was empty. The bottom shelf of the bookcase held a stack of photo albums and scrap books. Their misalignment in such an orderly setting caught his eye.

A teacup rested on its side at the edge of a small table that sat next to the rocking chair. The matching saucer held some spilled tea as if, in the moment of her first symptoms of distress, she had tried to replace the cup. He leaned close to the body and inhaled deeply of the very faint, sweet scent of death.

When he straightened, he stood still and let the room settle around him. Prescott had been right. Something about this death didn't seem right. Maybe it was only that the sight of Bebe had caught him off guard, unsettled him. Or maybe it was the fact that she had been the one to discover the body.

Better to scratch the itch, Hugo thought. Otherwise, he wouldn't be able to let it go. He moved to the doorway and called down to Junior. "You got the camera?"

THE STANDING LAMP was the only source of light in the attic so Hugo slanted the shade to illuminate the body. The glare brought the scene into high relief. It was the best he could do in the dim space.

Junior only managed to get three shots because the roll of film was near the end. It would have to be enough. Once he finished, Hugo took a handkerchief from his pocket and righted the cup. There was a razor thin slice of lemon in the bottom of it. He poured the contents from the saucer into it.

"What're you thinking?" Junior asked.

"That she had a heart attack."

"So, why the photos? And the spilled tea?"

"Mr. Prescott isn't satisfied with the obvious."

Junior grinned. "Brownie points."

Hugo made no reply as Hunt Slaughter stuck his head through the doorway. "Ready for me?"

Hugo nodded. "I'll take Bebe and her father to the kitchen while you get her down to the wagon. Don't do anything to the body other than a temp reading until you hear from me." He turned to Junior. "Go down the drive and talk to the mailman."

Junior headed through the door. Hugo called him back. "Just listen. Let him tell you his story."

Hugo caught the look Junior sent his way but he didn't care. He wanted this thing tied up with no loose threads and no room for innuendo or speculation. The gruesomeness of the scene would cause enough talk. That, plus the fact Ruth Camden had a lineage all the way back to d'Iberville. Old name, old money, big headache.

As the mortician and his assistant began preparing the body to remove it from the attic, Hugo went downstairs. He cleared the last tread of the stairs just in time to see Bebe's tail lights flash as she braked the little Mercedes coupe before turning out of the driveway onto Dauphin Street. She headed west.

He found Haywood Prescott in the kitchen with a neat glass of whiskey in his hand.

"Christ," Haywood said as Hugo came through the swinging saloon style doors. "What a sight."

"Yes."

Haywood gestured with his drink and Hugo shook his head.

"What kind of papers did Bebe bring by?"

Haywood's brows shot up and he shrugged. "Just routine legal documents to do with the business."

"Your aunt was involved in the day to day of Haywood Mills?"

"Well, not the day to day." He turned to look out the kitchen window. "But she held a small interest and occasionally there were things that required her signature."

Hugo let the silence grow. Finally, Haywood drained his glass and glanced at him. "I guess I should start the process of finding Archie."

"Archie?"

Haywood nodded. "Her grandson. He's on his way to Vietnam by now, I expect. Left for training about two months ago." He hesitated. "How was it?"

Hugo touched the knot of his tie. "A walk in the park."

Haywood grunted and set his glass on the kitchen counter. "What happens now?"

"Hunt's moving her. They should be done in about ten minutes."

"I suppose Fellowes will call the mortuary when he gets back to town." Prescott seemed uncertain about what to say or do.

"I'd like to look around once Hunt's gone."

"Sure." Haywood ran his hand through his hair, glanced around the kitchen. With a sigh, he turned toward the door. "There's a key in the fern to the right of the porch steps. Lock up, if you don't mind." With that he left the kitchen and Hugo heard the outer door close behind him.

HUGO WAITED UNTIL the sound of the mortician's hearse died away. Junior sat on the front steps smoking and reading the Saturday edition of the *Mobile Press Register*.

He started in the kitchen. The kettle sat on the back burner of the stove, long since gone cold. A diffuser containing used tea leaves rested on a spoon shaped dish. They were still damp. He looked through the cabinets and found a clean, empty jar with a lid. He dumped the tea leaves into it.

A slow walk through the house revealed nothing that caught his eye. The house was much larger than it appeared from the street. An alcove under the stairs held a secretaire. Envelopes, stamps, various correspondence were all neatly tucked away. He saw no sign of legal documents.

Finally, Hugo went back up the stairs and entered the attic. He noted for a second time how cool it was and wondered how long Ruth Camden's body sat there waiting to be discovered. He'd get on the horn to Rhys, find out who the medical examiner was. The body was in full rigor. Under the circumstances, Hugo felt certain the coroner would at least have him swing by O'Sullivan's and give the body a cursory examination.

He removed a flimsy white curtain from one of the dormer windows. It allowed a bit more illumination but revealed nothing new. On a whim Hugo lifted the stack of photo albums and scrap books from the bottom shelf of the bookcase and took them and the teacup, the handle protected by his handkerchief, downstairs with him.

JUNIOR DROVE TO the lab in the basement of City Hall. Evie looked up from the *Mobile Press Register* crossword puzzle at the sound of the door closing. She straightened and quickly removed her glasses. She slipped them into the pocket of her lab coat then smiled as Hugo and Junior crossed the room toward her.

"Well." She blushed. "Hello, you. I heard you'd come home and were on the job."

Hugo gave her a smile. "Good to see you, Evie. What's a nice girl like you doing in a place like this?"

Junior piped up. "Caused a stink until they let her have the job is what."

A look of admiration came into Hugo's eyes. "Did you now?"

Evie's blush deepened. "Yeah, well, for all that, I get to work week-ends. Which means I mainly get to twiddle my thumbs." She held up the crossword puzzle to emphasize her boredom, and slapped it down on the workstation. "What's this? You bringing me coffee?" She eyed the china cup in Hugo's hand.

"Evidence."

"Of what?"

"Nothing, probably."

"This have anything to do with Ruth Camden?"

"Why do you ask?" Hugo placed the cup on the lab worktable.

"Helen Marie called."

"How'd she know?"

Evie tilted her head to one side in a look Hugo remembered from their school days together at St. Andrews. "Earth to Hugo. Did you forget where you are?"

He gave a small shake of his head. "I guess everyone in town knows by now."

"Not everyone." She grinned. "A lot of folks are at the game."

"You wouldn't happen to know the final score, would you?"

"Twenty to thirteen."

"Well, there's that." He shoved his handkerchief back into his pocket. From his jacket he fished out the small jar of loose tea leaves. "Can you check these?"

"What? You think she was poisoned?"

"No. I think Haywood Prescott isn't happy that Chief Goode wasn't at his beck and call when his aunt died."

Evie opened a drawer of the work station and pulled on a pair of gloves. She retrieved her glasses from her coat pocket and lifted the jar just above eye level and peered at the contents. "I don't know, Hugo. It looks like tea leaves to me." She sniffed the small amount of liquid in the cup. "Smells like tea."

"Humor me."

"It'll cost time and money." The question behind that observation remained unspoken.

Hugo thought about it a moment, then shrugged. "We'll let the chief decide. He's the one who has to answer to the family."

"Then I'd better send it off to Auburn."

"You can't do it here?"

"Not the kind of tests we need unless it's your every day, garden variety arsenic poisoning. It's only that simple in mystery novels. In the short term, we'll know more when we have the autopsy results. The organs will give us an idea of anything irregular. Blood, urine, stomach contents will have to be tested. A month, maybe? More likely, two." She pushed her glasses up the bridge of her nose with her forefinger. "If there's going to be an autopsy."

"That'll be up to Haywood Prescott, I guess. He's the one with questions. Or the chief. Either way, it would be good to know if we're wasting our time or if it's simply what it appears to be, a heart attack."

Evie watched him for a moment then took a small jar with a lid from a drawer in the work station. She poured the tea into it and placed the tea cup in a paper bag and labeled both of them. "I'll see what I can do."

❧

JUNIOR'S THOUGHTS WERE still with Evie when they walked down the steps of the police station. He thought she had looked especially nice today. He frowned. As usual, she hadn't spared him a second glance. Now that Hugo was back in the picture, she probably never would. Everything would be like it was before Hugo left. His frown deepened into a scowl.

The day was rapidly fading as they walked down Royal Street to the car. Hugo got behind the wheel and held out his hand for the key.

Junior stared at the outstretched hand and shook his head.

"Come on, Junior. I just need it for a few hours."

Junior stared off into the distance for a moment then dropped the key into Hugo's hand. "You're going to get me in trouble."

"We're not in high school anymore, Junior. I just want to check something out before the chief is back in the office and starts asking questions."

Junior got in on the passenger side. "You need to get a car." He slouched down in the seat. "Let me out at the Dew Drop. I can walk home from there."

Two

Hugo drove through the gloaming, through Midtown, and up the hill. At Hawkers Lane he eased the Ford Fairlane down the narrow alley fifty yards before killing the head lights. He let the car roll to a stop and sat behind the wheel staring into the dense darkness caused by the houses that backed up to this service access. With a shake of his head, he got out of the car.

He eased the door closed and set out across the forty or so yards of wooded lot. As the growth thinned, he saw the warm glow of the lights of the country club.

The Club. He shook his head again, leaned against a tree, and waited.

After a while, she sauntered out the open double doors of the card room and crossed the patio to the edge of the brick pavers where it met the golf course. There she paused, lit a cigarette, and waited.

She had come. Just like all those Sunday nights of their last year at St. Andrews. He would make the long bicycle ride from Tina's Boarding House and wait for her to finish dinner with her family at the club. Then she would walk out onto the patio and wait.

He chuckled deep in his throat and watched as she smoked, the tip of her cigarette glowing in the low light with each drag.

He pushed away from the tree at the same moment Bebe stepped off the patio and onto the green of the ninth hole. *Always the middle,* Hugo thought. Bebe came to no one. They came to her. Or met in the middle.

Why had he come? Because he had stayed away for two months and he couldn't stay away another day. Another hour. Another minute.

She didn't speak until they were standing almost toe to toe. "What are you doing here?"

They had reached the center of the ninth hole and he realized it wasn't a cigarette she was smoking.

"Just taking the night air."

"The club is off limits to orphaned Catholic school boys."

"So I heard." It was the game they played. "Not all Catholics, apparently."

But Bebe was bored with their childish game. "What are you doing here, Hugo?"

"I thought it was obvious." He could smell gin on her breath.

"In Mobile." Her voice was suddenly as hard and sharp as flint. "Why did you come back?"

"Nowhere else to go."

"There's a whole wide world out there. Remember?"

"I've seen enough of the world. In the end, it's all the same."

"Hot and humid." She dropped the roach onto the lush grass of the golf course, ground it out with her boot, and exhaled the last of the smoke into the night air.

"That. And lost. And drug addled and in need of a good wash."

"Good God, Hugo. Don't tell me you've become philosophical in the jungles of Asia."

"No." He gave her a fleeting smile. "The streets of San Francisco."

They were silent for a few moments, the muted sound of piano music drifting out onto the night air from the country club.

"Well?" There was impatience in her voice now.

"How's Rich?"

"You'll have to ask him."

"Oh?"

"What do you want, Hugo?"

He hesitated. "Your aunt, how was she when you saw her on Friday?"

Bebe narrowed her eyes. "Is that what you came to ask? Really?" The flint of her voice cut through the night air.

No, Hugo thought. That wasn't what he wanted to ask her but they both knew those questions could never be given voice. They had moved beyond that. The choices they had made that fateful day so long ago left them no path back.

She turned her profile to him. "Distracted, I'd say. Annoyed." She took a couple of steps in the direction of the country club.

"Annoyed?"

She stopped and looked back at him. "She didn't want to sign the papers Daddy sent over. Said she had more important things to deal with."

"Like what?"

Bebe shrugged. "She didn't say. She was probably just being her usual irritable self. All her scrapbooks were spread out on the floor around her chair and she didn't want to be bothered."

"Did she do that often? Sit and browse through the photos?"

"I have no idea."

"How was she when you saw her? Other than distracted. Did she look ill?"

"No. She looked like she always did. Straight backed, imposing, impatient for me to be gone." Bebe set off again in the direction of the doors leading into the country club.

Hugo watched her the whole way. She never looked back. He had known she wouldn't.

☙

HUGO PULLED TO the curb in front of Junior's house. His hand rested on the gear shift as he sat thinking. Then he shifted into drive and turned the car toward Dauphin Island Parkway.

The parking lot at The Fin Restaurant was full. He recognized the chief's car.

The smell of fried fish hit Hugo as he stepped through the door. Chief Goode sat at a round table in the corner of the bar facing the door. Two other off duty officers sat with him. Goode watched Hugo cross the room, a look of calculation on his face.

"August."

"Chief."

"I get the impression you're about to ruin my supper."

"Not intentionally."

Chief Goode nodded at an empty chair and Hugo sat down.

"We have a suspicious death."

"Suspicious how?"

"Ruth Camden dead in her attic."

"Christ," Goode said under his breath. "How did she die?"

"Won't know until the autopsy. If there is one."

"What the hell was she doing in the attic? Did she fall?"

"No. She was sitting in a rocking chair."

Chief Goode sat back in his chair and leveled a look of pure malice at Hugo. "You think you're a real funny guy, don't you?"

"Not particularly. It looks to me like she had a heart attack. Her nephew thinks otherwise."

That was the line Hugo had been dying to deliver. The fact that he had an audience of two of the chief's cronies was icing on the cake.

Chief Goode's son was a year younger than Hugo. Someone had pulled strings and Virgil Goode managed to get a coveted slot in the National Guard when draft notices began to blanket the nation. The fact that Hugo had volunteered stuck in Goode's craw and he did everything in his power to make Hugo's life a misery.

The truth was, Hugo could care less that Virgil had skirted the horrors of Vietnam. In hindsight, Hugo might have played his cards differently given a second chance. But then, residents of St. Thomas More's Catholic Boys Home weren't likely to be lucky with the draft lottery.

At some level Hugo understood Goode's animosity toward him. Understanding didn't make it any more bearable.

Hugo kept his expression bland as he held the chief's gaze.

Finally, Goode broke the silence. "Right. We'd best have a look. It'll quiet any rumors started by Prescott's squeamishness. Let's face it, everyone thought the old girl was too mean to die."

He waved dismissively at Hugo and lifted a Budweiser bottle for a long pull. "Have Rhys send her to the hospital for the autopsy."

Hugo stood and crossed the bar to the door. He could feel three pairs of eyes boring into the back of his skull. He grinned.

Three

He was alone in a listening post deep in the rocket zone. The rains of May formed a curtain of mist where shadowy figures appeared and disappeared like the gentle undulation of a sheer fabric billowing in the breeze. Charlie was out there. Charlie owned the night.

The Tokay lizards screamed their carnal obscenities all around him, taunting him, echoing the sentiments of the VC. Back at you, *Hugo thought.*

His platoon hadn't dug in properly. He had railed at them to dig deeper, to set the perimeter with claymores. His men had looked at him with dead eyes and his words had fallen on deaf ears. Didn't they realize they were on their own? The slicks couldn't risk an evacuation in the dark. They wouldn't be flying in to the rescue.

Hugo struggled but the jungle growth held him immobile, unable to take a step, unable to bring his M-16 into firing position. The metallic taste of fear rose in his throat. Helicopter gunships raked the hillside behind him, setting it on fire, lighting up the night sky like a million roman candles. He needed to move, alert the unit. Charlie was coming for him, was coming for all of them.

Hugo lunged against the constraints binding him and with a bellow came awake and upright in the bed, arms flailing at the tangle of blanket. His heart pounded and it took a moment to realize where he was. He fell back against the sweat damp pillow and lay there breathing hard, his heart racing.

The telephone rang insistently. He pushed the knotted blanket to the foot of the bed. He didn't know how long the phone had been ringing but he figured that whoever it was could wait.

As he stood on the cold linoleum flooring of the bathroom waiting for relief, the caller gave up. He turned his gaze to the view from the tiny bathroom window.

"Shit."

The police car sat parked on the narrow vacant lot next to his house on S. Cedar Street. Maurice was visible through the kitchen window of the house on the next lot over. He looked up from whatever he was cooking, smiled, and waved a spatula at Hugo.

"Shit." He picked up the half empty beer can sitting on the back of the toilet and drained the stale dregs.

The phone started ringing again and Hugo caught it on the third ring.

"I was beginning to think you'd changed your ways." Evie sounded bright-eyed and upbeat.

"Not likely. What time is it?"

"Half past nine."

Hugo mentally said shit a third time. "What you got for me?"

"I can't send the tea to Auburn because it's Sunday. Someone will have to make the trip tomorrow."

"And you called to tell me that?"

"I called to tell you I heard the hearse brought the body over from O'Sullivan's. It got me thinking so I decided to do a little test."

"Are you at the hospital?"

"No. I'm at the lab. I wanted to do a little experiment with the tea. I figured if Rhys had ordered an autopsy, there could be something serious going on."

"What did you find?"

"It's not conclusive, but we do have poison in the tea."

"I don't understand. It's either poison or it isn't."

"Oh, it's poison, all right. I wanted to make sure it wasn't an accidental overdose. Most people don't take their prescriptions by dissolving them in their tea so I thought we could eliminate that as the source. Instead, it confirmed your suspicion. I can't identify what, specifically, at this stage. I did a flame test and it isn't arsenic. That's all I can say for sure. We'll need more sophisticated testing to see if we can identify it."

"How long will that take?"

"Depends on the back-log in Auburn. Six weeks, six months. Unless someone shakes the tree."

Hugo grunted. It would have to be the chief. Two months on the job didn't earn any favors, especially at the state level. After last night, he didn't think his standing had improved much with the chief and his cronies. But, then, he wouldn't be the one with Haywood Prescott breathing down his neck.

The chief had held the position for about twelve years. His longevity had as much to do with his adaptability as it did with politics and skill at his job. Hugo had no doubt the poisoning of one of Mobile's old grand dames would be cause enough for him to call out any favors due him at the state level.

"You're sure it's poison?"

"Hamlet died."

"What?"

"I gave a few drops of the tea to Hamlet. He died. That's proof enough for me."

"Me too. Thanks, Evie." He started to hang up but stopped and asked, "We are talking about one of your hamsters, aren't we?"

"Mouse."

"You really should give them less tragic names, Evie."

"I prefer to consider them prophetic names."

There was a moment of silence. "I hope he wasn't one of your favorites."

"You know what they say."

"What's that?"

"To be good at your craft you must be willing to kill your darlings."

"That's awfully deep for so early on a Sunday morning."

"Blame that on Sister Madelaine's literature class. And shake a leg already. Make Hamlet's sacrifice worth it."

"Right." Hugo stared at the receiver then gently replaced it in the cradle. Evie had always been different. Mostly quiet and observant, but she had a streak of iron running down her spine that had helped her cope through the taunts of being a smart girl, of being an orphan. He had no doubt she could kill her darlings if that's what it took to succeed.

He slipped on the trousers he'd worn the previous day and hopped barefooted across the rough patch of Johnson grass of the empty lot. He retrieved the photo albums and scrap books from the police car.

He wasn't sure what he had expected to find but all the albums held were a lot of old, sepia toned pictures of people from decades past, invitations to parties and balls, pressed flowers, thank-you notes, wedding invitations, and birth announcements. The minutia of Ruth Camden's life neatly compiled in chronological order.

⁂

THE DAUPHIN WAY Historic District was a beautiful area of Mobile. Most of the houses had been built from the mid-nineteenth to the mid-twentieth century. The old families still clung to this large neighborhood in the face of white flight to the suburbs. The houses here were a combination of working class frame structures interspersed with impressive mansions in a wide variety of styles from Greek Revival to Queen Anne.

Ruth Camden lived in a raised bungalow at the end of a long driveway. The word bungalow was deceptive. While it lacked the wedding cake embellishment of many of the houses in this section of Dauphin Street, or the old world feel of others, it was neither small nor unimpressive.

The old oaks on the property created a deep shade around the front of the north facing home. Moss hung in long tendrils from the trees. Hugo stood in the V of the open door of the police sedan and surveyed the house and grounds before him.

The lawn was leaning more toward brown than green as what passed for winter in the port city approached. Everything was immaculate, a testament to the owner's yard man, no doubt. Hugo felt the mild chill in the humid air. The autumn sun would not reach these shadowy recesses until midday.

He heard a scraping sound that appeared to come from the side yard behind a brick wall. Carefully he closed the car door with a soft click. A black, wrought iron gate gave passage into the side garden. It stood ajar. Hugo passed through and along the east wall of the house banked with hydrangea bushes still in bloom this late in the fall. Another muffled noise reached him. He followed it to the rear of the house. He pushed his coat back to expose the revolver holstered at his waist and stepped quietly around the southeast corner of the building.

In a flower bed near the back door of the residence a small, frail looking woman was on her knees, a trowel in her gloved hand, her white hair a mass of soft curls in wispy disarray.

Hugo relaxed and covered the gun with his sports coat. He cleared his throat and the woman's head jerked up in surprise. Her blue eyes were startling in the pale canvas of her face and snowy hair.

"Who're you?"

"Hugo August. Who are you and what are you doing?"

She threw the trowel into a wicker basket next to her and began spreading pine straw over the disturbed soil of the flower bed. "The tulips. Ruth's tulips." She shook her head. "William was supposed to plant them last week but he was sick." She reached up and caught a spindle of the back steps railing with one hand and pulled herself to her feet. A grimace passed quickly over her features and she exhaled a small grunt. "They need the cold nights ahead."

"You've been planting tulips?" Hugo watched her knock the excess dirt from her gloved hands.

She took off the gardening gloves and threw them into the basket with the trowel. Her fingers were horribly gnarled. "Aimeé Marlowe." She reached out to Hugo. "Ruth's cousin."

He shook the offered hand. It felt boney and small in his grasp. Hugo wondered how she had managed to get the brilliant sapphire ring over the swollen knuckle of her finger.

"Silly of me, I suppose." She blinked back the tears forming in her eyes and looked away from his steady regard. "Ruth loved her garden and she had her heart set on tulips in the spring." She placed a hand at the base of her spine and straightened to a more upright stance. "When Bebe called I was in shock. I shouldn't have been. Ruth had a bad heart. Still, sudden death is always like that, isn't it?" She gave him a fleeting smile then picked up the basket and put one foot on the bottom step to the back porch. As she laid her hand on the railing for support, she paused as if the knowledge that she was having a conversation with a strange man in the isolated rear of a house where death had just occurred might be a cause for concern.

"What did you say your name was?"

"Hugo August." He took his shield from his coat pocket. "Mobile Police Department."

"Police." She frowned. "Did Haywood call you?" She looked east toward the brick wall separating the Camden house from its neighbor. "Margaurite. That busybody." She took another step up. "Thinks I'll steal the family silver, does she?"

"Mrs. Marlowe, have you been in the house?"

"Of course I've been in the house." She cleared the third step. "Ruth gave me a key ages ago in case something like this should happen. And now it has." She climbed the last step. "Besides, there's a key in the fern on the front porch. Everyone knows it."

"Would you please stop, Mrs. Marlowe?"

"Stop?"

"You can't go into the house."

Her face flushed a deeper pink. "Well, really. Haywood, my own flesh and blood, thinks I would. . . Well, I don't know what he thinks. And Ruth my dearest friend in the world."

"Mr. Prescott didn't call and neither did the neighbor. I'm here to look into Mrs. Camden's death."

Aimeé Marlowe frowned. "I should think that would be a job for her doctor."

"Her doctor's out of town."

"Homecoming." She tut-tutted. "Well, he'll be back later today. Probably have Sunday brunch at the Deke House before he sets out."

"And until we've talked to him and the coroner has examined the bod—Mrs. Camden, it's best to keep the house secure."

"Well, I never." She drew her shoulders back and looked down her nose at him from the height of the back porch top step.

"All the same," he reached up his hand for her to take to help her back down, "I'm afraid we need to follow protocol."

She hesitated, then took the offered hand. As she stepped off the last step onto the brick walkway, she stopped and looked up at Hugo, apprehension visible in her features. "The coroner, you said. What has the coroner to do with it? Can't Dr. Fellowes take care of her?"

"I'm sure Dr. Fellowes will be able to answer certain questions but since the police were called in, it's best to let the medical examiner have a look as well."

Her grip on his hand tightened. "They won't. . . Oscar Rhys is the coroner, isn't he? Ruth would be mortified to have that man do whatever it is he does. Surely, Haywood won't allow it?"

"Oscar doesn't do anything other than make a determination if there's anything out of the ordinary about her death. I'm sure he'll take her medical history into consideration. If the medical examiner needs to take a look at her, Oscar will set that in motion. It's not something you need to worry about. Mrs. Camden will be treated with respect."

She shook her head. "Poor Ruth," she said softly. "Such indignity. She doesn't deserve to be disrespected this way."

"You were close?"

"As I said, she was my best friend. I don't know what I'll do without her." Her voice broke on a little tremor and she cleared her throat. She smiled sadly at Hugo. "You're too young to understand the true depth of a lifelong friendship. We are bound much more strongly than the mere ties of family."

"Who else was close to Mrs. Camden?"

"Her family, of course. Haywood, Skip, Bebe. Archie is her grandson. He lived with her after his mother died and before he went off to war."

"Anyone else that she might have confided in? Someone who might know if anything was troubling her?"

"Troubled? Ruth?" She shook her head. "She told me everything. I'd know if she had anything on her mind. Other than Archie, of course. She took his departure very hard but I do think she had resigned herself to the situation." She thought for a moment. "And, there's the Archbishop, of course. They've been friends for years. The gardening club members and the historical preservation society. Ruth had many friends."

"Did she get along with people? Generally, I mean."

"Ah. You've been talking to Haywood. They were at odds about Archie and the business. But they've been at odds for years about one thing or another. Too much alike, if you ask me." She hesitated, as if searching for the right words. "She could be difficult. You had to know how to handle her. As close as we were, we had our moments. Our little ups and downs. But not for many years now. Youth, you know, makes the blood run high."

She reached into the pocket of her sweater and took out a key. She stared at it a long moment, then placed it in Hugo's hand. "You should probably remove the one in the fern if you don't want anyone in the house. I don't know if Haywood has a key or not. Or anyone else, for that matter. I can't imagine Ruth giving one to Viola, but maybe she did. That's the maid. Viola."

"What's the maid's last name?"

Aimeé Marlowe had turned back to the garden path and she stopped and looked up at Hugo. "I don't know. She's the maid. Ruth probably has her number written down somewhere." With that she followed the brick path around the house and continued down the long driveway to Dauphin Street where she turned east.

THE PHONE WAS ringing when Hugo entered the Camden house. He followed the sound to the living room and just as he located it, it stopped. The sudden cessation amplified the silence. It was the sound of emptiness, Hugo thought.

He pulled on a pair of gloves as he went down the hallway to the bedroom that he knew belonged to the victim. There was a subtle hint of fragrance as he entered the room, so fragile you barely knew it was there. This was a woman's room and he wondered how long she had lived alone here. He tried to call up any memory he had of the name Camden but there was nothing. But she was a Haywood by birth and that was a name everyone recognized.

The room was large as was the custom for homes of the well-to-do built in its time. The ceilings high with transoms above the doors to help alleviate the heat of Mobile's subtropical weather. A comfortable arm chair with a shawl folded over the back stood in a corner with a standing lamp beside it. A foot stool was pushed against the wall and out of the way. The top of the chest on that wall held a dozen or more framed photographs of all vintages from barely recognizable sepia daguerreotypes to Kodak moments in full color. Bebe was there among the silver framed faces, wearing her homecoming crown, smiling for the camera on the arm of the governor. He remembered that day. Homecoming in Tuscaloosa five years ago. It was the last time he had seen her until yesterday.

He recognized some of the people in other photographs as well. Haywood Prescott and his bride at their long-ago wedding, a man he couldn't identify with the former mayor at a ribbon cutting ceremony from some years back, an infant in its christening gown that had to be Archie, he figured. There were photos of the Mardi Gras court taken at varying years with new, fresh debutantes smiling in their finery. Bebe featured in one of those as well.

He pulled the chain on the art deco lamp sitting on Ruth's dressing table to illuminate the items collected there. A couple of strands of gray hair were caught in the bristles of a hairbrush that bore Ruth's initials. An ornate silver backed hand mirror featured the same svelte image of a woman as that captured in the design of the lamp. The pieces reminded Hugo of a lost week spent in a San Francisco loft with the lovely Shelley who thought she was Marion Davies. She had the silent screen icon down to the hair, pencil thin arched eyebrows, and body skimming evening gowns that revealed more than they concealed.

He pushed the memory aside and examined the rest of the items on the table. A silver topped crystal jar contained loose white powder. A vase held a single hydrangea blossom.

In the top drawer he found a jewelry box that contained a wide array of pieces from hat pins to pearl necklaces. A note card was stuck into the frame of the mirror above the table. The name on it read Gisele Fournet. It was an old card, the yellowing of the portion unprotected by the mirror's frame suggested it had been there for many years. He turned it over but there was nothing else on it to give it any significance. He replaced it in the edge of the frame.

Nothing of any real interest caught his eye. In the bathroom adjacent to the bedroom he found a prescription for digitalis for Mrs. Camden's heart condition, aspirin, cough syrup, and a small bottle of paregoric that appeared to be years old. He gathered it all into a paper bag along with the canister of tea from the kitchen pantry. He had also found some rat poison and several types of cleaning products. All of it would go to the lab for Evie to check.

Something was missing. He stood quietly in the center of the kitchen, closed his eyes, and let himself imagine Ruth's last moments. She would fill the kettle with water and put it on the burner to boil. While she waited she would fill the brewing ball with loose tea leaves which she would place in the tea pot. He opened his eyes. The tea pot, where was it? He began opening cabinets until he found the china tea pot. It had been washed and dried and put away.

He returned to the living room and picked up the phone. The dispatcher's voice on the other end of the line was new and female. He told her to get a scene of crime investigator over to the Camden house to collect prints.

While he waited, he returned to the attic. It gave him no further insight and a search of the rest of the house produced nothing else of interest. He discovered the bedroom that her grandson had used when he lived with her. There was a small library with a desk. It had obviously been her husband's. Everything in the desk drawers was yellow with age. An armchair sat next to a window that gave a view of the side garden.

The missing legal documents from Haywood Prescott nagged at the edge of his mind. Had Prescott taken them?

At the secretaire in the stairwell he found an address book. The entry for the maid was under V. No last name. In parenthesis beside the phone number was the name John Henry.

Hugo dialed the number and after several rings an ancient male voice answered. "John Henry."

"I'd like to speak to Viola, please."

"She gone to church, I 'spect." There was a hesitation. "Who dis is?"

Hugo knew that if he identified himself as a policeman it would make Viola wary. Mobile had been spared the violence that erupted in the wake of Martin Luther King's assassination in April but the long simmering distrust between blacks and whites was a palpable energy that was evident in a brashness of attitude and a sullen, un-cooperativeness with authority. The nation was a powder keg waiting for the next spark, even in backwater Mobile, Alabama.

"Hugo August," he replied. "I understand Viola works for Mrs. Camden. I'm looking for some papers and thought Viola might be able to tell me where Mrs. Camden put them."

The silence lengthened until Hugo thought John Henry wasn't going to answer. "Hello?"

"How come you looking for Miz. Camden's papers?"

"She died sometime Friday night or early Saturday morning."

"Dead, you say?"

"Yes. We need to find her will and insurance papers."

"You axe Mr. Prescott?" A wary note in John Henry's voice reso-nated over the phone line.

"He's the one looking for her papers. Maybe I could come over to your house and speak with Viola after church."

"She don't live here."

"Then why is this number in Mrs. Camden's address book?"

"Viola don't have no phone. She give this number to folks who needs to call her."

"She's your neighbor?"

"She live two houses down."

"What's that address?"

John Henry didn't answer right away. "Who you say you is?"

"Hugo August. I'm taking care of Mrs. Camden's death for Mr. Prescott."

"How she die?"

"Not sure until her doctor has a look at her. She had a bad heart."

"Unh."

Hugo waited.

Finally, John Henry said, "I tell Viola to call the house after church. You be there then?"

Hugo decided not to push the matter. It was obvious John Henry didn't want anything to do with the death of a white woman, even in the most peripheral way. "Ask her to call. I'll try to be here."

Four

Evie arrived with a short, freckled, red-head who looked like he belonged in high school. By his attitude, it was obvious he knew that's how people saw him.

Hugo grinned at Evie. "I thought you were on duty yesterday."

"The whole week-end."

Hugo watched the red-head bustling about in a very officious manner. "Your assistant?"

She kept her features expressionless. "My boss."

Hugo's brows shot up but he said nothing. He went over the areas he wanted most particularly fingerprinted because of what they knew about the tea. He watched Evie's jaw flex and relax but her expression remained unchanged.

She thought he was second guessing her ability but his intent was to make a point with the junior scientist. He knew how some men could be if they felt threatened by the more accomplished and intelligent among them. Especially if they were women. He didn't want Evie's boss to flex his muscle to the detriment of his case. Ruth Camden's prominence in Mobile made her death too political for any screw-ups.

As Evie and her boss set about their task, Hugo checked his watch. It was almost twelve o'clock. If Viola was at church it would be another hour at least before he could expect a call from her. He wondered which church she attended.

Hugo's stomach growled. He couldn't remember the last meal he'd eaten. He gave Evie the house key he'd acquired from Aimeé Marlowe so she could lock up when they were done. Then he dug around in the fern on the porch until he found the one he had replaced there the day before. With it in his pocket, he turned the car toward downtown.

⚶

THE AFTER-CHURCH CROWD was already forming a line at Morrison's when he walked through the doors into the foyer. Junior and his grandmother were near the front of the line. Hugo paused but not before Junior saw him. The look he sent Hugo was straight from their shared childhood, a look of long suffering and disappointment.

Mrs. Knight turned and saw Hugo. There would be no escape now. He skipped in line to accept her embrace, ignoring the scowls of the patrons who had strategically parked at church to affect a quick get-a-way to a coveted spot in the buffet line.

"Why haven't you been to see me, you bad boy? It's been weeks." Mrs. Knight patted his cheek.

"Working, Mrs. K." Hugo returned her smile. "You look nice today. I especially like that hat."

The color in her face deepened and she gave a wave of her hand. "This old thing?"

Hugo told her what he knew she needed to hear. "You always look like the pages of a magazine, Mrs. K. I bet that's a new nail polish you're wearing."

She cut her eyes at him with a coy tilt of her head. Then she held up her hand, her fingers splayed, and admired the polish. "Blushing Pink. I picked it up at Woolworth's yesterday."

When they had made their selections from the array of dishes on display at the buffet, a black waiter in a white jacket, tie, and black dress pants took their trays to a table and unloaded the various vegetables, meats, and drinks. It was still early for the bulk of the lunch crowd so the noise level was low.

"Bless us, O Lord, and these, Thy gifts, which we are about to receive from Thy bounty. Through Christ, our Lord. Amen," the three of them prayed in unison.

Junior started in on Hugo as soon as they had made the sign of the cross. "Where's the car?"

"Outside."

"You're going to cost me my job." It was obvious by the aggrieved tone of Junior's voice that he was spoiling for a fight.

Hugo looked across the table at him, started to speak, then glanced at Marilyn Knight. He cleared his throat. "It was late when I found the chief and brought him up to date on the situation. I didn't want to disturb Mrs. K at that hour." He spread butter on a roll. "Besides, what's the chief going to do? I need to be able to track down the details of the case, tie up any loose ends."

"So, it's a case now, is it?" The sarcasm in Junior's voice wasn't lost on his grandmother.

"Boys, am I going to have to separate the two of you?" She added sugar to her already sweetened tea. "It's Sunday. Behave yourselves or I'll ask Father Gregory to have a word with both of you."

"We're not school boys any more, Mrs. K." Hugo felt his mouth water in anticipation as he speared a fried shrimp with his fork.

"Then stop acting like it." She reached for the salt. "Now tell me what this is all about."

"Work." Hugo and Junior spoke in unison.

"I think it's about Ruth Camden. I heard she had some kind of fright that left her looking like a monster at the Halloween fair."

Hugo stared at Junior who shook his head in reply to the unspoken question. "She had a heart attack."

"In the attic?" Mrs. K fixed Hugo with her I'm-not-falling-for-that stare. She renewed her attack on the fried chicken breast on her plate. "Hiding from her murderer, if you ask me. Why else would she be in the attic?"

"She was up there looking through old albums and trunks," Junior volunteered.

"Uh huh. A likely story. Myrtle Crum told me she couldn't sleep a wink last night. Afraid she'd be killed in her sleep."

"Grammy," Junior's voice held a note of exasperation, "Mrs. Crum thinks the wetback at the Piggly Wiggly is going to kill her in her sleep. Or that old Otto Schwartz at the shoe shop is going to climb through her window one night and have his way with her."

"Well, she saw what she saw. Said Ruth Camden had been frightened to death."

Hugo knew that when Mrs. K's imagination kicked into high gear the story would evolve into a gang of Nazi criminals torturing Ruth for the hiding place of her jewels. For her and her friends like Myrtle Crum, The War was still the thing in the night that gave them nightmares. He needed to derail her imagination.

"Everyone thinks she had a heart attack. Haywood Prescott called the police because he couldn't reach Dr. Fellowes, that's all. People don't know what to do when they come unexpectedly upon a sudden death." He patted Mrs. K's hand. "I wouldn't put too much faith in what Myrtle Crum has to say. She calls the police every time a cat knocks over her trash can in the night. And there's no way she could have seen the body."

"Well, Wayne saw the body. The poor man could hardly speak of it, it was so gruesome."

Hugo glared at Junior who arched his eyebrows and shrugged in denial.

"Death does that to a body sometimes, Mrs. K. It's part of the natural process. Don't let someone's imagination frighten you. Her doctor was treating her for a heart condition. Aimeé Marlowe says she had health issues so I'm sure that at the end of the day we'll find out that's all it was."

"What does Aimeé Marlowe have to do with it?"

"I spoke with her this morning. Apparently, she's Mrs. Camden's cousin."

Mrs. K looked out across the cafeteria, her gaze distant with thought. "Yes. Now I remember. She's not a Mobilian, you know."

"I'll keep that in mind," Hugo teased. "But I found Mrs. Camden's heart medication in her bathroom so I feel pretty sure she wasn't lying to me about that."

Junior's grandmother blushed to the roots of hair. "That's not what I meant at all, Hugo August. It's just that, well, there was talk."

"There's always talk, Grammy." Junior spoke around a mouthful of food.

"She's foreign," Mrs. Knight insisted. "Came over here as a young woman. Hardly more than a girl, I hear. Before the Great War. From France." She lowered her voice on this last revelation as if it was evidence of poor character.

Hugo thought he had detected the faintest hint of an accent on certain words when he spoke with Aimeé Marlowe but time had successfully melded it with the cadence of the deep South to the point that most people would be unaware.

"The two of you can laugh all you want," she continued, "but Mobile lives and dies by its bloodline. You ignore it and you end up on the wrong side every time."

"And Ruth Camden would be the right side?" Hugo asked.

"Nothing righter."

"So, according to that logic, her cousin would be on the right side by default?"

"Honestly, Hugo, I'd swear you forgot where you're from over there in that Viet-nam." She sat back in her chair, a frown on her face. "Still, she is a foreigner. Not that I ever had any reason to think ill of her. Never had much occasion to be around her, really, though she does attend St. Andrews. Not important enough, I reckon."

"Better off, I say." Junior wiped his mouth with his napkin and sighed with contentment. "Folks like that don't know you unless they need something from you. Once they get what they want, you're forgotten until the next time."

Hugo knew as well as anyone that to get ahead in this city you had to know who was on what side of every issue. Invariably that followed the bloodline of the old families of Mobile. The problem was, he'd never given much thought to getting ahead. Getting by had suited him just fine except for that brief time in high school when he had thought college could open any door. He blamed Father Gregory for that delusion. He blamed Father Gregory for a lot of things.

He'd been surprised that he'd been hired for the job with the police department, and as a detective at that. Small reward, he decided, for two tours in Vietnam and a year on the streets of San Francisco as a beat cop. Both occupations had left their scars.

Five

Hugo followed Junior and his grandmother in their old Buick Electra to their home in Midtown after lunch. He declined her famous banana pudding. The meal at Morrison's had left him on the verge of a food coma. As he and Junior rolled back down Dauphin Street he relayed the news that Ruth Camden had, indeed, been poisoned.

"So, what did Evie say, exactly?" Junior asked.

"There was something in the tea."

"Prescott was right then."

Hugo was silent for a couple of blocks. "Odd, don't you think?"

"What's odd?"

"That Prescott called the police rather than Hunt Slaughter."

"Like you said, folks don't know what to do with a dead body except call their doctor or the police."

"But they didn't send out a patrol car, did they? They sent two detectives. Why would they do that?"

"Because it was Haywood Prescott who called it in."

"In that case, we'd better be thorough, don't you think?"

"As in canvas the neighborhood?"

"Exactly. And we'd better hustle up a subpoena for her phone records. That might help us with our time line."

"Sure thing."

Hugo turned the sedan into the driveway of the Camden house.

Sitting on the parking bay was a gold Plymouth Barracuda. As they approached, a small black woman got out of the passenger side.

"Viola," Hugo said.

"Yeah?"

"The maid."

As Junior and Hugo got out of the police car, the driver's door of the Barracuda opened and a slim black man wearing a long leather coat with a huge fur collar that trailed down the lapels rose from the driver's seat. He had a pointed goatee and wild long hair that blended with the fur of the coat collar. His nose was long and pointed and he had small, black pebbles for eyes.

"I thought I recognized that car." Junior's voice rose in greeting. "Tyrone Pritchett. What brings you here?"

"The cat." Tyrone's voice was surprisingly deep for a man of such slight stature. He looked from Junior to Hugo. "What brings the po-lice here?"

The sharp intake of breath by Viola turned all eyes on her.

"Are you Viola?" Hugo asked.

She nodded.

"I'm Hugo August." He took his shield from his coat pocket and showed it to her. "I'm investigating Mrs. Camden's death."

"John Henry said she had a heart attack." Viola's voice trembled on the last word.

"We won't know the cause of death until the medical examiner looks at her. I've been told she had a bad heart. I'm sure he'll be able to tell us what happened."

Viola looked from Hugo to Junior then to Tyrone Pritchett. She reached for the door handle of the Barracuda.

Hugo stepped closer. "I was expecting you to call the house. Why did you come instead?"

Her hand rested on the door handle but she didn't open it. She looked up at Hugo. "The cat. I was worried about the cat."

"I see." He gestured toward the house. "Why don't we go inside and look for him? He'll more likely come to you than a stranger."

The flesh on Viola's knuckles paled as her grip tightened. Hugo thought she would refuse his request but after a moment she slowly released the door handle and took a couple of hesitant steps toward the house. She paused then squared her shoulders and went up the steps to the front porch.

Hugo noted that she made no move toward the fern where the spare key had previously been hidden. Was that because she had already looked for it and discovered it missing? Or could it be possible she had no knowledge of it? He doubted that.

He moved past her, unlocked the door and waited for her to enter ahead of him.

They stood just inside the door at the foot of the stairs. Hugo didn't push. He wiped the black print dust from his hands with a handkerchief and allowed Viola to gather herself. She cast a long look down the hallway toward the bedroom before moving to the left and the kitchen.

The print dust all over the kitchen gave her pause but after a quick glance at Hugo, she took a small can of salmon from the pantry. In the overhead cabinet she found two matching bowls and placed them on the counter. She flaked the salmon into one bowl and filled the other with water before placing them on the floor near the back door.

They waited in silence for a couple of minutes then Hugo asked, "When did you last see Mrs. Camden?"

"Friday. I catch the eight o'clock bus and it leaves me off two blocks down. About eight thirty. I work 'til two thirty. The bus picks me up about three. A few minutes before three."

"Do you come every Friday?"

"I come every day. Monday to Friday." She rubbed her upper arms with work roughened hands. "Sometimes if she have a party, I come on a Saturday or Sunday." She fell silent for a moment then asked in a desperate whisper, "What I'm gone do now?"

That was the problem, wasn't it? For someone like Viola the sudden loss of her livelihood was the paramount issue. Hugo had no answer. "How long have you worked for Mrs. Camden?"

"Since 1940. Before the War. Before her son went off and got hisself killed in Korea."

"Then you must know her better than anyone."

Viola cut her eyes at Hugo then returned her gaze to the kitchen window and the view beyond. She said nothing.

Hugo stared at the bowl of salmon. The smell had permeated the kitchen. Where was the damn cat? "What's the cat's name?"

"Beauregard."

Right, Hugo thought. "When did you last see him?"

"I put him out Friday before I left. That's what I always do. Last thing. Be sure the cat's out, wash and dry the bowls and put them away."

"And Mrs. Camden lets him back in at night?"

"Before she go to church she let him back in. She like to let him have a ramble she call it, for an hour or two. She let him out every morning for a bit then I let him out before I quit work. She don't want no litter box in her house. But she don't want him out after dark either. Afraid something will happen to him. He always here when I gets to work."

"Have you always worked five days a week for Mrs. Camden?"

"Always. Never miss a day. Not one in twenty-eight years except one time. She give me three days off to bury my mama."

Did Viola punch the clock as regular as rain because of her work ethic and loyalty to the family, Hugo wondered, or because Ruth Camden was a tyrant and Viola dared not jeopardize her job? Probably the latter, he thought, as he remembered Bebe's words about her aunt's disposition.

"It looks like Beauregard isn't in the house. He would have come out of hiding to eat don't you think?"

"He always hungry when I gets here. Waits by the back door where I put his food and water."

"It was thoughtful of you to come to take care of the cat."

A frightened look came into her eyes. "She was most particular about Beauregard. He's old. I just thought someone needed to see to him."

Hugo wondered if the cat had been in the house when Bebe arrived. He made a mental note to ask. There had been no evidence of him on either occasion when Hugo searched the premises.

"Mr. Prescott said he sent some papers around for Mrs. Camden to sign. That Bebe dropped them off. Were you here when that happened?"

"Yes. She went up to the attic. That's where Mrs. Camden was. Looking at her things."

"Did she do that often?"

"She spent a lot of time up there after Mr. Archibald died. Grieving. But that was years ago. Last couple of months she started spending time up there again." Viola shrugged. "I suppose it was because of Mr. Archie."

"Her grandson."

Viola nodded. "It upset her mightily. She didn't want him to go to war. Called Mr. Prescott about it. Wanted him to do something."

"But he didn't?"

"Said it was out of his hands."

"What about the papers? What did she do with them?"

Viola glanced at the swinging doorway of the kitchen. "They was on the table in the dining room when I left."

Hugo thought about this a moment. "Did she have a safe place she kept important papers? Somewhere other than the secretaire in the hallway?"

"You looking for her will? Her insurance papers?" She turned toward the doorway to the hall and went down it. Just before Ruth's bedroom, she opened a door to a small room. Her gaze skittered around the space. It served as an oversized closet. With the aid of a straight-backed chair she reached a hatbox on top of one of the three armoires.

Hugo took the hatbox from her and helped her back down off the chair. He placed the old box on a low dresser and removed the lid. It was nearly full of papers, envelopes of varying sizes, blue bound documents.

"Thank you. I'm sure we would have found this sooner or later but you've saved us a search."

"Mr. Prescott do know you here?"

Even though he was the police, it was obvious Viola feared Haywood Prescott's reaction more than she did him.

"Yes. He knows."

His assurance did little to alleviate the worried expression on her face.

"Well. I'll be going then. Ain't nothing I can do about that cat." She glanced fleetingly away from Hugo toward a corner of the room. Her gaze returned to him, then she walked back into the hallway and headed for the front door.

Hugo followed after her and as she was about to open it, he asked, "What's your last name, Viola?"

The apprehension seemed to grow in her expression. "Pritchett."

"Tyrone is your grandson?"

She shook her head. "My nephew."

It was as if she were holding her breath. Hugo wondered what she didn't want him to ask. "Thank you, Mrs. Pritchett."

She stared at him a moment longer then nodded and walked through the door.

Hugo watched from the open doorway as she got into the car and Tyrone drove away, the deep throated rumble of the glass packed twin mufflers changing to a roar when he turned onto Dauphin Street and accelerated away. Junior came bounding up the steps and looked back at the departing Barracuda until it disappeared from view. "What's the maid doing with Tyrone Pritchett?"

"Her nephew."

"Huh." Junior put out his cigarette against the sole of his shoe. He dropped the butt into his coat pocket and followed Hugo into the house and back down the hallway to the room used by Ruth Camden as a closet.

Hugo stared at the corner of the room partially barred by a standing fan, a coat tree with a man's raincoat thrown over it, and a small trunk. "Let's see what Viola didn't want me to know." They moved the objects obstructing his view. Sitting on the floor in the corner of the room was a safe about four feet tall.

Hugo pulled a pair of gloves from his pocket and put them on. When he tried to slide the safe out of the tight corner for easier access, he realized it was too heavy. "Must be made of solid iron."

He squatted in front of it. When he pulled on the door handle it swung open easily. There was nothing inside. Hugo ran his gloved finger across the shelves of the empty interior and looked at the tip. Nothing. He swiped his forefinger across the top of the safe and studied the track left in the dust.

"Wonder when it was emptied?" Junior asked.

"No way to know." Hugo stood. "Let's take a look at the stuff in the hatbox."

❧

THERE WAS NOTHING in the hatbox that was of any value. A good number of the papers were concerning the death and estate of Edward Camden in 1954. The envelopes held cards of condolence, as well as correspondence from far flung friends. There weren't any recent postmarks.

"She probably has a safe deposit box at the bank." Junior folded one of the letters and returned it to the envelope.

"Maybe." Hugo stood looking at the papers on the dining room table, lost in thought.

Viola knew about the safe. He had no doubt of that. Had she really come to feed the cat?

"Tell me about Tyrone Pritchett."

Junior started stacking the odds and ends of paper back into the hat box. "A big fan of Malcolm X, I hear. Spent some time in the North but came home after he got into trouble with the law."

"What kind of trouble?"

"Rumor has it he killed a man. I don't set much store by it." He placed the lid on the box. "He was never anything but a skinny runt of a kid before he went to Chicago to live with some of his family."

"So why do people think he killed someone?"

"Because he likes them to. Claims he killed the wolf for that fur on his coat."

"Yeah?"

"It's a good story, but honestly, can you imagine him in the wild? There aren't any wolves on the streets of Chicago, I'll tell you that. Except maybe in the dives and projects. The only wolves in Chicago are the kind who walk on two legs."

"When was this?"

"He showed up about a year and a half ago." Junior gave a snort of laughter. "Wearing dark glasses like those Black Panthers. Strutting when he walked like a banty rooster."

"Has he been in trouble since he came home?"

"Naw. Got a little mouthy with old Otto over at the shoe repair shop. Went in there to have him do something with that leather coat he wears most of the year. Otto wouldn't touch it. Said Tyrone was being disrespectful and that he didn't have to put up with that in his own place of business."

"What happened?"

"Nothing. Big Mo Hitchens caught the call. The sight of a uniform was enough for Tyrone to decide he wouldn't do business with a Nazi anyway."

"Nothing else?"

"Not that I know of. I can pull his record if you think we should give him a look but do you really think the maid had anything to do with Mrs. Camden's death?"

"I don't know what to think. She knew about the safe but didn't mention it even though it would be the most likely place for any important papers."

"You don't think she came to see about the cat?"

"Do you?"

"Depends, I guess. If she expects something from the Prescotts as a type of pension or remembrance, she might have." Junior grinned. "Or she might have thought she could just take a few of these expensive nick knacks made of silver to compensate for the loss of her job. I imagine Tyrone would know how to convert them to cash pretty quick."

HUGO AND JUNIOR spent a couple of hours going door to door on both sides of Dauphin Street. The neighbors they talked with had lived in the area for decades. They all knew Ruth. No one had seen anything out of the ordinary on Friday or Saturday morning. At the house next door, no one was home. Neither was the neighbor directly across the street.

After comparing notes, Hugo left Junior at his home without any argument. He watched as his friend climbed the front steps, resignation obvious in his carriage.

A small prick of remorse niggled at Hugo. Before his return to Mobile, Junior had been free of his shadow. He had been a detective with a city issued car. Even if that distinction carried no monetary advantage over the beat cop, there was the prestige of being singled out by his betters. And, now, after only a few weeks on the job, Hugo was driving the car and taking the lead on their first case together that amounted to more than Mrs. Lofton's husband giving her a broken arm and a head wound that required twenty stitches.

Hugo pushed the thought to the back of his mind. He couldn't alter his relationship with Junior any more than he could be the passive member of the partnership. It wasn't in his nature and after two months of trying, he didn't want to resist any more.

Junior stood on the front porch, his hand on the door handle, and looked back over his shoulder at Hugo.

He should call him back, Hugo thought. Ask him to come to the VFW to have a beer, decide on a strategy for the case. Instead he put the car into drive and turned toward downtown. He pulled to the curb in front of St. Andrew's and debated with himself for a while. Finally, he got out of the car.

The interior of the church was dimly lit by the late afternoon sun through the stained glass windows of the apse. There was no one about that he could see. Hugo took a seat on a pew near the back of the nave. He let the silence and faint fragrance of the alter flowers settle around him.

It had been many years since he had entered this structure that had at one time been so central to his life. How little it had changed. But that was the nature of the church, wasn't it? To withstand the turmoil of the world that swirled outside its doors and never let such events impinge on the piety of those it harbored. He stood to leave and saw Father Gregory coming up the aisle.

Father Gregory stopped at the end of the pew and nodded at him. "Welcome home, Hugo."

"Father."

Father Gregory smiled. "I heard you'd returned and that you're working with the police department."

"Good news travels fast."

"Marilyn Knight is a faithful ally. She keeps me apprised of the goings on in my flock."

"I'm not part of your flock anymore, Father. I haven't been for a long time."

"Ah." The priest sighed. "Still pouting with the church, I see."

"Call it what you like."

"Then why are you here?"

Hugo wasn't sure why he'd felt compelled to find his way to St. Andrew's but for an answer he said, "Ruth Camden. You know her?"

"Yes, of course. Sad news about her death. She didn't attend St. Andrew's but she has always been a valued supporter of many of the church's programs. When her son died in Korea she built the new West dormitory at St. Thomas More."

"What about her grandson, Archie? Can you tell me anything about him?"

"Only that he's been called up for active duty. She went to the Archbishop to ask him to intervene but there was nothing he could do."

Hugo turned his gaze to the apse and studied the crucifix mounted there. *Corpus humanitas*, the human and the divine in one body. All he saw was suffering. "What *can* the church do, Father?"

"You know the answer to that, my son."

"Not much, then." He stepped around the priest and headed for the West entrance.

"Hugo. . ." The priest's voice echoed in the vaulted ceiling of the church but Hugo didn't stop.

Six

He pulled into the Seven-Eleven at Government and George. He was surprised when he saw Lorraine Shaw behind the counter. She grinned when she looked up and recognized him.

"Hugo August. Where the devil have you been?"

She had a deep drawling voice that reminded him of whiskey neat and smokes.

He returned her smile and shrugged. "Here and there." He pulled out his shield. "Don't suppose I could entice you to break the law, could I?"

"Since when did you need permission to break the law?"

They both laughed.

"Cigarettes?" Her brows rose in query.

"No. I gave up smoking. Beer."

Lorraine looked past him, scanning the parking lot. "Sure. What's your brand?"

"Budweiser." He walked to the back wall of coolers. The glass door of the section containing beer was covered with butcher paper in keeping with the Sunday blue laws. He reached in and grabbed a six pack. He placed it on the counter and dug in his pocket for his wallet. "I thought you'd be off to Hollywood by now."

She gave him a rueful smile. "So did I, but you know how it is. Life happens."

"That I do know." He hesitated. "When do you get off work?"

"At six." Her smile turned sexy and she arched an eyebrow seductively. "Why?"

"Thought you might be thirsty." He couldn't take his eyes off her full lips painted a deep scarlet. She'd always worn that color, applying it as soon as she walked out the doors of St. Andrew's every day. And she looked awfully good with that mini skirt showing a mile of leg.

"Sure." She leaned over the counter and counted his change into his hand, tilted her head to look up through thick black lashes. "I'll meet you. Where?"

"I'll swing by for you."

She wrinkled her nose. "Not a good idea. I don't want to leave my car here."

"Okay. How about I come by your place? Say about six thirty?"

She pursed her lips and gave a small shake of her head. "That's not a good idea either."

"Still living at home?"

"You could say that." She held up her left hand and waggled her ring finger. "For a policeman you're not very observant."

Hugo leaned back and examined the ring. "Well, in my defense, I was distracted. Who's the lucky guy?"

"You wouldn't know him."

"Pity."

She sighed and puckered her lips into a pout. "I could come to your place."

Hugo shook his head. "As tempting as that sounds, I think I'll have to pass." He popped the top on a beer. "Maybe another time."

Lorraine laughed. "I remember when you wouldn't have cared about something as insignificant as a husband."

"Look at me. All grown up."

"And ain't that a shame."

Hugo took his beer and saluted Lorraine as he turned toward the door. "Yes, it is," he muttered to himself.

He was getting into his car when a gold Barracuda cruised down Government Street headed west, the deep throated rumble drawing his attention. Tyrone Pritchett. Hugo sat with the motor of the police sedan idling, sipping his beer, lost in thought. He put the car into gear and turned toward the station. It was time to take a look at the Wolf Man's sheet.

⁂

TYRONE PRITCHETT'S RECORD didn't reveal much beyond Junior's recollection of his history. Hugo was able to discover an address. He made a note of it and left the nearly deserted police station. The town was quiet, the kind of Sunday night quiet that generally blanketed the inhabitants of Mobile year-round. Hugo made his way home to a house that lay in darkness. Even his neighbor's house was quiet with a lone, bare blub burning on the front porch.

Hugo sighed and gathered the remaining four beers and went inside. The house held a damp chill and he lit the space heater in the front room. He stood and watched the ceramic grate begin to glow with the heat of the flames then took the luke-warm beers to the refrigerator. His debate over whether or not to have a third one to top off the night was interrupted by the ringing phone.

"August," he said into the mouthpiece.

"I need to see you." Bebe's voice sounded about two gins into the bottle. He could hear piano music in the background.

"Sure. Where are you?"

"The Quarter Note."

He looked at his watch. "I'll be there in fifteen minutes."

The line went dead.

He grabbed a fresh shirt from the armoire and checked his tie to see that it didn't have any obvious spots on it. A quick glance in the bathroom mirror, a comb through his hair, and he started for the door. He paused only long enough to extinguish the flame in the heater.

A GUY IN a tuxedo was playing at the piano bar, crooning a Frank Sinatra song. Bebe sat to his left, away from the other patrons who had gathered around. Hugo slid onto the stool next to her.

"Hey, you."

She offered up a smile, mellowed by alcohol. "Hey, yourself."

He studied her a moment. "How're you doing?"

"Great." She stood and picked up her drink. "Let get a table where we can talk."

He followed her across the room to a corner table with a reserved sign on it. She slid around the semi-circle banquet seat and he slipped in beside her.

"You need a drink." Bebe looked toward the bar.

A waiter appeared at their table. He picked up the reserved sign and slipped it into the pocket of his apron. "What will it be, sir?"

"Bourbon."

And then they were alone.

"Why didn't you call me when you got home?" Her voice held a note of aggrievement.

He saw the shimmer of tears in her eyes but also the steel resolve to hang on to the anger that simmered just below the surface.

"I didn't think you'd want to hear from me." He placed his hand over hers where it rested on the white linen tablecloth. She pulled away from his touch, picked up her drink, and drained the glass.

"Bebe. . ."

The waiter reappeared and she smiled up at him as he placed Hugo's drink on the table. "Thanks, Ernie. Will you get me another?"

Hugo waited until the waiter was out of hearing. "Do you think that's a good idea?"

"It's a perfect idea."

He let the silence grow between them as Bebe stared straight ahead. Ernie came and went, delivering her drink.

Sitting so close in the confines of a booth designed for lovers, the scent of her filled his senses. It was distinctive, seductive, and fragile. Just like Bebe. He had hallucinated this scent in Vietnam. When the stench of his own unwashed body was so pervasive that he could no longer smell himself, he could evoke the memory of Bebe's fragrance, how it lingered in the crook of her elbow, behind her jawline, in the bend of her knee.

He tore his gaze from her profile and cleared his throat. "Why did you call?"

Bebe turned her drink around and around on the table but didn't taste it. "Archie."

"Your cousin?"

"He's missing."

"You mean you don't know where he is, exactly, or missing in action?"

"He left for Fort Bragg on September thirteenth. He never checked in with his unit."

"AWOL? He never made it to basic? When did you find out?"

She turned to face him. "Daddy was trying to reach him to tell him about his grandmother. That's when the Army told Daddy there was a warrant out for Archie's arrest for draft evasion." She paused, a frown creasing her forehead. "I think Aunt Ruth knew. She hasn't been herself for a while."

"Where do you think he might be?"

Bebe shrugged. "Who knows. If Aunt Ruth had anything to do with it he's in Canada or Europe."

"Do you think she did?"

"She was furious with Daddy because he couldn't do anything to get Archie out of serving. She accused him of not trying. I think she would have done anything to keep Archie safe if he was willing to go along with it."

"Was he?"

Bebe sat quietly for a moment. "I don't know." She toyed with the olive in her drink. "I thought you might be able to find out what the Army plans to do if they find him."

"I can pretty much tell you the answer to that. He'll be court-martialed and sent to prison."

"Dear God." The words whispered past Bebe's lips. She pressed her fist against her chest. This time she didn't fight the tears that sprang to her eyes. "You have to do something, Hugo. You have to help him."

"Bebe, this isn't something that's in my power to fix. You're dealing with the Army and the serious problem they have with draft dodgers. They'll want to make an example of him."

"But what if something happened to him on the way? What if he was in an accident or. . .oh, I don't know!" She took the paper napkin from beneath her cocktail and dabbed at the corners of her eyes. "His grandmother is dead. We need to bring him home."

Hugo wanted to comfort her. He resisted the urge with a will of iron. There would be no going back if he did. So he sat quietly while she struggled to regain her composure.

"This is so horrible. All of it."

"Yes, it is. I'm surprised your father wasn't able to get him into a National Guard unit. That's the safest place to be right now."

"Aunt Ruth certainly thought he could have." She shook her head in a gesture of exasperation. "I know he tried. The Archbishop called and they talked about the options. And I know he was in contact with our senator."

"Did you talk to your father about it?"

"It was the subject of dinner conversation for weeks. Aunt Ruth kept hounding him." She turned her face from him and her voice caught when she spoke. "How did everything go so terribly wrong?"

The sadness in her voice tore at his resolve. She was no longer talking about Archie or her aunt. He wanted to kiss her. The desire ripped through him and he looked away. Then he took a good, long drink of bourbon. When he looked back at her, she was watching him.

Bebe leaned away from him, putting more distance between them as they sat side by side. She touched her hair, arranging the fall of waves. The moment was gone.

"I'll make some calls and see if I can find out what the Army knows. How did Archie travel?"

"By Greyhound."

"Who besides your aunt might have seen him off?"

She lifted a shoulder in a faint shrug. "No one, really. We had dinner the night before at the club. There was quite a crowd of us, maybe eight or ten?" Her forehead creased with thought. "Nine. Cissy didn't come. Skip said the baby was teething. And Aimeé wasn't there either."

"I can't promise anything."

"But you'll try?"

"Yes."

She nodded and gathered her handbag. "Thanks, Hugo. I. . ." She didn't finish whatever it was she was about to say. Instead she offered up a sad, fleeting smile then slid out the far side of the banquet seat. She crossed the room to the door of the lounge, shoulders back, self-assured. She was herself again.

Hugo knew he should probably drive her home but something held him back, something about that straight back and raised chin. That debutante walk delineated the differences in their worlds as effectively as the Berlin Wall.

Seven

Hugo started by calling the local Army recruiting office. Four years in the service didn't give him any inside knowledge about how to find out what Archie Camden's status might be and who could answer his questions. He got lucky because Buck Sissons was the in-take officer in the Mobile recruitment office.

"Long time, no see," Buck said when he answered the phone.

"How's the military career going, Buck? I thought you'd be in charge of a battalion by now."

"Funny. At least I'm not humping the boonies."

"There's that."

"What can I do for you?"

"I'm looking for Archie Camden."

"You're not the only one."

"So I heard."

"What's your interest?"

"His grandmother died."

"Yeah, I heard. What's that got to do with you?"

"It's my job. Mobile police."

"You? A cop?" Buck laughed. "Now I've heard it all."

"Truth is stranger than fiction." Hugo leaned back in his chair and tracked the chief's movements as he made for his office. "Seriously, what can you tell me?"

"He was MIA on his arrival at Fort Bragg on the fourteenth of September. The in-take officer put in a call to our office three days later. I went to his address of record and it was all closed up, a couple of pieces of mail in the mailbox. The neighbor said he'd left with his grandmother for the Greyhound bus station earlier in the week."

"Odd, don't you think, that he would travel by bus."

"Not really. That's how most recruits arrive unless they're traveling across country to catch their FTA. Uncle Sam is spending all his money on fireworks."

"But the Camden's have money. Wouldn't you think his grandmother would spare him an eighteen-hour bus trip?"

"You mean keep the heir apparent from rubbing elbows with the common folk?"

"Something like that."

"That's not how it works. Or have you forgotten? He was issued a ticket and the station manager remembers him and his grandmother. Not a lot of their passengers arrive in a new Cadillac Coupe de Ville."

"What do you think happened between Mobile and Fayetteville?"

"I think he decided the Army life wasn't for him and he got off the bus somewhere along the route. That happens a lot more than it used to."

"Where would he have gotten off, do you think?"

"My guess would be Atlanta. Big city, easy to get lost. And that's where the driver turns around and heads back south. Camden would have changed buses and picked up a new driver, one that didn't know he was supposed to be on the bus."

"What's the Army doing to find him?"

"The usual. There's a warrant out, naturally. There's been an inquiry into any sources of funds that might be available to him. The bus drivers for both legs of the trip were interviewed. I went with the MPs and talked with his grandmother, of course. She's listed as next-of-kin on all his records."

"What did she have to say?"

"I got an ear full from her. She was very vocal about him even being called up in the first place. Because his father died in Korea, she seemed to think he should have been given a pass."

"You speak with anyone else?"

Buck sighed. "Look, Hugo. I've got a dozen open files on guys from this region that have disappeared after their conscription letters went out. I've done this enough to know this one isn't going to be unearthed any time soon. Where there's money, there's a way. You know what I'm saying?"

"Yeah, I know what you're saying."

Archie Camden was in the wind and no one was looking very hard to find him.

CHIEF GOODE WAS on the phone when Hugo tapped on his open door. The chief ended his call and motioned for Hugo to come in.

"Did you know about Archie Camden?"

"AWOL. I got the warrant along with every other law enforcement agency nationwide."

"You didn't think I needed to know?"

"It didn't occur to me to mention it because it's old news. And, I didn't know Ruth Camden may have been poisoned until this morning." He flipped open a file jacket on his desk and held up a note from the lab. "I don't see how his desertion has anything to do with his grandmother's death. He's probably in Mexico living on a beach somewhere. Or freezing his ass off up in Canada."

Hugo turned to leave but paused at the door. "Did Buck Sissons contact you about it?"

"Don't recall. He might have. Like I said, that was two months ago." The chief stared him down, both of them aware of the implication behind Hugo's question. He reached for the phone and, as he dialed a number, said to Hugo, "Dr. Allen is doing the autopsy this afternoon. See what he can tell us."

∴

EVIE LEANED AGAINST the wall in the corridor outside the autopsy room. Her expression said it all.

"Kicked you out, did he?" Hugo mimicked her position against the wall.

"Never let me in." Her brows formed a thunder cloud. "Not suitable for a woman, he said." Her expression turned to one of pleading. "Talk to him, Hugo."

"It's not something you really want to see."

"What do you think I did during my training?" Her anger was now aimed at him. "It's 1968 for God's sake. All those nurses in Vietnam, you think they're being told to stay out of the operating room?"

Hugo suspected the medical examiner's objections came from Evie's appearance as much as his age and resistance to women being exposed to the realities of the autopsy table. Her petite stature and the horn-rimmed glasses accentuated her little-girl-lost look. The name didn't help much either. She should have been a Bernadette or Geraldine if she was going to compete in the world of science. The sisters did her no favors by giving her a name she so prophetically grew into.

He pushed away from the wall. "Come on, then. But don't say I didn't warn you."

"I've worked on cadavers, you know."

"What I know is you fainted when the bus I was hitching onto took a sudden left and my bike kept going straight into a parked car."

"First off, it wasn't your bike but mine. And, second, that was different. I thought you were dead."

"So did I." He chuckled as he held the door open for her. "And I still have the scars to remind me."

Dr. Allen looked up from the corpse on the table. "Get her out of here."

"She's seen a dead body before. She'll be okay."

"This is no place for a woman."

"But it's where a forensic scientist needs to be and that's what Evie is."

Dr. Allen's gaze flicked up and down Evie. He scowled. "Forensic scientist, huh?" He looked for a moment like he would argue the point. Instead he said, "Don't be sick in my morgue." He had already made the Y incision.

Evie stood beside Hugo, her hands clasped behind her back, as Dr. Allen proceeded.

"Well, the liver is certainly inflamed in this lobe. There's also fatty tissue but that's to be expected in someone her age."

"So, the inflammation is evidence of poison?" Hugo asked.

"I'm saying she has disease consistent with a less than healthy diet and areas of the liver show signs of acute inflammation that, in my opinion, suggests the ingestion of some kind of highly caustic substance. That can be anything from bourbon, over time, to acute arsenic poisoning."

"Any idea what?"

Dr. Allen looked up from the scale where he was weighing the liver. "Nope. You'll have to wait for toxicology to tell you that."

He made a notation on a chart. "There're hemorrhagic points visible across the surface of the heart and lungs indicative of oxygen deprivation." He pointed his pen toward the body's right hand. "The nail bed suggests cyanosis."

He took a long Q-tip and swabbed inside the mouth and the back of the throat. "This foamy liquid in the endotracheal cavity suggests she asphyxiated." He flipped a page on his clipboard. "It says she was found upright in a chair."

"Yes."

"No vomit at the scene?"

"No."

He examined the eyes with a pin light. "Petechiae around the eyes. Consistent with loss of air supply." He pulled an overhead light closer and examined the throat. "No signs of manual strangulation."

"What's your best guess as to cause of death?"

Dr. Allen looked over the top of his glasses at Hugo. "I don't guess, but," he flipped through the pages on the clipboard, "since this young lady determined the presence of poison in her tea, I would hypothesize that, *if* she drank it, the probability is she died due to paralysis of the autonomic system due to poison. My findings, however, could simply demonstrate that same loss of oxygen due to heart attack. She does have an enlarged heart and evidence of previous episodes of ischemia."

Hugo sighed. "That's not very conclusive."

"You'll have to wait for the tox report if you want a better answer. For now, all I can tell you is we have a suspicious death given the circumstances of the poison found in the tea."

⁂

HUGO AND EVIE stood on the sidewalk in front of the Mobile General Hospital. The wind off the river funneled down St. Anthony Street with a bite to it. Colder weather had arrived. "So, what do you think?"

"He's right." Evie pushed her hair back from her face. "We have to follow the science. Especially since I think she was poisoned and this will open a real can of worms if we can take it to trial."

"Agreed." Hugo opened the passenger door of the car. "Come on, I'll give you a ride back to the station."

"Take me to the library instead. I want to check on something."

⁂

HUGO LEANED BACK in his swivel chair and stared at the notes taped to the wall behind his desk. At the center was one of the photos Junior had taken of Ruth Camden. Creating an orbit around this gruesome sight were three-by-five cards with notes in Hugo's handwriting. Above the photo were notes bearing the name of each person he had encountered since first arriving at the house on Dauphin Street. The family members were grouped together on the right, and Viola, Tyrone, Buck Sissons, and Wayne the postman, were on the left. Beneath the photo he had posted the name Beauregard, the word safe, and AWOL, each on its individual card.

Junior dropped the Mobile City Directory on Hugo's desk with a thud. "It'll take a while on the phone records. I got a court clerk to sign off on the subpoena but the girl at the phone company says these things take a while. In the meantime, here's 1967 at your fingertips." He studied Hugo's display. "You think one of them actually did it?"

Hugo glanced at Junior then back at the notes. "Someone did. We have to start somewhere."

"Why's the grandson up there? He high tailed it out of here two months ago to avoid the war."

"He's AWOL but he could be anywhere. Even right here in Mobile."

"He can't be that dumb."

Hugo made no reply. He swiveled around to face his desk and opened the large hard-bound book that held the details of the lives of the good citizens of Mobile between its covers. It documented the number of households, who lived in them, their occupations, employers, marital status, and children. He was searching for Viola Pritchett when the chief called to him from the doorway of his office.

"Close the door," the chief said when Hugo entered the room.

Hugo complied and stood waiting while the chief steepled his fingers together and studied him.

Goode sat forward in his chair and opened a file on the desk. "Dr. Allen called." He read a handwritten note in the file then closed it. "He can't find a definitive cause of death."

"What about the cyanosis?"

"It was very faint in the nail beds. Could simply be the result of post mortem pooling of blood."

"And the lungs and heart?"

"Signs of asphyxia. All of which can be attributed to a heart attack causing loss of air supply."

"So, what are you saying?"

"Don't go making this into a murder. There's nothing to indicate this wasn't a death from natural causes."

Hugo held his tongue for a count of three. "What about the tea?"

"We don't know that she drank any of it."

Hugo waited.

"Look. The Haywoods and Prescotts have a lot of clout. There's nothing to be gained by stirring up a hornet's nest when this could all just be what it appeared to be when you arrived on the scene." The chief sighed. "Rhys is sending everything to Auburn for analysis. Until they can tell us *definitively* that something is fishy, keep this low key."

Evie's words echoed in his mind. *Follow the science*. He shrugged. "Anything else?"

"Take that damn picture off your wall.

Nine

The screaming woke Hugo. He coughed and rolled over onto his side. The gritty, damp sand was cold against his cheek. He opened his eyes and saw the sun rising over the horizon. Sea gulls glided above the shoreline, their cries echoing along the beach.

He raised a hand to his face and felt grit. A wave of panic rushed through him as he struggled to his feet, fighting for his footing, his heart pounding. He dusted at the damp sand clinging to his clothes as he peered through the pilings of the house overhead. The police sedan was parked at a drunken angle just beyond the beach house.

"Christ." How had he gotten there? He scanned the nearby houses. All was quiet, no cars, no people. Everything looked deserted, all closed up for the winter.

He searched his pockets for the keys as he lurched toward the car. He yanked the door open and saw them dangling from the ignition. His heart rate began to slow to a more normal beat. He slumped in the driver's seat and ran his hands down his face.

For several minutes, he sat there trying to remember. He looked around the seat and into the back. No beer cans. No dead soldiers.

He was cold to the bone. Sand clung to his face, hair, and clothing. He turned the key in the ignition and adjusted the heater setting. His body was stiff and ached. He sat there, his head resting on his hands as he gripped the steering wheel at the twelve o'clock position. After a few minutes, warm air began to blow on his feet. Slowly the warmth filled the car. He backed out of the sand without getting stuck and headed toward the bridge connecting Dauphin Island to the mainland.

When he pulled onto the empty lot next to his house he saw Maurice sitting on the porch steps.

"Maurice." He closed the car door and crossed the yard. "You're up early."

"And you're up late." Maurice flicked the butt of his cigarette into the dead grass. "You look like shit."

"What can I do for you?" Hugo sat on the step next to him

"You had a visitor."

"Yeah?"

"She waited a long time."

"Did she?"

"Well, a long time for a woman like her."

"What's that like?"

"Too good for the likes of you."

Hugo gave a small grunt of amusement. "That applies to just about everybody except maybe the short time girls."

Maurice nodded. "True."

They sat in silence as the day grew brighter.

"You ever get it on with the boom-boom girls?" Maurice asked.

"No."

"Why not? You a virgin or something?"

Hugo shrugged. "The posters, I guess, at Basic. Or the hypodermic needle the size of a bicycle pump on the wall of the medic's shack at Long Binh."

"That would do it."

The silence began to lengthen again and Hugo said, "Well?"

"Good looking." Maurice smiled, revealing a gold tooth. "Really good looking."

"Blond? Brunette? Redhead?"

"Black hair. Like a crow's wing. Red lips. Curves like Highway 69. A sexy voice that would make a man stand right up."

Hugo felt a twinge of disappointment. "Lorraine. Did she leave a message?"

"Said she was thirsty." Maurice chuckled. He stood but didn't move toward his house.

"What?"

"I need a favor."

"I'm listening."

Maurice seemed to be struggling with what to say next. He shook his head. "It's probably nothing."

"But?"

"This friend of mine. . ." He paused. "It's probably nothing."

Hugo waited but Maurice simply shook his head again and lifted his hand in a dismissive gesture.

"Well, if it becomes something, let me know."

Maurice nodded. "*Didi.*" He started across the empty lot toward his house. "You really should give Hot Lips a call."

Hugo grinned and stood to enter the house. He paused on the stoop. "Hey, Maurice."

Maurice stopped halfway across the empty lot that separated their houses and turned to look back at Hugo.

"You know Tyrone Pritchett?"

"Know of him."

"What is it you know?"

"Nothing good."

"Like?"

"Small time. Drugs, guns, the usual."

"Anything specific?"

"Don't pay to know anything specific." Maurice turned and continued on to his house.

⁂

HUGO TOOK A long, hot shower. He let himself relax, let his mind float. But, by the time the water began to cool, he still had no clue how he ended up on Dauphin Island sleeping beneath the Haywood-Prescott beach cottage.

The phone started ringing and Hugo turned off the water and stepped out of the shower. It was Junior.

"Where've you been? I've been calling you since late yesterday."

"Out."

"Out where?"

Hugo hesitated. "What you got?"

"I found something interesting about Tyrone."

"What's that?" Hugo rubbed at his wet hair with a threadbare towel as he talked.

"He just bought that Barracuda three months ago."

"And?"

"Paid cash."

"That is interesting." Hugo stretched the phone cord across the kitchen. He opened the refrigerator and inspected the contents. He closed the door. "I'll pick you up in twenty minutes."

⚜

JUNIOR POURED ORANGE juice into a glass and grabbed the toast from the toaster. "Grammy. Breakfast's on the table."

When he got no answer, he went through to the living room and could see the milkman through the front window standing just below the steps in the yard. He was talking to Junior's grandmother as she stood on the porch in her house dress. The way she gestured with her hands and the coy turn of her head made the heat rise in Junior's face.

He knew people thought his grandmother was a flirt, that she couldn't seem to get enough male attention. What they didn't know was that she was the kindest, gentlest person he knew. She didn't mean anything by her flirtations. Junior told himself that it was only because her husband had died when she was so very young. Maybe if she had had a long marriage she wouldn't feel the need to be admired and flattered. She had only ever had the companionship of her daughter and then her grandson. She was lonely, the kind of loneliness that women felt, he supposed. Anyone who knew her knew she didn't mean anything by it. But still, it embarrassed Junior sometimes. He tried to ignore it but there it was.

He was halfway through his breakfast when he heard her talking as she entered the house. She spoke in the slightly higher pitch that came into her voice when she was talking to a man. Then he heard Hugo respond to her question and again felt the heat in his face.

She had always been that way with Hugo, even when they were kids. Something about him had been different from the start. It was as if he had already experienced life. He seemed apart from the childish antics of the other children in the neighborhood even when he participated in them. People recognized that in him. Even Junior.

It wasn't something he resented in his friend. In fact, it was something he was drawn to like everyone who came into Hugo's sphere.

Junior had been rescued by Hugo on his first day at St. Andrews. He had just come to live with his grandmother. Both he and Hugo had been in Sister Mary Elizabeth's third grade class and she was a bully who loved to dole out punishment for the slightest infraction, either real or imagined.

When questioned, Junior had given Sister Mary Elizabeth his name. He had been afraid of her, of a new school full of strangers, of not knowing anyone in Mobile, including his grandmother.

Sister Mary Elizabeth had demanded a second time that he speak up. Hugo had intervened by asking her if she was deaf. He repeated Junior's name very slowly and loudly. Sister Mary Elizabeth unleashed her fury on Hugo. In that moment, Hugo became Junior's hero and best friend. He still was.

It had been a relief when Hugo returned to Mobile after a five year absence with no word except a lone post card from Hawaii. If the truth be told, it was also a relief to Junior that Hugo had resumed his role as the dominate member of their friendship. He had felt lost without Hugo as the rudder of his life. The role of a detective had kept him anxious, fearful of failing, and, in the end, thankful that he had never had to deal with a real life and death case on his own.

It wasn't that Junior didn't think he could do the job. Or that he didn't have good instincts. It was something else that he couldn't define. Hugo gave him the confidence to be himself, to trust himself.

"Coffee?" Junior stood and took a cup from the cupboard and motioned toward Hugo.

"You bet. It smells good in here, better than the Tiny Diny."

Junior got down another plate and filled it with bacon, eggs, and grits. He placed it at the empty space at the kitchen table. "How about you, Grammy?"

"Just some toast, Junior." She smiled and cut her eyes at Hugo when he sat at the place Junior had laid for him. "And coffee."

Junior filled everyone's cup and sat back down. "Lorraine Shaw called last night. Looking for you." He sipped at the hot coffee.

"Yeah? What did she want?"

"To know where you lived."

"Such a pretty girl," his grandmother interjected.

"I heard she was married." Hugo took a drink of the strong coffee and nodded in satisfaction.

"She is. To Big Mo Hitchens."

Hugo looked up, a fork full of eggs midway to his mouth. "You're kidding me?"

"Nope."

"It's a good thing I wasn't home, then."

"More than a good thing." Mrs. K gave Hugo a look of admonition. "I hear he's crazy jealous of her."

"Good to know." Hugo wiped his mouth with a napkin. "So, what did you find out about the Wolf Man?"

Junior sat back in his chair and stretched his legs under the table. "It's pretty much like I said. He wants to be seen as a big man around the neighborhood. Seems to think his time in Chicago gives him some kind of macho or something. Word is, if you need a gun he can get it for you. Also a good source for weed. Nothing about hard stuff, though."

"Small time, then."

"That's what it looks like."

"And yet he has a nearly new Barracuda with all the bells and whistles."

"Yep. And he paid cash."

Hugo ate the last piece of toast smeared with fig preserves and finished off his coffee. "I think we need to pay the car dealership a visit."

"My thoughts, exactly."

IT TOOK THEM a good ten minutes to break free of Mrs. K once they finished breakfast. She made Junior promise to be home in time to take her to vote before the polls closed. She was fearful that Nixon would win. She fussed over Junior's tie, whether or not he had his wallet, and made sure Hugo wouldn't like another cup of coffee. In this most domestic of moments, Hugo felt one of those rare flashes of belonging.

The fact was, the few times Hugo had ever felt whole had been in Marilyn Knight's house. He had always felt unanchored, always searching. Something was missing and he had never been able to define it. Those rare moments of being whole, of belonging, came from the total acceptance without reservation that he felt from Junior's grandmother. Some people saw her as flirtatious but he knew her behavior for what it truly was. She was searching for something, too. Something she couldn't define any more than Hugo could.

"Where's the dealership?" He asked as they crossed the lawn to the police sedan parked at the curb.

"Over on Holcombe Avenue."

Hugo tossed the car keys to Junior. "You drive."

Eddie, of Eddie's Used Cars, came out of the trailer that served as the sales office as soon as they pulled onto the lot. Once he realized they weren't paying customers the jovial attitude became all business.

"Got the car off a kid headed into the Army. Said he wouldn't be needing it for a couple of years and he wanted the money to leave for his mama." Eddie nodded in satisfaction. "A nice ride, all tricked out with white wall tires, glass packed mufflers, leather seats." He nodded again. "A real sweet deal."

"Tyrone Pritchett paid cash, you said."

"Twenty-three hundred dollars. All above board, perfectly legit. Title transfer signed, sealed, and delivered. I gave him a discount for cash. The car isn't even two years old."

"Do you get a lot of customers paying that kind of cash?"

"Most of my customers are lucky to scrape together a couple hundred bucks for a down payment. I get the rest in monthly installments."

"What was the date of the sale?"

"I'll have to check my records."

When Eddie made no move to do just that, Hugo said, "Now would be a good time."

"Right, right." Eddie went back into his office.

Hugo strolled along the line of parked used cars, Junior trailing along with him. He stopped at a white Ford Thunderbird with a black landau top.

"Nice car."

Hugo thought so, too, but he said nothing.

Eddie came hurrying across the lot. "That's just the car you need. I can make you a sweet deal. It's a '63 but very low mileage. Nearly new tires and an automatic transmission."

"You got the date Pritchett bought the Barracuda?"

"Sure, sure." He handed Hugo a pink note. "August second."

Hugo looked at the date written on the note then slipped it into his pocket. "Thanks."

Ten

"I don't know how Tyrone figures into it." Junior turned the car toward downtown.

"Neither do I." Hugo squinted against the morning sun. "But there's something there. It might not have anything to do with the death but they're hiding something."

"They?"

"Viola and her nephew."

"Okay. What now?"

Hugo was silent for a couple of blocks. "The Waterman Building. It's time Prescott answered some questions."

"Like?"

"What was in the safe for one, and who benefits from her death."

They found a parking space on Bienville Square. Inside the foyer of the Waterman building, they skirted the huge rotating globe the building was famous for and checked the directory set out in polished brass letters. Haywood Enterprises had their offices on the fifteenth floor.

Haywood Prescott's secretary had the whole Twiggy thing going on but even though she was thin as a twig, she was no light weight. She was adamant that Mr. Prescott couldn't be disturbed and that Hugo needed to make an appointment.

After a bit of back and forth, Junior took out his notebook and began writing in it. "Your name?"

She glanced from Junior to Hugo. He could see the wheels turning.

Just how much trouble would she be in if she continued to stonewall the police?

"I'll just see if he can spare a minute."

She disappeared behind an elaborately carved, heavy, oak door only to reappear in a couple of minutes.

"Mr. Prescott will see you now." Her voice was very prim and her lips thinned to show her disapproval.

Haywood Prescott rose from his chair behind a desk the size of a small dining table. It, too, was made of a heavy, expensive wood. The windows at this height gave a view of the Mobile River, the docks, and the narrow causeway snaking across the bay to the Eastern shore. The mid-morning sun glistened off the water.

"What can I do for you August?"

"Just a couple of questions, if you don't mind, about the state of your aunt's affairs." Hugo took one of the chairs facing Prescott's desk without invitation. Junior took the other. "I'm sure Chief Goode has brought you up to date on the situation with her death."

Prescott resumed his seat. "Yes. A suspicious death." He cleared his throat. "I was probably hasty in my reaction. It was the shock of it all, I suppose. And how she looked."

"I think your instincts were right." Hugo glanced at Junior who took out his notebook and pen. "The testing process is lengthy and tedious but there's no doubt in my mind that she drank the poisoned tea. It's just a matter of time before we discover what the poison was."

Prescott swiveled his desk chair around and stared out at the view for a moment before turning back to face Hugo and Junior. "The chief seemed less certain."

"You'll forgive me, but the chief wasn't there. Unless we find that someone else was sipping poison from a china cup in your aunt's attic, I think we have a very deliberate murder."

"Why would someone want to murder Ruth?"

"That's what we intend to find out. And we can start with the terms of her will. Do you happen to know who inherits her estate?"

"No. Not really. I would imagine Archie will get the bulk of it. With

Uncle Edward, her husband, and Archibald, her son, dead, he would be the closest living relative she has."

"Exactly how is she related to you?"

"She's my mother's sister. There were three siblings. Ruth, my mother, and my Uncle Sebastian Haywood. In that order. My mother's dead. Bass—Sebastian, that is—lives in Arizona. He has no children. I have a sister. My brother was MIA in Korea."

"Two cousins lost in the Korean War. Odd coincidence."

"They joined up together. Everyone thought it would be over in six months. Both of them felt they'd missed out on all the action."

"You didn't share their sentiment?"

"I did my stint in North Africa chasing Rommel. I tried to discourage them but Walter was determined. He was twelve years younger than me and he felt he'd been cheated. Our cousin, Archibald, was closer to my age but he had given in to the concerns of his parents. He was their only child. He was bitter about being forced to stay home and finish his college degree then follow his father into the family business. His son was a toddler when the conflict in Korea escalated. Archibald should have had better sense but he felt Korea was his chance to experience war and victory. He never came home. Left his wife a widow and Archie fatherless."

"Who would know the contents of your aunt's will?"

"Her lawyer. Maybe Archie."

"The lawyer's name?"

"Tyler Redman." Prescott opened a drawer of his desk, took out an address book, and flipped through the pages. "His office is in the Van Antwerp building." He made a notation on a notepad, tore the page off and handed it across the desk to Hugo. "That's his phone number. I'm not sure how these things work but you may tell him that I have no objections to him sharing whatever information he sees fit with you." Prescott stood.

Hugo stood as well. He slipped the note into his coat pocket. "Thanks, Mr. Prescott."

"You'll keep me informed of your findings?"

"I'm sure the chief will be happy to keep you in the loop." He shook Prescott's hand and turned to leave. "What happened to the papers Bebe took to Mrs. Camden?"

"I don't know."

"You didn't retrieve them the day you discovered her body?"

"No. That was the last thing on my mind."

They were at the door of the office when Junior turned to Prescott. "What was in the safe?"

"Pardon?"

"Mrs. Camden's safe. It was unlocked and empty. Do you know what she kept in it?"

"I have no idea. I didn't even realize she had a safe. It was Edward's, I imagine. As far as what she kept in it, her jewelry maybe?" He hesitated. "Do you think she was robbed?"

Hugo shrugged. "It's hard to say. Until we can find out what she kept in it. Who would be the best person to do a walk through to see what might be missing from the house?"

Prescott shook his head. "Honestly, I don't know. The maid, perhaps. Or Aimeé Marlowe."

"Thanks." With that Hugo and Junior left the office and didn't speak until they were once again on the sidewalk in front of the building.

"That was easier than I thought." Junior rocked back on his heels as they stared across the street into Bienville Square. The splashing of the three-tiered fountain could be faintly heard during the lulls in the morning traffic.

"Too easy." Hugo turned toward the intersection of St. Joseph Street and Dauphin. "He already knows what's in the will."

"Probably." Junior fell into step with Hugo. "The money will stay in the family. Everyone's happy. Life goes on."

At Dauphin and Royal they entered the Van Antwerp building. The lawyer's office was on the second floor.

Hugo could tell by the receptionist's reaction to their arrival that Prescott had already given them a heads-up. She ushered them into

Redman's office. Unlike Prescott's lair, the lawyer's accommodations were well worn, cramped, and reeked of cigars.

Tyler Redman was also a stark contrast to Haywood Prescott in his dress and physique. Where the industrialist was fit, well-groomed, and attractive, Redman's suit looked as though he slept in it. His fringe of hair needed a trim, and his teeth were deeply stained from a life-time of either smoking or chewing on cigars. Or both. He appeared to be all bone and sinew.

He rose from his chair when Hugo and Junior squeezed into his office. They shook hands and took their seats.

"Now, then, what can I do for the police?"

"You're Ruth Camden's attorney?"

He nodded.

"We have some concerns about her death."

"Haywood said."

"He called you?"

"Said give you whatever you want though it's not up to him to decide."

"The terms of her will."

"In the main, it goes to Archie. If he should predecease Ruth, then it's divided among various members of the family with a few special bequests." Redman took a cigar out of a box on his desk and snipped the end with a cigar cutter. "At least, those were the terms until a month ago."

Junior took out his notebook and began taking notes.

"She changed it?" Hugo asked.

"The bulk of it still goes to Archie. But she cut her cousin Aimeé Marlowe out entirely. She also left a substantial bequest to her maid."

"Viola?"

"Twenty thousand dollars."

"That's pretty substantial. Had she left anything for her in the original version?"

"Five thousand dollars. And she's to get the cat, Beauregard."

"Have you told Haywood any of this?"

"No. I'm meeting with him and his sister and the rest of the family tomorrow afternoon. There are a few minor bequests to them. Haywood's sister, Sharon, gets the family silver, a few pieces of antique furniture, and some other personal items. Bebe gets the house on Dauphin Street."

"You call that a minor bequest?"

"If you consider what Ruth is worth, yes."

"When will you file with Probate?"

"I'd like to try to get in touch with Archie first."

"Do you know where he is?"

"No. Haywood tells me he's missing."

"And you don't have any information on how that came about?"

"Why would I?"

"You're Mrs. Camden's attorney. And now, I guess, you're his as well."

"I was Ruth's attorney and now I'm the attorney for her estate. Whatever Archie has gotten up to is none of my doing."

"Where do you think he is?"

"I couldn't say."

"Has any of Mrs. Camden's money been re-appropriated?"

"I won't know that until I have Letters Testamentary and can check her accounts."

"When will that be?"

"I'm trying to get a line on what the Army has to say about Archie. A Major Gregson is supposed to be in touch sometime later today. I'll meet with the rest of the family tomorrow, and then I'll file the necessary documents with the court. It usually takes about a month but I can get the clerk to speed things up. I should have everything I need within two weeks."

Junior looked up from his notepad. "What does Mrs. Camden keep in the safe?"

"I don't know. I guess I'll find out when I have the authority to open it."

"It's already open. And it's empty."

"You don't say." Redman took a lighter from the desk drawer and puffed at the cigar until it caught. "I guess I'd better get over to her house and secure it."

"That's already done." Hugo said. "For now, we're treating it as a crime scene. No one is to go in or out until we release it."

Redman studied Hugo and puffed on his cigar. "What do you think happened?"

"Someone poisoned her."

"With what?"

"We won't know that until we get the analysis back."

Redman leaned his head against the high back of his chair and stared above Hugo and Junior's heads. "Any idea who did it?"

"That's what we're trying to determine. Did Mrs. Camden have any enemies to your knowledge?"

"No. She was old fashioned which made her come off to some as stiff and proper. She was plain spoken which offended some. But she was honest, quietly generous, and devout. She was also my friend."

"Why did she write her cousin out of the will?"

"Ruth and Aimeé have tiffed off and on since Aimeé first came over from France. She was private and didn't air her grievances so I just assumed they were off again."

"What involvement did Mrs. Camden have in Haywood Mills?"

"Substantial."

"As in?"

"A one-third interest."

"Did you draw up any papers concerning her interest in the mill in the past week or so?"

"No. I only deal with Ruth's side of things. Whenever Haywood wants something, his lawyers do the paperwork and I review it on Ruth's behalf."

"She hasn't asked you to review anything lately?"

"No."

"Who has the other third?"

"That would be Bass."

"Sebastian Haywood?"

"Correct."

"What about Haywood's sister?"

"Sharon. I don't know if she got any of the mill shares. She was already married at the time. She got the bay house and some bonds from what I hear. I don't know what else. I wasn't involved in any of that. The Haywoods have a whole firm of lawyers who take care of them and theirs."

"She still live in Mobile?"

"Point Clear."

"Of course."

⁂

"TWENTY THOUSAND DOLLARS." Junior whistled softly. "That makes a nice little retirement bonus." He turned the key in the ignition of the police sedan and pulled out into the traffic on Dauphin Street.

"Yes." Hugo took out his notebook and flipped through the pages. "I think we need to pay Viola a visit." He found the address he was looking for in his notes. "But first we need to get something to eat and review what we know so far."

They went to the Dew Drop Inn. The lunch crowd was thinning out. Nancy brought them menus.

"I hear you think Ruth Camden was murdered." Her eyes sparkled with interest as she looked from one to the other of the detectives.

Hugo kept his eyes on the menu and his voice disinterested. "Where'd you hear that?"

"A cop."

"Yeah?" Hugo looked up. "Which one?"

"Dewey Nelson."

"Huh." He handed her the menu. "I'll have the Devil Dog. Extra chilli."

Nancy glanced from Hugo to Junior, her pen poised over her

pad. When neither Hugo nor Junior commented further, she wrote down their orders.

"Christ." Hugo pulled out his notebook. "The chief won't be happy."

Junior took a sip of his iced tea. "It was bound to get out sooner or later. The mailman's been telling everyone who will listen all the gory details."

Hugo read a page of his notebook. "We need to talk to the neighbor's yard man. He worked late on Friday, replanting the azaleas along their driveway according to the retired engineer across the street. Maybe he saw something."

"There are a couple of neighbors who weren't home Sunday. I'll keep at it until I catch someone."

"The timeline doesn't give us much to go on. The last person to see her appears to be Viola."

"Two-thirty, give or take a few minutes. We need to narrow the window."

Hugo stared off across the restaurant, not really seeing the other diners. "I agree. Someone came to the house on a very busy Friday afternoon or early evening."

"The house sits so far back from the street that the passing traffic wouldn't necessarily notice much."

"They would notice someone turning into the drive. Or leaving."

"Maybe."

"If it was a gold Barracuda with glass packed mufflers it would be hard to miss."

"True."

They fell silent as Nancy brought their lunch and placed it on the table.

"I can't get the cat out of my head." Hugo doused his hotdog with Tabasco sauce. "His disappearance would help us with the timeline if we could find someone who saw him."

"How?"

"Viola said she put the cat out on Friday before she left to catch the three o'clock bus."

"And?"

"No one has seen it since."

"Maybe they have and didn't think it was significant enough to mention."

"That's what I'm thinking." Hugo returned the notebook to his coat pocket and turned his attention to his meal. "We need to re-canvas the neighborhood and find out if anyone has seen the cat."

"If he was still roaming the neighborhood in the late afternoon then Mrs. Camden didn't keep to her habit of getting him back in before heading out for five o'clock Mass."

"Exactly."

Eleven

They made their way east down Old Shell Road to Broad Street and turned left toward the area of town known as The Bottom. It was an old community that dated from the Spanish Colonial period. Its boundary to the north and west was Three Mile Creek, hence the name, as in the creek bottom.

Viola's home was a shotgun house that stood out on a street turning toward decay and neglect. It was evident she took pride in her residence. It looked like it had been painted within the past year. The humidity of Mobile was the curse of homeowners who waged a constant battle against mildew and peeling paint caused by the proximity of the river and bay.

An aluminum glider sat on a front porch not much bigger than the stoop at Hugo's house. It was aqua. The trim of the house had been painted the same color. Neatly clipped privet formed a skirt across the front of the house hiding the underpinnings. A pot of bright red geraniums sat on either side of the steps.

Hugo counted two houses down on either side of Viola's address, trying to decide which one might be John Henry's residence. He and Junior got out of the car. Two teenagers coming their way on bicycles turned around in the middle of the street at the sight of them and headed back the way they had come. An old man sitting in a faded stuffed chair on the porch of the house across the street got up and went inside.

Viola opened the door after the first knock. Her hair was tied up in a red kerchief. She had an apron on over her dress. Her eyes grew large when she saw them.

"Mrs. Pritchett, we need to ask you a few questions."

"About what?"

"About Mrs. Camden's routine, about Archie."

She hesitated then removed the latch on the screen door. "Come in."

The small sitting room was neat but sparsely furnished. The pieces were of quality. Cast-offs from Ruth Camden, Hugo thought. There were two armchairs with a round occasional table between them that divided the sitting area from a dining table pushed against the back wall of the small space. She motioned for the two men to take the armchairs and she brought one of the two dining table chairs to sit opposite them. She perched on the edge of the seat, her hands clasped together in her lap, and waited for them to speak.

Junior took out his notebook.

Hugo glanced around the room. "You have a lovely home, Mrs. Pritchett."

"It's Miss Pritchett."

Hugo nodded. "Have you lived here long?"

"I was born in this house."

"Do you live here alone?"

"Yes."

"Where does Tyrone live?"

She shifted on the edge of the seat. "I don't know. He don't stay in one place for long."

"How did you know where to get in touch with him to bring you to Mrs. Camden's house to check on the cat?"

"He hangs out with some friends at a place on Chinquapin Street. I called over there and they got the message to him."

"What's the place? In case we need to get in touch with Tyrone."

Her knuckles paled as she clinched her fists. She glanced down at them where they rested on her lap and relaxed her hands. "Abe's Bar-be-que."

"Does Tyrone pick you up from the Camden house very often?"

She shook her head. "Once in a while is all. If I work on the week-end. Or it come a storm."

"And you call him at Abe's to let him know you need a ride?"

She nodded.

"When was the last time, before Sunday, that he came to get you? Do you remember?"

She shook her head. "A month ago, maybe. I can't rightly recall."

Junior flipped back through the pages of his notebook. "Did anyone else visit Mrs. Camden on Friday?"

Viola shook her head.

He made a notation and frowned. "Did the yard man come that day?"

"No. He comes on Wednesday."

"No phone calls?"

"Mrs. Fillmore called about the meeting of the historical society. The drug store called to say her prescription was ready." Viola's forehead creased in thought. "And Mrs. Marlowe. But Mrs. Camden wouldn't talk to her."

"Oh?" Hugo sat forward, his elbows on his knees, his hands clasped lightly together. "Why not?"

"I don't know. Mrs. Camden just say to tell her she busy."

"Did they talk often?"

"Most days. Until here lately."

"What changed?"

"Mrs. Camden upset with her about Mr. Archie. She nearly mad with grief when he have to go off to training and Mrs. Marlowe fuss at her about what she call her irrational behavior about it all."

"Did you think Mrs. Camden's behavior was irrational?" Hugo's tone was reflective, inviting speculation.

"She called Mr. Prescott and the Archbishop and her lawyer. She keep after them to do something but she was herself, you know? She don't shout or cry or break down. She just insist that something be done. Had to be done." Viola shook her head. "You had to know her to understand how much it bothered her. She don't show her true feelings to people."

"And Mrs. Marlowe was unsympathetic."

"Yes. It was like Mr. Archie was just someone she hardly knew. She couldn't understand what Mrs. Camden was so worried about."

"Were you worried for Archie?"

She swallowed and looked down at her hands. "Yes. He's such a good boy. Always remember my birthday. Brought that dining table over for me in a friend's truck two years ago. Said I should have it since I polished it so many times." When she looked up at Hugo and Junior, there were tears standing in her eyes. "Gave me a ride if he was home and the weather got mean."

"I thought he lived on his own."

"He do now. Come home from college in the spring and say it was time he moved out of the nest."

"Did he want to go to 'Nam, Viola?"

She shook her head. "He never said but I know he didn't want to go. Who would? What we doing on the other side of the world killing people we don't even know? Why we doing that?"

"I wish I knew." Hugo stood. "Thank you, Viola."

She rose from her chair, moved it back to the table, and waited as they left. Once they stepped onto her porch, she put the latch on. She spoke to them through the screen door. "She didn't have a heart attack, did she?"

"We don't know how she died yet. There are questions we need to answer before we can say for certain."

"The paper says the funeral is Thursday."

"Yes."

"What about Mr. Archie?"

"No one knows where he is. Do you?"

Viola shook her head and pulled back into the shadow of her house. She continued to watch from behind the screen door until Junior pulled the sedan away from the curb and headed back toward the heart of town.

✳

JUNIOR DROPPED HUGO at police headquarters at Government and Royal. He returned to the Camden house and sat in the car reviewing his notes.

The Goldings to the east of Ruth had not been at home when he and Hugo canvased the area on Sunday. He decided to start there.

The maid answered the door. Junior identified himself. She turned to fetch her employer but Junior stopped her.

"Were you here on Friday?"

She didn't respond immediately. Junior knew she was trying to decide how best to answer him and still escape the notice of the police.

Finally, she said, "Yes." She refused to make eye contact.

"Did you see the neighbor's cat? Beauregard?"

Her head jerked up, surprise evident in her expression.

"The cat?"

"Yes."

She nodded distractedly, her gaze distant as she called up the memory.

"I see him out the back." She nodded again, pleased to answer such an innocuous question. "I was getting my sweater and umbrella out the pantry. I see him out along the back hedge."

"What was he doing?"

"Doing?" Her brows came together and she stared at Junior. "He a cat!"

"Was he grooming himself? Chasing a mouse?"

"Ain't no mouse on Mrs. Golding's property!" She crossed her arms in a huff.

Junior waited.

"He just crossing the yard. He do that all the time."

"What time was this?"

"About two-thirty. Like I say, I was fetching my pocket book and things. I get off at two thirty and catch the three o'clock bus down the block."

"Where was the cat going?"

"How do I know?" She appeared to think about it a moment. "That fountain, I 'spect. She keep gold fish in it. She always raising a racket about that cat and her fish."

"She?"

The maid gestured to the east with a jerk of her head. "Next door. Miz Marlowe."

An attractive woman who looked to be in her late fifties or early sixties appeared in the foyer. She glanced from Junior to the maid and back again.

"Can I help you?"

"Mrs. Golding?"

"Yes."

Junior produced his shield and identified himself.

"You're here about Ruth, I imagine."

"Yes, ma'am."

She gestured for him to come in. "We'll be more comfortable in the living room. Would you like coffee? Or some iced tea?"

"No, ma'am. I'm just trying to determine the last time anyone saw Mrs. Camden."

They settled into the comfort of chintz covered arm chairs.

"Such a sad business. And so unexpected. But I guess all death is unexpected."

"Were you and Mrs. Camden close?"

"Not really. We've been neighbors for thirty years or more and we were involved in various organizations but we didn't socialize otherwise. You know, just the everyday courtesies in passing."

"How about her grandson, Archie?"

"A dear boy. He would bring my newspaper up from the lawn when the weather was bad. Or bring my trash can in from the street. So polite and always a smile on his face."

"Do you remember the last time you saw Mrs. Camden?"

Mrs. Golding took a moment to think about the question. "I recall seeing her at the A&P on Thursday. We discussed the merits of the turnip greens in the produce section. And I think I saw her coming home Friday night. That would be in the early evening. I had been to a meeting of my quilting circle and as I turned into my driveway, the car in traffic behind me went on down to her driveway and turned in."

"You said early evening. Can you be more specific?"

"Five-thirty? A quarter to six, maybe?" She gave a slight shrug. "She always went to five o'clock Mass. I imagine she was coming home from church. The time would have been right."

"Are you sure it was her car?"

"Well, not really. I just assumed. I only glanced right when I realized the car behind me had turned into her driveway. It was already full dark. The days are so short this time of year."

"Did it sound unusually loud?"

She frowned. "No. Like I said, I wasn't really aware of it until it turned into her drive."

NO ONE ANSWERED the door at Aimeé Marlowe's residence. Junior waited after the third knock but when no one appeared, he went back down the front steps and surveyed the house from the lawn.

The house was of an age of the other houses on either side of it. All of them had wide, deep lots. Built well before the turn of the century, he decided.

There was a pathway that lead to the back of the house and he followed it. The grounds back there weren't as formal or well maintained. He found the fountain with the gold fish. A cherub with an urn was designed to pour a continuous stream of water into a basin that was about six feet across. The cherub's vessel was empty.

The basin was at least two feet deep and Junior watched the sun flash on the scales of the fish as they glided lazily around the concrete cherub. Water lilies floated on the surface and a bright green moss traveled over the outer lip of the basin and up the cherub.

Three palm trees grew in a cluster in a corner of the back yard. Instead of the traditional azaleas to be found everywhere in Mobile, Mrs. Marlowe's back garden revealed a decadence antithetical to the laced-up formality of her neighbors. In fact, the back garden had an almost unkempt look, a bit of civilized jungle. No wonder the cat was drawn to it, Junior thought.

He spied a break between two sapling willow trees and crossed the back yard to discover an alley way of sorts. It was barely wide enough for a vehicle and it appeared to run from one side street to the next behind the houses facing Dauphin Street. Junior followed the lane back toward the Camden house. At the end of the hedge row that formed the property line of the Golding's, a distinct path opened onto a gate to Ruth Camden's back yard.

"Interesting." Junior proceeded all the way to the end of the block along the alley then turned back. When he was almost level with the Camden house again, he saw an old beat up truck turn into the narrow lane from the side street at the far end. It came to a stop five houses down. By the time Junior made his way to the truck, the yard man had unloaded his push mower, wheel barrow, a rake and hoe.

The yard man looked warily at Junior from under the brim of a battered straw hat.

Junior showed him his shield. "Junior Knight, Mobile Police Department. Mind if I ask you some questions?"

The man made no reply, just stood waiting.

Junior gestured with a jerk of his thumb. "Whose house is this?"

"Mr. Talmadge."

"You work for him a long time?"

The man nodded. "Five years."

"You know the other people who live along here?"

"I know who they is."

"Mrs. Camden?"

He nodded. "The one with the cat."

"How about Mrs. Marlowe?"

He nodded again.

"You ever do yard work for either of them?"

"No, suh. Not Mrs. Camden. She got William to do her yard."

"And Mrs. Marlowe?"

"Used to. Not for a long time now."

"Why not?"

"Miz Camden say I don't have to no mo'."

"What did Mrs. Camden have to do with you cutting Mrs. Marlowe's yard?"

"She pay for it. Besides, Mrs. Marlowe don't like the way I do things. Say I charge too much."

Junior considered this. "Do you?"

He shrugged. "You have to ask Mr. Talmadge 'bout that."

"Do all the people who do yard work use this alley?"

He nodded.

No much of a talker, Junior decided. "You see the cat lately?"

"Last Tuesday when I come. He likes potted meat."

"Tuesday, that's your day to do Mr. Talmadge's yard?"

"Yes, suh."

"That the last time you were in the lane?"

He nodded.

Junior decided he wouldn't get anything more from the yard man. He made a note of his name in his notebook then walked on down to the other end of the alley before returning to the Camden house. It would be an easy thing for someone to come and go this way without being seen by anyone unless they happened to glance out one of the upper story windows on the back side of the houses that faced Dauphin Street.

✣

HUGO PULLED ONTO I-65 at Government Street and floored the Thunderbird. It jumped to speed like a crouched tiger pouncing. He could feel the power of the big V-8 engine through the steering wheel as it propelled him forward like a bullet in flight. Big Eddie was right. This was the car for him.

In no time he reached the St. Stephen's Road exchange and exited only to race back on the south bound lane of the interstate with the window down, the cold air whipping through the car, and *I Got You, Babe* blasting on the radio. The rush was worth being joined at the hip to Big Eddie for the next two years. Hugo grinned.

He drove through the streets of Mobile just for the sake of the ride, enjoying the car and allowing his mind to wander. His thoughts kept returning to Archie. Where would he go? Bebe had mentioned Canada or Europe. Why those two places and not Mexico which was so much closer? Probably because Mexico was a poor man's answer. Archie Camden wasn't a poor man. There was the language thing as well. People would notice. Unless he spoke Spanish, which Hugo decided he needed to find out.

The Haywoods had started out with Haywood Mills but their interests had long ago spread into everything from lumber to pine by-products to shipping. That meant connections and Buck Sissions was probably right. Archie could go to ground without any hardship and live a long and full life with all the comforts of home.

Hugo turned the Thunderbird toward downtown.

At the court house, he explained to the Probate clerk what he needed. She brought him a stack of registry books dating back ten years. The look on his face caused her to take pity on him. She showed him what to look for and a quick way to scan over the entries to find pertinent information.

After two hours, the clerk reappeared and told him she had to lock up. Hugo heaved a sigh of relief. He thumbed through the notations he had made in his notebook but felt frustrated that it only led to a maze of references that told him very little.

"What're you trying to figure out, shuga," the clerk asked in a three-pack-a-day rasp.

"Connections."

She studied him a minute and smiled. "I have a special fondness for handsome young men. You wait for me over at the Royal Flush. I'll be along in a few minutes and see if we can't find what you need."

Over a couple of beers, Judy Fohl told Hugo she had been the clerk of court for twenty-one years. She had worked the summer of her junior year of high school and then went full time when she graduated. There was little she didn't know or know how to find. He quickly discovered that not only did she have all the legal documents of the citizens of Mobile county at her fingertips, she had her finger on the political pulse of the city as well as all the dirt. She knew who got divorced and why, who felt cheated out of the family property and who got it all, who was trying to hide their money and how. She assured him she wasn't a gossip but that in the interest of justice, she would help him.

Hugo liked Judy. Even though she was a dozen years older than him, he found her deep red hair, hot pink lipstick, and undercurrent of sexuality very attractive. He could see why men would confide in her. He ordered another round of beer.

Twelve

Hugo woke to the sound of hammering. He rolled out of bed and pulled on his trousers. Two men were taking down the front door of the house across the street. He pulled on a sweater and walked barefooted over the chilly concrete roadway in the gray morning light.

"Hey!"

The noise stopped and the men stared down at him from the porch.

"What're you doing?"

The men exchanged glances. The older and larger of the two came down the steps to stand about four feet from Hugo.

"Salvaging." He reached into his back pocket and pulled out a sheet of paper. "Mr. Beaumont gave us permission to strip it of anything usable before they tear it down." He unfolded paper and held it toward Hugo.

Hugo took the note and gave it a quick read. The second man, who remained on the porch, began hammering again.

"What's your name?"

"Clyde Minton."

Hugo returned the letter of permission to him. "And your helper?"

"That's my son. Clyde Jr."

The sun was barely up. "Salvage something that doesn't make so much noise."

He returned to his house and lit the gas space heater. In his bedroom he found a pair of socks and pulled them on before moving on through to the kitchen. Once he had the coffee brewing, he let his gaze linger on the albums and scrap books stacked on the kitchen table.

Something in Ruth's life had gotten her killed. Poison left no doubt that the murder was pre-meditated. It was also up close and personal. So, who had access to Ruth, the house, and the tea? And who had motive? Until he answered that question they wouldn't be able to narrow the field of suspects. He would start at the center and work his way out.

He began by arranging the books in date order. By the time he had them all laid out on the table he realized it was going to be a daunting task. The first book dated from the late 1800s. It held photos of Ruth as a baby, lace from her christening gown, a lock of her hair. There were pictures of her extended family, parents, grandparents, their friends and relatives. A few lines of script in white against the black pages of the book regaled the history of the family.

He read postcards from California, the St. Louis World's Fair, Niagara Falls. There were a couple of postcards from Paris picturing hand colored images of the Eiffel Tower. These brief messages were written in French, barely legible. He remembered Mrs. K's comments about Aimeé Marlowe.

Some photographs were missing, the little triangles that had held them in place drew attention to their absence. If there was anything from this distant past that was relevant to Ruth's death, Hugo couldn't discern it. He imagined most of these people were long dead.

He had worked his way through three of the albums, reading cards, letters, thank you notes. He was beginning to recognize the strong Haywood features through the generations, the high cheekbones, the wide forehead, the esthetically spaced eyes. All in all, a handsome family. He also began to have a feel for Ruth's life through the snapshots of moments in time captured in the photos and the memorabilia of the things that mattered to her.

Hugo was on his second pot of coffee when Junior interrupted his journey through Ruth Camden's life with a knock on the door.

"So, you bit the bullet," Junior said as he followed Hugo through the house to the kitchen.

"What?"

Junior nodded to the kitchen window and the view of the Thunderbird parked on the lot next door. "Big Eddie give you a deal?"

"So he said. All I know is I'll be on the hook for the next two years."

"How's it drive?"

Hugo grinned. "Like its name. A Thunderbird."

Junior nodded and grinned in return. He went to the stove and poured himself a cup of coffee. "What you got here?"

Hugo sat down at the table and flipped a page of album number six. "Ruth Camden's life."

"Anything useful?"

"Not that I can find. She had a big family. Relatives in France and Germany it seems."

"Aimeé Marlowe."

"Yes. There are old postcards from France but they pretty much stopped after WWI. I'm working my way through but other than a guide to fashion through the ages, I haven't learned much."

Junior bent down and picked up an engraved invitation that had slipped from one of the albums to the kitchen floor. "A bridal shower."

"There's a lot of that in here. Mardi Gras stuff. Tea parties. Birthdays."

"We're not going to find our killer in the past." Junior took a sip of his coffee, frowned, and emptied the cup into the sink. "How do you drink this stuff?"

"In the Army you learn to drink anything that's been boiled."

"Boiled is right. Grammy thought you'd come for breakfast."

"I got distracted with all this." Hugo's gaze traveled over the array of items on the table. "But I am hungry. Let me get a quick shower and we'll go to the boarding house for a bite."

TINA'S BOARDING HOUSE served breakfast until eight-thirty every day except Sunday. Hugo and Junior arrived at the end of that window.

Wanda scowled at them as they came through the door but she couldn't quite hide her delight at seeing them. "You're late," she scolded.

Hugo smiled and opened his arms. Wanda stepped into his embrace and gave him a hug. "Surely you can scrape the bottom of the pot for old time's sake."

She stepped back and smiled. "I'll see what I can do. It's been a long time, stranger."

"Five years."

"Where you living?"

"In the demolition zone."

"Which one?"

"South Cedar."

"You can always have your old room back."

"Your mom might not agree. I'm afraid I made her life a misery the whole time I. . ." The expression on Wanda's face stopped Hugo in mid-sentence. "What?"

"Mom died two years ago."

"Oh, Wanda." He was at a loss for words.

She shrugged and cleared her throat. "She would be pleased that you came home in one piece." She waved them toward a clean table. "Sit down. I'll have to brew a fresh pot of coffee. Not that you two are worth the trouble."

The hearty helpings of scrambled eggs, grits, and biscuits with gravy she pulled together from left-overs was more than enough. It also happened to be the best deal to be had anywhere in town for a cost of only seventy-five cents.

Hugo drained his third cup of coffee and stood to leave. He dropped a dollar on the table as did Junior.

The door of the boarding house opened and Big Mo Hitchens stepped into the foyer.

"Wanda!"

She appeared from down the hallway and when Big Mo reached for her, she evaded his grasp and jerked her head in the direction of dining room and Hugo and Junior.

Big Mo lifted his chin in greeting.

"Guess I'm too late for breakfast."

"And too early for lunch," Wanda said.

He followed her movements with his eyes as she entered the dining room and began to clear away the dirty dishes.

As Hugo and Junior approached the front door, Big Mo continued to stand in the middle of the small foyer, his thumbs caught in his gun belt, partially blocking their way. It was a blatant act, a manner of marking his territory.

"Mo." Hugo arched his eyebrows as he waited for the policeman to move.

"August." Instead of stepping aside, Mo turned his attention to Junior. "How's your grandmaw, Junior? Got her a new perm lately?"

Hugo touched the knot of his tie and stepped into Mo's personal space. "How's your wife?"

Mo held his gaze. "Satisfied."

"Yeah?"

"Mo!" Wanda called from the doorway to the kitchen.

Mo's upper lip lifted in a smirk and he stepped out of their path.

Junior was quiet after they got into the car.

Hugo silently cursed himself. He regretted his loss of control for Junior's sake. Instead of deflecting Mo's bullying from his friend, he'd drawn attention to the innuendo behind Mo's words. "What the hell can Wanda be thinking?"

"Yeah." Junior kept his eyes on the road.

They rode in silence a couple of blocks.

Junior cleared his throat. "It's not a good idea to get on Mo's bad side."

"Didn't know he had a good side."

Junior grunted. Then after a few more blocks of silence, he filled Hugo in on his activities of the previous afternoon.

"So where does that leave us?"

"With an indefinite time-line, access by just about everybody in Mobile by means of the alley way, general knowledge of a key known to be hidden in the fern, and no motive."

"Let's see if Evie can tell us anything new."

⁂

"THE MEDICAL EXAMINER puts the time of death between five p.m. and midnight." Evie pushed her glasses back up the bridge of her nose. "The blood and urine tests rule out heavy metal poisoning. I think we're looking for a biologic or an unknown compound."

Junior read down the sheet of paper Evie had given him from the file jacket. The charts and symbols told him nothing. "What does that mean?"

"It could be a plant-based poison, like something from the rhodo-dendron family all the way down to mushrooms. Or it can be anything from drain cleaner to paint thinner."

"Well, that narrows it down."

"I'm leaning toward a biologic."

"Because?"

"The taste. She drank it in her tea. Most compounds have a harsh chemical taste. Some plants taste awful as well, but some don't and can be more easily disguised. And compounds are usually so caustic that no one would consume them. Her throat showed no signs of irritation."

She glanced over at Hugo who was reading through the informa-tion from the autopsy report. "It's just a guess but someone had to know it was something she would consume. It has to be something ingestible, accessible, and potent. This wasn't a slow poisoning over time."

Hugo looked up from his perusal of the file. "Whoever it was knew what they were doing. They've experimented with this before."

"I agree. The dosing is the critical element. Otherwise, Mrs. Cam-den would have most likely become ill and then recovered. Or she would have been in a slow decline over a long period of time." A barely suppressed note of excitement crept into her voice. "I think we need to talk to her doctor."

Junior handed the report on the blood work back to Evie. "Rhys hasn't talked to her doctor yet?"

"I think the word has gone out to back pedal this one." Evie sighed. "The chief wants to know what killed her before we declare it's officially murder. And the more people you question, the more people will speculate."

"How long will it take before we know the lab results?"

"Maybe never. Unless you know what you're looking for it can be nearly impossible to identify the substance. There are thousands of poisons that haven't been compiled in any kind of comprehensive index. Many more haven't even been identified. And because of the number that have been determined, it's a slow process of comparisons. It's like finding a needle in a haystack. Each one has to be looked at to see if the molecular structure matches. That's why I think we should start with biologics and go from there."

"They can't speed that up?"

"It can go faster for someone who deals in poisons on a regular basis. They're able to recognize certain constructs they've come across before, things that are easily accessible and more commonly used. But generally, nope. We're lucky Auburn started out their forensic research looking at poisons when the department was first established. We might be dealing with something they're familiar with and have catalogued."

Junior watched Evie watching Hugo. He looked away.

Finally, he cleared his throat and took out his notebook. "I guess we need to see if her doctor has anything interesting to say." He flipped through the pages. "Dr. Fellowes. And see if Dr. Allen remembers any other deaths that look suspicious."

"Good idea." Hugo handed the file to Evie. "I think with the neighbor seeing Mrs. Camden return from church at about five thirty, we've narrowed the time of death as much as we can for now. I'll check with Bebe and see if her aunt complained of not feeling well."

Junior saw Evie's gaze drop to the file in her hand and all animation fade from her expression. "And the next step?" He returned his notebook to his coat pocket.

"We'll have to hammer away at everyone's movements. Get a timeline of their activities leading up to Saturday morning. See who had the window of opportunity to poison the tea."

"That could have happened at any time."

"I don't think so. The killer needed to know that Ruth, and only Ruth, would drink the tea. That means someone knew her routine well enough to put the poison in place at a time when only she would be likely to consume it. We need to know if she had a routine. If she always drank tea in the evening, say after Mass."

"Then we're looking at the family."

"Maybe." Hugo glanced from Junior to Evie. "Murder is most often a family affair."

"We've got to find the motive." Junior sighed.

"We've got to find Archie."

Thirteen

Junior dropped Hugo at home so he could retrieve his car. They agreed to meet back at the station after lunch.

Hugo enjoyed the feel of the Thunderbird as he eased down Levert Avenue. Ashland Place was a small enclave in the section of Mobile known as Midtown. The homes had, for the most part, been built in the early twentieth century around the original house called Ashland. They were all solid, spacious homes on large lots that whispered affluence and permanence in an understated way. Their styles ranged from Victorian to craftsman. He pulled to the curb in front of a brick cottage with a mullioned bay window on Lanier Avenue. The lush lawn and mature landscaping added to the sense of place and status.

Bebe's mother answered Hugo's knock. She was quick to hide the look of surprise that flashed across her features. "Hugo." She managed a fleeting, insincere smile. "What a surprise."

"Mrs. Prescott. Sorry to arrive unannounced."

"Bebe isn't here."

"I came to talk to you, if you have a moment."

"Me?" Her brow lifted in question.

"I'm trying to piece together the events leading up to Mrs. Camden's death and gather any background information that would help us determine what happened."

"I don't know how I could help you. I didn't see Ruth very often. Mostly at family functions. We weren't particularly close."

"Nevertheless, there might be some small detail that would point us in the right direction."

She stood in the doorway a moment, indecision warring across her features. "Very well." She stepped back into the foyer and opened the door wide for him to enter. "But I fear this will be a waste of your time."

She refrained from adding *and mine,* Hugo thought. He smiled in the face of her reluctance and followed her toward the rear of the house to a room that served as a family gathering spot. There was a sense of comfort and welcome about the way it was furnished and the evidence of everyday use that was in stark contrast to the polished perfection of the rooms they had passed through.

Voncille Prescott gestured toward a stuffed armchair covered in a pale plaid fabric for Hugo. She took a seat in a small scale, wing-backed chair across from him. "Now, what is it you think I know that will help with your inquiries?"

The chair she had taken allowed light from the windows along the back wall of the room to fall full on her face. It spotlighted her porcelain skin, remarkably unwrinkled by time, the rich fullness of her blond hair that held a few gray strands throughout that were becoming rather than aging. She was dressed in a simple skirt and blouse but for all their simplicity, they spoke of the impeccable tailoring and quality materials of wealth. She was no less formidable in her genteel, informal domain than her husband was in his aerie of an office looking down over the city.

"I'd like to start with the last time you saw Mrs. Camden."

She thought for a moment. "I suppose that would be about two months ago. I don't remember the exact date but it was at the club. We had a farewell dinner for Archie."

"You haven't seen her at church or social gatherings?"

"No. Haywood and I go to early Mass and I think Ruth's habit is to go to the five o'clock service."

"You go to the same church?"

"Yes. The family goes to Holy Spirit Catholic Church."

"Is it normal for you to see so little of your husband's aunt?"

"Yes. We don't have that much in common."

Hugo fell silent and leaned back in the chair, thinking. "Had she been sick recently?"

Voncille Prescott frowned. "I don't know. Certainly nothing serious or Haywood would have said."

"Bebe didn't mention her not feeling well?"

Voncille shrugged "No. But then I don't see that much of Bebe, either."

"Oh? Why's that?"

"She has a very busy life. As do I."

"Who inherits Mrs. Camden's estate?"

"Archie, I imagine. I wouldn't know for certain. You'd need to ask Haywood. Or Ruth's lawyer."

"Do you have any idea where Archie might be?"

"My guess would be France. I know Ruth was asking Haywood about old family contacts after Archie got his conscription letter."

"Did he have any information to give her?"

"I couldn't say. No one has heard anything from that branch of the family in decades, to my knowledge. Most of them died or were displaced during WWI and the remaining few haven't been heard from since before WWII. I only remember meeting a distant cousin a few years after Haywood and I married. She came over for a visit."

"Do you remember her name?"

Voncille shook her head. "No. It was one of those brief tea party events Ruth liked to host. I think she may have stayed with Ruth for a few days before continuing on her trip across the states."

"When did you last visit Mrs. Camden at her home?"

"I don't know. At Easter, maybe? Haywood and I picked her up for lunch at the club after Easter service." She paused, her brow drawn in concentration. "I can't remember any time since then."

"Would you know the contents of Mrs. Camden's house?"

"Well, I suppose. Most of them, anyway. Why?"

"We need to determine if anything is missing."

"I don't think I'd be the best help in that situation. I might remember furniture pieces, paintings, perhaps. I know her china pattern and her silver. But, really, more personal things would be beyond my knowledge."

"Did you get along with Mrs. Camden?"

"After a fashion."

"What does that mean?"

"Ruth considered herself the head of the family. She was the oldest of her siblings. Sebastian, being the male, should have held that position, I suppose, but he was the baby and spoiled. He never liked the mill and used his asthma as an excuse to move to Arizona. He plays golf and lives on the income from his interest in the company.

"Ruth and Haywood were very close at one time but since Haywood has had to take on the management of the family businesses, she's been difficult."

"Why did Haywood inherit the job?"

"After the war he started in the mill and worked his way up. Edward was managing everything after Ruth's father died. But then Edward had a heart attack in the mid-fifties."

"Edward? Ruth's husband?"

"Yes."

"Who will be the head of the family business after your husband?"

"Skip, I suppose. He oversees the mill now."

"What about the other family members? Bebe? Mr. Prescott's sister and her kids?"

"Bebe? What would she know about running a business?"

"Then one of your sister-in-law's children."

"Not very likely. Sharon was a late-in-life child. Haywood's mother was nearly fifty when she was born. Her children won't be of age to take on any responsibility for the business for some time to come. Her oldest is only ten."

"So basically, the reins of power for the family business now rest with Mr. Prescott and your oldest son, Skip."

"Yes, I guess that's true."

"Where does Archie stand in all this?"

"Archie wasn't interested in working for the family. He got his degree in architecture."

"How did his grandmother feel about that?"

"She indulged him in whatever he wanted."

"He was spoiled, then."

"I wouldn't put it that way. He doesn't have the personality to be spoiled. Perhaps a better way to put it is that he's independent. He's also creative and has vision."

"You like him."

"Yes. Everyone likes Archie."

"Do you think he's fled the country to avoid going to Vietnam?"

Voncille didn't answer right away. She gazed out the window overlooking a beautifully landscaped flower garden. "I wouldn't have thought it of him. He has a moral compass at his core. But Ruth was terrified that he would be sent over there and never return. I think she feared him being captured or maimed more than she feared him being killed. Death is so much easier than suffering, isn't it?" She looked back at Hugo. "But maybe he did. None of us can know what's in the heart of another, can we?"

"No. I don't suppose we can." He stood. "Did Mrs. Camden have any enemies that you knew of?"

"Enemies?" Voncille rose to her feet. "Why would she have enemies? She was just a housewife. A grandmother. People like Ruth don't have enemies."

"Thank you. I'll leave you to get on with your day."

He followed her back through the house to the front door. When she opened it for him, he turned to her. "Was Bebe close to her aunt?"

"She was probably closer to her than anyone else on our side of the family. When she and Archie were small they were inseparable. The family was closer then. She's always had a great deal of affection for him. They've seen quite a bit of each other since he came home at the beginning of the summer." Her brow creased slightly. "I do hope he hasn't done anything foolish."

"When will Bebe be home? I'd like to speak with her."

"Bebe doesn't live here anymore."

"Oh?"

Voncille offered no further information and after a brief hesitation, Hugo crossed the small porch and down the steps to the sidewalk. She continued to stand in the doorway until he got into his car and drove away.

ﷺ

JUNIOR SAT IN Dr. Fellowes waiting room flipping through a *Good Housekeeping* magazine. His grandmother would like the mustard yellow kitchen appliances with all the latest features, he decided.

He closed the magazine and looked at the date. Spring issue. He tossed it onto a side table and looked at his watch. He'd been waiting nearly twenty minutes. The doctor's receptionist was on the phone making a notation in the appointments book. She was very pretty.

A woman who looked to be in her mid-thirties came through the doorway that lead into the bowels of the building. She stopped at the receptionist's desk and made an appointment for a follow-up visit. Junior stood and went to the receptionist's desk as soon as the woman left the building.

"Look, I need to see the doctor and I can't hang around here all day. Either take me back to his office or I'll find it myself."

"He's with a patient." The young woman behind the desk stared up at him with an anxious expression. "You can't go back there."

The encounter with Big Mo Hitchens still ate at Junior. The not-so-subtle slight to his grandmother fueled his resentment. He headed for the doorway the patient had just come through and the receptionist jumped up from her chair and blocked his way.

"Please. You'll get me in trouble." She held her hand up as if she would forcefully stop him. "I've only worked here one week and I need this job."

She looked to Junior as if she was on the verge of tears. She had very blue eyes and was a petite little thing. He felt guilty that he had let his impatience and anger make him act out of character. "What's your name?"

"Bobby Jean."

He smiled down at her. "Don't look so frightened, Bobby Jean. The doctor won't bite. Just tell him it's official business."

"I don't know. He hates to be disturbed when he's with a patient."

Junior lowered his voice so no one in the waiting room could hear. "It's about a murder."

Her mouth formed a shocked O, and she backed toward the door then turned and fled down the hallway. He wondered if she liked to bowl.

She was back in a couple of minutes and she escorted Junior to Dr. Fellowes office. The room was empty. She told him to have a seat and wait. The doctor would be with him as soon as he finished the examination of a patient.

Junior spent the time checking out the curiosities of the doctor's office. He was reading through the names of the skeletal chart hanging on the wall when Dr. Fellowes came through the door.

The doctor was a short man, his salt and pepper hair more salt than pepper. An effort had been made to tame a head full of curls. He wore glasses but the piercing brown eyes behind them told Junior he was a busy man who resented being called away from his patients.

Junior got right to the point. "I came to talk to you about Ruth Camden. The police are treating her death as suspicious."

"Charles Allen told me. I went to the hospital and saw her before he did the autopsy. I don't know what I can tell you that he didn't."

"I understand she had a heart condition."

"Yes. She had arrhythmia, an irregular heartbeat. It caused her to have episodes of lightheadedness and shortness of breath."

"Could that have caused her death?"

"Certainly. It can lead to stroke or cardiac arrest."

"What does the digitalis do?"

"It interrupts the irregular beat and restores a regular pattern. Usually."

"Did she have any other health issues?"

"Her sugar ran a little high at times but not enough to require medication. She was disciplined enough to control it with her diet." The doctor looked at his watch. "Anything else?"

"How was her health generally, aside from the heart thing?"

"Good for her age. She did suffer a bout of flu-like symptoms a little over a month ago. It laid her low for a couple of weeks but when I saw her about ten days ago she seemed to have no residual issues."

"She had the flu?"

"Yes. Nausea, vomiting, extremely dehydrated. I put her on clear liquids for a few days and gave her something for her symptoms."

"You're sure it was the flu?"

"I didn't do a culture, if that's what you're asking. She presented with flu-like symptoms. We've had a bout of it going around the city. Ergo, I treated her accordingly." He looked at his watch again. "I have patients waiting. If there are any other questions, they'll have to wait for a more convenient time. And the next time, don't frighten that witless girl with innuendo. You can find you way back to reception, I assume?" With that he left the office and disappeared through a door down the hallway.

Fourteen

Hugo sat in the Thunderbird in a parking space behind the police station. He stared without seeing the rear entrance. Why had no one told him that Bebe was married? He searched back through the encounters they had had over the past five days. She didn't wear a ring. That was the first thing he checked when he came upon her so unexpectedly Saturday.

Her reaction when he asked after Rich wasn't that of a wife. Was it? *You'll have to ask him.* That implied she didn't know, didn't it? Or maybe that she didn't care. Someone else, then. He needed a name.

In all this time since he came home, why hadn't he asked Junior if she was married? Because he hadn't wanted to know. In his mind, he had known since he left Tuscaloosa that she would marry. She would marry the right kind of guy, someone who pleased her parents, someone with the proper background and social standing. Someone like Rich.

Rich had been the straw that broke him. Her parents had come up for homecoming. They had all been partying at the Kappa Delta sorority house before the parade. Everyone had flitted around Bebe, homecoming queen, like bees to honey. Hugo, for one of the few times in his life, had felt less than. He had felt ill at ease and begun to question everything from his clothing to his ability to interact with those people. And that had made him angry.

After being subtly snubbed by Bebe's parents and grandmother, he had run into Rich at the bar. They had sized each other up and Rich had delivered the castigating blow. He and Bebe would be home for Thanksgiving to participate in the Camellia Ball at the country club. It was one of the highlights of Mobile society's year, the announcement of the debutants for the coming Mardi Gras season, and the beginning of the round of parties and balls that would culminate on Fat Tuesday. Bebe would be among their number. Didn't Hugo know? He should have. Bebe was a Haywood, after all. Rich would be her knight. Hadn't she told Hugo?

He hadn't had a moment alone with Bebe that day until well past midnight. By then his anger had festered until he could barely speak coherently. While Bebe and her family had attended the game, and enjoyed a celebratory dinner afterward, he had bussed tables at the university's cafeteria. As the partying continued at the homecoming dance, she had been surrounded by her coterie of friends, Rich featuring prominently among them.

Even now he felt the rage building. And yet, knowing what her life would be, he hadn't allowed himself to acknowledge what he would surely find when he returned to Mobile. It had been five years, after all.

When she called him to the Quarter Note he had felt that rush of wanting that had been a constant in his life for as long as he could remember. Right now, he felt gutted, as if he had just relived that long ago homecoming showdown.

A police sedan pulled into the parking space beside him. He glanced over to see Junior give him a brief wave. Hugo took a deep breath and opened the door of the Thunderbird. He schooled his features. He couldn't bear anyone to see him so utterly devastated by something that had been lost a long time ago. In truth, it had always been beyond his grasp. Had he subconsciously made the decision to return to Mobile with the hope that it would be otherwise? He didn't know.

Junior practically hummed as he relayed what he had learned from Dr. Fellowes as he and Hugo climbed the stairs to their office.

"You say this was a month ago. Did you get the date?"

"The nurse pulled the records. September 29th. Apparently, she got sick the night before. The maid found her that morning so weak from being ill that she could barely stand. The neighbor to the west of her drove her to the doctor's office."

"The neighbor's name?"

"Westmoreland."

"And they didn't think to mention this when we first canvased the neighborhood?"

"I guess they thought she had the flu just like her doctor did."

"Still, you would have thought it was worth mentioning when the woman was found dead a month later."

"You would think."

Hugo picked up a stack of a half dozen or so pink message slips on his desk as he sat down. "We'll need to interview them again. And Viola." He leafed through the messages and stopped at one from Bebe. He dropped the rest back onto his desk. "We'll want to see if anyone can recall anything unusual around the time of the first attempt."

"Are you going to tell the chief?"

"Not yet. I want to have something on the poison, if possible, before I lay it all out for him."

"It would be nice to have some help."

"I think we should keep it low key, just like the chief wants. With just the two of us hopefully nothing will fall between the cracks. Keep your fingers crossed we don't get assigned anything else until we have a better handle of things."

"I've got to go over to the Oakleigh district on a call about a break-in of a shed in someone's back yard." Junior read the report sheet he had found front and center on his desk.

"Yeah. I need to return some calls. And there's the niece who lives across the bay. One of us needs to talk to her. I guess it'll have to be me."

"What did Bebe have to say?"

Hugo kept his eyes on the page of the phone book. "I talked to her mother. She didn't have much to offer. Apparently, there's no love lost between her and Mrs. Camden. They rarely saw each other. But everyone seems to think the world of Archie."

"No one's that universally liked."

"We'll have to keep digging until we find the exception. In the meantime, you might want to find out who the priest is at Holy Spirit. See if he remembers if Mrs. Camden was at five o'clock mass on Friday. See if she had anything on her mind that she might have shared with him."

They each spent some time returning calls. Hugo typed up his notes on the Camden case. He looked through the file of a court hearing that was on the docket for the next morning. Only after Junior left to check out the theft in Oakleigh did he pull out Bebe's message.

Bebe Prescott. She had called at 11:12. There was a phone number. The two desks closest to Hugo's were unmanned giving Hugo a modicum of privacy. He picked up the phone and dialed. He listened to the ringing at the other end of the line for a long time. Finally, he hung up.

Bebe Prescott. He stared at the name on the pink message slip. It felt as if a weight had been lifted from his chest. He had jumped to the wrong conclusion. Again. He knew it was foolish to feel such a sense of relief but he had no control over it.

He opened the phone book to look up Haywood Prescott's sister and realized he didn't know her married name. He decided to call Tyler Redman. He would know all the principals of the family.

The secretary put his call straight through. Redman told him Sharon Prescott's married name was Shipley. He also gave Hugo her phone number.

"Did you know Mrs. Camden was sick in late September?"

"Yes. She came down with the flu."

"You still think it was the flu?"

Redman didn't respond immediately. Finally, he said, "I take it you think that was another attempt on her life."

"I do. Did she confide anything to you about being afraid or that she was having an issue with anyone?"

"No. If she had, I'd have told you."

"And you don't know of anything that was out of the usual?"

"She was worried about Archie. She didn't talk about it but his departure left her depressed, I think."

"Did anyone from the Army interview you about Archie?"

"I already told you I didn't know about that until Haywood told me. Why would they?"

"Perhaps as a show of being thorough."

"I assure you I had nothing to do with Archie's disappearance."

"His grandmother is dead and he's missing. Does that concern you?"

"Yes, it does. It concerns me because he'll be in a lot of trouble when the Army catches up with him. I've known him since he was a boy."

"Did you like him?"

"I wasn't around him much but he was bright, always pleasant, and Ruth doted on him."

"What would be your guess as to his whereabouts if he decided to dodge the draft?"

"I can't say."

"Can't or won't?"

"I can't help you as far as Archie is concerned. I hope he's safe. I spoke with Major Gregson and he paints a very bleak picture if the Army locates him. Naturally, I'll help him in any way I can if that happens."

"Did Mrs. Camden talk to you about relatives she might have in France?"

"Not in many years. I think two world wars pretty much scattered the remnants of that branch of the family. If there were any left after the fighting." Redman paused. "Ruth used to talk about a cousin. I think one of her children immigrated to Canada. She came over from Paris for a visit after the second war, I believe. Or was it before? You might ask Aimeé Marlowe about her."

HUGO TRIED TO call the Shipley home before setting out for Baldwin County. When he got no answer, he decided it was for the best. An unprepared subject would be more likely to reveal something useful. By the time he could get to Point Clear school would be out and hopefully Sharon Shipley would be home with her kids.

He drove through the Bankhead Tunnel to the Causeway that linked Mobile with the Eastern shore through a series of raised earthen embankments and bridges. The wind off the water was brisk but a few hardy fishermen were dipping their hooks in hopes of fresh fish for dinner.

There were a few cars in the parking lot of Argiro's, a local establishment that could provide you with all your fishing needs from the fresh catch of the day, if you were unlucky, to beer, if you worked up a thirst.

The drive from downtown Mobile to Point Clear was about twenty-five miles. Once on the Eastern shore, Hwy 98 traveled south through the bay side communities of Spanish Fort, Daphne, Montrose, and Fairhope. It was a pleasant day for the ride. There were still areas where you could catch glimpses of Mobile Bay through the trees from the high embankment that formed the coastline.

Daphne and Fairhope were small communities that were quiet during the winter months. The truck route cut a more direct path to his destination but Hugo preferred the winding original highway that followed the shoreline.

Montrose consisted of a long strip of highway with homes mostly hidden from view down near the water's edge. The same was true for Point Clear although it did boast of the Grand Hotel, the Punta Clara Kitchen, and a post office.

Hugo stopped at the post office and the post mistress gave him directions to the Shipley house. Unless you knew where you were going, most of the addresses were hard to find. The people who lived there or had their summer homes there liked it that way.

The low, discreet sign out near the highway read Bay Breeze. As Hugo eased down the long winding driveway to the home of Sharon

Shipley, he saw an older Mercedes sedan parked under a carport. The structure sported a weather vane of a sailing ship mounted on the cedar shake roof. There was an equally old Jeep in the circular driveway from which a blonde woman and two small children were disembarking.

The woman looked up at the sound of his car on the oyster shell driveway and sent the children ahead into the house that was a sprawling clapboard building. The wood siding had aged to a silvery gray.

She waited for Hugo to come to a stop behind the Jeep.

He felt a little jolt as he got out of the Thunderbird and showed her his shield. She could pass for Bebe's sister. Not her twin, but the resemblance was striking. "Mrs. Shipley?"

She nodded.

"I'd like to talk to you about Ruth Camden."

She glanced away, looking out over the bay. Then she nodded. "Come into the house. The wind is nippy today."

She had a rich voice, not too deep and not too high. Strong coffee with rich cream, Hugo decided. There was no doubt she was a Haywood. She had the blonde hair, blue eyes, the assurance, and the walk, he decided as he followed after her.

They entered through a small ante room where the children had dropped coats, shoes, and books. It opened into a bright, sunny kitchen where the boy and girl sat at a sturdy wooden table with glasses of milk and peanut butter and jelly sandwiches. They fell silent when Hugo entered the room behind their mother.

"Virgie, be sure they clean up when they're done and they can go check the crab traps afterwards."

Virgie nodded as she wiped her wet hands on a dish towel.

"Who are you?" The little boy hadn't taken his eyes off Hugo.

"Hugo August."

"What do you want?"

Sharon didn't allow Hugo time to respond. "Don't be rude, David. Mr. August is here on business."

"What kind of business?"

"The none-of-your-business kind of business," his mother replied in a teasing voice.

Hugo followed her through a sunny living area with a huge stone fireplace where the embers burned low. They went down a hallway on the other side of the house and came to a small study.

Sharon gestured for him to take a comfortable leather armchair. She sat behind a heavy oak desk that had the look of many years of service. Except for the double windows that looked out onto the bay, the walls were lined with bookcases filled with a wide range of titles. Interspersed with the books were silver framed family photographs. There was one of Sharon with a tall dark headed man with the Eiffel Tower in the background. Another showed her laughing up at the camera from the steps of an ancient ruin.

"Now, Mr. August, what do you want?"

Her question brought his gaze back to her. "Have you talked with your brother about your aunt?"

"I have."

"Did he inform you that we have some concerns about her death?"

"Yes."

"Were you close to your aunt?"

"Probably closer than anyone other than Archie."

"Did you like her?"

Sharon swiveled her desk chair to turn her profile to him. She sat with her head resting against the high back as she stared out the bank of windows at the whitecaps on the bay. "I adored her."

Hugo let the silence lengthen.

"She was my champion. It was her idea that I live over here away from the pressure and bickering of the family after my husband died two years ago."

"Many found her to be difficult."

Sharon turned back to face him. "She was proper and she was proud, but not of the things that mattered to most of my family and acquaintances. She was proud to be of service to her community. She was proud of doing what was right, always."

"Do you think she would be proud of Archie for dodging the draft?"

Anger hardened her features. "Archie wouldn't do that. Not as an act of cowardice, anyway. If he did, there would be a damn good reason why."

"He's considered AWOL by the army."

"I know. They came to see me in September."

"Who came?"

"Buck Sissons and two military policemen. They were all done up in their uniforms, chests huffed out to look threatening. That's why David is so curious about who you are."

"The children were here when they came?"

"Yes."

"What did you tell Buck?"

"The same thing I'm telling you. Archie wouldn't shirk his responsibility. Certainly not because Aunt Ruth wanted him to."

"Do you think that's what she wanted?"

"Yes. She was terrified. This is the fourth war she's experienced in her lifetime and she was afraid of losing any more people she loved."

"Even though it would have been dishonorable?"

"That's what she struggled with. We talked about it a lot. She felt we have no right to be in Vietnam. That the war is morally wrong. And she'd lost so much of her family already in the three previous wars."

"What was her plan?"

"I don't know."

"And yet you're the only person who admits to knowing she was actively trying to convince Archie to shirk his military service."

"We spent a lot of time together over here this summer. Archie was home from college and she hoped that he would be skipped over with the lottery. The truth of the matter was he thought he was safe from the draft. He was at Harvard in '65 when they instituted the Vietnam Exam for college deferred men. He scored high and thought that was the end of it. The Army was drafting eighteen year olds. He turns twenty-six this December, the upper age limit of draftees."

"But your aunt was still worried?"

"Yes. It was almost as if she had a premonition. She tried to get Haywood to find him a spot in the National Guard. It wasn't what Archie wanted. He'd been away at school for so long and he was ready to get on with his life. Besides, she should have known better."

"Why's that?"

"Haywood played his cards to get Skip into the Guard. He knew he couldn't go to that well twice."

"During all that discussion of Archie's plight, she didn't tell you her plan?"

"No. I asked her what she thought could be done if he actually got drafted and all she said was she had a card up her sleeve that she would use if she had to."

"Did it have anything to do with her family in France?"

"There isn't any family in France anymore. I lived in Paris the summer after my freshman year of college. I went over there to do volunteer work to help find displaced people. Aunt Ruth came over and spent a month with me. We visited the cemeteries and searched for records in the churches and courts but so much had been destroyed over the course of two wars. The only person we found was a distant cousin. He was ancient then. He and I wrote for a few years but then his letters stopped coming."

"Do you remember his name?"

"Of course. François Jemet."

"Do you still have any of his letters?"

"I'm sure I do. I'm a bit like Aunt Ruth. We cling to our personal and family history."

"Could I see them?"

"They're in French."

"Still, I'd like to see them."

A shriek of laughter penetrated the quiet of the room and Hugo looked out the windows to see the children chasing each other on the lawn leading down to the pier.

Sharon watched as well. Finally, she broke the silence. "I'll have to unearth them. It might take a while. I'm not as clever or organized as my aunt."

"I don't mean to be pushy but it's really important."

"I'll get right on it. Do you have a card with your number?"

Hugo took a card from his pocket. It listed his information at the station. On the back, he wrote his home number.

Sharon studied the card a moment then placed it on the desk. "Anything else?"

"Why did your aunt write Aimeé Marlowe out of her Will?"

"Did she? That seems extreme. Although I can't imagine she intended to leave her much. Just a token of friendship or something Aimeé particularly coveted."

"Did Mrs. Marlowe covet many of Mrs. Camden's things?"

"She coveted everything."

"Oh?"

"I don't like her. Never have. She's good at being helpless."

"And that bothers you?"

"She's the least helpless person I know. It's just a ruse to get her way."

"I see. Did your aunt feel the same way about her helplessness?"

"Aunt Ruth understood her. She felt responsible for her. Aimeé came over here when she was not quite sixteen. The family sent her because things were desperate in France. Her father gambled away everything so they shipped her to America to live with relatives and to find a rich husband to provide for her."

"Did she?"

"Oh, yes. Aimeé gets what she wants, one way or another."

"Why did your aunt feel responsible for Mrs. Marlowe?"

"They have known each other since they were small children. Aimeé is three years younger but Aunt Ruth remembers playing with her when she was a toddler in Paris. The family went there every summer to spend several weeks. I suppose that image of Aimeé, a mere baby, became imprinted at that early age. Aunt Ruth paid dearly from that view."

"How's that?"

"When Aimeé arrived in the states, her journey was interrupted by a train derailment in Boston. Her governess died in the crash. Everyone fell all over themselves to be of assistance to the poor, fragile fifteen-year-old cousin with the charming accent. The following year Aunt Ruth made her debut. Richard Marlowe was Aunt Ruth's escort and they were in love although he hadn't yet proposed. You can guess the rest."

"She married your aunt's sweetheart?"

"Yes."

"I'm amazed, in light of such a betrayal, that she felt protective of her."

"Family. That was the most important thing to Aunt Ruth. And, of course, Aimeé played the innocent. How could it be her fault that a handsome, rich man fell in love with her? She had simply been a young girl who spoke very poor English, helpless, far from home, and destitute. She hadn't seen any of the American side of the family since she was three or four. They were like strangers to her. What male wouldn't respond to that?"

Hugo heard the bitterness. "The impression I have of your aunt isn't of someone easily duped."

"No. But at the time she was barely nineteen herself. Her mother, Tia, clung to her family connections, felt torn from them after they no longer traveled to Paris. I remember her as being a rather melancholy woman. I don't think she ever truly adjusted to living in America."

"Still, such a wound would be hard to overcome, I should think, especially when it comes to matters of the heart."

"You would think. But then Aunt Ruth met Uncle Edward and she once told me that she felt Aimeé had spared her by marrying Richard. He was too much Ashley Wilkes to Uncle Edward's Rhett Butler."

Hugo gave a grunt of amusement at the comparison and stood. "Thanks for being so candid with me Mrs. Shipley. I won't take up any more of your time."

Sharon led him back through the house. She stood in the doorway of the little ante room as he started across the lawn toward his car.

Before he got behind the wheel, he turned back to her. "What did your aunt keep in the safe?"

"I don't know. I'd be surprised if she kept anything in it. She has a safety deposit box at the bank."

"I take it you're familiar with your aunt's house, her belongings."

"I suppose I am."

"Would you be willing to walk me through the house to see if anything is missing?"

She hesitated. "Couldn't Voncille do it? Or Bebe?"

"Mrs. Prescott doesn't feel she would realize if any personal items were missing."

Sharon walked down the shallow steps and crossed the distance between them. "Do you think she was robbed? Is that why she's dead?"

"I honestly couldn't say. There's no outward appearance of a robbery but whoever did this might have been after something specific."

Hugo could see the indecision in her eyes.

Finally, she nodded. "I can't come tomorrow. It will have to be Friday."

"That'll work. Just let me know when to expect you. They'll get a message to me if you call the station."

As Hugo retraced his path back along Hwy 98 he decided the Prescotts and Haywoods were a very good-looking bunch. He wondered how much younger Sharon was than Haywood. She couldn't be much older than thirty. Thirty-five at most, he decided.

Coming down the hill from Spanish Fort to the Causeway in the gathering dusk, he could see the large sign for the Thunderbird Inn. It rose high above the low building on the narrow strip of land, the massive head of the bird and wide spread wings detailed in glowing neon. It was a place where you could get whatever you needed from a hot breakfast at five in the morning to a room for an hour or two in the middle of the day. He was tempted to stop in for a beer but he didn't.

Hugo didn't know what had prompted the return of his episodes of lost time but he realized he liked being a detective. If his black outs became known, he knew the chief would jump at the opportunity to get rid of him.

He had thought those episodes of hours, and sometimes days, lost were behind him, that in leaving San Francisco he had escaped them. The police department there had allowed him to resign rather than fire him.

Since taking this case it had happened twice. The dreams had returned. The black outs and the dreams, they always came together. He had to keep his guard up. No one could know. They would think he was crazy.

Maybe he was.

Fifteen

Hugo tried to call Bebe when he got home. There was still no answer. He spent a couple of hours going through Ruth's scrap books. This time he knew what he was looking for. In the end, the only thing he had was a faded postage stamp on a postcard that was barely legible and a first name scrawled at the bottom of a message.

He sat in the armchair in the front room and tuned the radio to WABB. He turned up the volume as the Beatles blasted Revolution across the airway. With his head resting against the back of the chair, he closed his eyes as he ran the facts through his mind. What was he missing?

The flash of headlights streaked through his window as a car pulled beside the Thunderbird parked on the empty lot. He turned off the radio and went to the door. Junior came up the steps with a bag in his hand, the smell of bar-be-que made Hugo's mouth water. He held the screen door open and Junior lifted his other hand to reveal a carton of Cokes as he stepped into the house and went straight through to the kitchen.

"Thought you'd be hungry so I ran out to Dick Russell's. Grammy worries that you don't get enough to eat."

"I am kinda hungry, come to think of it." He trailed behind Junior and began clearing scrap books from the table.

"Did you find the niece?"

"Yes. You'd think I would have encountered her at some point but apparently not. She's not someone you're likely to forget."

"That good looking, huh?"

"She is that. Probably in her early thirties. Does the name Shipley mean anything to you?"

"Big farming and timber operations over in Baldwin County. They're into funding The Boys' Club."

"How do you know these things?"

"I stayed home, remember? Besides, the police try to steer kids toward the club when we catch them getting up to no good."

Hugo took an ice pick to the frost encrusted ice trays in the freezer and managed to find two glasses in the cupboard. They poured their Cokes and dug into the pulled pork sandwiches.

When they had finished, Hugo leaned back in his chair with a groan of contentment. "That was good. Thanks. I was down to what I have in the pantry."

"What's that?"

"Canned peaches."

"I like canned peaches. Especially with a little dollop of cottage cheese."

"Not if you eat them once a day every day for a year."

"Didn't they give you anything to eat over there?"

"The guys in the rear with the gear did all right but if you were out humping the boonies, not so much. We had cookies and cocoa. That was my preferred breakfast. The turkey loaf or beans and wieners were tolerable at supper. That was the only time you could heat something up when you were in the field. But not even the Vietnamese would eat the canned bread."

"Who ever heard of canned bread?"

"Exactly. We called it white dread."

"No wonder you're so skinny."

"I prefer to think of it as lean." He clasped his hands behind his head and stared at a granddaddy long legs making his way up the kitchen wall. "Besides, we were all in the same boat. After humping thirty-five pounds around the undergrowth and through the streams all day every day nothing was left but stringy, bite riddled, muscle and bone. We were too tired to be hungry."

Junior wiped his mouth on a napkin. "If you don't like canned peaches, why do you have them in your pantry?"

Hugo grunted and after a pause said, "Emergency rations." He couldn't tell Junior that the can of peaches had been one of the first things he had bought when he moved into the house. He couldn't tell Junior why he had done so because he didn't know himself. As a reminder, perhaps? No. Life in 'Nam required no reminders.

Junior was silent for a couple of minutes. "What did you do after you got to San Francisco?"

"Bummed around a while. Watched the free show in the Haight-Ash-bury district. Got bored. Came home."

"The hippie life not for you, huh?"

"I guess not. Look at me. I'm a cop, for Christ's sake."

"Still, the summer of love and all that. Must have seen some things."

"I've seen a lot of things since I left Alabama. Now I'd like to forget most of them."

"Don't mean to pry."

Hugo drew himself up and stood. "You're not prying, Junior. I wish you'd been in San Francisco with me, and that's the god's truth. Lots of pretty girls, street music, free love, total abandon. You won't experience anything like that here in the heart of the bible belt."

"Still, you're glad to be home, right?"

Hugo gave him the answer he knew Junior wanted to hear. "Sure."

"What did you miss the most?"

Hugo grinned. "That's easy. A hot shower. Soap. Being clean. Sometimes we wore the same clothes for weeks at a time. They'd be rags by the time they choppered in fresh fatigues. Stank to high heaven though by then we didn't realize it." He gave a slow shake of his head. "Seems I can never get clean enough."

He collected their trash from the table and took it out the back door to the garbage can. When he came back in, Junior was studying the postcard from Ruth Camden's album.

"*We* something, something. . .*package,*" he angled it for better light, "*and are most grateful. You are kindness.* That doesn't sound right. Maybe *too kind?*"

"You can read that?"

"I took French, remember. For four years."

"Yeah. Because of that girl at Murphy. What was her name? Lydia?"

"That, and because I didn't want to be in Father Thomas' German class. He was too handy with the ruler."

Hugo opened the album and flipped the pages until he found another post card. "Here, read this one."

"*Things are very. . .*" Junior frowned. "I can't make out this word. . . .*cannot continue this* something... *Henri is our hope.*" He handed the card back to Hugo. "That's the gist of it. Signed the same, by this Giselle."

"Maybe Sharon will know who this is."

"Sharon, is it?"

"She's coming over on Friday to go through the house to see if anything is missing."

"What did she have to say about the safe?"

"Nothing. She knew about it but said her aunt has a safe deposit box at the bank. We should see if her lawyer will let us have access to it."

"I don't see why not. He'll have to file a list of all her possessions with the court anyway to probate the estate. No reason we can't get a peek to see if there's something that will lead us to Archie or give us a clue as to why she's dead."

"He might stall to protect Archie."

"The niece didn't know anything about Archie's disappearance?"

"She says he wouldn't go AWOL. Not without a good reason."

"Then where the hell is he?"

"Good question."

Sixteen

Hugo jerked awake, his heart pounding. He realized the noise that had awakened him was the ringing phone. He threw back the blanket and found his way in the dark into the kitchen. "Hello?"

"Why didn't you return my call?" Bebe's voice held that sultriness he remembered from all those long ago, late night calls.

"I tried but you never answered."

She sighed. He could hear in his mind the rustle of the sheets.

"I had to go to O'Sullivan's to finalize the plans for Aunt Ruth. I wanted to get into the house to pick out a dress." She sighed again. "She looks so much better now."

"I'm sorry you couldn't reach me. I can meet you there first thing tomorrow."

"No. I don't think I'll ever be able to go back into that house. Besides, it's today already. The funeral is this morning."

That sound again, of Bebe against the sheets. She was in bed talking to him. He stood there in the chill of his dank, crudely furnished house and steeled his mind against the image of her.

"What about the dress?"

"I went to Hammel's. Found something that she would have worn."

"And earlier this evening? I tried to call."

"Dinner. At the club."

There was a long silence.

"Why you, Bebe? Couldn't someone else have taken care of all that?"

"Daddy arranged everything but some things only a woman can

do." She fell silent. When she spoke again her voice was thick with emotion. "Her hair. Her make-up. Someone. . ."

"I'm sorry, Bebe."

She didn't say anything for a long moment. He thought she would hang up but then she said, "Why did you come home? I was better. After a while I stopped hurting."

Hugo's grip on the phone tightened into a fist of iron. His throat was so tight that for a moment he couldn't speak. "I'm sorry."

"Me too." The phone went dead.

⁂

HUGO GOT A hot shower and dressed. He put the coffee on and went next door to Maurice's house. It took a few minutes for him to answer Hugo's banging.

"What?" Maurice stood there in his briefs, still half asleep, his Afro squashed on one side.

"Yesterday's paper. Do you still have it?"

"What?" Maurice rubbed at his eyes. "What the hell time is it?"

"I need the paper from yesterday. Do you still have it?"

Maurice gestured with a jerk of his head for Hugo to come in. "It's here somewhere. Shut the door. It's cold."

Maurice disappeared into the bedroom and came back out in the floral woman's dressing gown Hugo had seen him wearing on his front porch earlier in the week. "What do you need with the paper that's so urgent it couldn't wait until a decent hour?" He looked through some magazines on the end table then turned and walked through the house to the kitchen. Hugo could hear him curse under his breath. He returned with the *Mobile Press Register* in a disheveled mess.

Hugo took the paper and began leafing through the sections. He found the obituary page and scanned down it until he found the notice about Ruth Camden. He held it up. "Can I keep this?"

"Take the whole damn thing. It's old news." Maurice yawned. "Want some coffee? Now that I'm up I might as well brew a pot."

"Thanks, but I gotta run." He folded the newspaper under his arm and turned for the door.

"Fine, but don't be making a habit of this. Get your own damn paper next time."

"I'll do that."

※

HUGO RACED TO the courthouse and headed straight for criminal court. An assistant D.A. was going down the list of cases on the docket. He looked up when Hugo entered the room.

"Good news." He flipped through his files and came up with the one that had brought Hugo to the court house. "Your guy pled out. Six months with credit for time served. He'll be home for Christmas."

"Then you don't need me?"

"Not today."

Hugo checked the time. He could make the funeral if he hurried.

※

THE OBITUARY HAD been well written and thorough. Hugo noted all the things that Ruth Camden had accomplished in her long life, making an abbreviated genealogical chart of her family in his mind as he went. The parking lot at the church was full to overflowing when he arrived for the 10:30 service. He had plenty of time to note a number of people who figured prominently in her life as they sat attentively through High Mass at Holy Spirit Catholic Church.

The Archbishop performed the service which said a lot about her involvement in the church and influence in the community. He was surprised that they hadn't held the service downtown at the Cathedral.

Hugo counted five more priests in attendance and his thoughts flashed back to the young private lying in a muddy stream in the jungles of Vietnam holding his shrapnel torn gut and begging for a priest. *And here they all are*, he thought. *Fat lot of good that does anybody.*

Hugo stood against the back wall of the crowded church and observed the congregants, the music of the Latin liturgy filling his soul. It was this ritual in all its beauty that in the past had been a balm to the hurts and had helped him escape the realities of his life. It had stayed with him since leaving the church. He felt the power of it even now. Once a Catholic, always a Catholic. He smiled grudgingly at the thought.

Strange that he had not felt any of this when he had been in Vietnam, or later in San Francisco. Like so many of his fellow soldiers, he had blocked all feeling, all emotion, and gotten through each day with a moment to moment immediacy. Nothing had mattered beyond the next foot fall, the next river crossing, the next dig-in. He had looked on as if viewing a silent film as the soldier who had marched in step beside him since basic lurched backward with a bullet between his open eyes. *There it is*, he thought at the time. *It don't mean nothing.* He had helped load the body onto the evac chopper and closed his mind to it. Even now, he couldn't remember his name.

⁂

BEFORE THE SERVICE ended, Hugo slipped away from the church. He went to the cemetery to ensconce himself under a magnolia tree on the periphery so he could observe Ruth Camden's inner circle.

Bebe wore a black cape with a stand-up collar. The high heels and short skirt accentuated her long, lean legs.

Hugo tore his gaze away to scrutinize the other mourners.

Bebe, Voncille, and Sharon. *The three graces*, Hugo thought.

He didn't know the priest who presided over the internment in the family mausoleum. It was probably her parish priest. He recognized most of the dozen people gathered in the noon sun of a beautiful, clear day.

Tyler Redman stood out from the rest of the mourners, his rumpled suit setting him apart. He looked sallow in a crowd of well heeled, physically attractive members of the rich and notable. Even the priest, in his pristine robes and adornments, looked like a runway model awaiting his close up.

Ruth would be pleased that her last day in the physical world was such an idyllic one, Hugo decided. He was beginning to know the enigma that was Ruth Camden. He realized he wanted very much to find her killer.

A man with auburn hair and an expensive suit stood talking to Haywood after the service concluded. Hugo didn't recognize him. The man moved on to Bebe. They exchanged a few words before she turned away abruptly. She cut across the cemetery to the pathway where the cars waited, her long legs moving stridently with a sense of urgency. The stranger watched her walk away before turning to speak to Voncille.

A movement out of the corner of his eye caught Hugo's attention. He turned to see Buck Sissons walking toward him at a leisurely stroll.

"August." Sissons said as he came to stand in the chill shade of the tree next to Hugo.

"What brings you here?"

"A hunch."

They watched as the handshakes and hugs were dispensed among the gathered family and friends. Sharon took Viola's arm and the two of them walked toward the vehicles.

"And you?"

"A killer."

"You're sure it's one of them?"

"Yes." Hugo's scrutiny returned to the unknown man with the auburn hair. "Who's that?"

"Which one?"

"Red hair, expensive suit."

"Don't know the last name. Trey something, but then aren't they all? He's with the bank."

"Yeah?"

"About a year, I think. He was sent down here from the main office in Birmingham."

"They must be looking for the economy to improve."

"Wishful thinking with Brookley Field set to close any day now."

"Johnson's revenge."

"That's politics for you."

"'Nam has the last laugh. His presidency will be defined by the war."

"Haven't you heard? We're winning."

"You don't say."

They watched the remaining mourners pull away in a long line of limousines and expensive cars.

"No Archie." Hugo scanned the area, seeking any movement, anything out of the ordinary that would give away a hidden looking post.

"Apparently not."

"Surely the army has some idea where to look."

"The best scenario, from a deserter's stand point in this part of the country, would be Mexico. You can live dirt cheap, their borders are as porous as a sieve, and as long as you have a little money, the authorities will look the other way. If it was me, that's where I'd go. Down on the Yucatan peninsula, live the good life. Might be a little rustic for his taste but it's a short plane hop for family and friends."

"And yet I get the feeling from everyone else that he's either gone North or to Europe."

"The whole lot of 'em are trying really hard to make you think that way. But that's a greater risk for a deserter. The Canadians are sticklers for law and order. If you get a sympathetic border guard, they get around the law by conveniently failing to ask about a man's military discharge. But without proper immigrant status he'd have to live below the radar. I don't see our architect doing that. Europe has become much more regimented. People take notice, especially of foreigners.

It's harder to travel across borders without proper documents. There's a greater chance of leaving a paper trail."

They waited in silence under the magnolia tree. The door of the mausoleum stood open. There was no sign of the grounds keepers who would reseal it.

"He's not coming." Hugo once again scanned the cemetery.

"No, I don't believe he is."

Buck headed across the graveyard toward the mausoleum. Hugo followed. There was no one inside except the lately departed.

Seventeen

When Hugo reached the station, he found a message from Judy Fohl. He caught her at the court house just as she was preparing to leave the clerk's office.

"Perfect timing. Let me get my purse and you can buy me lunch."

"Sure. Where would you like to eat?"

"The Sea Ranch."

The restaurant was only ten minutes away. They took Hugo's car and nipped through the Bankhead Tunnel to the Causeway. It was a favorite eating place during the week for businessmen working downtown and had the added appeal of overlooking Mobile Bay.

Most of the lunch crowd had thinned out. They were seated by the windows to take advantage of the view. As soon as the hostess disappeared, a waiter arrived with a martini in a chilled glass.

"I get the impression you've been here before." Hugo watched over the top of his menu as Judy took a sip of her drink.

She gave a grunt of appreciation. "One of my favorite watering holes." After another sip she looked over at Hugo. "Don't tell me you're abstaining."

"I'm on duty."

"So am I." There was a twinkle in her eye and the shadow of a smile on her lips.

"I can't afford to be caught drinking on the job."

"The rest of the police force doesn't seem to be troubled by the prospect."

"Maybe not, but the chief isn't one of my fans."

"I see." She glanced down the menu then set it aside. "Tell me what happened to Ruth Camden."

"She was poisoned."

"Someone close to her, then."

"That would be the most obvious place to start."

"Hence the interest in the family business. Chasing the money."

"After sex, the top motive for murder."

"You seem awfully knowledgeable for someone so young."

"I read a lot of Dashiell Hammett."

"Hmm."

The waiter reappeared and Hugo and Judy placed their orders. Once he was again out of earshot she lit a cigarette and leaned in close. "The Haywood-Prescotts have used Haywood Mills as a corporate structure to branch off into a number of different enterprises that have nothing to do with the original business. Everything from shipping to an import-export concern in Morocco. They have offices all over the place from France to Argentina."

"That's impressive."

"The thing I think you'll find interesting is the operational by-laws. It takes a two-thirds majority vote of the principals to make any substantial changes to the company operations."

"Who are the principals?"

"The company was started by Willis Haywood. His oldest son was killed in a boating accident so he left his entire estate to his only remaining child, Francis, who proceeded to have three children. Ruth was the oldest. The other two were Diane and Sebastian. You with me?"

Hugo nodded.

"During Willis' lifetime, the mill was the whole of the family's interests. It produced lumber and the sawdust was sold off to the paper mills for pulp. It was under Francis that they began to branch out into shipping. When he died, the company was left in three equal parts to his children."

"Ruth, Diane, and Sebastian."

"Right. Diane married Reginald Prescott. He worked in the mill but it was Ruth's husband, Edward, who began the transformation. So all three were equally vested in all the subsequent areas of expansion."

The waiter brought their meal of the house specialty, baked flounder *muniere*. The fish was light and flaky and dripping with butter and lemon. Judy and Hugo tucked into their lunch. Once the dirty dishes were removed and they had been served coffee, Judy left off prying into Hugo's personal life and took up the thread of their earlier conversation.

"Now, here's the major rotten apple in the pie. Haywood and Sharon's father died fairly young. When their mother, Diane, died three years ago, her one-third interest was divided between the two of them."

Hugo sat back in his chair and stared out across Mobile Bay. "Haywood has only a sixth interest in the company."

"Give that boy a gold star." Judy lit another cigarette and blew a plume of smoke toward the ceiling. "Haywood is the figurehead but anytime he wants to do anything outside the standard operating procedure of the company, he has to have his sister vote with him as well as one of the other principals."

"The missing papers."

"I don't know anything about missing papers. But I do know a catch-22 situation when I see one."

Hugo looked at Judy with admiration. "How do you know this? This can't all be in the records in Probate."

"The law requires companies to register within the state of operations. It's then a matter of public record. After all these years dealing with a mountain of recordings, I've learned how to read the dry details and come away with the gold nuggets buried in the legalese. You have to have an imagination to make the connections sometimes but it's all there."

She ground out her cigarette in the ashtray. "But the real key is gossip." She opened her purse, took out a tube of lipstick, and, with that most feminine of talents, applied it perfectly within the lines of her lips in three swift moves without the aid of a mirror. "People like to know things. They like to feel important, in the know. They can't do that unless they tell someone."

"And they tell you."

She winked at him and smiled. "All the time, handsome. Gossip is power and I always lend a friendly ear." She took a folded sheet of paper from her purse and slid it across the table to Hugo. "I think you'll find this helpful."

He opened the piece of paper and read it. "These are all the subsidiaries."

"Probably not all. They might have wised up and started separating their interests under different firms operating out of different states. Or even the Bahamas. But I think this will give you something to think about."

"France, Italy, South America. . .and Canada."

"Bingo."

"I don't know what to say, Judy. I owe you one."

"Then pay the bill and let's get back." She grinned. "I'm just a working girl, you know."

She was anything but a working girl.

⚜

HUGO LEFT JUDY at the foot of the steps leading up to the side entrance to the court house. He parked at the police station and walked four blocks to Whitehall Bank.

Mobile was home to two banks. The Whitehall Bank had been in business since before cotton was king. It was a family owned institution. It was *the* bank. The newcomer in town was The Bank of the South. It had arrived on the coattails of Reconstruction.

In the lobby of the Whitehall, Hugo found a roster of bank officials. The burnished brass of Charles Whitehall, III, told him he had found Trey.

He went to the first desk in the bullpen across from the teller cages and asked to see Charles Whitehall.

The clerk looked up from the doodle he was drawing on a legal pad. "Do you have an appointment?"

Hugo took out his shield. "No."

The clerk sat up straight and picked up the phone. After a brief exchange with whoever was on the other end of the line, he directed Hugo to take the elevator to the third floor.

Hugo stepped off the elevator into a reception area that spoke the language of wealth. An oriental carpet hushed any footfall and the oak paneled walls mounted with oil paintings created an exclusive club feel.

The receptionist had jet black hair. The deep red of her lipstick contrasted dramatically with her pale complexion. Her eyes were the blue of sapphires. She brought to mind the screen sirens of Hollywood's heydays.

After a long ten minutes, Hugo put aside the copy of *Newsweek* and stood. "Are you sure Mr. Whitehall's in his office?"

"He'll be with you shortly." Her voice was just as rich as her surroundings.

"That's what you said earlier. How long is shortly?"

At that moment the phone on her ivory inlaid desk buzzed. She answered it, then stood. "Mr. Whitehall will see you now."

Hugo noted that she had the debutante walk down pat. Did debutantes work, he wondered? Maybe in plush surroundings like this, he decided. Not that he'd seen her do anything that resembled work unless you called leisurely flipping through the pages of *Town & Country* work. She led him down the wide hallway to the third door on the left.

Charles Whitehall rose from behind his desk when Hugo entered the room. He buttoned his suit coat as he came around and shook hands.

"Mr. August. Come in. Sorry to keep you waiting. I was on a call to the west coast." He gestured for Hugo to take a chair facing the desk. When he was once again settled in his own seat he asked, "Now, what can I do for the police?"

Hugo thought it was interesting that Charles Whitehall, aka Trey, knew his name when he hadn't given it to either the clerk downstairs or to the receptionist.

"I wanted to talk to you about Ruth Camden."

"I thought I saw you at the cemetery. That was you, wasn't it? Watching from the shade of the tree?"

"Yes. That was me and Buck Sissons. He was there looking for Archie Camden."

"And what were you looking for?"

"The same."

"Why's that?"

"I'm trying to find Mrs. Camden's murderer."

"Murder!" Whitehall pulled back, physically repelled by the idea. "Haywood never told me she was murdered."

"What did he tell you?"

"That, under the circumstances, there had to be an investigation to determine the cause of death."

"Poison."

"Good God."

"This is the first you've heard that she was poisoned?"

Trey Whitehall looked genuinely shocked, Hugo had to give him that. The truth of the matter was that he had made a bee line for the bank to take the measure of the man since seeing his exchange with Bebe at the cemetery. But in light of his conversation with Judy, he thought he might be on to something of a less personal nature.

"For someone who recently moved to town, you seem to be close to the family."

"Yes." He picked up a letter opener and toyed with it. "I arrived in Mobile in January but I've known the family a long time. Skip and I were at Alabama together. So were our fathers. The same fraternity and all that."

And all that. "The bank handles the family's finances?"

Trey looked up and set aside the letter opener. "The company banks with us, yes."

"And the family's extended interests? Does the bank manage that money as well?"

Trey didn't answer right away. Finally, he said, "I can't discuss the business of the bank's patrons. I've admitted the Prescotts are customers but that's as far as I'm willing to go. It's a legal issue, you understand." He sat back in his chair. "Besides, what could their business have to do with Ruth's death?"

"Money. The oldest motive there is."

Trey frowned. "You don't think someone in the family is responsible?"

"Do you think a stranger would kill Ruth Camden for her money?"

"I see your point."

Eighteen

Junior finished typing up his notes on the break-in in Oakleigh the day before. As far as the home owner could determine, the only thing missing was a shovel. The owner had been more upset that the lock was broken and now the door sagged on its hinges and wouldn't close properly.

He placed the typed pages in a folder and dropped it in the pending investigations basket on his desk. Then he swiveled his chair to look at the Wall of Death as he and Hugo had come to refer to the names and bits of fact taped to the plaster wall of the second-floor bullpen.

Contrary to the chief's demand that Hugo take down the death shot of Ruth Camden, it was still there. For motivation, Hugo had said.

Junior got up and took the photo from the wall. He held it under the intense light of the banker's lamp on his desk. He took a magnifying glass from a drawer and scrutinized all the items visible in the image.

There on the floor near one of the three legs of the pie crust table was a tiny black spot.

Hugo came through the double doors leading into the bullpen. Junior looked up.

"How was the funeral?"

"Well attended."

"Anything interesting?"

"Buck Sissons was at the cemetery for the internment."

"Looking for Archie, I suppose."

"Yes, but no luck." Hugo picked up a pink message slip on his desk and read it. "How about you? Anything new?"

"I finally talked to the Golding's yard man. He worked on the yard all afternoon. Didn't finish up until late. Around four, four-thirty. He didn't see anything unusual."

"No one came by the Camden house during that time?"

"No. He saw Viola leave. She and the Golding's maid walked down the block to catch the bus."

"Anything else?"

"He didn't see Mrs. Camden leave for five o'clock Mass but Holy Spirit is only ten minutes away. He was probably gone by the time she left."

"No cars in or out?"

"None."

"Any other news?"

"Dr. Allen had one other suspicious death about three months ago. He determined the man died of bad moonshine."

"Huh."

"Look at this." Junior handed Hugo the photo and the magnifying glass. "You see that speck on the photo there?"

Hugo nodded.

"Do you remember seeing it when we were there?"

"No."

"What do you think it is?"

Hugo angled the photo and looked through the magnifying glass at different depths. "I think it's one of those little black triangles that hold a photo in place. It must have fallen out of one of the scrap books."

"A photo corner." Junior took the picture and looked at it again. "You're right. Maybe someone took something from an album and dislodged it in the process."

"Maybe. Or maybe the glue is old and it simply fell out when Ruth was looking through the books." Hugo stared off across the bullpen to the windows on the far wall of the building and the view beyond. "I remember there were a few empty spaces in one of the early books."

"It's probably nothing."

"You never know." Hugo taped the photo back to the wall. "Good eye."

Junior nodded. It was probably nothing he reminded himself, but he couldn't help but be pleased that Hugo thought it was worth noting. "What's on the agenda for this afternoon?"

"I took Judy Fohl to lunch and she gave me quite an ear full. It seems Haywood has been lying to me." He reached for the phone and began dialing a number. "I plan to find out why."

BEBE ANSWERED THE phone on the second ring.

"I need to talk to you about your aunt's death."

There was a brief hesitation. "Can't it wait, Hugo? It's been a rough day."

"I'm sorry, Bebe but I'm afraid it can't."

She sighed. "If you must. Come to my apartment. I'm a mess."

"What's the address?"

"Oh." She paused. "I thought you knew. Maison Imperial. Number nineteen."

"I'm on my way."

It took him nearly twenty minutes to get from the police station downtown to Maison Imperial apartments located at the foot of Spring Hill. They had become the go to residence of newly separated men in the throes of divorce who had once lived in the exclusive neighborhood at the top of the hill. It allowed them to be near their children during the protracted legal process. Perhaps just as importantly, it was close to the country club and the golf course. Many a heated and expensive battle had been waged over the club membership. It was also a handy place for men who were still married to stash their mistresses.

Gossip is power. Hugo smiled. He cruised through the complex until he spotted Bebe's little Mercedes convertible parked in front of the building that housed her apartment. She opened the door at his first knock.

Her hair was down and she had changed into jeans and a sweater. She was barefooted, the bell-bottoms covering the tops of her feet and dragging a little at the heels. She gestured for Hugo to come in.

"I'm sorry about this, Bebe." He looked around the space. There was still a newness about the apartments. The ground floor was an L shape with a bump out for a dining table. The kitchen could be closed off with a pocket door. A massive abstract oil painting hung over the sofa. Everything was very modern except for an oriental cabinet in blood red. Otherwise the furnishings were sparse.

She took the lone armchair and Hugo sat on the sofa. She still hadn't spoken.

"You do know that your aunt was murdered?"

"Yes. Daddy told me."

"It's my job to find the killer. That means I have to look into her life. All aspects of it. That includes her family."

"You're saying you going to pry into our lives."

"You could put it like that."

"How else would you put it?"

Hugo had no answer to that. "Did your aunt have any enemies? Anyone who resented her enough to do something like this?"

"No." Bebe drew her feet up onto the chair and tucked them beneath her. "Well, obviously someone did but I don't know who that might be. She disapproved of me but I didn't kill her because of it."

"Why did she disapprove of you?"

"Conduct unbecoming." Bebe uncoiled, stood, and moved to the oriental cabinet. She opened it to reveal a bar. She held the gin bottle up and looked over her shoulder at Hugo. When he shook his head, she poured two fingers into a cocktail glass and returned to her seat.

"You weren't close to your aunt, then?"

"Not recently. I admired her. She was a strong woman who held her ground in a world dominated by men. But she did it quietly, behind the scene."

"Did those men include your father?"

"Of course. He's been in charge of the company since Uncle Edward died and that was in the mid-fifties."

"What were the papers you took by her house on Friday?"

"Something to do with the business."

"Do you know what was in them?"

"I didn't read them."

Hugo sat quietly and studied Bebe. He soon realized she didn't feel the need to fill the silence. "Why did you deliver the papers? Do you work for the company?"

"No. I was downtown for lunch at the Trade Center. I stopped by the office to pick up a check. Daddy asked me to deliver the envelope to Aunt Ruth." She shrugged, took a sip of her drink. "So, I did."

"Walk me through that visit."

Bebe gave him a long look. "Fine." She stared at the painting over his head. "Viola answered the door. She told me Aunt Ruth was in the attic. I went upstairs and found her there." Her forehead creased and she turned her gaze to Hugo. "I startled her, I think."

"Because she didn't hear your arrival?"

"I don't know. I think it was because she was so focused on what she was doing. She had her magnifying glass out and was examining a photograph from one of her books."

"What was the photograph of?"

"I don't know. She wanted to know what I was doing there and I told her."

"And her reaction?"

"She said she didn't have time for Haywood's foolishness. Those were her words. That she had more important issues to deal with."

"Then?"

"I told her I'd leave the papers in the dining room but that Daddy really needed her to look at them. She was to call if she had any questions."

"Her response?"

"Nothing. She ignored me and went back to studying her pictures. So I left."

"Did you see the cat when you were there?"

Bebe shook her head. "No." She hesitated. "No, I don't think I did." Her eyes widened. "Oh, God. I forgot all about Beauregard."

"He's missing."

"Poor old thing. Are you sure he isn't hiding in the house?" She worried her lower lip between her teeth. "Viola would be able to coax him out of hiding. Have you talked to her?"

"Viola hasn't seen him since she put him out Friday afternoon after your visit. You didn't see him Saturday when you went to check on her?"

"No. What could have happened to him?"

"Maybe he simply wandered off when there was no one to let him back into the house."

"I feel awful. I never even thought of him." Tears formed in her eyes. "She loved that mangy old cat."

"Maybe he'll show up. One of the neighbors may have taken him in."

"He might have gone to Aimeé's. She complained about him and her gold fish. He was fascinated by them."

"I'll be sure to check with her. Did Beauregard stray very often?"

"I don't think so, but really, I don't know. He was always around whenever I dropped by. In fact, he actually let me pet him when I took Aunt Ruth to lunch a week ago."

"Did the two of you go to lunch regularly?"

"No. We didn't see each other much, actually. I was worried about Archie. I knew she was upset so I thought lunch together would make us both feel better."

"Did it?"

"Not really. She was preoccupied. It worried her that she hadn't heard from him. Not a single letter since he left and that was nearly two months ago."

"Maybe he called."

"That's just it. She expected him to call her after he got settled at camp in Fayetteville but he never did. Then she thought that surely he would be able to write and let her know how things were. But nothing so far."

"You like him."

"Of course. He was never the kind of pest that some kids can be. When we were small and our families were close, we played together all the time. I can't believe you don't remember him."

"Did he go to St. Andrews?"

"No. He went to Highcliff."

"I'm surprised. He lived with your aunt and she was a staunch Catholic."

"I never understood that either. As we got older, we weren't as close. After Uncle Edward died, the company business caused a lot of friction." Bebe stared down at her drink as she swirled the clear liquid in the glass. "He was so sweet natured when he was a little boy." She blinked back tears. "I was afraid for him to go to Vietnam. So many men who have gone never came back."

"Have you had any ideas about where he might have gone?"

She shook her head. "I can't really believe he simply skipped out. I wouldn't have thought him capable of it."

"Maybe he isn't as brave as you think."

"You think it's brave to go?"

Hugo had no reply.

"I think it takes more courage to refuse." Bebe took a sip of her drink.

They sat in silence for a long moment.

"Would you tell me if you knew where he was?"

"I don't know where he is. That's the truth."

Hugo stood. "Lunch at the Trade Center, huh?"

"Yes."

"That's an odd choice."

"If you must know, I was entertaining some of Daddy's associates."

"By that you mean people he's doing business with?"

"Yes."

"Do you do that often?"

"Occasionally. Mother usually hosts parties at home or the club but she's not overly fond of the Japanese."

"I see."

He turned toward the door and Bebe followed him. "What do you talk about with Japanese businessmen?"

"I tell them about Mobile, Fort Conde, the Magnolia Cemetery, Oakleigh. Sometimes I arrange trips to Bellingrath Gardens. Horticulture is big with them." She held the door open for him. "And I smile a lot."

Hugo was half way down the sidewalk when he turned back to Bebe. "Did you know Mrs. Camden left you her house?"

"Yes. Tyler Redman told me at a meeting of the family yesterday." She walked out onto the cold concrete of her entry way.

"What will you do with it?"

"I don't know. I like my life the way it is right now." She crossed her arms and hunched her shoulders against the chill in the air.

Hugo nodded. "Do you know why she wrote Aimeé Marlowe out of the will?"

"I didn't know she had ever been in it."

"Right." He touched the knot of his tie then fished his keys out of his pocket, stalling, trying to think of something more to say. "Thanks for seeing me today."

"Sure." She turned back into her apartment and closed the door.

Nineteen

Hugo debated going back to the station but it was nearly five o'clock. He didn't really want to fight the afternoon traffic.

He tried to decide which direction to take with the investigation. He couldn't help but think that Archie's whereabouts was key to answering the question of who killed Ruth Camden and why. Tomorrow he would meet with Sharon Shipley and go through the house. Maybe something would come from it.

He decided to call it a day. At the service station at McGregor and Airport, he filled his car with gas then used the pay phone to call the police station. He discovered that Junior had gone home. It was Bingo night, Hugo remembered. Junior would be taking his grandmother to St. Andrews.

The idea of a nice steak at The Quarter Note tempted him, especially since he was already in the vicinity, but his wallet was getting pretty thin. Lunch with Judy hadn't been cheap. He went instead to the A&P at Sage and Dauphin Streets. He needed something in his pantry other than peaches.

After strolling around the aisles of the grocery store for fifteen minutes he made his way to the check-out. He realized, as the cashier was ringing him up, that he had a wide disparity of items in his cart. The bread and peanut butter would satisfy him tonight, he decided. He'd figure out what to do with the rest of it later.

It was hard dark by the time he pulled onto the lot next to his house. He still hadn't replaced the burned out light bulb on the front porch. He took the two bags of groceries from the back seat and was halfway to his front steps when a shadow came swiftly out of the night from his left and he felt the blow to his jaw.

The bags went flying and Hugo stumbled, trying to regain his balance as the second blow caught him just below his left rib cage. He went down and tried to roll away from his attacker only to be caught in the gut by a vicious kick.

"Stay away from my wife, pretty boy, or next time you'll be sorry."

Hugo sucked in a painful breath and rolled onto his back. A minute later he heard an engine turn over and the screech of tires as the vehicle tore away down the street.

"Christ." He lay there in the dirt of his yard for a few minutes. Tentatively he ran his tongue around in his mouth checking for loose teeth. He tasted blood. Slowly he rose to a sitting position and took a couple of deep breaths. Finally, he got to his feet. His shoe struck something. He reached down and picked up an orange.

The bathroom mirror revealed a scrape just below his left eye. The inside of his mouth had a cut high on the left cheek. The punch below the ribs was a dirty blow. He would probably piss blood for a few days as a result. Mo Hitchens would pay for this when the opportunity presented itself. And it would be soon.

He washed his face, rinsed his mouth with Listerine, then found the flashlight. He went out into the yard to retrieve the remainder of his groceries. A marmalade cat was feasting on the package of hamburger meat. He left her to it and gathered up the rest of his shopping.

The loaf of bread had suffered in the scuffle so he opened the box of saltine crackers and ate peanut butter and crackers for his supper. He should have splurged for the steak, he decided.

⁂

FRIDAY DAWNED CLEAR and cool. Hugo sipped coffee as he turned the pages of another of Ruth's scrap books. About half way through, he came to a page where a photograph or an invitation of some type should have been. You could tell by the paler shade of the empty space delineated by photo corners. What had been there, he wondered, and who had removed it? Or had it simply fallen out as he suggested to Junior yesterday?

He was due to meet Sharon Shipley at ten o'clock at the house on Dauphin Street. It had occurred to Hugo in the night that he didn't know where Archie had lived before his disappearance. He decided it would be helpful to find out and to search it as well. He was angry with himself that he hadn't thought to do so before this late hour in the investigation. They might find something to shed some light on Archie's state of mind or even a possible hint as to where he might have gone.

As soon as the clock rolled around to seven, he called Junior at home. After he declined an invitation to breakfast, he told him he wouldn't be coming in to the station until after he went through the Camden house again. He put Junior on the task of finding out where Archie had lived and to see if they could get access to it.

Hugo decided he would call on Aimeé Marlowe before his meeting with Sharon. He was curious to see her reaction to the terms of Ruth's will. If Sharon had been right in her characterization of Aimeé, then she would have expected to inherit something. He wanted to know what they had fallen out about. Viola had said it was over Archie. Could it have been something so insignificant as a lack of compassion?

After a steamy shower, Hugo shaved gingerly around the scrape on his cheek. He had some serious swelling around his eye and a deep purple bruise beneath it. There was major bruising above his left kidney as well. There was nothing he could do about any of it for now but there would be pay-back. That was for damn sure.

He ate a banana and an orange for breakfast. He had forgotten to get milk for the cereal. Lunch would have to be his meal of the day, he decided.

At eight thirty he pulled into the Camden driveway and parked. He walked down to Aimeé Marlowe's house and rang the bell.

He was beginning to think she was a late sleeper. Or she could have gone to early Mass and not yet returned home? It occurred to him that neither he nor Junior had spoken with her since his encounter in the back yard of the Camden house. Just as he was about to ring the bell again, the door opened.

"I thought I heard the bell." Aimeé was dressed in what Mrs. K would call her church clothes. She studied Hugo's battered face but made no comment. Instead, she stepped back from the open door. "Come in, come in, Mr. . ."

"August. Hugo August."

"Now how could I forget a name like that? High born, exalted." She started down a hallway toward the back of her house. "It's French, you know. Hugo."

Hugo followed after her, taking in the overpowering array of paintings on the walls of the hallway, the ornate mirror over a long narrow table with ball and claw feet. The surface of the table was covered with bric-a-brac and an art deco lamp. "I didn't know."

"Oh, yes. And of course, August. King of the jungle. Brave and true."

They entered a sunny breakfast nook at the back of the house. The room felt small due to the profusion of nick nacks everywhere. A cup of tea was steaming on the table that was placed to overlook the back yard.

She gestured for him to take a seat. "Is that you, Mr. August? Brave and true?"

"I don't think Sister Mary Claire gave much thought to the meaning. She named me after her favorite brother I've been told."

"Ah. Was she French?"

"Irish, as it so happens."

"Yes. Quite a lot of the nuns here are from Ireland." She turned toward the kitchen cupboard. "Would you like a cup of tea?"

"Thank you. That would be nice."

She brought a china cup and saucer and placed it on the table in front of him. "Milk or lemon?"

Hugo remembered the thin slice of lemon at the bottom of Ruth Camden's tea cup. "Milk, if you don't mind."

"Not at all." From the refrigerator she poured milk into a spouted miniature pitcher in the shape of a cow and brought it to the table. Then she filled Hugo's cup from the teapot. Finally, she settled in the chair across from him. "Now, what has you paying calls so early in the day?"

A subtle rebuke, Hugo thought. "I wanted to talk to you about Mrs. Camden. We've determined that she didn't die of natural causes."

"Poisoned, Haywood said." She took a sip of her tea. "I don't believe it. Who would want to poison Ruth?"

"It's my job to find out."

"Well, maybe your name will serve you well after all."

"I don't think my name will have anything to do with solving this case. But I will solve it."

Aimeé studied him over her teacup. A hint of a smile softened her lips. "Not much experience at this sort of thing, have you?"

"What makes you think that?"

"You're so young. Can't be older than your late twenties, if that. Am I right?"

"My age doesn't have anything to do with it."

"I'm sure you're very capable. But poison, that's a hard thing to prove, isn't it?"

"Not as hard as it used to be. Science is catching up."

She topped up her cup of tea and glanced at Hugo's untouched drink. "Still, I'd think those things could be tricky."

"Yes, they can. Let's hope they don't prove too tricky. We all want to bring Mrs. Camden's killer to justice, don't we?"

"Of course."

"When did you last see her?"

"Wednesday of last week. There was an ad in the newspaper about a sale at Hammel's. I thought we could go shopping and have lunch afterwards."

"Did you?"

"No." Aimeé frowned. "She's been so obsessed with Archie these days that nothing interested her. She had become a veritable hermit, rarely leaving home for anything except Mass. So, I went on my own."

"You didn't see her on Friday?"

"No. I called and Viola told me she was busy."

Hugo poured milk into his tea and stirred it. As he placed the spoon on the saucer, he realized it was engraved with the image of a building. It was a souvenir from the St. Louis World's Fair.

"I thought the funeral yesterday was very nice. I was impressed that the Archbishop performed the service."

"Yes." Small brackets of annoyance formed on Aimeé's forehead. "Everyone kowtowed to Ruth. They were all about the money, you see."

"What will become of all that money, I wonder?"

"Archie should inherit it all except a few incidentals. If he ever comes home."

"What if he doesn't? What if he has decided to skip out on his enlistment? What happens then?"

Aimeé shrugged. "I don't know. Haywood will keep managing the company and I guess her lawyer will try to find Archie." She leaned slightly forward. "I never liked that man, Tyler Redman. I don't know why Ruth trusted him with her business."

"Will Redman have the power of Ruth's vote?"

A look of surprise flashed fleeting across Aimeé's face. She quickly hid it. "I suppose he will. I don't see any other way they could conduct business."

"All Haywood has to do is get Sharon on board with his plans and there's no issue. I understand that Sebastian will go along with whatever Haywood wants."

"Sharon will never fall in with Haywood."

"Why?"

"She'll be ruled by what she thinks Ruth wanted."

"You don't like Sharon?"

A subtle change fell over Aimeé. Hugo couldn't say exactly what it was. She sat less erect, the features of her face softened. "Of course, I like Sharon. She's always been there for Ruth. She helped her come to grips with Archie going off to war. It's just that she doesn't always stop and think what's in the best interest of the rest of the family."

"Does she have anything to gain by Ruth's death?"

"That's a shocking thought. It implies Sharon might want to harm Ruth."

"I'm just curious about the terms of the will. I'm sure, if Sharon was so close to her aunt, that she received something."

Aimeé looked down at her teacup. "The necklace. She gets the family necklace."

"Which is?"

She raised her eyes to meet Hugo's unblinking regard. "Sapphires. A waterfall of sapphires. It's been in the family for generations."

This, Hugo decided, was what Aimeé Marlowe coveted.

"What did Ruth leave you?"

She looked away from Hugo and focused on the fountain in the back yard. "Nothing."

"I'm surprised. I thought you were her best friend, plus being her cousin."

"I told you Ruth and I sometimes had our little spats. I had thought we were long past that years ago but it seems I was wrong."

"Had you been at odds lately?"

Aimeé turned her pale blue gaze on Hugo, her expression sad. "No. I've always been there for her. It would have been nice for her to have remembered me with a small token but, at the end of the day, her things were hers to dispose of as she saw fit."

"Did you like Archie?"

The change of direction seemed to unsettle her briefly. She took a sip of her now cooling tea. "Archie was always a pleasant child. Ruth spoiled him. He didn't have any interest in the business, went off to live in the Oakleigh district in one of those run-down houses. Always taking photographs and drawing."

"You disapproved of his profession?"

"I wouldn't say I disapproved. He was needed in the business.

He could have better protected Ruth's interests if he had taken his rightful place."

Her tone softened again. "But he was Ruth's whole world and for that I can forgive him."

"Where do you think he is?"

"I don't know. I only learned yesterday that he was missing."

"Who told you?"

Aimeé took another sip of her tea. She returned the cup to the saucer with great care. "The maid."

"You didn't attend the family meeting with Redman?"

She looked down at the table and aligned the spoon at the proper angle to her teacup. "No. I suppose that since I didn't inherit, it wasn't considered appropriate. But it would have been a courtesy to at least let me know something as important as the fact that Archie had vanished, don't you think?"

"Have you seen the cat?"

Again, the abrupt change of subject seemed to throw her off stride. "Ruth's cat?"

"Beauregard."

"No. Not in over a week now."

"Weren't you worried about him after Ruth's death?"

"Truthfully, I'm not a cat person. He didn't like me either. Always scurried away under a piece of furniture whenever I visited." Once again, she gazed out the window at the fountain. "This is the first time I've spared him a thought, if you must know."

"Ruth loved him."

"She was ridiculous about that animal. He was old and unwell. He should have been put down long ago."

Twenty

Junior started his day in a good mood. At Bingo the night before his grandmother had won the pot. Simply winning had her bubbly and happy. To have twelve dollars to spend on something totally frivolous had her itching to go to Woolworth's. She had squeezed oranges for fresh juice for their breakfast. When he left the house, he promised to take her shopping on Saturday.

The chief was in his office when Junior settled at his desk. The door was closed and he was talking to a man Junior didn't recognize. From the body language, it didn't look like a friendly exchange. Junior kept his head down, looking up phone numbers and noting them in his notebook. The last thing he wanted was for the chief's anger to spill over onto him.

There wasn't a listing for Archie Camden in the phone book. Directory Assistance informed him that the number was unpublished. The City Directory didn't have the information he needed to locate his residence either. Considering that he had only moved out of his aunt's house in the late spring, Archie's new address wouldn't show up until the next edition of both publications.

Buck Sissons would know the address. According to Hugo, he and his men had gone there during their search for Archie. But, Junior didn't want to tip his hand. If no one had gone through the house yet, he wanted to be the first on the scene. He knew that was unlikely, but still.

He didn't think Haywood Prescott would be in his office at this early hour so he decided to try Tyler Redman. The lawyer didn't seem the kind of guy who kept bankers' hours. Surely, he would be able to tell Junior what he needed to know.

Redman's secretary informed Junior that her boss had already gone over to the courthouse to file some documents with the court and to go before the Judge of Probate at nine o'clock on behalf of another client.

Junior decided it was a good idea to be out of the office for the morning. The chief's visitor had left with a scowl on his face, closing the door with enough force to rattle the glass panel. The chief didn't appear to be any happier.

Redman was chewing on an unlit cigar when Junior found him in the halls of the courthouse. A battered briefcase sat at his feet and he was frowning over a sheaf of papers in his hand. He looked up when Junior spoke his name.

"Detective Knight. What brings you to the courthouse this early on a Friday morning?"

The detective bit made Junior stand a little taller. "Looking for you, Mr. Redman."

"About Ruth, is it?"

"Actually, I'm trying to find out where her grandson, Archie, lives."

"Think you'll find out where he high-tailed it to, I suppose."

"Something like that."

"He bought a place over in the Oakleigh District. A rundown old house on Washington Square. Augusta Street, I believe. Don't know the house number."

"Who would have a key?"

"I do. Ruth wanted me to have some work done on it to keep it dry and secure until Archie came home."

"When did she ask you to do these things?"

"A week or so after Archie left town."

"It sounds as if she was expecting him to come home."

"Of course she was."

"Some folks think she had other plans."

"Knowing Ruth, I don't think she would actually go through with a scheme that would jeopardize Archie's future."

"He could have a future somewhere else considering all the money she had to give him a cushy life."

"There's no way he'll see a penny of Ruth's money if he deserted. I've already had two visits from the authorities. Her estate is locked down tighter than a drum."

"Who, exactly?"

"A Major Gregson. He wanted a copy of her will and the addresses for all the beneficiaries. The Federal Prosecutor also paid me a visit."

"So, everything's in limbo."

"Until we find Archie." Redman glanced at his watch. "I'm due in court."

"I'd like to have a look at his house, if you don't mind."

Redman tucked his chin and looked over his glasses at Junior. He seemed to be debating with himself. Finally, he said, "I don't see any reason not to give you the key. You'll end up with it sooner or later. No need to waste time with the courts. Go by the office and tell Brenda to give it to you."

"Thanks."

"I'd appreciate a heads-up if you find him."

"I can't promise that."

"I'm not going to interfere. I just want to be prepared. A military tribunal is a different animal. I've lined up a lawyer in Birmingham who has experience dealing with this kind of situation."

"I'll keep that in mind."

Redman nodded and opened the heavy door leading into the court room.

As Junior turned to leave, he saw the man who had been closeted with the chief earlier. He was headed up the stairs to the second floor of the courthouse.

❦

THE CAMDEN HOUSE was colder than outside when Hugo unlocked the door. He realized no one had been in Ruth's home since the temperature drop Sunday night. In the service nook between the dining room and kitchen he found the thermostat and turned on the heat.

The house reeked of fish and Hugo swore under his breath. He had forgotten about the canned salmon left out for Beauregard. He emptied it into a garbage can out by the detached garage behind the house and washed the bowl.

He started at the secretaire under the stairwell. Before he had only given it a cursory look. Now he read every piece of paper, pulled the drawers from their slots and checked for anything that might be taped to the bottom of them. He even pulled it from the wall and checked the back.

Satisfied that there was nothing to be found, he moved on to the room Ruth used as storage. He made quick work of the armoires. Two of them contained Ruth's clothing. The third held items Hugo thought must have belonged to her husband. A large travel trunk held table linens, lengths of silk, embroidery work, and some lace.

He had just replaced the top tray of the trunk when he heard the front door open and close. He stepped out into the hallway to see Sharon unwinding a scarf from around her neck. A breath of cool fall air arrived with her. She looked stunning with her hair slightly mussed and her cheeks pink from the cold. When she raised her eyes and looked at him, the sensuality of her movements, the toss of her hair back from her face, the slight parting of her lips, was like a feather light caress along the length of his body.

"Hello."

The soft alto of her voice returned to him like a memory of past lives, past loves.

"Hi."

She came down the hallway toward him. At the entrance to the storage room she stopped and studied his face. "Ouch."

Hugo grinned. "Walked into a door."

"I'd steer clear of that door. It looks like it has a pretty good right hook."

"I plan to take care of it."

"Ah. A man of action."

"Not really but you can't let little things slip by without notice. If you do, you'll end up with a problem."

"Under other circumstances I'd say that was good advice."

"Under any circumstances it's good advice."

"Good to know."

"Thanks for coming."

"I saw you at the cemetery yesterday."

"I thought I was being discreet."

"The military uniform next to you put paid to that."

"One does tend to notice things like that, I suppose."

Sharon looked into the room. "I see you started without me." She sniffed the air. "What's that smell?"

"Canned salmon. Viola left it out for Beauregard on Sunday. We were trying to lure him out of hiding. I put it in the garbage when I got here this morning."

"You found him, right? He's with Viola?"

"No. He hasn't been seen since Viola left last Friday."

Sharon closed her eyes and shook her head. She opened them with a sigh. "Poor old Beau. He's been out in the cold all this time. I wonder if any of the neighbors saw him? Maybe someone took him in." Her expression was hopeful.

"Maybe."

"Aunt Ruth wanted Viola to have him. She's cared for him since he was a kitten and they were used to each other. I naturally thought she had taken him home. I feel so guilty. I should have thought to ask about him. I should have been out looking for him."

Hugo touched her lightly on the arm, directing her toward Ruth's bedroom. "We'll see if the neighbors have seen him when we're done here, if you like. Let's start in here and see if anything is missing among your aunt's personal things."

Sharon stood at the threshold and let her gaze travel around the bedroom. She went straight to the chest beside the reading chair and lifted one of the photographs. It was of a young girl with a little boy with white-blond hair sitting on her lap. Hugo realized it was a photo of Sharon holding Archie.

She held it to her chest, her back to Hugo. Her voice was tight when she spoke. "I'm taking this with me."

Hugo shrugged. "It's nothing to me."

Sharon slipped the picture into the deep pocket of her barn jacket. She stood perfectly still for a moment then moved on to the dressing table. She sat on the stool and let her hand linger over the hairbrush. Hugo watched her reflection in the mirror.

Finally, she began opening the drawers, moving items about. She took the jewelry box out and set it on the table. She shook her head. "I can't say if anything is missing. These are the pieces she wore regularly. Her good jewelry is in the safety deposit box at the bank."

"I understand she left some of it to you."

Sharon looked up sharply and held his gaze through his reflection in the mirror. "Where did you hear that?"

"Did she?"

"Yes. In fact, she left all of it to me except her diamond and sapphire engagement ring. Archie gets that for his future bride."

"Did she have a lot of good pieces?"

Sharon swiveled on the stool, rested her hands on her lap, and looked up at Hugo. "Yes. Not only did she have jewelry that belonged to past members of the family, Uncle Edward was quite generous."

"What does someone do with all those expensive baubles?"

"There was a time when people dressed. Especially for formal occasions. They traveled a lot for the business. Uncle Edward and Aunt Ruth. New York, Washington, Boston, entertaining and being entertained. She was Queen of Mardi Gras in her day. Did you know that?"

"No. I'm afraid I don't keep up with the society page."

Sharon continued to hold his gaze. Her brow lifted slightly and she turned back to examining the contents of the rest of the dressing table. When she closed the last drawer, she stood but she didn't move. After a few seconds she shook her head and faced Hugo.

"What else should we look at?"

"Did she have a special place she kept important documents? Where they would be safe from prying eyes?"

"Did you check the secretaire?"

"Yes. Not exactly a hidey-hole for things of value."

"What about Uncle Edward's study?"

Hugo nodded.

Sharon gave the question some thought. "I know where she kept the key to the silver drawer. Maybe, if it was something she didn't want to leave lying around, she put it there."

In the service pantry she took down a sugar bowl of a deep blue, blurry pattern. Inside was an ornate, old-fashioned key with a tassel attached. The key turned smoothly in the lock of the top middle drawer of the breakfront china cabinet.

"When you unlock the top drawer, it also unlocks the two below it." Sharon stood back to give Hugo room to open it.

A gray silver cloth covered the contents. Hugo folded it back to reveal rows of polished place settings in silver. "How many knives and forks does one person need?"

"Twenty-four."

"You're kidding."

"I told you. Aunt Ruth and Uncle Edward entertained quite a lot in their younger years."

"How do you fit twenty-four people around a table?"

"Mostly at lawn parties. She could seat twelve here in the dining room. And another six or eight in the card room."

Hugo closed the top drawer and moved on to the one beneath it. Inside were an assortment of large forks, ladles, cake knives, and things he had no idea how they were used. In the bottom drawer a long silver tray was stacked with very small, shallow silver plates that featured a decorative scroll around the edges. "What are these?"

"Butter pats."

He looked at Sharon, his brows raised in question.

"Individual plates for butter for the use of each dinner guest."

"This stuff must be worth a fortune."

"I couldn't say. But they are lovely."

Hugo started to close the drawer when he noticed that the tray supporting all the lovely butter pats wasn't sitting exactly level. He lifted the tray and there in the bottom of the drawer he found a stash of large envelopes.

"Bingo."

They emptied the contents of the bottom of the drawer onto the table and replaced the silver.

Hugo debated whether or not to include Sharon in the inspection of what they had uncovered and decided she might be able to give him some insight into the contents of the envelopes.

Haywood Mills, Inc. was imprinted as the return address of the top envelope and when he peeked inside Hugo knew he had found the missing documents Bebe had brought to her aunt to sign.

There were a couple of envelopes that had Tyler Redman's name and office address in the upper left corner. The other two envelopes carried no designation of origin.

Hugo decided to save the documents from Haywood Mills until after he determined what was in the remaining envelopes. One from Redman's office contained a copy of her most recent will. Since he already knew the high points of it, Hugo chose to set it aside for further scrutiny later. The other one from her lawyer had to do with a note she held from Haywood Prescott. It was in the amount of one hundred thousand dollars.

He passed this over to Sharon. "Did you know about this?"

Sharon quickly read over the document. She frowned. "No." She scanned down to the bottom and the date. "It's from 1953."

"Why would Haywood borrow money from Ruth?"

"I rather wonder why Ruth would lend him money."

Hugo read through the document again. "Maybe back then he was in financial straits."

"I doubt it. He went to work at the mill after the war. By the time she loaned him this money he should have been making a substantial salary. Skip and Bebe would have been in grammar school." She frowned. "I can't think of any reason he would need to borrow this kind of money."

"It's dated early December. Maybe something to do with the holidays? Did he buy a new home or some other big out-lay along that line?"

"No. They've always lived in Ashland Place. The house was a wedding gift from Voncille's parents."

"I wonder if it's been repaid."

"Knowing Haywood, if he had settled the debt, he would have demanded the original note. Especially considering their combative relationship since Uncle Edward died and Haywood took over the business."

"Any particular reason they were at odds?"

"She didn't approve of some of his business decisions."

"And why are you on the outs with Haywood?"

"Who says I'm on the outs?"

"I heard it somewhere."

"There are many reasons. His current desire to get into business in Asia is one of the more current ones. Haywood has been rather ruthless in some other venues the company is involved with. He's become quite the robber baron."

"Is he breaking the law?"

"Let's just say I don't like his ethics in certain enterprises."

"Are you involved in the management of the business?"

"No. But they have to provide me with all the annual reports. Any major changes require my vote so I receive a copy of all proposals."

"Can't they simply have a majority vote without you?"

"The by-laws require a written and signed response of record from each shareholder. So even if I'm out-voted, I have to be kept informed of all significant actions."

"I see. Do you understand all the ins and outs of the businesses?"

Sharon leveled him with a look he couldn't quite read.

"I majored in international finance. So, yes, I understand."

"No offense intended."

"None taken."

"So, with such a background I'd think you'd be helpful to the company."

"That was what my father hoped for. I find I don't like the squabbling."

"That's why you live in Point Clear?"

"Partly. But I lived there even before I inherited the bay house and an interest in the company. My late husband's family and business are in Baldwin County."

Hugo returned the promissory note to the envelope. He opened one of the unmarked envelopes. Inside he found three photographs. They were all old, probably taken around the turn of the century.

"Who are these people?" He passed them to Sharon.

She studied each one. "I have no idea. None of them look familiar to me." She looked on the backs of each. "This one has the names listed but I don't recognize any of them."

Hugo remembered the blank spaces in Ruth's scrap books. He turned over the photo of a groups of four people. Only three names were noted on the back, those of the three women in the picture. He wondered who the man might be. "Do you think these were originally in her albums?"

Sharon shrugged. "I wouldn't know. She kept all her keepsakes in the attic. I know she would sometimes look through them. She even. . ." She picked up one of the photographs and looked at it more closely. "When we went to France she brought some pictures to show around to see if anyone recognized the people in them. I think these might be those same photos."

"When was this?"

"The summer the Korean War heated up. I went over in mid-May. Aunt Ruth joined me toward the end of June. She saw this new conflict as another costly disruption in families and lives. It motivated her to find what remnants she could of our French relatives." Sharon lined the three photographs up on the table in front of her. "Archibald joined the UN Forces while she was there. She didn't even get to say good-bye."

Hugo opened the last envelope and emptied the contents onto the table. It contained a scrap of paper that appeared to be torn from the bottom of a letter. It was written in French. He passed it over to Sharon. "Can you read this?"

"Roughly, it translates, *It's as if we're dead to her. She doesn't. . .* and that's it." Sharon turned the piece of paper over but there was nothing on the back. "I don't know what it means. It appears to be old, though."

"Does the handwriting look familiar?"

"Why would it?"

"You said you corresponded with one of your relatives after your return from France."

Sharon reached into her left coat pocket and pulled out a stack of about a half dozen letters tied up with string. "I've brought them for you. And I can tell you this is not François' writing."

"Who could it be?"

"I don't know. Aunt Ruth had a wide circle of acquaintances from around the world. When she was a child her family would return to Paris for a month each summer. They stopped doing that when she was about seven or eight, I think." She picked up the piece of paper again. "This is very old. It's possible it could be from that time. It might have been written to Grandmother Tia."

"This was Ruth's mother?"

"Yes. That's the French connection for the family. My grandfather was in Paris on a business trip when he met her."

The other item from the envelope was a piece of blue ribbon, the cut ends slightly frayed.

Hugo returned both items to the envelope and sat staring at the china cabinet. What was so important about a scrap of a letter written decades ago and a piece of blue ribbon that Ruth Camden felt the need to secure them under lock and key?

Probably nothing, he decided. They most likely evoked a memory from Ruth's childhood.

Twenty-One

Sharon hadn't discovered anything missing as they made their way through the house. Hugo left her going door to door to ask the neighbors about Beauregard. He took the envelopes they had discovered to the station.

The chief was standing at Hugo's desk reading the notes taped to the wall when he arrived. Goode made no comment about the photograph of Ruth Camden. Instead he eyed Hugo's face.

"What the hell happened to you?"

"Stumbled in the dark when I got home last night."

Hugo could see the chief trying to decide whether or not to accept this scenario.

"Drunk?"

"Porch light burned out." He rounded his desk and sat down.

"That should be an easy fix."

"It will be."

The chief returned his attention to Hugo's notes on the case. "I hope you've got more to go on than this."

"It's beginning to come together. I'm still waiting for word on the poison. If we knew what it was, that would help us discover who had access."

"Uh huh." Chief Goode put his hands in his pocket and rocked back on his heels. "No motive yet?"

Hugo knew he had to give the chief something. It was within his power to decide there wasn't enough evidence to make a case and that he and Junior were needed elsewhere. He also knew that if he gave him too much the case could be snatched from them and given to more senior detectives. He decided to throw Tyrone Pritchett to the wolves.

"The safe was open and emptied. The inside clean as a whistle. She kept something of value in there. Tyrone Pritchett sometimes picked up his aunt when she got off work. She's Mrs. Camden's maid. And he recently paid cash for a tricked-out Barracuda. He got in trouble in Chicago and now he's back in Mobile. Known as a go-to for guns."

"I know who he is."

"Better to see where it leads, don't you think?"

The chief grunted.

"And she changed her will recently."

Goode considered this a minute. "Tread lightly." He turned on his heel and went into his office.

Hugo checked his messages. There was nothing pressing so he opened the envelope containing the papers from Haywood Mills. It was several pages long and full of legalese. The best he could make out, this was to be a shipping partnership with a Japanese company named Tankaa. Whether it was a good deal or not was outside Hugo's expertise. He wondered if Sharon had received a copy of this proposal. He was sure she could explain it to him.

He sat at his desk and leaned back in his chair, his hands clasped behind his head, staring across the room and out the windows. Nothing was adding up. Ruth had been ready to ship Archie somewhere out of reach of the Army. Neither Bebe nor Sharon felt Archie was the kind of man to shirk his duty. Haywood had done nothing to help prevent his conscription. With Ruth dead, no one knew where Archie was.

The phone on his desk rang. It was Junior. He was at Archie Camden's house. Hugo jotted down the address and hung up. Now maybe they would make some headway into Archie's vanishing act. He stopped in the midst of adjusting his tie. Vanished. That was the word Aimeé Marlowe had used. It was as if Archie had vanished into thin air somewhere between Mobile, Alabama and Atlanta, Georgia.

He went downstairs and approached the duty sergeant. "Hey, could I have a look at the duty roster?"

The sergeant hesitated, his eyes narrowed as he studied Hugo's black eye. "What do you need the roster for?"

"I forgot the name of one of the officers doing a door-to-door on a case I'm working. I'd like to goose both of them about their reports."

"What officers?"

"Dewey Nelson, for one. Thought if I saw the name of the other one on the roster it would jar my memory."

The sergeant leaned back in his chair. Finally, he took a clipboard from the corner of his desk and slid it under the security screen.

Hugo scanned down the pages until he found what he was looking for. "Thanks." He returned the clipboard to the sergeant. "I owe you one.

***

JUNIOR STOOD IN the foyer. Archie's house smelled musty so he turned back to the front door and left it standing open. The humid climate of Mobile could wreak havoc on an empty structure. Mold crept into every crevice and corner here in the sub-tropics. He felt the damp chill and decided that if no one had disconnected the phone, the house probably still had gas and electricity. He flipped the light switch and discovered he was right. He went in search of the furnace control. It was in a hallway that ran down the middle of the house.

The structure was a rambling Victorian house. In a room that had been adapted for use as a study or office, a big bay window overlooked Washington Square. Junior did a walk through to get the lay of everything. Upstairs was mainly empty. All of Archie's energy had been concentrated on the ground floor.

None of the furnishing were new. They weren't exactly cast offs but rather had a comfortable, lived-in look. Probably expensive, Junior thought. That's the way rich people lived. Where Grammy would give her eye teeth for a new, brightly covered sofa, the likes of Archie Camden were content to cocoon themselves in the burnished, well-worn familiarity of quality pieces. Grammy would not have had the faded rug beneath his feet. Certain areas on the periphery revealed that it had at one time been a more vibrant red with blues and gold. Now it was faded almost pink.

The desk was positioned in the center of the study and gave a view of the square. A nice place to work, Junior thought. He sat in the high-backed leather office chair and began going through the contents of Archie's desk.

An uncapped pen rested on a calendar that served as a blotter in the center of the desk as if the user had just stepped away for a minute. The top sheet marked the days of September. The last notation said *Dinner. The Club*. The date was the twelfth. The thirteenth was circled in red.

Junior found an address book in the left top drawer. He took his time reading all the entries. It was pretty much what you would expect. A few contacts for workmen; plumber, electrician, a painter. There were also numbers for various departments for the city for permitting and licensing. The rest appeared to be family, friends, and school contacts. Some of the names were familiar. Most weren't.

He found the usual things you would have in a desk. In the top right hand drawer he discovered a brass compass. It fit nicely in the palm of his hand, comfortably weighted. The back held an inscription. *"May you always find the way home. M.J."* Junior flipped through the address book trying to identify a name that would match the initials. There wasn't one. The compass wasn't new. You could tell it had been much handled over the years. He wondered if the inscription had been meant for Archie or for someone in the past.

Bookcases had been built into this room. This was Archie's handiwork, Junior decided. They looked too new in a setting where everything was time worn. They were a work of art, the medium stain bringing out the veining of the wood. The shelves were only partially filled. He browsed the titles. A lot of books on architecture, history, photography, travel. Not much fiction.

On one of the bookshelves three framed photographs held pride of place. The first was of Archie and his grandmother at a graduation ceremony. Both of them smiled with pride for the photographer. The next was an old photograph of a bride and groom. Probably his parents, Junior thought. Lastly was a recent photograph of Archie, Bebe, and, due to the striking resemblance, probably Sharon Shipley. Behind them the sun glinted off the water of the bay. They were lounging in a trio of Adirondack chairs grouped together. Something about the picture arrested Junior's attention. The photographer had captured an ephemeral moment in time. A moment of contentment, promise, and anticipation. They could have been brother and sisters, Junior thought.

A finely carved wooden cabinet stood between two of the floor-to-ceiling bookcases. An old oil painting of a stucco villa descending into ruin mounted above the cabinet made Junior think of Italy.

When Junior pulled on the handle, he discovered that the top third of the front panel of the cabinet rolled up and back. It concealed files placed in vertical slots. A handsome way to camouflage the mundane functions of an office, he thought. There were three such rows, one above the other, each with its own roll-down covering like a roll-top desk.

Only the top tier held any files. Most of them contained information concerning the restoration of the house. There were a few that had to do with Archie's education. A diploma for an undergraduate degree from the University of Alabama. A master's degree in architecture from Harvard. In one of the files Junior found a copy of Archie's birth certificate, a passport, a sheet of paper with his driver's license information, and, lastly, the deed for the house.

Junior flipped through the pages of the passport. It appeared their missing man liked to travel. There were stamps from England, France, Spain, and Italy in the early pages. The most recent stamp was to Israel. That had been over a year ago.

Yet another file held bank statements. Junior whistled softly at the balance.

The room gave him a strange feeling. Apart from the musty smell, it felt as if the owner might walk through the door at any moment. When Hugo stepped into the room on the heels of that thought, Junior felt a prickle at the nape of his neck.

"Jesus." He did a double take. "What happened to you?"

"Took a tumble in the dark."

Junior studied Hugo's face and knew from his expression to leave it. "What do you think of this place? It would make a great setting for a Halloween spook house."

"Looks like he started in this room."

"He didn't make much progress. The bathroom's clean and usable but everything in it is ancient. He's repaired the plaster in there and the bedroom." Junior looked overhead at the trayed ceiling with intricate plaster work around the base of the chandelier. "By the time he comes home he'll have to do it all over again because of the damp."

"I don't think he's coming home."

"You think he's done a runner?"

Hugo studied the calendar on Archie's desk. "Something happened to him. No one disappears that completely." He picked up the pen on the desk and rolled it between his fingers and thumb. "No one vanishes into thin air."

"I don't know. The Haywoods and Prescotts have the kind of money and connections that can make an elephant disappear from under your nose."

"I think that was the original plan. Ruth cooked it up and planned it out. But she didn't count on Archie putting a kink in her scheme."

"Viola said he didn't want to go to Vietnam."

"No one wants to go. That doesn't mean they won't."

"You think he refused to run?"

"Yes."

"Why?"

"It's too out of character. Both Sharon and Bebe feel he's too ethical to ditch his responsibility. He comes from a long line of men who fought. Some of whom died, including his father. And Ruth wasn't worried about her check. She was desperate to hear from Archie. To learn that he had arrived safely in North Carolina to begin basic. But the letters and phone calls never came."

"Well, why didn't she tell the mailman what she was expecting? Why say it was about her check?"

"Because after the military police showed up on her doorstep, she was afraid Archie had changed his mind at the last minute and followed through with her plan. If that was the case, she couldn't afford to draw attention to any mail she received from him. It would have had to be mailed along the way or at his final destination. Too easy to track him down with that kind of evidence."

"Then why make a big deal about the mail to begin with? The less attention she called to it, the better off everyone would be."

"Because of Viola. And possibly Aimeé Marlowe. She couldn't afford to let the mail be seen by either of them. Viola especially. She would know immediately that it was from Archie. He lived with Ruth most of his life. Viola would recognize his handwriting at the very least."

"Do you think Viola would tell? And isn't Mrs. Marlowe one of the family?"

"Redman as much as told us. He said Ruth was private with her business. She didn't discuss personal things with anyone. Besides, she wouldn't want to put Viola in a position to have to lie to the authorities."

"I think you're beginning to like Ruth Camden."

"I think I am, too."

"I still don't understand your logic. Ruth wanted Archie out of the hands of the Army. She made that happen. Obviously, at the end of the day, he went along with it."

"She wouldn't leave the house. Aimeé Marlowe tried to get her to go out but she wouldn't. Bebe took her to lunch and she was preoccupied the whole time." Hugo had been checking out the contents of the office as he spoke. He picked up the photograph of Archie with Bebe and Sharon and scrutinized it. "Something went wrong. Her sudden interest in having her check placed in her hand only began after Archie left for training." He slipped the framed photograph into his coat pocket.

"So what do we do next?"

"Let's finish up here. Tomorrow we're going to Atlanta."

"Atlanta! The chief isn't going to go for that."

"We'll go in my car. And tomorrow's Saturday. Finch and Hardman are on the rota."

"What do you think we'll find in Atlanta?'

"It's the last place Archie was seen. The bus driver told Sissons he didn't get off before the change in Atlanta. It's the only hope we have of picking up his trail."

"It's nearly two months old."

"There's that."

"Okay. I'll have Mrytle Crum take Grammy to Mass." The prospect of a real pursuit gave Junior a little thrill. He tried to keep the excitement out of his voice. "What time you want to leave?"

"Early. Six o'clock. It's six hours to Atlanta. We can make it in five, if we're lucky. That will put us there before lunch."

"It's a Saturday. Wouldn't it be better to wait until Monday? You're not going to find anyone to give you any answers on the week-end."

"We have to be back on the job Monday. The bus terminal doesn't shut down for the week-end. Besides, I feel lucky. Don't you feel lucky?"

Junior grinned. "As a matter of fact, I do." Lucky, and ready for a road trip in Hugo's new car.

Twenty-Two

Hugo left Junior to finish up the search of Archie's house. He didn't hold out any hope that they would find anything there. He felt certain Buck had executed a search of the premises. If anything had been discovered, he wasn't sharing. No, to Hugo's thinking, all the planning had been on Ruth's part. Whatever she worked out to slip Archie out of the country would be somewhere in her house or it wouldn't exist at all.

He wanted to hear what Haywood had to say about the promissory note. It didn't fit anywhere in Hugo's knowledge of the family finances. He felt sure Haywood could write a check for that amount and not even blink an eye. So what did he do with the hundred thousand dollars?

Twiggy informed Hugo that Mr. Prescott was out to lunch with clients and that he didn't plan to return to the office until Tuesday. When he pressed her, she told him her boss had a hunting trip planned with those same clients and would be entertaining them at the camp over the week-end.

Hugo stood on the sidewalk outside the Waterman Building mulling over his options. He debated paying Buck Sissions a visit. He didn't think the Lieutenant would be any more forthcoming on the Army's progress on their search for Archie. The names of the bus drivers had been a throw away. Buck hadn't thought there was anything else to be learned there so he had given Hugo a bone.

Fair enough. He would gnaw on it and see if he couldn't find something in the marrow the MPs had missed.

Hugo walked over to Dearborn Street to the pay phone at the YMCA. He thumbed through the phone book and found Mo Hitchins' number and address. With a slap of the pages, he closed the book and headed for his car.

No one answered his knock. The driveway was empty. Hugo stood on the front porch and surveyed the surrounding neighborhood. It was a quiet street in Midtown. Very few houses had a vehicle parked out front. Where would Mo be?

Drinking, Hugo decided. Somewhere down on Dauphin Island Parkway. He looked at his watch. It was already three o'clock. Mo would have to wait. He had one more stop to make.

Two cars were parked in front of the Seven-Eleven. Hugo sat in his car and waited until the drivers came out of the convenience store and left.

Lorraine looked up from the magazine she was reading at the sound of the bell over the door.

"Oh, Hugo." She came from behind the counter. "I'm so sorry."

"Are you okay?"

"Yes." She gingerly touched the puffiness around his eye. "I'm fine."

"You would tell me if you weren't, wouldn't you?"

"Yes. Honestly, Hugo, I'm fine."

"Does this happen often?"

Lorraine hugged her waist and looked up at Hugo with pleading in her eyes. "It's all my fault."

"He's a bully, Lorraine. Always has been."

She shook her head. "You don't understand. It really is my fault. I told him."

"Told him what?"

She looked down at the floor. "That I was at your house the other night."

"Christ, Lorraine. What were you thinking?"

"I'm so, so sorry." She reached for the lapels of his coat.

The sultry Lauren Bacall voice, the soulful eyes peering up through heavy dark lashes, and the slightly parted lips didn't cut it this time. He stepped back from her.

"I can't help myself. I don't know why I provoke him." She ran her hands through her hair, glanced at him then away. "Even as I'm saying things that I know will send him into a rage, I know I should stop but I can't."

Hugo studied her. He couldn't tell if she was truly repentant or not. Or if she was telling the truth. "Well, you got his attention. Now you have mine. Where does he hang out and drink?"

"Hugo." Her voice held a note of pleading. "Let it go."

He turned toward the door. "Somewhere down on the DIP, right?"

"Please, Hugo."

"Sorry, Lorraine. I can't."

A couple of grammar school children entered the store under Hugo's arm as he held the door open. They headed straight for the Icee machine.

Hugo gave Lorraine one last look and left the Seven-Eleven.

What was Lorraine playing at, Hugo wondered as he drove back to the station. She had always bounced from one extreme to the next. The bold red lipstick, cutting classes, making out in the Church Street Cemetery.

He remembered those nights. She would snitch vodka from her parent's house. He would sneak out of the dormitory at St. Thomas More. The intensity of those nights swept over him in a wave of heat even now. Christ, had they only been fourteen?

But the next day she would linger in the hallways of St. Andrews, flirting with other boys, Mo Hitchins among them, giving Hugo the cold shoulder. It was as if she wanted to provoke him. The problem was that Hugo couldn't be provoked. As much as he liked Lorraine and as much as he lusted for her, it had always been Bebe. The fact that she was out of his league and out of his reach had never dampened his desire for her.

By the time he arrived at his destination, Hugo realized it didn't matter what kind of game Lorraine was playing, what kind of savage satisfaction she got out of baiting Mo. He couldn't let this slide.

At his desk he typed up his notes on the case. Something about the mundane task helped him clear his head. Just as he told the chief, things were coming together. But he still had no motive for Ruth's death.

JUNIOR SAT IN Archie Camden's big old leather chair and looked out across Washington Square. What would it be like to live in a place like this, he wondered, to have the money to fix it up just like you wanted? He thought of Evie. She'd like a house like this, he'd bet. No shared sleeping arrangements. A bathroom all to herself. Yeah, she'd like it.

He sighed and stood. When pigs fly, he thought. His salary allowed him to live comfortably with his grandmother. It would be a different story if he had to afford an apartment of his own. He liked having the little extra money to take Grammy to the movies and out to eat. In fact, he decided, he'd take her to the Wagon Wheel over in Creighton tonight. He and Hugo were going off to Atlanta on an adventure and she deserved a little treat. Especially since the promised shopping trip to Woolworth's tomorrow wasn't going to happen. Besides, it was Friday night. He didn't have an appetite for the fish fry at St. Andrews. So, the Wagon Wheel it would be. Maybe they'd have oysters. November ended in an R. Someone said the oysters were especially good right now.

It was long past lunch time and his stomach growled. He turned off the furnace and locked up the house. From the trunk of the car he got his lunch and opened the brown paper bag. Pimento cheese sandwiches. He sat in the car and ate. When he finished the two sandwiches, he picked up the apple his grandmother had polished and put in with his lunch. He turned it over and over in his hand then put it in his pocket before he headed toward the station. It might be a good idea to check in with Evie and see if she had learned anything about the poison.

A stack of books of various sizes and ages sat on the work station with pieces of yellow legal paper stuck in dozens of places through most of them. She was feeding bits of carrot to her mice when Junior entered the lab. The sound of the door closing caused her to look up. She pushed her glasses up the bridge of her nose. "Hey, Junior."

"Whatcha got here?" He nodded toward the piles of books.

"Looking for our poison. I thought I might as well read up on botanicals that would give us the same symptoms as Ruth Camden."

"Any luck?"

"Too much luck. A lot of poisonings present the same symptoms."

Junior tapped on the cage. "Who have we here?"

"Meet Horatio, Socrates, and Ophelia."

Junior picked up one of the small bits of carrot and held it between the bars of the cage. Ophelia snagged it before the other two could react and turned it rapidly in her paws as she ate. "Feisty little thing, isn't she?"

"When you're the runt you have to be quick or you don't eat."

It wounded Junior to know this sentiment came from experience. If it had been possible, he would have shielded her from life in the orphanage. He had been lucky to have his grandmother. Otherwise, he had no doubt he would have been in the same boat. Only, he would have been stranded in California and never have known Evie. Or Hugo.

"You still living at the YWCA?"

"Yeah. It suits me. I'm used to small, shared spaces."

So much for a big Victorian mansion overlooking Washington Square, Junior thought. Just as well. He'd never be able to afford it. He smiled at the thought.

"What?" Evie popped one of the carrot bits into her mouth and chewed.

"Just thinking of Archie Camden's house. It's big enough for a dozen people to live and not bump elbows."

"The grandson, right?"

Junior nodded. "Searched it earlier today."

"Find anything?"

"Not really. It's like he walked out his front door on September thirteenth and disappeared into a vacuum." He sighed. "Any news on your front?"

"No. I called the lab at Auburn and tried to steer them toward a biologic. They have their own way of doing things so I guess I just have to be patient. How's the case shaping up? Any motive?"

"Lots of motive. The problem is picking one."

"How's that?"

"There's a squabble over control of Haywood Mills. The voting shares are set up in a convoluted fashion so that almost everyone has to agree on everything. There's an empty safe that they all swear never contained anything. And Mrs. Camden changed her will a few weeks ago."

"Huh."

"The fact she was poisoned makes it hard to pinpoint the killer's window of operation more accurately. You have to figure the poison was already in the tea leaves when she made her last cup of tea. It could have been placed there anytime, even though that would be tricky. The killer would run the risk of poisoning the wrong person."

Evie sat staring at one of her mice running on a wheel. She looked up at Junior. "What did the old will say?"

Junior blinked and a slow smiled lifted the corners of his mouth. "Evie. You're a genius." He caught her by the upper arms and gave her a gentle shake. "We never looked at the old will." He reached in his pocket and brought out the apple. "For you." Then he turned and hurried from the lab.

He quickly covered the three blocks to the Van Antwerp Building and Tyler Redman's office. To his dismay, the office was locked up tight. The gold lettering on the glass pane of the door gave the office hours for Fridays as eight o'clock in the morning until two in the afternoon. Who took off work at two in the afternoon?

This meant it would be Monday before he could get his hands on Ruth's original will.

Twenty-Three

Hugo searched through the Camden file and found the name of the driver for Greyhound's southern leg of the bus route. Charlie Neuman lived in Ocean Springs, Mississippi. He drove to downtown Mobile and started his route from there. He made the round trip to Atlanta and back on a rotating basis with another Greyhound driver seven days a week.

The clock above the file cabinets of the squad's bullpen read five twenty-five. Hugo dialed the phone number and Charlie answered on the second ring.

Hugo identified himself.

"I told that other fella all I know. This Camden guy got on with the rest of the passengers. He sat on the left about six or seven rows back."

"How many stops did you make along the way?"

"The usual. Evergreen, Montgomery, Opelika and LaGrange. Final stop, Atlanta. Picked up a few passengers in Montgomery. Three or four. You'd have to check with the agent at the terminal if you need an exact count. And a woman got on in LaGrange."

"Did Mr. Camden get off the bus at any of those stops?"

"Montgomery. Everybody got off. The bus was gassed up. That's our longest stop."

"How long?"

"Twenty-five minutes, give or take. Depends on when we roll in. Can't leave before the scheduled departure time."

"What did Mr. Camden do during that break?"

"Beats me. I pulled the bus to the pumps and then went to the bathroom. Usually drink a Co-Cola and eat a sandwich my wife packs for me."

"What about the passengers in general?"

"Same things for most folks. Three hours of riding and you're ready to stretch your legs. Relieve yourself. A few grab something quick and easy at the café. It's a little early for lunch but most passengers have been up a long time by then."

"What time do you depart from Mobile?

"Seven-thirty. On the dot."

"Anything unusual happen along the way?"

"No. Just an average run. A little traffic hold up around Opelika. An accident."

Hugo tried to think of anything that might result in information he didn't already know. "How did he seem to you?"

"What do you mean?"

"Did he appear to be upset? Was he in a good mood?"

"How do I know? He was one passenger on a bus load of people. If you want to know what kind of mood he was in, you might try to track down the girl who had the seat next to him."

Hugo sat forward in his chair, his pen poised over his notebook. "What girl?"

"She got on in Montgomery. We were pretty full so this Camden fella let her have the window seat beside him."

"Did they appear to know each other?"

"I couldn't say. I was busy driving the bus. I only glance in the rear-view mirror once in a while to be sure everything's okay."

"What did she look like? Do you remember?"

"How could I forget? A doll like her? Blonde hair, long legs. Smart dresser."

Hugo make rapid notes then leaned back in his chair. "Would you know her if you saw her again?"

"I think so."

"Thanks, Mr. Neuman. If you think of anything else give me a call here at the station."

"Sure thing."

Hugo hung up the phone and sat in thought for several minutes. He went to the file cabinet and pulled Tyrone Pritchett's record. There was an old mug shot. It would have to do. He stuck it in the Camden file which he took with him as he left the station.

⁂

HUGO DROVE OUT Old Shell Road to Bluebird Hardware. He barely made it before they closed. He bought a light bulb and a step ladder. With the aid of his flashlight, he installed the new bulb on the front porch when he got home. He wasn't afraid of Mo Hitchens but he didn't relish a repeat ambush either. If 'Nam had taught him anything, it was that nowhere was safe. Everywhere was a rocket zone. It was a lesson he wouldn't forget again. *Do the time, stay alive, return home in one piece.*

He had forgotten to get milk. Again. So, for supper he opened a can of tuna fish and finished off the saltine crackers. There were still three beers in the refrigerator but he resisted the temptation and drank two of the Cokes Junior had brought over earlier in the week.

With the tuna can disposed of in the garbage can on the back porch, he opened Ruth's scrap books. This time he went through the most recent addition to her collection. He found a photo of Archie. It had been taken at the bay house. Hugo could see the cedar shake rooftop of the boat lift at the end of the pier in the background. To complete his photo spread, he found a recent photo of Sharon and one of Bebe. These were added to the Camden file. There wasn't a recent photo of Haywood.

Next, Hugo went through the armoire and pulled out a clean shirt and his suit. It was still in the plastic sheathing from the laundry.

He examined all three of his ties and finally decided on the blue pin stripe. He was ready for Atlanta.

He took the Camden file into the kitchen and spread the contents on the table. From his coat pocket he retrieved the photo of the three cousins and stood it in the center of the material. For a long time he studied it. Something about the images evoked a longing in him that he felt in the marrow of his bones. It wasn't the people in the image, but rather the sense of permanence, of belonging, of an impenetrable world that was both desired and yet unattainable that aroused this deep wanting.

Hugo stood and went to the back door. He opened it onto the cool night and stood on the small back porch breathing in the smell of the river with a faint overlay of decay. Above the low illumination of the lights of the state docks, the black of the night sky was studded with stars.

He returned to his chair and began to examine all the documents. He read his typed notes, and placed the photographs of all the players in a row. He had fed the chief the story about the safe. Now he couldn't get it out of his mind. It seemed unlikely to him that it had always been empty. Ruth hadn't kept her jewelry in it. The new will had been in the silver chest. Ditto the promissory note from Haywood. What else did you keep in a safe? Money. It was a fairly large safe. *Lots of money.*

✺

JUNIOR WAS READY to go when Hugo pulled up to his house. Mrs. K came out onto the porch wrapped up in a fuzzy housecoat, an anxious look on her face. She sent them with a thermos of coffee, a sack lunch, and admonished them to drive safely.

The morning was cold, the sky a bright blue, the sun slanting low in the east as the winter solstice approached. At Atmore they got on I-65 and Hugo let the big V-8 engine roar. They didn't slow down until they reached Evergreen.

They found the bus stop. It was at a mom and pop service station that served hot coffee and hot dogs rotated on a rotisserie. After they made use of the facilities and tanked up the car, Hugo bought them a hot cup of coffee. Neither the man nor his wife who ran the station recognized any of the people from Hugo's photo array.

The husband informed Hugo that the bus generally stopped anywhere from ten to fifteen minutes at the station. Sometimes the passengers got off, sometimes they didn't. It all depended on whether or not the driver was running ahead or behind schedule. The owners couldn't tell Hugo and Junior whether or not anyone got off the bus that particular morning.

On the road again, Hugo made as much time as he could since the interstate would end at Georgiana. They wouldn't pick it up again until they were east of Montgomery when they could connect with I-85. The traffic on Hwy 31 would make for slow going.

During the course of the drive, they attacked the case from every angle, looking for that *aha* moment that came from a tidbit that had meant nothing originally but might be key when considered in the light of new information. When nothing presented itself, Junior read Hugo the day's edition of the *Mobile Press Register.*

Hugo listened with half a mind as Junior shared the details of a City Council meeting set for Monday afternoon to consider complaints from the Mobile Historical Society about the devastation of whole neighborhoods of iconic shotgun houses. The Camelia Society of Mobile would host their annual competition in January. A deadline for entries was given. A Coke machine vendor had his photograph in the paper. His employer was threatening to have him arrested for stealing a gold coin found in one of the machines. In his defense the employee claimed he had replaced the coin with a quarter. No one would have been the wiser if his wife hadn't bragged about it. Junior thought he remembered the employee as a lower classman at St. Andrews.

By this time, Hugo had stopped listening. Finally, Junior finished the paper and put it aside with a sigh of boredom.

They listened to the radio, Junior fiddling with the knobs when they drove in and out of areas of reception. By the time they reached Montgomery, both men had run out of things to say.

They stopped at a service station on the edge of town and bought a city map. Junior navigated to the bus station on Court Street. Hugo thought there might be something that would mark the violence of the attack on the Freedom Riders in 1961. There wasn't. The building was small and modern with wrapped windows at the corners pretty much like the station in Mobile. You could see the Federal Courthouse rising behind it on the next street over.

They parked on the street in front of the station. It was a Saturday and this part of town revolved around the activities of the courts so there was very little traffic. A few passengers were in the waiting room. At the ticket counter Hugo showed his photos to the attendant. He shook his head. He didn't recognize any of the faces.

A porter in the baggage area remembered Archie because he had asked him for a light and had, as an afterthought, bought the book of matches from him for a quarter. He didn't recall seeing anyone with him. It had been a busy day for the bus line, as most Fridays were, and he couldn't say what Archie had done after their encounter.

They found an empty table in the restaurant. Junior lit a cigarette as the waitress stopped by. She was young. Probably not more than eighteen, if that. She had the whole Cleopatra eye thing going. The photographs were lying face up next to Hugo. They immediately caught her attention. Archie's picture was on top.

"Is he in trouble?" she asked.

"Why would you think that?" Hugo looked up from the menu.

"I know a cop when I see one."

Hugo smiled. "You nailed us. Have you seen him?"

She seemed reluctant to say.

"He's missing. His grandmother died. We're trying to find him."

"That's a shame. He was a nice man. Kinda sad. But then they all are, aren't they?"

"Who are they?"

"The boys on their way to basic."

"Did he tell you that?"

"He didn't have to. You can read it in their faces."

"You waited on him?"

"Yeah. He didn't eat much of his club sandwich."

"Was he alone?"

"Yeah."

"Did you notice what he did after he left the restaurant?"

She blushed. "He saw someone he knew. Out the window. He had only eaten part of his sandwich and he got up in a hurry and left money on the table. I watched him lope down the street toward the corner."

"Where did he go?"

"To a car parked down the block. I couldn't see anything but the back end. He leaned down and talked to someone through the window on the driver's side."

"And?"

She shrugged. "I don't know. I had other customers. I picked up the money for his meal and saw that he'd left a ten dollar bill."

"And that bothered you?"

"His meal was only two dollars and change."

"Nice tip." Junior said.

"I felt kinda bad about it, you know? He didn't get to finish his sandwich and hardly touched his Co-Cola. Just ran out after he saw that car pass, I guess. He was due some change."

"You didn't see what he did after that?" Hugo felt that they were finally on to something.

She shook her head. "When I realized how much money it was I went back to the window. The car was gone and so was he."

"What kind of car was it?"

"Black. Big."

"Did you recognize the make? What model it was?"

"Sorry. I was watching him, not the car." She smiled. "What can I say, he's good looking. And classy. We don't get a lot of that in here."

"Was it a foreign make? Or a sports car?"

She shrugged. "It was just a car. I wasn't really interested in what kind. I was just curious about someone who would walk away from their meal like that. If I had to guess, I'd say it was a sedan of some kind. They all look kinda alike."

It was a letdown. Would Archie know someone living in Montgomery? Possibly. The Haywood family money made them a powerhouse in the state. Everyone knew that politicians greased the wheels of commerce. And businessmen provided the lucre used to grease them. What was the likelihood that such a person would conveniently drive by the bus station when Archie was sitting facing the window eating lunch? Zero. Especially when you consider whoever it was stopped along the curb half a block away and waited for Archie to catch up to him. Or her.

⁂

THEY DECIDED AGAINST lunch at the bus station although Hugo left the waitress a fifty-cent tip. The V-8 was a gas guzzler and they'd have to fill up one more time before they got back home. They got paid on the first and fifteenth of the month. It was only the ninth and Hugo's wallet was nearly empty. No one would ever get rich on their salaries. The lunch Mrs. K had packed would suffice.

Even though it was Saturday, by the time they arrived in Atlanta the traffic was brisk. Hugo had planned for them to be there before lunch but traffic on the state highways messed up their timing.

They got lost looking for Cain Street and the bus terminal. After they passed the distinctive Coca-Cola plant sign the second time, Hugo found a service station and Junior got directions and a map.

The terminal was a departure from any bus station Hugo had seen. The image of the racing greyhound stood out against a baby blue background. The interior reminded him of some of the stations he had experienced on his journey home from California. This one had a large restaurant, a barber shop, and a beauty parlor.

Since they only had one set of photos, he and Junior couldn't split up. After forty-five minutes of questioning everyone they could find from ticket vendors to the shoe shine boys, they decided they had made a wasted trip. They were standing outside in the departure area watching people boarding a bus for Savannah. A porter was sitting on a concrete ledge a few feet away in the baggage area smoking a cigarette.

Junior walked over and asked him for a light. Then he showed him the photographs. After studying them for a minute, the guy nodded and pointed with the fingers holding his smoke. "I seen that one. He axe me what time the number nine left for Augusta."

Hugo overheard the comment and joined Junior and the porter.

"Was he alone?" Junior asked.

The porter nodded.

Junior fanned through the other photos. "You didn't see any of these women?"

He studied them, going back through a second time. Then he shook his head. "Naw. Might of been in the car, though."

Hugo felt his pulse jump. "A black sedan?"

"Naw." The porter gave Hugo the once over, his gaze lingering on his face and the deepening purple of his eye. "A gold car. Sporty. Loud."

"A Plymouth Barracuda?" Junior had his notebook out, jotting down the details.

"Could be."

"Who was driving it?"

"Don't know. All I seen was the passenger side. It pull up just over yonder out the way of the busses." He pointed to the exit of the parking bay. "Sat there idling. I notice it right off. Fine looking car." He nodded his head in remembered admiration.

"Anyone get out?" Hugo asked.

"Not that I seen."

"How do you know this man," Hugo tapped the photo of Archie, "had anything to do with the gold car?"

"'Cause he got in it." The porter dropped his cigarette butt to the pavement and stood to grind it out with his shoe. "I seen him come from behind number nine. He stopped and looked around then walked, quick like, and got in straight away. No messing about. The car took off as he was closing the doh."

Tyrone Pritchett. Hugo felt vindicated. His gut had told him that Tyrone was somehow involved.

"Did you tell anyone else about this man?"

"Who I'm gone tell?"

"No one came around asking about him?"

"They didn't axe me."

"What's your name?"

The porter hesitated. "Who you?"

Hugo took out his shield. "I'm a detective with the Mobile Police. This man is missing and we're trying to find him."

The porter considered this. Finally, he said, "Eubie Watts."

"Have you worked here long?"

"Gone on twenty years."

Hugo shook his hand. "Thanks, Mr. Watts. You've been a big help."

⚜

JUNIOR FELT THEY couldn't get back to Mobile fast enough. After Montgomery, Hugo had given him the keys and told him to drive the rest of the way. While Hugo slept in the passenger seat, Junior's mind raced with possibilities. They had decided it would be best to wait until morning to bring Tyrone in for questioning. It would be late when they got home and both of them were dog tired from the long day of driving. No one was privy to their discovery so Tyrone would keep. Better to be fresh, on their game, when they confronted him.

The unexpectedness of a Sunday morning visit would be to their advantage. Tyrone's last known address was in the file. They didn't know if he still lived there or not. Viola had told them he moved around a lot. But the Barracuda would lead them to him. It would be the give-away. They'd start with what they had and work from there. Junior was familiar with the bar-be-que joint and the riff-raff that could be found sitting on the stoop peddling weed, illegal cigarettes, and moonshine at any given hour of the day. Their man would show up there sooner or later. It was the center of his fiefdom.

Junior felt bolstered by their discovery. The Army, with all its manpower and might, had gone in search of Archie but they were the ones who had found him, or at least his trail. He and Hugo. He was about to burst to tell someone, to tell Evie. The thought dampened his excitement. *Let it go.*

As the Thunderbird hurtled through the dark night, the roadway illuminated only by a narrow tunnel of light piercing the lonely stretch of highway, Junior's thoughts drifted to the black sedan in Montgomery. It had to be explained somehow. And the woman on the bus. Was she simply a passenger who happened to take the seat next to Archie? Or was it too much of a coincidence that the driver had described Bebe Prescott to a tee? Hardly.

Twenty-Four

The nap on the last leg of the drive home left Hugo unable to sleep. Even though it was pushing midnight when they arrived, he did nothing but toss and turn. A sense of disappointment settled over him as the realization that Archie had, indeed, skipped town in the wake of his draft notice. He didn't know why it should bother him. Perhaps it was because he had come to see Archie through Sharon's eyes.

Hugo tried to sort out how he felt about the matter. Thousands of American boys of draft age had fled to Canada in the growing protest against the war. Archie could have requested immigration status before he received his draft notice. Hugo couldn't understand why he hadn't. The U.S. was a favored nation as far as immigration policy went. The Canadians were known to turn a blind eye to the requirement of proof of military discharge to well-educated American applicants with useful skills. Deserters lived in a cash society without work permits or legal status. He couldn't see Archie seeking that life.

Everything about Archie's decision to run was troublesome. His deferment while he finished college gave him plenty of time to plan for this eventuality. Why had he come home and waited to be called up? With his college degree he could have circumvented the problem entirely by joining the Air Force or the Navy as an officer, far removed from combat. His term of service would have been longer but it would have been relatively safe. None of his actions made any sense unless, as Sharon said, he truly believed he would be one of lucky ones. Or that his old family name and money would somehow exempt him.

What did any of this have to do with Ruth's murder? That was the knotty question that seemed to have no answer. Her death had to be a separate thing but until they found Archie and questioned him, there was no way to separate his defection from the case.

Had it been Bebe on the bus? He would need to interview Charlie Neuman and find out. Every time his thoughts came around to that question, they skittered away, unwilling to address the possibility.

꧁

SUNDAY STARTED OUT clear and noticeably colder. Hugo and Junior decided they would be less conspicuous in the police sedan than the Thunderbird. They rolled by the address of record for Tyrone Pritchett. The house was on Spruce Street in Happy Hills. It was early and the street was still asleep after a typical Saturday night.

"Welcome to the jungle." Junior circled the block but there was no sign of the Barracuda. Dilapidated cars sat on cinder blocks, a mangled trash can lay like a dead soldier in the roadway, almost every porch held a collection of discarded items from old boots to sagging chairs bleeding cotton batting. Screen doors sported ripped mesh or none at all. Not even a stray dog stirred.

Junior continued to circle in ever widening blocks until they had cruised the neighborhood. He returned for a last crawl down Spruce Street. Nothing and no one stirred except a little girl sitting on the steps of a sagging porch wearing only fleece pajamas. She was barefooted and hunched in on herself against the cold. She watched them as they drove past to the street corner.

Hugo studied her in the sideview mirror. She couldn't be more than three or four. How could she sit there like that in the cold? Because the alternative was worse. The need to escape outweighed the fear of everything else. The dark, dusty, bat infested bell tower had been his bolt hole. He had been afraid of heights so no one ever thought to look for him there. He was no longer afraid of heights. Or anything else.

Hugo shook off the memory. "Spin the block." He took off his coat and started shedding the sweater he wore over his dress shirt.

"You'll give us away."

"Do it."

Junior sighed and did as he was told.

They pulled up at the house where the little girl sat. Her eyes got wide with fear as Hugo approached but instead of running into the house, she balled herself up into a smaller knot.

"It's okay." Hugo had the sweater in one hand and Junior's brown bag lunch in the other. She followed his every move with fear in her eyes. He could see the pulse in her neck jumping in terror. "Let's put this on, okay? It's cold out here." He set the lunch on the step next to her and held up the sweater. "Come on. This will keep you warm."

He thought she was going to bolt but instead she slowly unknotted her small body and held up her hands. He slipped the sweater over her head and threaded her arms into the sleeves. It came down over her feet. He bunched the sleeves up her arms and opened the sack. There were two sandwiches and a banana inside. He took out the banana and gave it to her.

She clutched the banana to her chest. Her eyes never left Hugo's face.

"It's okay. You should eat it. And the rest of it." He picked up the sack, gave it a little jiggle, and returned it to the step.

She snatched up the sack and ran to the far corner of the porch. A pile of discarded items anchored the space. She dug into it and placed the sack there, carefully covering it with a bent hubcap. Satisfied with her handiwork, she came back to sit on the step and peeled the banana.

Hugo tugged on the bottom of the sweater, stretching it to wrap her feet in it. He rubbed them through the wool material to warm them. There was nothing else he could do at the moment except hope there was a Mrs. K in her life somewhere.

As he walked back to the car, his gaze swept the area for any signs of life. All was quiet but that didn't mean he hadn't been seen. Word would travel fast that the police had been in the neighborhood looking for someone. A niggle of fear that the little girl would suffer for his actions caused him to look back at her.

She smiled at him. The banana was already gone. She got up from the step, looked all around, then threw the banana peel under the porch before returning to her perch. She pulled the sweater down over her feet as Hugo had done.

He got into the car. "Chinquipin Street. Let's see if we can catch Tyrone before the grapevine does."

THEY SPENT THE morning cruising all the neighborhoods they thought Tyrone might haunt. They had no luck. The Barracuda seemed to have vanished off the streets of Mobile. They even made a foray outside the city limits into Prichard.

Eight days into the investigation and they had little to go on. They returned to the station and put out an APB on Tyrone's car. Strict instructions were given that he was to be brought in but no one was to question him other than Hugo and Junior.

Hugo called John Henry's number but no one answered the phone. He looked at the clock. Viola would be at church.

No one answered the phone at Charlie Neuman's number either. Hugo felt the frustration building. He needed something to pop, one little kernel of truth to link Ruth's death to her killer.

He thoughts turned to Bebe. She had lied to him. The whole charade of concern for Archie was simply that. She had called him to the Quarter Note knowing that he would read more into it than was there. It gave her the perfect opportunity to muddy the waters, to throw him off the scent.

They all knew where Archie was. It had all been a shell game to distract the foot soldiers while their superiors went about their business.

Like the brass in Vietnam, the Prescotts and their hirelings were in the rear with the beer while Hugo and Junior chased shadows.

Hugo was tired of being toyed with. He wanted to hit something. Someone. He stood and caught his jacket off the back of his chair. "Go home. They'll call if there's any sign of Tyrone."

"What about you?" Junior looked up from the typewriter.

"I've got an errand to run."

Junior pushed back from his desk. "Okay. I'll drop you."

"I'll walk. Maybe it'll clear my head."

"Sure."

Junior's response held a note of speculation. Almost a question, possibly a warning. Hugo ignored it.

The air outside was biting and the wind off the water had picked up. Hugo turned his collar up and walked with purpose down Church Street five blocks to S. Cedar. He turned left. His house sat another two blocks south at the corner of S. Cedar and Eslava. He could hear music coming from Maurice's as he drew near. There was the 1956 turquoise and white Chevy parked on the street in front of it. A very distinctive car, one sure to draw attention.

Hugo shook his head, went into his house, and got his car keys. Although his ears and nose were cold from the wind and he'd jammed his hands into his coat pockets for warmth, the walk had done little to cool his temper.

He turned the Thunderbird in the direction of Midtown. Lorraine's car was in the driveway of her home when he drove by but there was no sign of Mo's truck. He cut through the neighborhood to Government Street and headed down the DIP. It was mid-afternoon on Sunday. His best guess was that Mo would be at the VFW. He was right.

Twenty-Five

The VFW Post on Dauphin Island Parkway was a long, low building of little distinction. A strip mall with a doctor's office, an insurance agency, a florist, and a beauty shop stood off to the north of it. Mobile Memorial Gardens lay across the street, the final resting place of thousands who had lived and died in the city and its surrounding communities.

Someone had put up a notice on the VFW billboard about the annual turkey shoot scheduled for the week-end before Thanksgiving. The top prize listed was a twelve-gauge shotgun.

Mo's old Chevy truck was parked in the lot, the back bumper dinged, mud splattered against the underbelly, and a rifle on the gun rack across the back window. A couple of old timers sat at a card table set up under the overhang of the awning over the front entrance. Their goal, it appeared, was to sell tickets to the turkey shoot. Both of them looked too comfortable with their beers to bother.

The old geezer in overalls pushed his baseball cap onto the back of his head and whistled softly. "That's some shiner you got there, young fella. Looks like you could use a cold one."

His sidekick chuckled. "It'll not only soothe your hurt feelings, but it'll help that swole up eye, too."

"I'm afraid it'll take something more than a beer."

A knowing look came into the old geezer's eyes. "A matter of pride, I take it."

"Just setting the record straight."

"Well, keep it outside. I don't want the place busted up."

Hugo made no reply as he pulled open the heavy door.

The light inside was dim but adequate. A pool table stood at one end of the building. A bar ran along one side. Tables were positioned around the center of the floor and a raised platform formed a stage with a space left open for dancing at the other end of the rectangular structure. *Mustang Sally* played on the jukebox.

A few of the tables were occupied. Mo Hitchens sat at the bar laughing with a couple of his friends. One of them saw Hugo standing in the doorway and nudged Mo.

Mo turned around on his stool, leaned back, his elbows on the bar, and gave Hugo that taunting sneer. "Well, looky here at what the cat drug in. Looks like someone finally whupped your ass, pretty boy."

"I wouldn't say that exactly," Hugo said as he crossed the room to stand in front of Mo and his buddies.

"Well, what would you say, then, 'cause it sure looks like someone had their way with you."

A rumble of low laughter passed through Mo's friends and he grinned at Hugo.

"I'd say some candy ass hid in the dark like a little girl and took a cheap shot."

Mo shot to his feet. The stool crashed back against the bar. His two buddies spread out on either side of him. "Are you trying to imply something, pretty boy?"

"Nothing implied about it, Mo. Just stating the facts."

"Why you little punk! You think you can take me down?" The sneer was back on Mo's face. "I've wiped the floor with the likes of you without breaking a sweat."

Hugo eyed his opponent. Mo had a good forty pounds on him but he was slow, cocky, and bolstered by his companions. Hugo was a good three inches taller with a longer reach and he'd spent two hard years in hell humping the boonies. He liked his chances.

He took a half step closer to Mo, his hands at his sides, his stance balanced, his core one tight coil. Hugo could smell him. It was the scent of a coward, of the VC who sent women and children into the fray to do their killing for them. "Not with someone like me you didn't. There's no one like me." He felt the blood lust descend like a veil. He caged it, controlled it. He was ready. "We can play this pissing game all day long. Or we can step outside and get on with it."

Hugo saw the swing before it came. He saw the moment of decision register in Mo's eyes. Hugo was an instant ahead of him and he put his whole body into the blow to Mo's jaw.

Mo's jab barely brushed Hugo's chin because he was already falling back against the bar from the force of Hugo's punch. Hugo gave him a sharp left, right tattoo to the gut before the upper cut that brought Mo crashing to his knees.

Hugo danced back a couple of steps, eyeing Mo's buddies. The action had been so quick they hadn't had time to react. Now it was too late. They looked at each other then at Hugo. Neither of them seemed to want to take the matter any further. One of them reached down to help Mo sit upright.

Hugo backed toward the door. As soon as it closed behind him, he shook his hands against the pain in his knuckles. He looked down at the two old men. "No real damage."

The old geezer grunted and gave Hugo a two-finger salute.

⁂

HUGO OPENED HIS eyes and saw the moon riding high in the sky. The wind whistled around him and caused the rope hanging from the bell clapper to jump and dance. He shivered and pulled his coat more closely around him. He felt as dry as parchment paper, as if the wind could blow him on the breeze as easily as a dead leaf in autumn.

The rage that had been slowly building for days had left him. Now he felt empty to his core. He rose from the corner of the bell tower and looked out across St. Thomas Moore's Catholic School for Boys. His inner demons had driven him here, to sanctuary. As a boy it had seemed he was above the whole world, safe, out of harm's way when he stood here. Now, everything looked small, insignificant.

He checked his watch. Nearly eight o'clock. Better, he thought. But, still, time lost. Time in which he couldn't account for his actions, how he had gotten here, what he had done in the aftermath of his encounter with Mo.

This time he didn't struggle with the how and the why. He did what he had done in 'Nam, in San Francisco. It had served him well enough then. It was how he would move forward now. He viewed this gap, this lost time, as something separate, apart, removed from his actions, his emotions. *There it is,* he thought. *It don't mean nothing.*

He climbed down the rickety ladder from the bell tower to the floor below, then down the narrow, twisting staircase to ground level. The door was secured from outside entry by a board wedged against the knob. Even in his dissociative state, he had taken the necessary precaution to dig in, secure the perimeter.

The Thunderbird was parked a block from the boys' home, keys in the ignition. Hunger drove him to Creighton and one of the few places he knew he could find something to eat at this hour on a Sunday night.

The McDonald's parking lot was abuzz with teenagers cruising, connecting, playing their car radios too loud. The music was just as restless as the kids, as questioning and demanding.

A boy with a buzz cut was making his move on a pretty brunette as she leaned against the fender of a late model Ford Fairlane. He stood out in a crowd of long hairs. Waiting for his FTA, Hugo thought, enjoying one last leave before flying off to hell.

He ordered two cheeseburgers, two fries, and a Coke. The combination of hot, salty goodness and sugar left him feeling sated and sleepy. He turned toward downtown and home.

The bare bulb of his porch light gave sufficient illumination to the dark corner of the street where he lived. Across from him, two houses stood in various stages of salvaging by Clyde Minton. Their partially dismembered husks loomed like skeletons on Halloween. He spared a passing thought to his landlord and when he might decide to give in to the relentless pressure of urban renewal sweeping the city. Sooner rather than later, he thought.

The hint of fragrance hit him when he opened the door. It was Bebe's scent, the perfume she wore. His breath caught. Was she here in the dark recesses of the room? He flipped the light switch and the sparse furniture jumped at him in the sudden, harsh light. No sound disturbed the silence. Was he hallucinating? He had experienced this scent so many times in his mind while in 'Nam. It had become the embodiment of her in his thoughts and dreams.

No, he decided, she had been here. In this room. Tonight.

The urge to go to her gripped him with such force that his body shuddered. Why had she come? He wanted desperately to see her, to pretend that the reason for her visit had been pure, had been spurred by the same need that rushed through his veins.

He steeled himself against that desire. Something had triggered her visit but the events of the past week told him it was only another move on the chess board. If he ran to her, he would be her pawn and she would control the outcome of the game. Eight days ago he would have given in to that urge. He wasn't sure what prevented him from doing so now.

Father Gregory's words echoed in his mind. *Your need to know has too much power over you, Hugo. It will cost you in the end.*

It was already costing him the thing he most desired.

⁂

AFTER SUPPER, JUNIOR and Grammy watched the new television show *60 Minutes* with Mike Wallace and Harry Reasoner. They did a segment on the war. The interviews made it more real somehow than the daily snippets they were accustomed to seeing on the evening news.

Neither of the newscasters had the gravitas of Walter Cronkite but the images that flashed across the television screen did their job for them. They showed up close the defeated, weary reality experienced by the soldiers in the field. Bleak young faces stared into the camera, the fear, the hopelessness, and homesickness evident in their eyes.

Junior's thoughts drifted to Hugo. The war had changed him. The change had been immediately evident when he arrived home from San Francisco. It wasn't something you could put your finger on but it was there nonetheless. He wondered what Hugo was doing tonight.

He had worried about his friend since they parted company at the station in the late afternoon. The rumor had reached Junior that Big Mo Hitchens had given Hugo the black eye. Junior could imagine why. The question was, what would Hugo do about it? Junior knew him well enough to know he wouldn't let it go.

He pushed such thoughts from his mind. Hugo would do what Hugo would do and that was that.

Grammy stirred restlessly on the sofa next to him, as if she couldn't be comfortable. The images had done that to both of them, left a sense of unidentified unease, foreboding.

Junior cleared his throat. "How about some popcorn for the show, Grammy?"

"Oh, that sounds nice, dear. I bought some Jiffy Pop at the A&P."

Junior shook the pre-packaged pan over the heat of the burner until the exploding popcorn kernels created a mushroom cloud of expanding aluminum. He settled in with his grandmother to watch The Ed Sullivan show. They enjoyed Connie Francis but Grammy didn't like Joan Rivers' comedic performance. She felt her type of humor was mean spirited and unladylike. Junior thought that Rivers was funny but took things a little too far occasionally. Her act was better suited for The Tonight Show when people of Grammy's sensibility were less likely to watch.

He glanced at the clock above the TV as the show drew to a close. He'd tackle the crossword puzzle, he decided, then call it a night.

His grandmother kissed him on the cheek as she left the living room to prepare for bed. He settled in with newspaper and pencil. A crossword clues about double names sent his thoughts drifting to the receptionist at Dr. Fellowes' office. Bobby Jean. He wondered what her last name was. As he was deciding how he could find out, the phone rang.

"Detective Knight?" The feminine voice on the phone was vaguely familiar.

"Yes."

"This is Margaurite Golding. Sharon Shipley is here with me. She thinks someone has broken into Ruth's house."

"I'll be right there."

Junior disconnected the call and immediately tried Hugo's number. There was no answer. He went down the hallway and tapped on his grandmother's door. When she opened it, he told her he had to go out on police business.

She had already started putting the pink foam curlers in her hair. She inhaled sharply and her hand clutched her nightgown into a knot at her chest. "Oh, Junior. At this time of night? I don't know if you should."

"Grammy, it's my job. It's nothing but a call about a prowler. Myrtle Crum makes them all the time. It'll turn out to be nothing."

"Can't a patrol car look into it?"

"Grammy." Junior tried to keep the exasperation out of his voice. "I have to go."

He ducked into his room and grabbed his overcoat.

His grandmother was still standing in her doorway when he came back into the hall. He kissed her cheek. "Go to bed. It's nothing."

But Junior's pulse raced and he felt a thrill of excitement running through his veins as he pulled the police sedan away from the curb and raced toward Dauphin Street and the Camden house.

Blue lights atop a patrol car flashed across the lawn of Ruth Camden's house. Junior parked between it and an older model Mercedes sedan on the oyster shell bay. He showed the officer his shield. "What have you found?"

The patrolman shook his head. "Nothing. The place is locked up tight, including the garage. No open or broken windows, no evidence of anyone about."

"How long did it take you to get here?"

"Less than five minutes. We were at the Loop monitoring the movie theater. Kids have started hanging out there after the place shuts down."

Junior counted the time in his head. Something aroused Sharon Shipley's suspicion that the house had been broken into. How quickly did she go to the next-door neighbor? Three minutes? Five? She'd have to gain entry, explain herself, and get Mrs. Golding to call the police. Three to four minutes. The patrol car arrives. Five minutes. Twelve to fifteen minutes minimum.

"Where's your partner?"

"At the back door."

Junior considered the facts. In twelve minutes someone could have easily slipped away in the dark. There'd be the risk of being seen if they left by way of Dauphin Street. Was it a risk worth taking? At this hour of the night, yes. But if they knew about the alley it would be easy to escape with no one to notice. Twelve minutes. *Damnit!*

"You tried the doors?"

The patrolman nodded. "Locked. No light or movement inside. Nothing around the garage in the back."

"Call another car. I want someone on each door and I want you and your partner to walk the alley that runs behind the hedge at the back of these houses. Stay off the track as much as you can. Look for any sign of a car being parked there or footprints in the dirt." He opened the passenger door of the police sedan and looked in the glove box hoping against hope. The extra key to the Camden house wasn't there. Probably still in Hugo's pocket. The only options would be either forced entry or send a car to the station to get the key in the case file.

"I'll go next door and talk to Mrs. Shipley. Keep this place locked down."

⁂

MRS. GOLDING HAD obviously been watching for him as she opened the door the moment he removed his finger from the doorbell.

Sharon Shipley was all that Hugo had claimed. She reminded Junior of Bebe but a touch more. More what, he couldn't define. She had the same bone structure, same blonde hair. The only thing that marred her good looks was the strain on her face. That, and, as he settled on the chair across from her, the beginnings of dark circles beneath her eyes.

After the introductions, Junior asked, "Why were you here at this time of night, Mrs. Shipley?"

"The mail." She gave a slight shrug. "I thought there might be a letter from Archie. We haven't been able to locate him and it occurred to me that no one has checked the mail in days." She looked down at her hands clasped in her lap. "I guess I wasn't thinking clearly. There was no mail in the box. There wouldn't be, would there? The mailman was the one to find her so I suppose they're holding it at the post office."

Junior gave himself a mental kick. Like with Archie's house, he and Hugo had overlooked an obvious avenue of information. "That would be my guess." He took out his notebook. "Why do you think someone broke into the house?"

"I saw them. The light through the window. I went onto the porch to check the box and I saw light bouncing off the walls. Like a flashlight."

Junior's whole body tensed. "Could you tell who it was?"

Sharon shook her head in exasperation. "I didn't really see anyone. Only the movement of the light."

"What did you do?"

Sharon began rocking her body ever so slightly. "I ran." She became aware of what she was doing and stopped, unclenched her fingers, and took a breath. "I just ran down the steps and across the lawn to Mrs. Golding."

"Then what?"

Mrs. Golding answered. "I called the police. Sharon has a card with a number for another detective and she tried to call it but got no answer. Because of all that's happened, I decided to call you."

"I'm glad you did. It may be unrelated to our inquiry but it's better to err on the side of caution." He studied Sharon. She had a look of deep sadness about her. It was evident not only in her face but in her whole body, as if a veil had been draped over her, enshrouding her in grief. He had learned from Hugo that she had been very close to her aunt. "Why did you decide to drive all the way from Point Clear to check the mail at this hour of the night?"

"I didn't. I was at dinner with the family. At the club. It used to be a family ritual. Dinner every Sunday evening. It's not something I've done in years but Haywood asked if I would join them tonight. In the wake of Ruth's death there were things to discuss."

"Who was at dinner tonight?"

Her forehead creased in a fleeting frown. "Haywood and Voncille, of course. Bebe, Skip and Cissy. And Trey Whitehall."

The banker at the family dinner. *Interesting*, Junior thought. "Is Trey Whitehall related in some way?"

Sharon hesitated then looked down at her hands. "No. He and Skip were at school together. The families have known each other for a long time."

"So, you left the club and decided to stop by your aunt's house."

"Yes. I was driving down Dauphin Street and as I got close to Aunt Ruth's house I felt such loss, such sadness. Archie doesn't even know his grandmother is dead." Tears formed in her eyes and the subtle rocking motion started again. "I just need to see him, to know he's safe." She blinked rapidly and sniffed, gathered herself and became very still. "I don't know. It suddenly popped into my head that maybe there was a letter. Maybe he had finally written to her. So, I stopped."

"I see." Junior stood. "Do you feel up to going back to the house with me? I'd like to know if anything looks out of place."

Sharon didn't answer immediately. Finally, she rose from the sofa. "I suppose it has to be done."

"Only if you feel up to it."

She nodded. "Let's get it over with. I need to get home to my children."

"I'm afraid you'll be delayed even longer. A car has to bring the key to your aunt's house from the station."

"I have a key."

Junior paused in the act of turning toward the entrance of Mrs. Golding's living room and looked back sharply at Sharon. "You do?"

She nodded. "I've always had a key."

Junior groaned inwardly. How many more mistakes could he and Hugo survive without blowing the case entirely. Who else had a key? Archie would, he decided. They had failed to ask Haywood Prescott if he had one. Hell, the banker probably had one as well. Who on god's green earth didn't have a key to Ruth Camden's house?

Junior thanked Mrs. Golding for her call and apologized for keeping her up so late. He and Sharon cut across the lawns of the two houses. The blue lights were still flashing on the patrol car. Junior spoke with the officer on the front door.

When he unlocked the door and swung it open, a breath of frigid air greeted him. He spoke over his shoulder to Sharon. "Stay here with the officer while I do a walk through."

He removed his pistol from the holster under his left shoulder and stood with his back to the closed door as his vision adjusted to the darkness of the foyer. The intermittent flashes of blue light suggested movement where there was none. He listened for any sound that might indicate the intruder was hiding out in the house. The only thing he heard was his heart pounding in his chest.

It occurred to him that the doorway would be viewed as the source of any threat to anyone lurking in the shadows. He took a deep breath and eased around to the entrance to the dining room. He knew the light switch was just inside the entryway. He found it and flooded the area with light from the chandelier as he remained behind the wall outside the illuminated area. Nothing stirred.

Cautiously he did the same with the formal living room on the other side of the foyer. It was a painstaking process as he worked himself around the ground floor of the residence. By the time he got to the task of checking out the second floor, the lump of fear in his throat had abated somewhat and the drumming of his heartbeat no longer deafened him.

At last, he ushered Sharon Shipley into the house. Everything seemed to be in order as they made their way through the rooms. She looked in the drawer of the dressing table in her aunt's bedroom and the jewelry box was where she had last seen it. Nothing upstairs seemed to be disturbed. They returned to the foyer, satisfied that nothing was amiss.

As she tucked the ends of her scarf into the V of her cashmere coat, something caused her to pause. She walked to the entry into the dining room.

"There." She pointed at the china cabinet.

Junior moved to her side and followed the direction of her pointing finger. "What?"

"The key. It shouldn't be there."

A key with a blue tassel rested in the lock of the top drawer of the silver chest.

"I put it back in its hiding place after. . ."

Junior circled the dining table in one direction as Sharon came around the other end. They stared at the key. Then she reached down and pulled open the top drawer.

"Someone's been in here. Someone who knew where to find the key." Sharon shivered. When she drew back the silver cloth, the highly polished place settings winked at them from their resting place in the reflected light from the chandelier. All twenty-four of them.

"Anything missing?"

She closed the drawer and opened the second. After a quick inspection she closed it and moved on to the bottom drawer. She inhaled sharply and took a step back. "They're gone."

"What's gone?"

"The butter pats."

Twenty-Six

After he sent Sharon Shipley on her way, Junior took a flashlight from the trunk of the police sedan. He made his way around the Camden house, shining the light in every nook and crevice in search of anything unusual.

The alley behind the house was empty of any living thing. He switched off the flashlight and stood there as his eyes adjusted to the darkness. Ambient light from the houses that backed up to this lane gave enough illumination that someone could navigate it. Especially if they were familiar with the area. He walked the length of the alley, checking to see which houses showed evidence of activity at this hour. Then he returned to the Camden house and his car.

Once he settled in the driver's seat, a lethargy washed over him as if he had taken a draught of sleeping medicine. He felt his weight settle into the seat cushions as if his body was boneless. It was a chore to lift his hand to the ignition and start the car.

He realized that it wasn't fatigue that made his arms and legs so heavy. The heightened sense of danger, the fear that had tightened his whole body into a coiled spring, now left him drained, so tired he didn't know if he could drive home.

How had Hugo endured two tours in Vietnam where every hour of every day was like walking into that dark house not knowing if a killer lurked there? The discomfort of earlier in the evening returned to Junior. He wasn't a coward. Neither was he brave. He accepted this about himself.

When Grammy persuaded Father Gregory that she couldn't manage without him, the priest had filled out the paperwork to designate Junior as her sole support. That, and his job in law enforcement, had gotten him an exemption from service.

At a different time in history such a designation might have created resentment from his peers. No one gave it a thought now that the race riots, anti-war protests, and a general disrespect for authority created a different attitude to the war in Vietnam and military service in general.

The only person to ever remark on his draft status had been Big Mo. If he were more like Hugo, Junior would have had the perfect come-back. Especially considering the fact that Big Mo hadn't been called up either. He wondered who had been bullied into making that happen. Or was it simply the luck of the draw?

Junior wasn't sure how he felt about the war. Grammy had lived through two world wars and lost her husband. She was afraid of everything; Germans, Mexicans, communists, and Jews. Cubans held the number one position until Hugo went to Vietnam. Now the focus of her enmity rested on the Viet Cong.

When you took all that into consideration, Grammy had been right. She couldn't survive in such a fearful, violent world on her own.

Sometimes Junior thought that if he didn't have Grammy dependent on him there could be something more in his life. Such thoughts made him feel guilty.

Grammy had saved him. Just like she'd saved Hugo.

He hoped Hugo was all right, that he hadn't let his bull headedness lead him into a more thorough ass whipping by Big Mo. But the truth was, he couldn't summon the energy to drive all the way downtown to check on him. It was fast approaching two in the morning and all Junior could think of was his bed.

✻

HUGO STOOD ON the back porch of his house watching the mating dance of a pair of cats. They faced off against each other from their precarious perches on the fence that ran along the back of his yard. They had been at it, off and on, for half the night it seemed, but in reality it had only been an hour or so.

The sky had gone from charcoal to a light misty gray and now a white-yellow with piercing shafts of light streaking across the sky. The pre-dawn chill seeped into his bones and he shivered. He'd been standing there over fifteen minutes watching the arrival of a new day.

This was one of the things he had missed during his time in Vietnam. Over there, the day came all in a rush, no tiptoeing arrival of the sun above the jungle. One minute it was night and the next it was day.

He pulled the lapels of the bath robe close against his throat. It fit tightly across his shoulders, the terry cotton worn and thin from many washings. The university had sent it, along with a precious few other personal items, to Mrs. K when he suddenly left Tuscaloosa all those years ago. For want of anyone else, she had been listed as his next-of-kin. The bath robe had been a gift from her the Christmas he had come to live with her and Junior when he was almost fifteen. She had been dismayed that it had been so big on him. In her eyes he had always been so much larger than he was. He ran his palm across the faded lapels of the garment and returned to the kitchen.

The aroma of coffee filled the house. He poured a cup and let the warmth travel through him as he drank the strong brew. The space heater had begun to make headway against the cold damp of the room.

Hugo had slept well the first part of the night, only awakening to fitful sleep with the early morning courting call of the feral cats. The encounter with Mo Hitchens seemed to have cleared the pipes. He looked down at the red knuckles of his right hand. It had been the right move. He would now be able to put aside all the distractions and get on with the job at hand. *Do the time. Stay alive.*

It was time he paid another visit to Viola. He had no doubt that Tyrone knew he was on their radar. Finding him would be difficult.

He'd had twenty-four hours to dig in somewhere. It was time they shook the tree. He still felt that finding Archie would unravel the mystery of Ruth Camden's murder and Tyrone was the last known person to see Archie.

Hugo glanced at the clock. Still too early to call Junior so he ate a bowl of dry cereal and headed for the bathroom and a steamy, hot shower.

THE STATION WAS a beehive of activity. The parking lot overflowed with officers in full dress uniform. A squad of police motorcycles was backed in at an angle all along Royal Street. The fire chief's car sat at the intersection of Royal and Government with the fire department's newest and largest fire engine lined up behind it blocking the street. The desk sergeant looked harried and angry.

Hugo climbed the stairs to the second floor. Junior sat behind his desk, the phone caught between his shoulder and chin as he made notes on a legal pad. He also wore his dress blues.

When Junior hung up, Hugo asked, "What the hell's going on?"

"Veteran's Day. Don't you ever look at your calendar? Or the department memos?"

Hugo stood with his back to Junior as he took his time removing his sports coat and draping it across the back of his chair. He touched the knot of his tie and sat down.

"Any new leads?"

He listened to Junior's report on the happenings at the Camden house in the night. He swiveled his chair back and forth, his head back, staring at a water stain on the ceiling of the squad room. Why the butter pats? There was enough silver in the chest to make a tidy payday for someone. Instead of taking the pieces that could be easily pawned or sold to an antiques dealer, the thief had taken the very distinctive butter pats.

He heaved a deep sigh. "Right." He sat up straight. "Any word on Tyrone?"

Junior shook his head. "He's disappeared like a rabbit down a hole."

"You think he was in the Camden house last night?"

Junior thought about it. "Doesn't fit somehow. Everything was too orderly, too normal, you know? If Sharon hadn't noticed the key in the silver chest drawer no one would have missed the silver until someone did the tallying up."

"Sharon, is it?" Hugo used the same taunting phrase Junior had employed when Sharon first crossed his path.

Junior's face reddened and he grinned sheepishly. "I wish." He cleared his throat. "So, what next? Do we bring Viola in for a chat?"

"Not yet. She knows we're looking for Tyrone. And she knows we'll eventually get around to her. Let's let that simmer a bit. We should do a haul at Abe's in the late afternoon when the usual suspects will be hanging around. Go in with cars and lights. Make a statement."

Junior hesitated. "Not a good idea. The parade starts at ten. Both the fire and patrol units will either be in the parade or doing crowd control." He watched Hugo for a long moment then added, "Kids are out of school today. They'll be in and out of Abe's all day."

Hugo avoided eye contact with Junior. He simply nodded, opened the case file, and picked up the list of holdings of the Haywood-Prescott family that Judy Fohl had given him. The only investment in Canada was *Liberte' Partenariat* in Sherbrooke, Quebec.

It took a while to find a phone number but after a quarter of an hour of being switched from one exchange to another, he had one. The woman who answered his call in French switched smoothly into English when he asked for Archie Camden. She informed him that no one in their company answered to that name. Could someone else help him?

Eventually, he was transferred to Basile Moreau.

"Who did you say you were?"

"Hugo August. Detective. Mobile Police Department."

"Mobile police department?"

"Mobile. Alabama. In the southern U.S."

"Oh, I know Mobile." This time he got the pronunciation right.

"I thought you might."

"What can I do for the Mobile Police Department?"

"I'm trying to locate Archie Camden."

"Can I ask why?"

"His grandmother died."

"I'm sorry to hear that."

"Do you know Archie well?"

"Actually, I don't know him at all but Bebe has spoken of him to me. Bebe? Bebe Prescott?"

"I know who you're talking about. In what regard did she speak to you about Archie?"

Basile hesitated. "Surely you know we're related?"

Hugo grinned. "Cousins."

"Right." There was a note of relief in Basile's voice. "She said he might be interested in working in an architectural firm here in Sherbrooke."

"Was he?"

"No. At least he wasn't when I last spoke with Bebe."

"When was that?"

A long silence made Hugo mentally curse. He had pushed too hard.

Finally, Basile spoke. "I don't think I can help you with your inquiries detective. I didn't know Ruth was dead. No one in the family informed me. I've had no interaction with Archie and I can't help you find him."

Hugo closed his eyes briefly in triumph. Basile Moreau knew Ruth was Archie's grandmother. Was he lying about knowledge of her death? "I'm surprised Haywood didn't check with you about Archie. They're desperate to find him. He missed the funeral."

"I haven't spoken with Haywood in some weeks. Bebe either."

"Did Archie interview with the architecture group in Sherbrooke? Could you give me the firm's name?"

"I couldn't say. I'm sorry I can't be of any further assistance but I'm late for an appointment."

The line went dead.

Hugo replaced the phone in the cradle. It was time to call Bebe to task.

⁂

THERE WAS NO sign of Bebe's convertible at her apartment building but Hugo rang the doorbell anyway. There was no answer. He stood on the small, covered stoop and surveyed the complex, the anger simmering just below the surface. He had driven straight from the station, primed to confront Bebe about all the evasions and manipulations since the very beginning of this case. Where would she be at this hour of the morning?

Anywhere. The beauty parlor, shopping, visiting a friend. *The Club.*

He drove up the hill and cruised the parking lot of the country club. It was full to overflowing. There, near the tennis courts, sat the little cream colored Mercedes. Hugo parked and approached the pro shop. On the covered entry stood a tripod with a poster announcing the Veteran's Day Tennis Tournament.

Hugo entered the foyer that gave access to the pro shop to his left and a lounge that lead to the changing rooms on his right. He walked through to the glass doors leading out onto the veranda that spanned the width of the building and sat about six feet above the courts.

Bebe was on the first court playing a game of mixed doubles. Her partner was Trey Whitehall. Hugo knew the moment she realized he was there. Though the veranda was shaded by an awning and lined with large tubs of lush ferns to keep the movements of the onlookers from distracting the players, she had seen him out of the corner of her eye. On the next point, she hit an easy cross court shot wide.

Most of the café tables were taken by club members watching the match, sipping their bloody Marys and gossiping in soft voices. They sent inquiring glances Hugo's way but he ignored them. He sat at one of the tables and watched the rest of the set.

The easy camaraderie between Bebe and Whitehall, the way they moved on the court as a team wasn't lost on Hugo. He turned his focus to Trey. As the set progressed, there was no doubt the banker was aware of Hugo's presence. He was sending a message.

The opposing team won the set and Hugo decided he had given Bebe her way long enough. He rose from the chair and moved to the top of the steps leading down to the courts so she couldn't ignore him any longer. She threw her racket onto a bench and came off the court.

"What are you doing here, Hugo?"

"You lied to me."

"I don't know what you're talking about." But she wouldn't look him in the eye.

"Basile Moreau."

She turned her profile to him. The color rose in her face. "That has nothing to do with Aunt Ruth's death."

"I'll be the judge of that."

"This isn't the time or place for this discussion."

Hugo felt his control slipping. He stared at Trey Whitehall who chatted with his fellow tennis players on the court below, all the while snatching glimpses of Bebe and trying to monitor their conversation. He remembered Junior's comment that the banker had been at the family dinner at the club last night.

Then he remembered something else. Something Bebe had said. *I like my life the way it is right now.*

"Hugo?"

He blinked. Bebe was watching him.

He clenched his jaw in an effort to moderate his reaction. He felt and heard the anger in his voice but he was powerless to control it. "Soon, Bebe. At the station. An official statement."

A quick intake of breath from a nearby table made him send the eavesdropper a scathing look.

"Hugo," Bebe pulled back slightly and frowned, "you can't think I had anything to do with. . ." She looked away, her eyes wide in shock. The color drained from her face as the moments ticked away in the build-up to an explosion.

But there was no explosion. Ever the debutante, the image of propriety and control, she blinked rapidly then went down the steps and back onto the tennis court.

Trey Whitehall's arm snaked around her waist as he leaned in and kissed her on the temple. He caught and held Hugo's eyes. When he pulled back from Bebe, he smiled. Hugo balled his hands into fists then turned on his heel and left. It was time to stop tip-toeing around the Haywood-Prescotts and make something happen.

Twenty-Seven

Hugo made a swing through Happy Hills then The Bottom. Kids played in the street. Sullen teenagers clustered around a small grocery store with burglar bars on all the means of access. They followed the progress of the Thunderbird with their eyes. One of them, sporting an impressive afro, hawked and spat in Hugo's direction as he rolled past.

It was quiet on Viola's street. He debated knocking on her door but, in the end, he didn't.

Driving relaxed him. He felt his anger slowly dissipate. As he made his way through the marginal neighborhoods that housed the majority of the city's black population, he let his mind wander.

Redman was the executor of Ruth's estate. With Archie on the lam that meant he controlled her voting shares. Even if he couldn't cast a vote, that inability still made him the lynch pin for the company to do business. He claimed to be more than her attorney, that they had been close friends. Yet he also claimed to know nothing of Ruth's plans to keep Archie safe from the draft. Was he aiding and abetting Archie's escape?

Aimee Marlowe didn't like Redman. Hugo wondered why.

It would be interesting to know what Haywood thought of him. But Haywood was at the hunting camp entertaining a group of Japanese businessmen. On Veterans' Day. Probably a wise choice, Hugo thought.

There was always Sharon. She probably knew the true nature of the relationship between Ruth and Redman better than anyone.

Besides, he wanted to talk to her about the butter pats. The oddity of the choice didn't sit right when all those twenty-four place settings of gleaming antique silver were there for the taking.

Hugo debated the drive to Point Clear and glanced down at the fuel gauge. Less than a quarter of a tank. The Shell station at Broad and Government would be blocked off by the parade. He tried to remember how much cash was in his wallet. Less than twenty dollars and four days until payday.

He stopped at the traffic light at Broad and Old Shell Road. He could see the blue lights on the police motorcycles up ahead at Government Street as he idled, waiting for the light to change. They were diverting traffic off the main thoroughfare onto South Broad in anticipation of the parade.

Hugo decided he could turn around, drive to Telegraph Road, and cross the Cochrane Bridge to get to the causeway. He could gas up at Argiro's. With that thought, he realized he was justifying the expenditure of the precious little cash he had in his pocket to drive twenty-five miles with only the hope of catching Sharon Shipley at home.

He had to do something, he decided. With the city shut down to celebrate Veterans' Day there wasn't much hope of finding Redman or the priest at Holy Spirit who they still hadn't interviewed. Hugo needed to escape the decorated warriors of past conflicts, the proud cadets of future service, the speeches of praise and justification, the clash of accolades and jeering protests.

And, if he was being honest with himself, he was drawn to Sharon. There was a gravitas about her that appealed to him. Decision made. He would drive to Point Clear if for no other reason than escape.

The driver behind him tooted his horn and Hugo looked up to see that the traffic light had turned green. He started forward and at that moment saw the gold Barracuda two blocks ahead being directed off Government Street onto South Broad by traffic patrol.

He gunned the Thunderbird and raced toward the police barricade. The two motorcycle cops manning the intersection turned and gave Hugo a broad stance and wide shoulders as he honked and gestured for them to clear the intersection. While they bowed up aggressively, he braked into a slide that brought his front bumper within inches of the barricade. He dug his shield from his coat and held it out the open window.

"The Barracuda—" he gestured toward the Plymouth disappearing around the curve in Broad Street. "Radio it in. There's a warrant for the driver."

The moment Hugo flashed his shield the taller of the two officers began dragging the barricade out of the way. Hugo burned rubber through the intersection seconds ahead of the first convertible in the motorcade.

Tyrone's car was already out of sight around the curve at Canal Street. Hugo had to be mindful of pedestrians spilling over the sidewalks, making their way toward the parade route. Junior had told him he needed to keep a hand radio with him if he was going to use his car for police work. Hugo had wanted the freedom to not be found when it pleased him. Now he was on his own. He hoped the traffic cop had gotten through to dispatch. They couldn't let Tyrone slip through their fingers.

Hugo checked left and right at every intersecting street hoping to glimpse the Barracuda. Three blocks ahead he caught the tail end of a car turning right onto Virginia Street at Pollman's Bakery. It was Tyrone's car. He was certain of it. He sped forward and took the turn at such speed that the Thunderbird fishtailed. But there, half a block ahead, was the Barracuda parked on the lawn of a house with its rear bumper still in the street.

Hugo slid to a stop, blocking any avenue of escape for the car. On the front porch of the faded yellow house a girl with long, straight, brown hair had come onto the porch as a guy in a tie-dyed tee shirt mounted the steps. He turned to look at Hugo. A second man fumbled his way out of the passenger seat of Tyrone's car, clearly high. Neither of the men was Tyrone. Neither of them was black.

Purple Haze was blaring over the car's radio as it idled on the lawn. The front porch of the house was littered with hand lettered signs with the peace symbol, slogans against the war in Vietnam, a drawing of LBJ with a noose around his neck.

As Hugo closed the door of his car, realization dawned on the guy in the tie-dyed shirt and he leaped off the porch and took off running down the street. In the instant that Hugo debated chasing after him, he heard the chirp of a police siren and he motioned the driver of the cruiser to deal with the runner.

The girl had already disappeared back into the house and slammed the door. That left Hugo with the passenger from Tyrone's car. He wore a braided leather headband, a turtleneck with a vest over it, and no shoes. He grinned at Hugo.

"Yo, man. Wha's happenin'?"

"Nice car." Hugo reached into the open passenger door and turned off the car's motor. The blaring music died along with the engine.

Headband frowned at Hugo. "Hey, man, you messin' with my groove." He fell back against the fender of the Barracuda for support.

"Where'd you get the car?"

He smiled again. "Nice ride, man."

"Who's your friend?" Hugo jerked his head in the direction of the tie-dyed shirt being marched back to the yellow house by a patrolman.

Headband's smile widened. "Lupe! Where's the parade, man?"

Lupe had adopted a sullen expression and he hawked and spat when the patrolman brought him face to face with Hugo.

"Pigs!"

Hugo heaved a sigh and shook his head. "Now that's no way to make friends and influence people."

Lupe didn't respond.

"Where'd you get the car?"

"From a friend."

"That friend have a name?"

Hugo could see Lupe trying to come up with an answer but he was only mildly less stoned than his passenger.

Hugo motioned with a jerk of his head toward the patrol car.

"Take'em downtown and put'em in a cell. Have a tow truck come and impound the car. I'll stay here with it until they arrive."

The officer secured Lupe and his unnamed friend in the back seat of the patrol car and set off for the station. Hugo took the keys out of the ignition of the Barracuda and turned his attention to the house.

No one responded to his knock so he tried the door knob. It was locked. The windows that opened onto the porch were covered by what appeared to be sheets. He went down the steps and around to the rear of the house. The back door stood open.

He called out and when he got no response, he did a walk through. The girl had obviously run straight through the house and fled out the back door.

The place was a mess. Dirty dishes overflowed the sink and the garbage can stank of something sour. The kitchen table had been used as a place to paint the protests signs. Jars of psychedelic paint covered the surface and the surrounding floor was splattered. The paint had been tracked through to every room in the house.

A bong sat on the floor in front of a couch that looked so nasty that Hugo wouldn't even touch it with the toe of his shoe. The same went for the mattresses on the floor of the bedroom. Hugo nudged the bathroom door open with his foot and quickly retreated from the acrid smell of urine. It appeared the house had no electricity or running water.

He didn't find anything that could tie a name to the house. It was obvious the kids had been squatting there.

Next, he slipped on a pair of gloves and began a thorough search of the Barracuda. He didn't find much of any use there either. Tyrone had kept it spotless and except for a roach clip and a pen with Midtown Coin and Stamp Company printed on it in the glove compartment, the interior was clean. Hugo found nothing of interest either in the body of the car or the trunk.

He sat in the driver's seat and rolled up the window. When he took his hand away, he saw a sticky, dark smear on his gloved thumb. It looked like partially dried blood.

Twenty-Eight

Hugo was impatient to interview the tie-dyed shirt who turned out to be named Bennie Early, not Lupe. He decided not to wait for Junior to return from his participation in the parade.

Bennie reeked of pot and a general lack of hygiene. He had come down enough from his high to have a concerned look on his face.

"Hey, man, I ain't done nothin'. Why'd you scoop me up like that?"

"Your car has loud mufflers."

"What! You hauled me in because that rat's car has cherry bombs?"

"Where'd you get the rat's car?"

Bennie crossed his arms and sat back in his chair. "What's it to you?"

"I'm looking for a rat."

"You looking for Tyrone?"

Hugo could see the wheels turning. Bennie was trying to decide how he could play the situation to his advantage but his drugged brain was struggling to come up with a strategy.

"Do you know where he is?"

"I might."

Hugo thought about that a moment and started to rise from his chair.

"Hey, wait! Don't you want to know?"

"I'm sure your friend can tell me. I don't have time to waste. I'm missing the parade."

Bennie bowed up and kicked the leg of the table.

Hugo waited.

With a sigh, Bennie said. "I don't know, man. His car's been parked down behind the old ice house for days with the keys right there in the ignition. Hex and I decided he'd gone back to Chicago or something like that." He gave Hugo a sheepish glance. "We weren't going to keep it, man, just cruise by Tessa's and make the parade." He raised his hands in supplication. "Swear to God."

Hugo settled back into his seat. "How do you know Tyrone?"

Bennie's eyes squirreled around the room before returning to size up Hugo's gullibility. "He's a friend of Hex's."

Hugo made as if he was going to leave the room again.

"Wait, wait, wait. If I tell you what you want to know, will you cut me loose?"

"Depends."

"On what?"

"Whether or not it's something I don't already know and how useful it is to me."

Bennie clasped his hands together on the table and leaned in. "He's Hex's source for pot."

"Tell me something I don't know."

Bennie scowled and stared down at his hands. "Word is he's a hit man."

"That's old news." Hugo studied Bennie a moment. "If you really believed that, you wouldn't have stolen his car."

"We didn't steal it, man! I told you it was just sitting there for two, three days." He ran his fingers through his long, dank hair. "It was the Goofy, man. It messes with your head. Makes you do dumb shit."

The door to the interrogation room opened and Junior entered, still dressed in his uniform blues. He went to the corner and stood with his back against the wall, arms crossed.

Bennie looked from Hugo to Junior then back again. "Look, I've heard the stories about Chicago and never believed it. But this is different. Tyrone bought this car, see, about two, three months ago. Me and Hex thought he must be dealing a lot more than dime bags, you know?"

"I'm listening."

"So, we thought, maybe, we could hook up with him, get in on the good stuff."

"And did you?"

Bennie shook his head. "Tyrone and his gang hang out over at Abe's. You know the place?"

Hugo nodded.

"They got their own thing going but it ain't nothing much but moonshine, weed, and cigarettes. At least as far as me and Hex can figure out. So, I ask Tyrone how he can afford such a fine car." Bennie sat back in his chair. "Said he did a job for a man."

"What kind of job?"

"That's what I asked him and you know what he did? He just laughed, that deep booming laugh he has."

"That's it?"

"I asked him was it drugs, 'cause me and Hex could help him with his distribution, you know?"

"Well, was it?"

"He said, *do I look like a small-time drug dealer to you?* Said this was a job for a high roller, one that required his special talents and discretion. Discretion. That's the word he used."

"When did Tyrone start flashing all this money?"

"That's the thing. First, he gets this fancy new car and you see him all over the place in it but he's still doing the nickel and dime stuff, you know? Proud of that car. Wouldn't even give us a lift to the Piggly Wiggly in it. Had all those snotty nosed kids in the neighborhood washing and polishing it all the time. But he's still playing the same old game, you know?"

"So, what changed?"

"He left town. One day he's hanging out at Abe's, the next you can't find him nowhere. Left some kid carrying a big old revolver in charge of his dispensary." Bennie grinned. "That's what he called it. His dispensary. Like the drug store. You get it?"

"I get it."

"Went to his head, I'll tell you that. Straight to his head. Thought he was Wyatt Earp. Wouldn't sell us anything. Me and Hex had to hitch all the way to Creola to score."

"Where did he go?"

"Beats me. I figured Chicago. He likes to let on he's connected up there somehow. That he has *friends*. I always thought it was bullshit but when he came back he's buying his girlfriend a new TV and wearing a diamond ring on his pinky."

"When was this?"

"I don't know, man. A few months ago? August? September? Something like that."

"How long was he gone?"

Bennie shrugged. "Don't know. One day I'm standing at the bus stop in front of the library and he drives by."

"A week? A month?"

"Naw, not a month. I don't think. Maybe. I'm not good with times." He sighed and rubbed his eyes with the heels of his hands. "So, how 'bout it? You gonna cut me loose?"

"Not sure what you've given me is worth that."

He looked at Hugo and his whole body seemed to shrink. "Look, man. There's this other thing."

"Yeah?"

"A week ago. Two weeks, maybe? Me and Hex went to see Tyrone. We needed a little something, you know?" A veil of exhaustion washed over Bennie's features. He was fading before Hugo's eyes.

"So?"

"We were broke. Asked him if he could let us have a little something on the cuff. Maybe do him a favor, help him with distribution, something like that." Bennie yawned.

"And?"

His eyelids drooped. "What?"

"Did you do Tyrone any favors?"

"Naw. But here's the thing. He gave me and Hex a dime bag. Just like that. Said it was for business relations. Tyrone don't give nobody nothin'. Ever." He yawned again. "And since then, he's throwing money around like crazy. I mean rollin' in it."

Bennie's skin had turned pasty and clammy. "Could I get a Coke or something, man? I don't feel so good." He folded his arms on the table and rested his forehead against them.

Hugo and Junior left the room. He told the officer outside the door to get the kid a Coke.

They next tried to interview Bennie's friend, Hex. It was a wasted effort because Hex had obviously enjoyed the higher high. They put him back in his cell and headed out to the city garage to take a look at the Barracuda.

⁂

EVIE LOOKED UP from an array of sealed containers on a rolling cart when Hugo and Junior opened the heavy metal door to the city garage. Junior thought she looked cute with her ear muffs and pink cheeks.

"Jeez. It's freezing in here." He turned up the collar of his coat.

"Close the door. The wind doesn't help." She pushed her glasses up the bridge of her nose with a gloved finger.

Hugo pulled on a pair of protective gloves as he looked over the evidence she had removed from the car. "Anything significant?"

"The window handle has blood on it as you suspected. It's mostly dried out. If the car was parked in the shade, I'd guess it could be a couple of days old. At a max, three. I can type it when I get back to the lab. It wasn't much and I didn't find evidence of bleeding anywhere else in the car. It could be from a cut finger. A little too much blood for a mere scratch." She looked over the interior of the trunk of the car once more. "He kept it really clean."

"So, there's nothing else of value?"

"I wouldn't say that. I found some hair that's consistent with the owner. More interestingly, there are a couple of blond strands as well. I found them caught beneath the edge of the floor mat of the passenger seat."

"Archie Camden."

"Could be, I suppose. If we had a sample we could see if they're similar. Other than that, it's just short blond hair."

Junior leaned down for a closer look at the containers. "What's this?"

"Pot. Some stems and seeds mostly. Found them in the trunk."

"Any other drugs?"

"No. There's some reddish clay in the shape of a bare foot on the passenger floor mat."

"That would be Hex, I imagine."

Junior looked inside the open car door. "Prints?"

"Dozens. It'll take a while to collect and sort them all."

"You should have some help with that."

"I have my own system and I prefer to work alone. Less chance of a mix up that way."

Junior nodded.

"You look all spit and polish today. The parade, right?"

Junior grinned and felt the color rise in his face. "Yeah, well, the chief kinda insisted."

Evie glanced at Hugo then back at Junior.

Junior shrugged.

Hugo was oblivious to their exchange. He stared into the well of the car's trunk, lost in thought. Finally, he stirred. "Our car thief said the car was parked behind the old ice house. Anything here that can confirm his story?"

Evie thought about it a moment. "There's the same red clay in the threads of the tires as the footprint on the floor mat. You could start with that. If there's any clay around the structure, bring me a sample. I'll see if the composition is the same. The amount of silica to quartz and oxides can range widely." She began stripping off her latex gloves and put her hands in her coat pocket. "Is it important?"

"Just a gut feeling." He picked up a roll of crime scene tape from the cart. "Come on, Junior. Let's go look for Tyrone."

A DELIVERY TRUCK was backed up to one of the loading bays of the long, low, rambling structure of the Crystal Ice Company on Monroe Street. Across the parking lot a man came out of the office door of a secondary structure, a clip board in his hand. He stopped when he saw Junior's uniform.

"Can I help you, officer?"

Hugo showed him his shield. "We're looking for a car. Gold Plymouth Barracuda. I was told it had been parked here for several days."

The guy shook his head. "Not here, it hasn't. There's someone here every day except Sunday. That someone is usually me. I'm the manager. I'd have noticed."

An overhead door rumbled closed on the ice warehouse and the driver walked around the truck to join the manager. He glanced at Hugo and Junior then signed off on the receipt on the clip board. With a nod, he climbed into the cab of the refrigerated truck and pulled out of the parking lot.

"It's a very distinctive car." Hugo prompted the manager.

"And I'm a very observant guy. Besides, we close and lock the gate at night. Someone gave you bad information." He climbed the shallow steps to the office building but stopped before opening the door. "Does this have anything to do with drugs?"

"Why do you ask?"

"Once in a while I have a stoner turn up looking for the ice house. There's an old building over on Dekle Street north of the docks. It's been vacant as long as I can remember but folks say it was used as an ice house back in the day when they brought ice down here in boats from Maine."

"I know the place." Junior nodded at the manager. "Thanks."

They made their way back to Water Street and crossed the railroad tracks to the river side. The structure they were seeking was on a rutted pig trail of a street north of the city's main docks. A small group of three buildings huddled together, their timbers long ago weathered and splintering, their tin roofs rusted and curling. It looked as if a strong wind could blow them down.

They parked the car and made their way across the lines of track to the first building. There was no door. The interior was dim, cool, and had a strong, harsh odor.

"Christ. What's that smell?" Hugo coughed.

"Seagulls, rats, bats, you name it. Anything that burrows or nests, I imagine."

It was mainly a long empty space. Rafters had fallen in here and there. It appeared there might have been dividers to designate areas of various functions but most of that had also collapsed. All in all, it was covered in a remarkable layer of dirt and dung.

Hugo couldn't stand the stench. It tickled the back of his throat. He made for an opening in the long wall. A rat the size of a house cat scurried through the debris in front of him. His gut clenched. He stepped through into the fresh, cold air.

Before him, a berm rose to a scattering of scrub trees with the city skyline behind them. Sparse weeds and brambles grew from the red clay of the mound. Hugo crossed two rail lines and there, where the slope began to rise, he saw a tire track. This was where Bennie had found Tyrone's car.

So where was Tyrone?

He turned to look back at the structure called the ice house.

Twenty-Nine

Hugo put his shoes in an evidence bag and placed them in the trunk of the police car. He hawked and spat then walked in his socks around the Ford Fairlane. His throat burned and he felt the need to retch, anything to get the stench out of his nostrils, his throat.

As soon as he'd found the tire track in the berm, he and Junior began a grid search of the ice house. It was in the second building that they found him. This structure was obviously the meeting place for druggies seeking to buy. It hadn't deteriorated as much. The windows were intact. Empty crates stood about. Footprints tracked through the layers of dust and red clay. Filthy as it was, it wasn't nearly as bad as the warehouse.

At first Hugo thought he was seeing another huge rat nesting behind a wall that had partially fallen in. As he got closer, he knew it was the coat, the one Tyrone liked to tell people he'd killed a wolf for the pelt.

It hadn't been a pretty site. The blow flies and rats had found Tyrone long before Hugo and Junior did.

Hugo opened the passenger door of the patrol car and rolled down the window. He tore off his coat, flung it on the back seat, and yanked at the knot of his tie before getting in.

Junior slid behind the wheel of the car and sat there a long moment. He was very pale. "I've never seen anything like that."

"Let's get out of here. I need a shower."

"Yeah." But Junior continued to sit there a moment longer staring at the ambulance where two men were loading a stretcher with Tyrone's body into the back of the vehicle. "Yeah," he said again and turned the key in the ignition.

Junior dropped Hugo at his house. He left his shoes in the evidence bag on the front stoop. He walked straight through to the back porch and undressed there, leaving his clothing in a pile.

The shower was hot and steamy. Hugo repeatedly blew his nose trying desperately to rid himself of the horror of the past couple of hours. He brushed his teeth and gargled. Even after all that, he felt he could still taste the smell of the ice house and Tyrone's decomposing body.

The shoes were a problem. The only other footwear Hugo possessed was his Army boots. He dug them out of the bottom of the armoire and took a shoe brush to them. They would have to do. He figured his sports coat was a loss. Even if the cleaners could get the smell out of it, he didn't know if he'd be able bring himself to wear it again.

It was the only winter dress coat he had. He tore the plastic cleaner's bag from his twill summer sports coat. It would have to do. He put on an extra undershirt and a sweater over his shirt to compensate for the light-weight, tan summer garment.

⁂

THE CHIEF CALLED him into his office the moment Hugo entered the detective squad's bullpen.

"Chief?"

"How did he die?"

"Pretty straight forward. A bullet to the back of the head."

"The weapon?"

"Hard to tell. The rats got there ahead of us."

"Christ." The chief sat back in his chair. "Shell casings? Bullets?"

"Not yet."

Hugo waited.

"You think this is tied to Ruth Camden's death?"

"He was the last person that we know of to see Archie Camden. He was familiar with the house and Mrs. Camden's habits because of the maid. According to our witnesses, he came into a lot of money recently. We need to nail down the time on that but I think it's all tied together somehow."

The chief sighed. "This is getting more complicated by the day. What's your next move?"

"I'm going to bring in the maid. Tyrone is her nephew. I want to get to her before the news reaches her and she has time to think things through."

Goode waved in dismissal and opened a file on his desk. "Use whatever resources you need but keep me up to date on every development."

Hugo turned to open the door of the chief's office but Goode stopped him. "Tell me about Mo Hitchens."

"What's to tell?"

"Do you have something you'd like to share with me about him?"

Hugo shrugged. "I've heard it doesn't pay to get on his bad side."

The chief stared at Hugo for a long minute. He grunted and returned his attention to the paperwork in the file.

Junior came up the stairs and through the door to the bullpen as Hugo was crossing to his desk. His hair was still damp and he smelled of Old Spice.

Hugo steered Junior back down the stairs. "We need to pick up Viola now. Word will get to her soon enough. Let's hope we're ahead of it." They hit the ground floor and Hugo asked Junior for the keys to the patrol car. He handed them to the duty sergeant. "Have the garage pick up this car and have it detailed."

The sergeant took the keys. "You the two found the body?"

"That would be us."

"Heard it was a mess."

"You heard right."

❧

THEY TOOK HUGO'S car. The streets were quiet in the wake of the parade. City workers were dismantling barricades and sweeping up the streets. Children played in the street a couple of houses down from Viola's residence. They were momentarily distracted by the arrival of the two officers but quickly returned to their activities.

She opened the door after the first knock. Tears were standing in her eyes.

"May we come in, Viola?"

She nodded and unlatched the screen.

When they were once again seated in the same arrangement of their previous visit, she spoke. "You've come about Tyrone."

"Yes."

"He's dead, isn't he?" A tear rolled down her cheek.

"Yes, Viola, he's dead. I'm sorry."

She sat there soundlessly with tears trailing down her face.

Junior took a handkerchief from his pocket and handed it to her.

"We think he knew something about Archie Camden's plans to evade the draft."

Viola dabbed at her eyes. "I can't tell you nothing 'bout that."

"Is it that you can't tell us, or you won't?" Hugo's voice was kind but demanded an answer.

Viola made a choking sound and held the handkerchief over her face. After a minute she regained some control and shook her head. Her voice was thick with tears when she spoke. "Miz Camden was good to me. She was my friend. Tyrone didn't have nothing to do with what happened to her."

"But he did have something to do with Archie's disappearance, didn't he?"

Hugo could see her struggling with what to do.

"I think Mrs. Camden asked Tyrone for his help."

A wave of relief washed over Viola's features but she wasn't ready to give up Ruth Camden's plan. "I can't help you."

"Mrs. Camden is dead, Viola. Someone poisoned her. I'm not trying to find Archie to turn him over to the Army. I want to sort out this whole sorry mess and find your friend's killer."

He didn't push her. He gave her time to weigh the implication of his words. Finally, she looked him directly in the eye.

"Why would anyone care if Mr. Archie went to war or not? And he already gone when she die?"

That was the heart of the matter. Ruth's death occurred well after Archie received his draft notice and boarded a bus for basic. His fate was already determined. What could Ruth's death benefit anyone? Someone wanted Archie out of the way and Ruth dead.

"Mrs. Camden bought Tyrone the car, didn't she?" Hugo leaned forward, his forearms resting on his knees, his voice low, conspiratorial. He knew Viola wanted to tell him and he needed to have her open up. The case had stalled almost from the beginning. There were dozens of threads that lead nowhere. And now, they had another body.

Viola nodded. "After the fourth of July Miz Camden begin to fret. They spend a lot of time at Miss Sharon's over the bay all summer. Mr. Archie like to sail." Viola glanced from Hugo to Junior and back. "They all so happy when he come home in May. One more year, she say, and he have his doctor's degree. He safe. He buy that house downtown and work on it all of June and July." She smiled at Hugo. "He so proud. Take me to see it when he finish the bookcases."

"He obviously cares a great deal for you, Viola. He wanted to share something he loved with you."

Tears welled in her eyes and she looked away from Hugo's steady regard. "He a good boy. That's why I did what Miz Camden ask."

"What did she ask of you, Viola?"

"She want to talk to Tyrone. She want to make plans. Just in case, she say."

"Why do you think she needed a plan for Archie's future?"

She dabbed at her eyes and sniffed. "He change his mind. Say he don't want to leave home again. Don't want to go back to school. That he lonesome and wants to be with his family."

"And if he didn't return to finish his graduate work, he would lose his deferment."

Viola nodded. "She try to talk him out of it. Only one more year, she say. But he joke her out of her bad mood. Tell her he's too old to be drafted. Got too much education already. That the Army wasn't going to put that kind of education to waste in a foxhole."

"What did she want Tyrone to do?"

"Be ready. That's why she buy the car. Say, if it's needed, okay. If not, okay. Tyrone just keep the car and no one the wiser."

"He was supposed to drive Archie to Canada in the event he was drafted."

"Yes. Better not to fly or take the bus. Best to be off the radar, she say."

"Tyrone's car isn't exactly off the radar."

Viola frowned. "She not happy with the car. Say he should have bought something plain. Something that don't draw the eye."

"That's why Tyrone was to pick him up in Atlanta, so no one in Mobile would notice and recognize Archie leaving town."

She nodded.

"The plan worked. Tyrone picked up Archie in Atlanta at the bus depot. An employee saw him get in the Barracuda. The question now remains, where did he take him?"

"I don't know. Miz Camden say it for the best. What I don't know, I can't say."

"You didn't ask Tyrone after he came back to Mobile?"

"No. The Army come four days after Mr. Archie leave. Miz Camden tell them what's what. The Army come back later in the week when I'm waiting at the bus stop. They ask me do I know where Mr. Archie is. I say no. I don't see Tyrone for two weeks. He come back but I don't ask. Best not to know like Miz Camden say."

"So, Archie was in on the plan all along."

Viola shook her head. "He don't want no part of deserting. Got mad when she tell him what she's done. Say he not afraid to serve. He don't want to but he not afraid. Tell her he'll be back home before she can miss him."

"Then why did Tyrone go to Atlanta?"

"That's the strange part. She say tell Tyrone to come by the house late. They be at the club for dinner and she want to give Archie one last chance to go along with her plan. She say tell him to come down the alley and knock at the back door."

"Did he?"

"I don't know. She tell me not to come to work that next day, the day she takes Mr. Archie to the bus. That she wanted to be on her own for a bit."

"Did this surprise you?"

"Yes and no. She a private person. I 'spect she just wanted to have a good cry and nobody the wiser."

"Did she say why she sent Tyrone to Atlanta?"

"She make no mention of anything until the Army come looking for Archie."

"What was her reaction?"

"She say she's been a foolish, foolish old woman."

"Why?"

Viola shook her head again. "She don't say."

Thirty

Hugo pulled away from Viola's house deep in thought. At some time between the afternoon of September 12th and the morning of September 13th Archie had changed his mind about shipping out to Vietnam. What had brought that about? Or who?

He thought he knew the answer. That aside, who else knew of Ruth's plans for her grandson? Viola, for one. But she was loyal to both Ruth and Archie.

Tyrone was a loose cannon. Would he have spilled the beans on the plan, bragging to bolster his gangster image like he did about the supposed murder in Chicago or the wolf pelt for his coat? Even if he did, what would anyone in his circle care about the fate of a privileged white man?

Could Ruth have pulled this off without help? Bebe had put out feelers for Archie to have a safe harbor in Sherbrooke. It was time to hear her side of the story. He glanced down at his watch. It was after five o'clock already.

He looked over at Junior who was furiously making notes about the interview with Viola. "Have a patrol car pick up Bebe and bring her in for a statement."

Junior's head snapped up and he stared at Hugo. "Bad idea."

Hugo clenched his jaw and stared ahead into the gathering night as he drove to the police station. "Do it."

"I'll go get her."

"No, you will not. I want her picked up by a black and white."

"Hugo. . ." The protest died on Junior's lips.

⁂

HUGO STARED OUT the window of the squad room watching the sparse foot traffic on the sidewalk below. Usually at this hour the streets around the police station and the court house were deserted but a few parade goers had lingered downtown, perhaps having been to the afternoon movies then dinner at Morrison's.

It was nearly seven o'clock. The patrol car had been sitting on Bebe's apartment waiting for her to show up. Junior was at his desk mindlessly shuffling paperwork. Hugo knew why he didn't go home. He wanted to save his friend from the train wreck that was barreling toward them.

The phone on Hugo's desk rang and he crossed the room to answer it. It was the desk sergeant informing him that they had Bebe Prescott downstairs.

"Put her in interview room two." He dropped the receiver back into the cradle of the phone.

Junior stood, the nervous energy barely contained. "Don't do this, Hugo. At least bring her upstairs to the lounge."

Hugo took his sports coat from the back of his chair and put it on. "She lied to me, Junior. Now we have two dead bodies." He adjusted his tie. "She's not going to lie to me anymore."

"Think what you're doing. This is Bebe we're talking about."

"You should go on home. No need for you to get caught up in the back-lash of this."

Junior stared at the blotter on his desk for a long moment. Finally, he shrugged. "What are friends for?"

"I'm serious. All hell will break loose as soon as the chief finds out."

"Come on." Junior jerked his head toward the doorway. "Let's not make it worse by keeping her waiting." When Hugo made no move, he said. "It'll be okay. It's Bebe, remember?"

But Hugo knew it wouldn't be okay. He had gone a step too far. Now that he had set things in motion, he couldn't take it back. His anger and his ego had goaded him into this decision and he would have to see it through to the end.

She sat at the table with her entwined hands resting in her lap. Her gaze went from Hugo to Junior as they entered the room. The look she gave Junior was one of disappointment. She took a breath and released it, shook back her hair and stared straight ahead.

Hugo took a seat across from her. "Thanks for coming in, Bebe."

She studied him a moment. "I didn't have a choice, did I?"

"No. Not really. Do you want your lawyer with you? Or your father?"

"I'm not afraid of you, Hugo. And I don't need anyone to fight my battles for me."

"Is this a battle?"

"What else would you call it?"

"A murder investigation."

"And that justifies your behavior?"

"Two people are dead, so, yes, I'd say that justifies my actions."

"Two?" Bebe sat up a bit straighter in her chair, her hands palm down on the table, fingers splayed. "Who?"

"We'll get to that–"

"Archie!" She stood suddenly almost tipping her chair over with the force of her reaction. "Archie is dead?"

Hugo stood and stared across the table into Bebe's eyes wide with fright. "Why would you think I'm talking about Archie?"

"Is it Archie? For God's sake, tell me, Hugo!" She was trembling.

Junior moved to her side and gently took her elbow. "It isn't Archie, Bebe." He sent a scathing look at Hugo.

Bebe collapsed into the chair. Her face drained of color. She turned her profile to Hugo and blinked back the tears that had sprung to her eyes. "You bastard." Her voice was a harsh whisper.

Hugo sat back down and waited as Bebe regained control of herself. When she finally looked at him again he leaned forward, his elbows on the table, his chin resting on his clasped hands. "You lied to me."

She blinked rapidly then cleared her throat. "Not about anything that mattered."

He knew her answer encompassed more than the circumstances of the case but he refused to be distracted by her attempt to unsettle him. "You knew Archie was missing long before his grandmother died. You knew about the plan."

She lowered her gaze to the table. "I knew he was missing. Aunt Ruth told me. But I didn't know that until we went to lunch a week before her death. If there was a plan, I didn't know anything about it."

"That's not what Basile Moreau tells me."

She lifted her gaze. The ice in Hugo's eyes made her blink rapidly but she didn't look away. "I knew Archie didn't want to go back to school. He and Aunt Ruth argued about it over the 4th weekend. It frightened me that he would take such a risk. When I asked Basile about architecture firms in Sherbrooke, it was a spur of the moment thought. He had called me about something else and it occurred to me that Archie would have a bolt-hole if he was wrong about the draft."

"You said you didn't think Archie would shirk his duty."

"I didn't. When I told him about my conversation with Basile, he laughed at me. He said the whole point of skipping the final year on his doctorate was because he didn't want to be away from home anymore."

"Why didn't you tell me this at the Quarter Note?"

"I wanted you to find him. Aunt Ruth worried that something had happened to him. With her dead, no one knows where he is. What if something has happened to him? We would never know."

"And yet you chose not to tell me any of this. That he had been missing for two months."

"I was afraid."

"Of what?"

"I was afraid Aunt Ruth had taken things into her own hands. I didn't want to get anyone in trouble."

"She's dead. Murdered. I doubt the Army or the law could do anything more to hurt her."

"I didn't know who was involved in his disappearance. The Army has been snooping around looking for him all this time. I don't know what they would do to whoever helped him."

"Your father, you mean? Or Sharon?"

"I don't know. Whatever was going on, I was left out of the loop."

"You didn't ask your father after you discovered Archie was missing?"

She looked down at her clasped hands and shook her head.

"I find that hard to believe."

Bebe said nothing. Finally, she sighed. "I thought it would be better if. . ." she glanced at Junior, "if someone we knew found him."

"I suppose, by that, you mean someone you can control, manipulate."

"Hugo, that's not—"

"Someone who would find your missing *cousin* and turn a blind eye to the federal warrant for his arrest."

"Hugo! This is insane!" Her cheeks flamed with color. Her eyes narrowed. "I know better than anyone that you will do as you damn well please, no matter the consequences."

"You're telling me that the whereabouts of Archie Camden died with his grandmother?" Hugo looked down at the closed file setting in front of him. "Why do you think he was so dead set against returning to school when he only had a year to go? He was so close to reaching the pinnacle of his education."

"I honestly don't know. He was so happy this summer. The phrase carefree is so prosaic but it applied to Archie. This summer was. . ." She paused then shook her head. "He was all light and laughter. I've never seen anyone so happy."

Hugo sat back in his chair and stared at the peeling paint on the wall above Bebe's head. What made a man that happy? So happy that he would risk anything to cling to it with all his might? His gaze drifted down to Bebe's beautiful blue eyes. Love. Archie Camden was in love and he had been willing to risk everything to remain in the presence of the person responsible for that heady feeling.

"The two of you didn't talk about this sudden change of heart on his part?" Hugo could feel the beast welling up inside.

"No." Bebe stared down at her hands.

"No late-night confessions? No plans about what you would do?"

Bebe looked at him, her forehead creased with frown lines. "What are you talking about? What confessions? What plans? I told you. I don't know what made Archie change his mind. I don't know what Aunt Ruth planned for him."

"Did you help him with the house on Washington Square? Did you decide how the kitchen would look? Pick out new appliances? Decide where the nursery would be?"

Bebe stood abruptly. The bright pink fading from her face. "What are you saying, Hugo?"

He stood and came around the table. "You know what I'm saying."

Her lips formed a hard line, her eyes narrowed in anger. Her hand snaked out in a flash and she slapped him, the action quick and hot, the sound reverberating through the small room. "Archie's my cousin!"

Hugo didn't flinch or turn away from her anger. "Second cousin."

"You bastard!" She rushed toward the door which Junior opened for her.

Hugo made no attempt to stop her or follow her.

"What the hell, Hugo?" Junior stood in the doorway staring at him.

Hugo touched the knot of his tie. "Someone else knew about the plan. Ruth Camden couldn't work out all the details without help. We need to find out who that was." He turned toward the door. "We'll start with Haywood. I'll pick you up at eight in the morning." With that he left the room, went down the stairs, and out of the building into the embrace of a damp, chill winter wind.

Thirty-One

Hugo leaned against the tree trunk, the collar of his sports coat turned up against the cold wind, his hands deep in his pocket. This time he knew how he came to be where he wasn't supposed to be. He had suffered no black-out, no lost time. He had simply been incapable of altering his course. The pain had compelled him to come, to stand here in the night air waiting and wishing.

The Veterans' Day festivities at the club were winding down. He could still hear the faint sound of music from behind the closed doors. The occasional voice raised in laughter and farewell of the late crowd filtering out of the building in search of their cars reached him across the golf course.

Bebe would not be one of them. He knew this. And yet he came. He came and he stood in the cold night wind in penitence. He wanted to take it all back. The compulsion to race headlong into the destruction of the remnants of his relationship with her had been more powerful than his desperate need. His need to know, to be right, had forced him to tear the fragile thread that still bound them. Now they were no more.

Hugo doubled over at the waist. He thought he might be sick. After a while, he straightened, looked one last time at the soft glow of lights emanating from the hallowed halls of the *The Club*, and staggered through the stand of trees to his car.

✿

JUNIOR GOT INTO the car when Hugo pulled up in front of his house on this cold, crisp Tuesday morning. He had not rested well the night before and his grandmother had picked up on the fact that he was troubled. It wouldn't do for Hugo to come inside. Junior didn't think he would react well to Grammy's questioning and that's why he had waited for him out by the street.

He saw his grandmother looking out the window as they pulled away. Her concerns would have to keep. Junior glanced over at Hugo. His expression was unreadable.

Junior knew what it had cost Hugo to confront Bebe with what he most feared. That she was in love with someone else. He knew how it felt to hold on to that glimmer of hope. This investigation had forced Hugo to break that fragile lifeline.

It was no secret that Hugo had loved Bebe since they were in the fifth grade. At least not to Junior. She was a year younger than them and a year behind them in school. That year the fourth grade had been so small at St. Andrews that it had been combined with the fifth grade class. The following year a new teacher had been hired and the classes returned to a separate curriculum but those seven students remained where they were and graduated a year early.

Hugo's infatuation with Bebe began that first day of that school year. He never spoke of his feelings to Junior. The evidence was there for anyone to see who looked, to anyone who was observant, to anyone who really knew Hugo. Junior was an observer. He supposed that was what made him a half decent detective. But he didn't have to be a detective to know that Hugo's heart had suffered a near fatal wound the night before.

"So what's the plan?" he asked at last.

"Haywood. We'll go straight to his office. He's the one with connections, offices all over the world. It would be easy for him to set up a scheme to get Archie settled somewhere safe and comfortable."

"But wouldn't he know if Archie arrived? If he's safe? And wouldn't he tell Ruth and Bebe?"

"Something either went terribly wrong or they're all lying to us. I plan to find out which is the case."

Junior thought a moment before responding. "I don't think she was lying."

"Yeah?" Hugo bit out the word.

"You frightened her. She thought Archie was dead. There's no question her reaction was genuine."

"That doesn't mean she didn't know about the plan or where he was supposed to go."

"Okay. Supposing something went wrong, where do you think Archie is?"

"If Bebe's telling the truth and no one knows, then I think we probably have a third body."

"Why?"

"He would contact his grandmother. At the very least he would let her know he was safe. Too much time has passed. He wasn't the kind of man who would let her worry like this."

"Why kill him? What's the motive? He appears to have no enemies."

"To keep him from inheriting."

"I don't see how that benefits anyone particularly. Ruth's estate will be divided between family and a number of charities if he dies before her. All of them already have money and plenty of it. Who would kill him?"

"It's all tied up with the company and the voting shares. It has to be."

Junior saw Hugo's jaw clench. He had his teeth into a theory and didn't want to hear anything that would undermine that theory. But Junior wasn't convinced and he didn't think Archie was dead.

They parked a block down from the Waterman Building and were standing before Haywood Prescott's secretary at the stroke of nine. She looked far too pleased with herself when she replied to Hugo's request to see Haywood.

"He's not available."

"Make him available." Hugo's tone scotched her attitude.

"I can't. He's not in the office today."

"Where is he?"

"Paris."

Junior waited for Hugo's anger to spill over onto the secretary but it didn't. Instead Hugo became perfectly still, his gaze fixed on a painting on the wall behind the secretary's desk. The seconds ticked by.

"I want the name of the hotel where he's staying."

"He doesn't stay in a hotel. The company has an apartment near *Place des Vosges.*"

"An address and a phone number."

She hesitated then took out a directory from the top desk drawer. Quickly she scribbled the information on a notepad. With obvious reluctance, she tore the sheet from the pad and handed it to Hugo.

He stood a moment, staring down at the information. "When did he leave Mobile?"

Twiggy looked as though she would refuse for a split second but something about the look in Hugo's eyes changed her mind.

"Yesterday. He had an evening flight from Kennedy," she said. "Now, if you don't mind, I have work to do."

"The Japanese businessmen?"

A look of surprise passed fleeting across her face. "Enjoying San Francisco by now. They left yesterday as well."

Hugo gave Junior a look of satisfaction. Junior sighed inwardly. Hugo had the bit between his teeth and was ready to run with it.

⁂

AT THE STATION Hugo gave the note from Haywood's secretary to Junior. "We need to have someone at this address pronto. Archie is there, I know it."

"But who?"

"They have police in France, don't they?"

Junior looked at the note and shook his head. "But why? What do I tell them?"

"That we're investigating a homicide." Hugo glanced toward the chief's office. "And we need a search of this apartment."

"We don't have probable cause."

"Sure we do. The federal government has a warrant out for Archie. That should convince them to check it out."

"But that's a federal warrant."

"A warrant is a warrant. Get on the phone and find someone. We need to set this in motion before the chief's aware of it."

Junior looked across the squad room at the chief sitting at his desk in his office. He was on the phone.

Hugo saw the hesitation. "Look, the chief is trying to side-step the Prescotts. He doesn't want to know that they're involved. If he did, he'd have to act. By now Haywood's secretary has warned him that we're on to them. If we don't act now Archie is forever in the wind." He could see Junior weighing the cost to his career and livelihood. He felt a twinge of guilt but he couldn't stop. Not now, not after all it had cost him. "Come on, Junior. You know I'm right. I'll handle it but you've got to find me someone who speaks English."

"You're putting a lot of faith in my high school French." Junior picked up the phone and dialed for an outside line. He gave Hugo a look of resignation as he asked for an international operator.

Hugo swiveled his chair and looked at the notes taped to the wall. He moved the photo of Tyrone to the family group. Had Ruth really meant for Archie to go to Canada? Maybe as a jumping off point to throw off the Army.

Was Archie alive? Had he gotten it all wrong? He had been so certain it was about the voting rights for the company. If that wasn't the case, why kill Ruth?

They were back to square one.

Junior's voice faded into the background as Hugo concentrated on the bits and pieces of information they had gleaned thus far. He singled out each note and paired it with every other known fact. His gaze kept coming back to the empty safe. It didn't fit.

. . .tell him to come down the alley and knock at the back door.

Hugo sat forward in his chair. Someone would have heard the Barracuda at that hour of the night.

He jumped when Junior tapped him on the shoulder.

Junior had his hand over the mouthpiece of the phone.

"Inspector Victor Durand. His English is good but he has a lot of questions."

Hugo took the phone. "Inspector Durand. What do you need to know?"

"This Archie Camden, he is a fugitive of the Army, no?"

"Yes."

"But you are the civilian police?"

"That's true."

"Why then does not the military police seek this man? And would they not have personnel in place in France to facilitate your request? A liaison with our French military?"

"They do but this is a civil case. I think Mr. Camden is the key to locating the person who murdered his grandmother."

"Do you think he is the murderer?"

"No. But he's the key. If the Army gets their hands on him first, he'll be under federal jurisdiction."

"Um. And it is you who wishes to, as they say, crack the case."

"It's not that. Well, not entirely that. He's from a wealthy family. A powerful family. If I don't get to talk to him, we may never get the answers we need."

"Protected, eh?"

"Something like that."

There was a long silence on the other end of the line. Then Durand sighed. "I do not know how the *Sûreté Nationale* can be of service. There are international channels, *tu vois?*

Hugo's mind raced. How to convince this detective to his cause? "Two people are dead. This family has connections all over the world.

If Mr. Camden slips through our fingers now, we may never solve these murders."

"Two deaths?"

"Yes."

Another silence.

"A powerful family is not a good thing for one's career, eh?"

"Probably not."

"But you pursue this regardless?"

"Yes."

"It seems this is personal."

"Shouldn't murder be personal?"

Durand was silent for a moment.

"*Bien*. This I will do for you, Detective August. I will go to the address and see if this fugitive is there. If I find him, I will have no authority to arrest him. That is a jurisdictional matter beyond the powers of a mere detective of police."

"There's a federal warrant."

"That is of little use to me. But, *Monsieur Camden* does not know this, eh?" He sighed. "Since you are not going through the normal channels with the warrant, send the pertinent details and a photograph of *Monsieur Camden* by fax. As soon as I receive it, I will act upon your request."

"And Haywood Prescott?"

"That is another matter entirely. This tenuous action for *Camden* is as far as I am prepared to extend myself. Unless you can provide me with compelling evidence that *Monsieur Prescott* is your prime suspect?"

"No. Not at this time."

"*Très bien*. I will await the fax and act accordingly."

Hugo would settle for what he could get from Detective Durand. If he was right and Archie was in Paris, then he would be able to either link him to Ruth's death or discount him. He rolled a piece of stationary with the Mobile Police Department's logo as a header into his typewriter. He pecked out the information about Archie's AWOL status, the death of Ruth and its possible link to his flight to safety, and the suspected link with the second murder victim, Tyrone Pritchett.

He snatched the finished letter from the typewriter, signed it, took the photo of Archie, and disappeared down the hallway to the fax machine. He checked his watch. It was getting late in Paris. He hoped like hell that Durand would stick around for the fax to reach him.

When he returned to his desk, he placed the original letter in the bottom drawer of his desk and turned his attention back to the murder display. He tried to recapture the elusive thread his mind had been following before the phone call.

"August!" The chief stood in the doorway to his office.

Hugo saw the blood in the chief's eyes. In a low murmur he said to Junior, "I'll keep you out of it. Make yourself scarce."

Thirty-Two

Chief Goode glared at Hugo. He stood with his hands behind his back, his face red with rage, and rocked back on his heels. "Close the door."

Hugo did as he was ordered.

"Do you think I don't know what's going on in my own police department?"

"Chief—"

"That it wouldn't get back to me?"

"Look, Chief—"

"No, August, you look. And listen. I told you to tread lightly. And what do you do? You have a panda pick up Bebe Prescott at her apartment. The officers waited for an hour and a half in full view of all her neighbors." Goode paced. "Is that how you interpret my orders?"

Hugo gave a mental sigh of relief. For the moment it looked like he'd dodged a bullet. The chief didn't yet know about the call to involve the Paris police. "We have two murders, Chief. She's been lying to me since we discovered her aunt's body. I needed to rattle her."

"Well, all you've accomplished is to fire up the gossip mill. When Prescott hears about this, if he hasn't already, all hell will break loose." He held up his hand to keep Hugo from interrupting. "And as far as I'm concerned, the death of Pritchett is unrelated. He's a small-time drug dealer. You should be looking at that instead of trying to connect the two cases."

"He was the last known person to see Archie Camden."

"And that's another thing," the chief waggled his finger in Hugo's face, "Archie Camden is the problem of the Army. He's AWOL, not a murder suspect."

"I didn't say he was a suspect. But I think he's pivotal in discovering a motive."

"Motive." The chief spat the word. "We don't even have a clear cause of death."

"Poison." Hugo knew he was pushing the limit but he wasn't going to let the chief side-step the fact that Ruth Camden had been murdered.

The chief moved to the window and stared down at the street below. Finally, he pinched the bridge of his nose between fingers and thumb before turning back to Hugo.

"I want you to shake every bush in Mobile County starting with that bar-be-que joint. I want you to pull in every small time, dime-bag dealing, bottom-feeding, piece of scum in this city. Develop a time line of Pritchett's movements the past two weeks." He moved to his desk and sat down. "That's how you'll find his killer."

"And Mrs. Camden?"

"Get a damn toxicology report!"

The chief drew a file across his desk and opened it. Hugo took that as a dismissal and escaped before Goode decided to delve further into the status of the investigation.

⁂

JUNIOR STOOD ON Royal Street trying to decide the next logical move. Hugo had made up his mind on a course of action but Junior feared he was allowing his reason to be swayed by his emotions.

It occurred to Junior that he still needed to have a look at Ruth Camden's original will so he set off for Redman's office only to discover that he wasn't in. The secretary informed Junior that Mr. Redman had gone to the dentist and she didn't know when he would be back since he was suffering with a bad toothache. The office closed at two o'clock so she very much doubted he would return today.

Junior searched his memory for the secretary's name. "Brenda, isn't it?"

She smiled and nodded.

"I just need to get a copy of Mrs. Camden's original will. Mr. Redman told me she made some changes but that they were minor. Still, it might be helpful to know how minor."

"I wouldn't call a priceless piece of jewelry minor."

"Priceless?"

She leaned forward conspiratorially and spoke in a lowered voice. "I'd say. It's old but you wouldn't know it. It's what people would call timeless, I suppose."

"You've seen it?"

She nodded. "Mrs. Camden didn't want anyone to know she was the owner so she had Mr. Redman bring it to the office for the appraiser to photograph and determine the value."

"And what value did he come up with?"

Brenda hesitated.

"You might as well tell me. I'll find out eventually."

"One hundred thousand dollars." Her voice had dropped to almost a whisper.

"Wow. That must be some piece of jewelry."

"It's the most beautiful thing I've ever seen. Like water falling with every movement."

"And who was supposed to get it that, in the end, didn't?"

Brenda compressed her lips together and stared up at him.

Junior smiled. "I'll find out once I have a copy of the original will."

"Mrs. Marlowe."

Junior thought about that. "Who knew Mrs. Camden changed her will?"

Brenda shrugged. "No one unless she told them. Except Mr. Redman, of course. And me. I typed it up and witnessed Mrs. Camden sign it."

"And did you tell anyone, Brenda?"

She looked at him with a shocked expression on her face. "I never! I've worked for Mr. Redman since he left Haywood Mills and set up his practice. I'm bound by the same confidentiality as he is. I never discuss what goes on in this office. With anyone."

And yet she had just given Junior a heretofore unknown nugget of information. He let that little tidbit roll around in his thoughts then he asked, "When was it that Mr. Redman set up his office?"

"Right after Mr. Camden died. 1954 I think." Her brow furrowed. "Yes, 1954."

"But Mrs. Camden retained him for her personal attorney?"

"She was very loyal and a good friend. Besides, she thought Haywood Prescott treated Mr. Redman badly. He had worked for the company for ages. Simply ages."

"I see." Junior studied Brenda. "And you've worked for him all this time?"

"Yes."

"He keeps odd hours for an attorney, doesn't he?"

"I suppose. But most of his work has to do with estates and property. If he has to be in court, it's always Probate Court and usually in the mornings." She fidgeted with the items on her desk, the steno pad, pens, a ruler. "And he doesn't have very many clients."

"Oh? How many is not many?"

She clasped her hands together on the blotter as if to physically restrain her fidgeting. "I couldn't say."

"I'm not asking their names, just how many. Approximately."

She didn't answer immediately. Finally, with a sigh, she said, "Nine."

"Nine?"

She nodded.

"Only nine clients?"

"Since Mrs. Camden died, yes."

"How does he make a living with only nine clients?"

Brenda cleared her throat. "You'd have to ask Mr. Redman."

"Your salary, does he pay you for a full week?"

"It was never intended to be a full-time job. I have school kids—had school kids."

He wanted to ask her how much she made but refrained.

"Has he always worked such short hours?"

"No. When I first came to work here, I did the filing and ran errands to the courthouse or delivered documents to clients, notarized them, things like that."

"He had another secretary?"

"Yes. In the beginning."

"And a lot of clients?"

"Well, more than he has now."

"So, what happened?"

"They died." She frowned. "Not all at once, of course, but over the years."

"And he never added any new ones to his client list?"

"Only occasionally."

"Huh." Junior turned that information over in his mind, trying to determine if there was anything there. "Well, if you would, I'd like a copy of the old will for Mrs. Camden."

"I don't know." Her expression had turned more apprehensive with each of Junior's questions. "Mr. Redman might not like it."

"He gave me a key to Archie's house without hesitation. I doubt he'd mind. I can come back tomorrow, I suppose, but time is something I don't have a lot of. Why don't you just let me have it? After all, we have the current will."

"Well," she hesitated, then stood and went to the file cabinet. "I probably shouldn't be doing this."

"I'm sure it'll be fine. We'd get it in the end regardless because this is a murder investigation."

She turned from the file drawer and looked at him. "It's so hard for me to comprehend that she was killed. On purpose. She was just an ordinary woman, you know? And I knew her. You don't expect someone you know to be murdered."

"Yeah, I know. It always seems like that kind of thing is just something on the news, that it's unrelated to everyday life."

She pulled out a file and leafed through it until she had the document. She removed it from the binder and made Junior a copy.

Their conversation had somehow changed her demeanor. Perhaps it had made Ruth's death more real. Junior hesitated but didn't know what to say to alleviate the air of despondency that seemed to have settled around her. He tapped the document against his thigh and gave her a feeble smile.

"Thanks. This will save me another trip tomorrow."

Brenda nodded and tried to return the smile but there a look of worry on her face.

JUNIOR WALKED BACK to the station but didn't enter the building. Instead, he got in the police car and drove out Government Street to take a left at the Civil War canon at Houston. When he reached Halls Mill Road he took a right. The early crowd was already gathering at the Tiny Diny. In his need to escape his grandmother's concern, he had left home without his usual lunch.

He ordered the blue plate special with fried catfish and sweet tea. As he waited for his food, he let his thoughts return to the conversation with Brenda. Why hadn't Redman told them that he had once worked for the family business? He tried to recall the conversation in the lawyer's office on Monday after the discovery of Ruth's body.

I only deal with Ruth's side of things. That had been Redman's comment about documents related to the company. He had had a perfect opening to reveal he had once been one of the lawyers for Haywood Mills, maybe even *the* lawyer. True, fourteen years had passed but still it was interesting that he didn't think to mention it. Junior decided he was probably reading too much into the omission.

The waitress placed the steaming plate of hot food before him.

His mouth watered in anticipation and he put thoughts of Redman out of his mind.

HUGO KEPT ONE eye on the clock and the other on the chief. Time crawled. It had been over three hours since his conversation with Detective Durand and still no word. He had used the time to hound the forensic team in Auburn about the toxicology tests. They had given him a run-down of things they had excluded but that didn't help his case with the chief.

Hugo dared not leave the station. Why the hell didn't Durand call?

Patrol was working off a list of known associates of Tyrone's, bringing in a steady stream for questioning. He had obtained a search warrant for Abe's Bar-be-que. Junior was in the process of executing it now.

Hugo had interviewed the two men caught with Tyrone's car, Bennie Early and Hector Morgan. Both had sobered up and were anxious to be cut loose. Neither had anything new to add to their initial statements and he had decided not to press charges for the stolen car.

The best Hugo could determine, the Barracuda had been parked for two days at the ice house before they decided on a joy ride. There was no report from the ME yet on time of death but Hugo knew that the body had been there at least that long.

He looked at the grizzled old man sitting in a chair beside his desk. His hair was gray and a number of his teeth were missing but for all that, he had a strong build and he wasn't someone Hugo would want to meet alone in a dark alley. So far, the owner of Abe's Bar-be-que had given him precious little information.

"Look, Abe, things aren't looking so good for you right now. All those cigarettes in the false cabinet without a tax stamp are going to take some explaining. That's a federal charge you're facing. I'm sure they've found the moonshine by now, too. A little help from you would go a long way in good will before a judge."

Abe crossed his arms over his barrel chest and gave a single shake of his head. "I don't know what you're talking about. Ain't broke no law. I'm a upstanding businessman trying to get by."

"Well, from the wad of cash they found in an olive oil can, I'd say you're doing more than getting by."

"Ain't no law against having cash. I got a business to run. Don't trust no bank."

"Still, that's an awful lot of cash from selling bar-be-que."

"Been saving a long time."

"Ummm. And the cigarettes?"

"Don't know how they got there. Probably put there by the po-lice."

"Why would they do that, Abe?"

"Why white folks do anything? To keep the black man down."

"So, you being hauled into jail has nothing to do with your illegal businesses?"

"Like I say, my business is selling bar-be-que."

"With a little dope and cigarettes on the side."

"Anybody say I sell them dope?"

"What about Tyrone Pritchett?"

"What about him?"

"He spends a lot of time at your establishment."

"So do a lot of folks. Guess he knows good bar-be-que when he tastes it. Besides, I ain't seen him in a while."

"How long is a while?"

Abe shrugged. "Two, three days."

"And the two of you don't do a little business on the side?"

"Like I say—"

"Yeah, yeah, I know. You run a legit business. But Tyrone doesn't. He's been selling weed out of your place of business."

"News to me."

"And you just let a punk like that jeopardize your business? Let him sell drugs to the kids in your neighborhood?"

"I don't know nothin' 'bout that."

Hugo studied him. "Okay." He motioned for the officer who stood near the doorway of the detective squad. "Put him in a cell until the feds can collect him. We'll let them figure out the charges."

With a sigh, Hugo closed his notebook. He grudgingly acknowledged that the chief was right. They needed to nail down Pritchett's movements. It was possible that his death was connected to his drug dealing but Hugo didn't think so. Still, that possibility had to be discounted, just as Archie's vanishing act had to be explained.

Someone put a bullet through Tyrone's head and someone saw something. They always did. It was a tedious process of elimination. If he was right and Tyrone's death had nothing to do with his drug dealing, then whoever shot him knew what had happened to Archie. The question was, had they killed him too?

Hugo wanted to speak with Viola again to see what she knew of her nephew's movements in the days before his murder. It would also be a good idea to have her go through the Camden house with him and see if anything other than the butter pats was missing. After all the years she had worked for Ruth, she would know better than anyone, including Sharon.

Hugo glanced at the clock for the hundredth time. He was beginning to lose faith in the assertions of Detective Durand. Maybe he had decided that going against protocol was a step too far. He toyed with the idea of calling Buck Sissons.

The phone rang and Hugo snatched it up. "August."

The deeply accented voice of Victor Durand was a welcome relief. Hugo felt the tension ease in his shoulders but at the same time, a heightened sense of the chase made him sit forward in his chair.

"You will be disappointed, Detective August, that we did not find your man. Either of them. Neither *Monsieur Camden* nor *Monsieur Prescott* were at the apartment."

Hugo leaned back in his chair and ran a hand through his hair. "They knew you were coming."

"*Que?*"

"Prescott's secretary must have reached him by phone."

"No, no. You do not understand. No one was at the apartment. No one has been at the apartment for over a month. I asked the neighbor about the residents. She was very helpful. A young woman came in early October. American by her accent, and according to the neighbor stayed for two or three days."

"Who was she?"

"The neighbor did not know. She had seen her before but not in a long time."

"What did she look like?"

"Very attractive. Blonde and slender. Fashionable. Adequate French." The detective cleared his throat. "Let me see. Yes, yes. So, the neighbor, she gives me *le domestique*. How you say? The one who cleans?"

"Maid."

"Yes. Maid."

"And?"

"It took a bit of time to locate her. She was not at her residence when first we inquired. But when I did speak with her, she informed me of the arrangement with her employer. She cleans the apartment once a week. When someone will be staying, they call her and she lays in some provisions and makes sure the towels and bed linens are fresh, that sort of thing."

"Did she know the name of the visitor in October?"

"She did not see the visitor but knew she was coming. She brought in fresh bread, butter, coffee, the usual. It is always the way. It is usually businessmen but not always. She did not know the name of the woman."

"So, she prepared the apartment for Mr. Prescott's arrival?"

"That is the thing. She did not receive the call. No one was scheduled to arrive. There has been no guest since the woman in October."

"And you're sure no one has been there recently? Maybe the neighbor missed him."

"Forgive me, Detective August, but I have been at my job for a long time. The apartment has not been in use for some time. The maid allowed me inside to see for myself. I know the sense of absence in a space, *no?*"

Where was Haywood Prescott? Why had his secretary lied?

Hugo stared at the images and notes taped to the wall. "My apologies, detective. It's obvious my source lied about Prescott's whereabouts. I've wasted your time."

Detective Durand grunted. "It is the way of the chase, is it not? We must follow through with what we have and hope for the best. I have given my card to the neighbor and the maid. They will contact me if anyone shows up at the apartment."

"Thanks."

"*Bien.* It is no great sacrifice. The neighbor is most attractive."

Hugo allowed himself a smile.

Thirty-Three

Hugo needed to clear his head. He snagged his jacket from the back of his chair and headed downstairs. The day had warmed but this close to the river there was still a bite in the air. He crossed Royal Street and entered the courthouse. The clerk at the window of the records office summoned Judy Fohl from her domain deep within the court offices.

She smiled when she saw Hugo. "Well, well, you've just made my day. I heard you discovered a body yesterday."

"News travels fast."

"It's a small town. Besides—"

"People like to gossip."

Her smile broadened. "What can I do for you, handsome?"

"I don't know, exactly. I was hoping you might know something that would help the pieces fall into place."

Judy checked her watch. "I close up shop in less than an hour. Why don't we meet for a drink?"

Hugo nodded. "The Royal Flush?"

"Good a place as any."

Hugo walked west on Government Street past the bus station and the movie theater. Traffic was picking up as the work day neared its end. All of this barely registered. Where was Prescott? Maybe he never caught the flight from Kennedy. It could have been delayed. There was still the possibility that he would show up at the Paris apartment.

Regardless, there was nothing Hugo could do about it. The neighbor would call Durand. He had to be content with that.

He had been so sure they would find Archie. Why else would Haywood decide to make a spur of the moment trip? And it was spur of the moment. On Friday the secretary thought her boss would be at the hunting camp on Monday. Instead he put the Japanese on a flight to California and hopped a jet for New York. What had precipitated that hasty decision?

Hugo wanted Archie to be found. He wanted him to be alive. His gut was telling him that he was dead.

So, what now?

Tyrone. Determine who had last seen him. The best information they had was that he had visited Kwanita, his girl friend, on Friday morning. No one else they had pulled in for questioning admitted to having seen him after that.

Hugo crossed Government at the Elks's Lodge and started up North Jackson Street. Midway of the block the door of The Bird of Paradise burst open and a couple almost collided with him. They were well into their cups. In an instant Hugo realized it wasn't a man and woman. One of the men was dressed in drag. Hugo recognized Maurice. Their eyes met in a quickly averted glance before Hugo moved on toward the intersection of Conti. He had also recognized the man with Maurice. The problem Maurice had been unwilling to talk about, no doubt.

My, my, Hugo thought as he cut back down Dauphin headed toward the river. *We do live in interesting times.*

Judy was already at a booth near the back of The Royal Flush when Hugo entered the favorite watering hole for the lawyers, judges, and minions who worked the legal system. He slid into the seat across from her. The waitress placed a frosted mug of beer before Judy.

"No martini?"

"Too high class for this joint. They make a mess of it."

Hugo wondered how you could make a mess of gin with a splash of vermouth and an olive but he bowed to her superior knowledge of such things. He nodded to the waitress to bring him what Judy was drinking. "Thanks for meeting me."

"It's your dime."

Hugo decided it was a good thing he hadn't spent his last few dollars on gas for a wasted trip to Point Clear. He was thankful that it was only two days until payday.

"What do you know about Chief Goode?"

"Well," Judy lit a cigarette and blew smoke above Hugo's head, "he's been Chief for twelve years or so. He's probably a pretty good cop but he's a better politician."

"How's that?"

"Twelve years. That doesn't happen unless the right people are happy. And by the right people, I mean the city council and their supporters. And by that I mean their supporters."

Hugo grunted.

"You think he's protecting someone?"

"I didn't say that."

"But you think it."

"I think he's being very cautious. Like I said, he's a good politician." She took a drink of her beer. "But if I were you, I'd keep those thoughts to myself."

"Noted."

"What else can I do for you?"

"Tell me about Trey Whitehall."

Judy studied him for a minute. "New in town. Sent down here by his daddy to keep an eye on the family money." She inhaled on her cigarette and let the smoke slowly drift from her mouth and nostrils. "But that's not what you want to know."

"I heard he had a thing for Bebe Prescott."

"So that's what's got you looking so hang dogged."

Hugo looked away from her scrutiny, his gaze following the movements of the waitress.

Judy sighed. "He probably does. Half a dozen men, at any given time, have a thing for Bebe."

"Is there anything to it?"

"Not my bailiwick. I hear the gossip but I don't run with the Old Mobile crowd." She stubbed out her cigarette in the ashtray as the waitress placed Hugo's beer before him. "What does any of that have to do with your murder case?"

"Double murder."

"I see." She sat back against the vinyl of the booth and gave this turn of events some thought. "How are they connected?"

"That's what I can't figure out."

"But you're certain that they are?"

"Yes."

"Well, then, I'd better keep my ears open." She shook another cigarette from the pack. "I did hear that the attorney general came down from Montgomery. He's been bending the chief's ear lately. He's not happy about something."

"Like what?"

"I don't know but I suspect there's a grand jury on the horizon."

"Good to know." Hugo took a long drink of his beer. It was ice cold. That was the only thing the Army had gotten right in Vietnam. Base camp always had plenty of cold, cold beer. The problem had been that most of the grunts had had precious little time at base camp. Only the brass and their underlings remained in the rear with the beer.

He replaced the frosted mug on the table precisely in the wet ring it had already created. "The thing I can't get a handle on is the voting shares for Haywood Mills. If Haywood holds sway over Sebastian and Sharon votes with Ruth, then they're at a stalemate."

"And the only way for Haywood to break the stalemate is by gaining control of Ruth's shares."

"Exactly. But she left them to Archie so that doesn't solve the problem."

"But Archie is missing."

They sat in silence for a while, each pondering the problem and drinking their beer.

Hugo leaned forward, his elbows on the table. "Do me a favor?"

Judy eyed him a moment then smiled. "Since it's you asking."

"Who controls Ruth's vote if Archie isn't found? There has to be some provision in the documents of incorporation."

"Possibly. If the lawyers thought that far ahead to such an eventuality. I can check."

"What happens if they didn't?"

"That's an easy one. They battle it out in court."

"But what happens to the operations in the meantime? How can they conduct business?"

"You might get lucky and convince Haywood to tell you but if I were you, I'd ask Ruth's lawyer." She drained her glass, gathered her cigarettes, and put them in her purse. "I'll see what I can find and give you a call tomorrow."

She slid out of the booth and left. Hugo sat back and listened to the Mamas and the Papas as the waitress leaned over the jukebox and fed quarters into the machine. She had long, shapely legs and a very short skirt. Hugo decided to have another beer.

HE SHOULDN'T HAVE had the third beer, Hugo decided. And definitely not the fourth and fifth. He had no memory of a sixth but probably there had been. Roxanne hadn't finished her shift at the Royal Flush until ten and he'd had to fill the time.

He stood in the shower and remembered what he could of the evening. In the cold light of morning the smudged eye-liner of the Cleopatra eyes and tangled mess of teased hair no longer bore any resemblance to Elizabeth Taylor. He had eased out of her bed and made his escape without waking her.

It wasn't that Roxanne wasn't attractive. She was. Or that she wasn't willing. She had been. Their romp had been mutually satisfying in the casual, here today, gone tomorrow culture of the moment. There would be no weepy eyes, no longing looks when next he strolled into the Royal Flush. Just two stones sparking against each other when tumbled together in passing. It was the hollow feeling that came afterwards that he knew was ridiculous. The irrational feeling of a small regret, another chip against his tarnished armor, that he now pushed from his thoughts.

His clothes smelled of cigarette smoke. He hung his sports coat and slacks across the railing of the back porch to air as he went about brewing a pot of coffee. He really needed to get a replacement for his winter coat and pants. Mobile rarely suffered more than a few days of intense cold weather. But even here, in the sub-tropics, a damp chill persisted downtown because of the river and the bay.

In the bedroom he retrieved his wallet. Four dollars and twenty-seven cents was all he had left. It was a good thing tomorrow was payday.

At seven thirty he called Junior and told him to meet at the Camden house. They needed to question the neighbors about sounds in the night. If Tyrone had followed Ruth's direction to visit her late on the evening before Archie's departure, surely someone heard something.

Next, he called the switchboard at the station and asked the operator to alert him of any calls through dispatch to Junior's radio. He didn't hold out much hope that Detective Durand would reach out with news that Haywood had appeared on the scene at the Paris apartment but he wanted to know immediately if it happened.

He would pay Twiggy a visit after the re-canvas of the crime scene and one of them was going to be very unhappy when he left.

THEY STARTED FROM either end of the block, working their way toward Ruth's house.

Talmadge remembered hearing a loud muffler late one night but he couldn't remember the date. He had been listening to the classical music station and when he turned it off and was preparing for bed, he heard the deep rumble. The sound came from the rear of the house and that gave him a moment of unease. He had looked out his second story bedroom window to see the running lights of a car that was just turning out of the alley onto the side street.

He had debated calling Ruth to see if everything was all right because he knew the car. He had seen it when the driver occasionally picked up Ruth's maid. Despite the late hour, he called because he knew he wouldn't sleep with the worry on his mind.

Ruth told him that she had been out to dinner and that Tyrone had come by to pick up some items to take to Catholic Charities to be priced for the annual fund raiser. She apologized for the late hour and having disturbed his sleep.

"How long was the car there?" Junior asked as he scribbled in his notebook.

"I don't know. I only heard it when it was leaving. I suppose the radio drowned out the noise when he arrived."

"And what time was this?"

"Just before eleven. I remember because it was the lateness of the hour that caused me to be concerned. Workmen come and go during the day but it's rare that anyone is on the lane in the evening."

No one answered the door at the next house so Junior moved on to Aimeé Marlowe's. He identified himself when she answered the door.

"What happened to the other one?"

"Ma'am?"

"The other detective. August."

"He's working the other end of the block."

She studied Junior then held the door wide. "Well, come in then. No point in letting all the heat out."

They went into the living room where she had a low flame licking the fake logs in the fireplace. The house had a Mediterranean look to it, the furnishings ornate, sofas and chairs overly plumped and rounded. There was a profusion of knick knacks and works of art mounted so numerous that there was very little wall space visible. Two chairs were angled comfortably on either side of the fireplace, a richly colored wrap was thrown across the matching footstool of one of them. A small table drawn up to this chair held a decanter of liquor with a matching glass of cut crystal. There was also a box of chocolates with the lid loosely placed on the top. It all looked rather rich and indulgent to Junior's eye.

"So, have you come to tell me you've found Ruth's murderer?"

"Not yet."

"Then why are you here?"

"Just double checking some facts."

She waited in silence.

"Were you home on the night before Archie's departure to basic?"

Her eyebrows shot up in a look of surprise. "That was months ago." She sat back in her chair, entwined the fingers of her hands, and laid them across the little pooch of her stomach. "I don't recall."

"You weren't aware of the departure date?"

"Well, not specifically. I know it was early September."

"I don't understand. I was led to believe that you and Mrs. Camden were very close."

"We were."

"Yet the date her grandson left for the Army made no particular impression on you? Even though Mrs. Camden was terribly upset by the occasion, had tried repeatedly to find some way to keep it from happening?"

Something changed in her eyes. "Well, of course, I was aware. It's just that the calendar date isn't committed to memory. I have always been there for Ruth."

"But you can't remember whether or not you were home the night before he left town?"

"I was home. I'm sure I was home." She smiled at him. "Where else would I be?"

"You didn't go to dinner with the family at the club?"

"No." She fell silent, her gaze fixed on the flames of the fireplace. "I was meant to go but I had been working in the flower beds all week with the yard man getting everything ready for winter. My arthritis was acting up." She rubbed her gnarled hands together and looked up at him with a hint of a smile. "I brewed myself a little herbal tea to ease the pain. Then I took a long, hot bath."

She reminded Junior of a cat, serene, content, watchful.

"Did Mrs. Camden have any visitors that evening?"

"Archie, I imagine. He was living downtown on Washington Square. It would be on his way to pick her up."

"But you don't know for certain."

"No."

"Did anyone else come by her place, to your knowledge?"

She shrugged. "Sharon, perhaps. Or any of the other family members. I couldn't say."

"You didn't hear anything? Any cars coming or going?"

"She lives two houses down. Margaurite Golding would be better able to tell you about that."

"Nothing in the alley out behind the houses?"

"If there was, I didn't hear it. I went to bed early and turned on the electric blanket to ease my stiff joints. My bedroom is on the front of the house so I wouldn't have likely heard anything out back."

Junior looked down at his notes, trying to decide just what it was about Aimeé Marlowe that struck him as a little off. He realized that for all her wispy white curls, bright blue eyes, and shy smile, he simply didn't like her.

"Have you seen the cat?"

She blinked slowly, almost owlishly to Junior's mind. "Beauregard?"

"Yes. Beauregard.

"No. I told the other detective."

"I thought he might have found his way back to the area after all this time. I understand he was drawn to the goldfish in your fountain."

"If he did, he didn't come into my yard."

⚜

HUGO HAD EVEN less luck than Junior. All the neighbors to the west of Ruth either couldn't remember what they were doing on the night of September 12th or they hadn't heard anything in the late evening.

It was obvious from Mr. Talmadge's statement that Tyrone had entered and left the alley from the east side street. Whatever he and Ruth had talked about at that meeting had sent him to Atlanta.

Hugo decided they needed to interview the girlfriend again.

Thirty-Four

Kwanita, also known from her school records as Joanne, lived on Herman Street. Three little stair-step children played in the dirt patch of a front yard. They stopped and gaped at the two white men who got out of the Thunderbird, their ball rolling into the street unheeded.

No one answered the knock until Hugo banged on it for the third time. Kwanita appeared in a fleece bath robe, her hair done up in a bright yellow print turban tied in a complicated knot. She recognized Hugo and turned from the door, leaving it open for him and Junior to follow her into the house.

She was a very attractive woman, tall and slender, her skin the color of caramel. Hugo could see that she had been crying. She crossed the room to a couch on the far side where a lit cigarette rested in the ashtray with an open Budweiser beside it. She drew her feet up under her and waited.

"What time did Tyrone leave here on Friday?"

"I already told you."

"Tell me again."

"After ten. He went to the store and got cereal and what not for the kids. At the Piggly Wiggly. He sat in the kitchen with them and they all ate. Made a right mess."

"And after?"

"Said he had business to take care of, needed to straighten out a misunderstanding. Say ain't no man gone play him the fool."

"What kind of misunderstanding?"

"I already told you. He don't tell me his business."

"He didn't come home afterwards?"

"That's the last I seen him."

"Tell me about Mrs. Camden."

"Who?" She raised her brow and tilted her head, a bored look on her face.

"The lady who died just over a week ago."

"I don't know nuthin' about nobody dyin'."

"Tyrone worked for her."

"Tyrone don't work for nobody."

"In September. He took a little trip out of town. Gone for about a week. Ring a bell?"

She lifted one shoulder in a shrug, turned her profile to them and took a drag off the cigarette.

"She bought him the car. The Barracuda."

She cut her eyes at Hugo then looked away again but said nothing.

"When he came home, he bought you the TV." Hugo looked around the room. The furnishings appeared too new to have endured three small children for very long. A mirror on one wall was made of brass and had spiked rays radiating from the center. On the floor, a zebra print rug covered part of the worn plank boards. The television in a huge cabinet held pride of place on the opposite wall. "Looks like he spent a lot of money on you."

"What?" She faced him now, fury in her expression. "A black woman can't have nice things? I'm supposed to be all meek and 'yes, suh, no suh'? Whatever you say, honky?"

"You're supposed to want to help us find out who killed him."

"Why? That gone bring him back? That gone pay my rent?"

Hugo studied her, then shrugged. "Right. He was just a meal ticket. Someone to buy you nice things, pay the rent. Why else would you be with a man like that, acting like a big dog when he was only the runt of the litter?"

She leapt from the couch like a mighty bronzed Valkyrie rising, her hand the avenging sword poised to slay the blasphemer. Hugo caught her wrist just before the palm connected with his cheek.

"You bastard!"

"That, I am. But I'm the bastard who's going to catch whoever killed Tyrone."

The silent tears trailed down her face and she jerked free of Hugo's grip. "Why do you care? He's just a dog shit on your shoe. Good riddance to the white man."

"I know about killing, Kwanita. Taking a man's life is no small thing. I will find him and he will pay."

She turned her back to them and used the lapel of her bath robe to dry her tears. When she faced them again, she cleared her throat and said, "Wait here." Capitulation strangled the words, rent the clothing, reduced her to ashes. It was the same admission of futility that had played out across the course of her young life.

A hallway ran along one side of the house and she disappeared down it. In a couple of minutes, she returned. She held out her hand and opened it. The coins caught the light and it radiated from her palm. Nestled there were five fifty-dollar American Eagle coins and two Canadian Maple Leafs.

"On Friday he give me these. Hide'em, he said. For a rainy day. Don't try to spend them. Folks ask too many questions. Trade'em for cash if things get desperate."

"Where did he get them?"

"He didn't say." She looked at the gold cupped in her hand and tears filled her eyes again. "She bought him the car. At first, he wouldn't tell me but one night he got high and said she needed him to deliver something for her. That the car was payment."

"Where was he supposed to make the delivery?"

"He wouldn't tell me. He just laughed and smiled that secret smile." A wistful look came into her eyes. "The end of August he make a trip. Say he's going north for a while. A week later he's was back. Then in a couple weeks he get up one morning real early and left. Kiss me on the cheek and say he'll be gone a few days."

Hugo took one of the coins from her hand and examined it. The gold gleamed at him, shiny and pure. It had a light of its own, deep within, like a living thing. He placed it back in her palm. "Keep it somewhere safe. Somewhere no one would think to look."

She closed fist and drew it to her chest, hugging the coins there. "You ain't gone take it?"

"No. Keep it. Use it wisely. Use it for the kids."

She stared after him as he and Junior turned and left the house.

⁂

"THE SAFE," JUNIOR said as they got back into the car. "That's what Ruth had in the safe."

"Yes." Hugo mentally cursed. He had found the pen advertising Midtown Coin and Stamp Company in Tyrone's car two days ago but had failed to see the significance. He turned the Thunderbird west and sped toward Airport Boulevard and Williams Street.

"How did he get them? Do you think Ruth gave them to Tyrone?"

"No."

Junior was silent for several blocks. "They were for Archie. To bank roll his new life."

"Probably not in the beginning. I imagine she's been stock piling for a long time. We have to remember she lived through three wars. She saw the devastation in Europe, France in particular. Desperate people without the means to escape."

"But she was safe in the states. All those wars were fought on someone else's turf."

"And yet, Archie, her last link to her husband and her son, the last of her immediate family, left on a bus two months ago to serve in yet another war far from home. It wasn't her personal safety that she was worried about."

"You think there were a lot more coins in the safe?"

"I think it was probably full or close to it."

"It's a big safe."

"Yes, it is."

They rode in silence until they reached the intersection at Holcombe Avenue. Junior had been glancing through his notebook. "Do you think that's all the coins Tyrone left with Kwanita?"

"I sincerely hope not."

⁂

THE COIN SHOP was across the street from Korbett's Restaurant just past the railroad tracks. Sly Rotterman pushed the buzzer that released the locking mechanism on the door of his establishment when Hugo held his shield against the glass. His eyes shifted back and forth between Hugo and Junior as they approached the counter behind which he stood.

"Officers." He bobbed his head in greeting. "What can I do for you?"

Junior ran his eye over the various coins on display in the case before him. "How's business these days, Sly?"

"Can't complain."

"Been buying a lot of gold lately?"

"Some."

During this exchange Hugo wandered the store, looking into cases that contained old coins, silverware, some jewelry, a hand mirror with a 1920's motif worked into the silver backing. There was a section near the back away from the windows with row upon row of stamps. Sly followed his movements with quick glances.

"How much is some?" Junior asked.

"A bit more than usual, I guess. Times are tough what with Brookley in the process of closing. People are trying to get cash ahead of the squeeze."

"Everything on the up and up?"

"Yeah. Sure. I don't deal with people I don't know."

Hugo had made the circuit of the room. He took the photo of

Tyrone from his inside pocket and dropped it on the glass case in front of Sly. "You know this man?"

The hesitation was a mere blink of the eye but both Junior and Hugo registered it.

"Could be," Sly said.

"Either you do or you don't." Junior pushed the photo closer. "He has a very distinctive face."

"Yeah. Yeah, he came in with some coins."

"How many?"

The hesitation was longer this time. "Is this the guy on the news? The one they found dead at the old ice house?" Sly looked from Junior to Hugo and back. "Coins are the same as cash, you know. You don't have to have proof of ownership."

"How much did he sell you?"

Junior could almost see the calculations going on behind Sly's beady, dark, simian eyes. How much did he have to own up to? What figure would hide how much he had fleeced Tyrone?

Hugo stabbed the photo with his forefinger. "He's dead, Sly. Do you really want to come under the microscope in a murder investigation?"

Sly took a handkerchief from his back pocket and wiped his brow. "Okay, okay. He came in here maybe two weeks ago. Had a hundred Maple Leaf coins. They're more pure than the Eagle. Ninety-nine point nine nine percent."

"Fifty-dollar denominations?"

Sly nodded. "Look, the value of gold is way down. Less than forty-five dollars an ounce. I explained that to him. Just because it's a fifty dollar coin doesn't mean it's worth fifty dollars."

"How much did you shave off the value?"

His gaze skittered around the room. "It's a buyer's market, you know? It isn't against the law to offer a low bid."

"How low?"

He sighed. "Thirty dollars a coin."

Hugo whistled softly. "That's a good twenty-five percent discount."

"He could have gone somewhere else. Pensacola has a dealer. Or New Orleans."

"But you convinced him he wouldn't get a better price."

"It's the truth. As I said, it's a buyer's market."

"You gave him three thousand dollars for his coins?"

"That time."

Hugo and Junior exchanged looks. "He sold more to you?"

"Last Friday."

"Total?"

"Almost seven thousand, all in all."

"That's a lot of coins. It didn't occur to you that there might be something not quite legal about a man like Tyrone having that many valuable gold coins?"

"Like I said, gold is legal currency. Possession is ownership under the law. Besides, I gave him a better price on the last batch. He had a ten-dollar 1933 Indian head gold eagle in the lot."

"Worth what?"

"Depends on the collector."

"Guess."

"Five hundred or more."

"For one coin?"

Sly nodded.

"Let's see it."

Sly hesitated and Hugo leaned a little closer. Sly stepped back and went to a long heavy drape hanging across windows at the back of the room. When he pulled at the edge of the fabric, it glided easily to reveal that it didn't conceal windows after all, but a big walk-in safe.

With a glance over his shoulder, Sly spun the dial a few times and opened the vault. His hand went straight to the desired coin. He placed it on Hugo's palm.

The coin was moist with sweat. Hugo noted that Sly's upper lip was dotted with perspiration as well. He returned his attention to the coin. It bore the image of Lady Liberty wearing an Indian headdress.

In an arc above her head were thirteen stars. The back side depicted the American eagle.

Hugo flipped it into the air and caught it. He watched Sly's face as he did so and saw the hungry way he followed the coin twisting in the air. He gave it to Junior to examine.

"I don't suppose you explained to Tyrone the enhanced value of such a rare coin."

"I told him it was unique. That I didn't often come across one. That's why I gave him a little extra."

Sly never took his eyes off the coin.

When Junior had finished examining it, he placed it on the glass counter. Before Sly could scoop it up, Hugo placed his hand over it and slipped it in his pocket.

"Hey!" Sly's small round eyes widened. "You can't take that!"

"I'm confiscating it as evidence."

"Of what?" A look of belligerence darkened Sly's fleshy cheeks.

"Didn't I say?" Hugo raised a brow. "We're investigating Tyrone Pritchett's murder. I think he was killed over these coins."

"Why that one? Why not the others?"

"I think this one will be sufficient for the court. But I'd be glad to take the others, if you like."

Sly's face was beginning to mottle with outrage. "I'm trying to run a business here. I paid for those coins."

"I'm trying to solve a murder. I sincerely hope I don't have to revisit my thoughts on your involvement."

With effort, Sly held back a retort.

Hugo sauntered out of the shop with Junior close behind.

They sat in the car and watched through the storefront as Sly locked down the safe and pulled the heavy curtain back into place.

"You think he had anything to do with it?"

Hugo shook his head. "He's just a jungle rat looking out for number one. There's no way he thought those coins belonged to Tyrone."

"The Indian eagle, you think it's worth what he said?"

"I think it's worth a hell of a lot more."

"When did you learn so much about gold coins?"

"I don't know much at all about gold coins. I know a little about people. Sly couldn't take his eyes off it. He's kicking himself right now for bringing it up but he couldn't help himself. It's the same as gossip. Some people can't resist the self-congratulatory pat on the back. He had to crow a little about his find."

"Why did he let on to Tyrone then? Why didn't he just keep his mouth shut and gouge him on it since it's only a ten dollar coin? Tyrone wouldn't know the difference."

"Greed. He wanted Tyrone to keep coming back. He sensed that Tyrone had a lot more stashed somewhere and that if he threw him an occasional bone, he would be perceived as doing right by him."

"You think Tyrone had more?"

"Some. But whoever killed him has the bulk of it."

Junior grunted. "You hungry?"

"I hadn't thought too much about it."

"Let's cross the street since we're here and eat at Korbett's."

"I'm broke."

"My treat."

Hugo turned the key in the ignition. "Could you spot me ten until tomorrow?"

Junior took out his wallet while Hugo navigated across the four lanes of traffic to the restaurant.

HUGO CALLED THE station from the pay phone at Korbett's. There was no message from Detective Durand.

They were seated in a booth and placed their lunch orders. Hugo took out his notebook and began skimming through the pages.

"Let's assume that Haywood left town in search of Archie. Something happened to prompt him to change his plans with the Japanese and hop a flight to New York, and from there to Paris. Supposedly. If that's the case, then the family still thinks Archie is alive. We know that as of late yesterday, Haywood had not arrived in Paris. Where is he?"

Junior sighed and shook his head. "The old will left an expensive necklace to Aimeé Marlowe. The secretary said it was valued at a hundred thousand dollars. Can you believe that? We don't know why Ruth changed her mind. She doesn't seem the type to do so in a snit over Mrs. Marlowe's lack of compassion. Something motivated her."

Hugo sat back against the high seat of the booth, closed his eyes, and listened to Junior's recitation of the facts.

"Someone knew that Ruth had a safe full of gold. Some of it wound up in Tyrone's pockets. Who would have known about the gold? Everyone in the family seemed to think she kept her valuables in the bank. Is one of them lying? Are all of them lying?

"Ruth made elaborate plans to slip Archie out of the country so he wouldn't have to go to Vietnam. She had to have had help. No one claims to know anything about her intentions except Sharon.

"We know Archie was on the bus to Atlanta. He was observed by three witnesses. A woman got on the bus in Montgomery and rode the rest of the way in the seat next to Archie. Was it a stranger? Was it Bebe? No one has identified the female passenger.

"Ruth was poisoned. Tyrone was shot in the head. Did the killer change his M.O.? Do we have two killers?" Junior sighed again. "This case is all over the place. We're making no headway. We don't even know what was used to poison Ruth."

Hugo wasn't as pessimistic as Junior. The dots were beginning to connect. There was something he had missed or discounted, something like the pen advertising the gold dealer. That something teased at the fringe of his thoughts. It was there in the mist slowly creeping in from the jungle. The killer thought he was hidden from view but Hugo could sense him. He had to let the target emerge from the undergrowth of odd facts and bits of gossip. It would come to him. He slowly opened his eyes.

The waitress placed a plate of hamburger steak with mashed potatoes before him. He was starving. "Let's eat."

Thirty-Five

Twiggy wasn't happy to see Hugo come through the doors of Haywood Enterprises. Her mouth thinned to a fine line. But her eyes gave her away. Something had put a chink in her badass, career girl, tell'em like it is and make'em like it, attitude.

"Where is he?" Hugo asked.

Pale as she was, she noticeably blanched.

"I don't know."

"Have you talked to him?" Hugo held up a finger in warning. "And don't lie to me."

"No."

"Is that normal? Does he go off like this routinely?"

"No."

"What was his excuse for going to Paris?"

Tears almost formed in her big, wide, eyes with the spiked eyelashes. Almost but not quite. "He didn't say. He just called and told me to change the reservations for the Japanese. Get them on a plane on Monday. Then book a flight to Paris for him."

"Only him?"

"Yes."

"And he gave you no reason for any of it?"

"None."

"You didn't ask?"

"He's the boss."

"And you haven't talked to him at all since that conversation? You didn't call the apartment and warn him that I was looking for him?"

"No. He called me at home Sunday afternoon from the camp. Told me to go to the office and make the arrangements. That he planned to be back in town late Thursday. Cancel everything until Friday afternoon."

"So he should be arriving tomorrow night."

"Yes."

Hugo thought about that. "Did you leave a message for him in Paris? At the company offices or with the maid who looks after the apartment?"

"No." She paused.

Hugo could see the internal debate.

"I tried the apartment. And I called the vice-president at the company offices. No one there knew he was coming."

"Is that unusual? Was he prone to surprise visits?"

"Everything is always planned out in advance so the necessary company officers and information is waiting for him when he's needed over there." Those almost tears rimmed her eyes again. "He always checks in when he's out of the country." She made a feeble gesture with her hand. "You know, the old feeling that things would fall apart without his personal oversight of every little detail." Her forehead creased with worry lines. "But not this time."

"It's only been two days."

She nodded. "I suppose you're right."

"Maybe he didn't want anyone to know where he was or what he was doing. Maybe he's off with a friend, enjoying a little R and R."

Twiggy glared at him. "I don't think so."

"And you would know?"

Her cheeks blushed a bright pink but she said nothing.

⚘

JUNIOR WAITED IN a little ante room off the vestry of Holy Spirit Catholic Church. Father Ambrose would be with him momentarily he had been told by the church secretary. The silence settled around him and Junior relaxed. He had always felt at peace when he was in the church. Something about the silence, the muted light, and the tall ceilings arching toward the heavens did that, he supposed. He relaxed and waited.

Father Ambrose was not what he had expected. For one thing, he was young. For another, he was strikingly handsome with dark Mediterranean coloring. Junior felt the incongruity of the priest's appearance and his purpose. He supposed one did not exclude the other but it seemed not right somehow.

He tried to imagine Ruth Camden confiding her fears and her sins to this man but couldn't quite picture it. A swarthy Errol Flynn would not inspire thoughts of God and piety in the breasts of many women, he thought. Either because his appearance kept him too grounded in the here and now, the earthy nature of life, or because his youth and beauty did nothing toward reflecting the gravitas of religious duty and wisdom.

"Detective Knight?" The priest extended his hand in greeting.

"Father. Thanks for seeing me."

"Of course. You have questions about Ruth Camden?"

"Yes."

"There's little I can tell you except she was kind, generous, and deeply grounded in her faith."

"She was regular in her attendance?"

"Yes. Five o'clock mass. I don't recall a single absence during my time here."

"How long have you been the priest at Holy Spirit?"

"Almost two years."

His answer surprised Junior. A priest so young in charge of one of the largest Catholic parishes in the city was unusual.

"Ties to the community? Family?"

Father Ambrose smiled. "No."

"Huh."

"I am not as young as I appear, Detective, and I did not come to this parish by any means other than the will of God."

"I wasn't implying that you had, Father. I'm just trying to establish how well you know the temper of your congregation, so to speak."

"You'd be surprised how quickly one can get up to speed with, as you put it, the temper of his flock, when regularly hearing their confessions."

"Then you should know what was on Ruth's mind in the last days of her life."

"I cannot speak to the specifics of the confessional but I will say that she was troubled. She worried about her grandson. Her son died in Korea, as you may know, and many relatives living in Europe died or were displaced during the two world wars."

"I'm aware of all that. What I need to know is what Ruth was thinking along the lines of how to keep Archie safe."

"The military was here before you, Detective. I know that Archie is AWOL. I had no answers for them and I have no information for you."

"We have no way of informing him that his grandmother is dead."

"I've been made aware of that fact. Still, I cannot help you."

"Because you don't know?"

"Are you Catholic, Detective Knight?"

"From the cradle."

"Then you know this is an exercise in futility. Nothing Ruth confessed to me will ever be repeated. I pray each day for Archie. I hope he is well and safe."

Junior knew there was no way around the sanctity of the confessional and he wasn't going to waste his time trying.

"Did she attend mass on the Friday before her death?"

"Yes."

"Did she seem unduly upset or troubled?"

"Not that I saw."

"Did she make any mention of plans for the evening? A social engagement? Anything like that?"

"Not to me."

"Did you speak to her?"

"I did."

Junior fell silent for a moment then smiled at the priest. "Thanks for your time, Father." As they shook hands, he asked, "You're accent. I can't quite place it."

"Fréjus, Provence."

"Right."

※

ON THE SURFACE, nothing of value had been gained by Junior's conversation with Father Ambrose except to establish that Ruth was alive and well at five o'clock on the Friday evening of her death. But something stirred in the recesses of Junior's memory. He turned toward downtown and the police station.

He dug Ruth's old will out of the case file and read through it. Then he took out the copy of the current will and found what he was looking for. She had left a piece of property in Provence, France to one Ambrose Enzo Caron. It was listed as a minor property consisting of a cottage and small orchard. One of the minor bequests, no doubt, that Redman had informed them of.

Junior decided he needed to speak with Redman again. He glanced at his watch. If he hurried he could catch the lawyer before he left the office.

The secretary was coming down the stairs as Junior entered the lobby of the Van Antwerp Building. He groaned in disappointment.

Brenda chuckled. "He's still up there. You'll have to bang on the door because I locked it on my way out."

"Thanks." Junior held the exterior door for her.

It took three tries to get Redman to respond to his knock. Junior heard the key turn in the lock and the door jerked open, Redman's face a thundercloud of annoyance.

"What!"

His expression changed as soon as he realized that it was the police calling. Again.

"Sorry to bother you, Mr. Redman."

Redman ushered Junior into the reception area with a jerk of his head. "What now?" he growled.

"Just a couple of questions to clarify some things."

"Couldn't you have done that on the phone?"

"I was in the neighborhood." He followed Redman into his office. The doors of a floor to ceiling cabinet against the far wall of the office stood open, the key dangling in the lock. Beyond the doors a safe containing shelves of files also stood open. It was overflowing with file jackets crammed tightly together with the exception of one row. There were very few folders in it. A briefcase sat on a straight-backed chair next to the cabinet. It was obvious to Junior that he had interrupted the lawyer in the process of stuffing a bunch of files into the case. "That's some file cabinet."

"Fire safe. To protect sensitive documents for my clients."

"Taking work home with you?"

Redman glanced at the briefcase as he sat in his desk chair. "Moving old files to storage."

"They're not sensitive anymore?"

"Most of these clients are dead. I've kept all this paperwork for the legally required length of time."

"Any of them have anything to do with Haywood Enterprises?"

Redman eyed Junior before answering. "Why would they?"

"Because you used to work for them. And you continued to work for one of the major shareholders."

"You've been busy."

"It's the nature of the job."

"This has nothing to do with that."

Junior sat in the visitor's chair across from Redman. "Tell me about Ambrose Enzo Caron."

"What about him?"

"Your client left him a piece of property in her will."

"Ruth's reasoning for why she made certain bequests were her own."

"But you were her friend. And her lawyer."

Redman took a cigar from the wooden box on his desk and began the ritual of preparing it, buying time, deciding how much to tell him, Junior figured.

"Ambrose was sent here by the diocese. The ways of the church are many and mysterious. My feeling is he was sent down here as a reprimand for something but you and I'll never know the why of it. I confess I thought Ruth had something to do with his assignment to Holy Spirit, especially after she made that bequest. I'm not sure what the connection was. He isn't family."

"That's seems awfully generous to someone she's known for less than two years."

"He was her priest." He shrugged. "And as I said, I had the feeling he was known to her before he came here."

"He's a handsome devil. Looks like he'd be a candidate for the cover of *Gentleman's Quarterly*. And the accent. I bet mass is well attended."

"Are you implying something, detective?"

Junior gave a little meh gesture with his shoulders and head. "Stranger things have happened."

"Not in this instance."

"Does he know about the inheritance?"

"Yes. I've informed him."

"Was he aware of it before her death?"

"Not to my knowledge. He seemed genuinely surprised when I told him."

"Why a property in France?"

"I suppose, if she was going to give him something, it would be the logical choice since that's his native country. She's owned that bit of real estate a long time."

"How long?"

"I couldn't say off the top of my head, but for many years."

"And she gave you no explanation for any of it?

"None."

"Okay. So, tell me about your time at Haywood Enterprises."

"It was Haywood Mills when I started. Edward hired me after he took charge of the business. I became lead counsel after Benedict retired."

"Sounds like you did all right for yourself."

"I can't complain."

"Even though Haywood sacked you first chance he got?"

Redman lit his cigar and puffed it to life. "It was a mutual parting of the ways."

"How's that?"

"Haywood had new ideas about the direction of the company. We had expanded into several areas under Edward. I thought it was reckless to commit further resources at the time."

"Because?"

"Edward had a level head. He didn't overextend the business beyond what was prudent. I felt Haywood was untested and that he needed more time in the role of leadership before committing to further expansion."

"The two of you don't like each other?"

"Not particularly."

"Bad blood between you?"

"I wasn't happy with the way things worked out but business is business. Haywood was president of the company. He was my boss. When you find yourself in an untenable situation, it's best to move on. I did. End of story." Redman glanced at his watch.

"Sorry to have kept you, Mr. Redman." Junior stood. He felt there was something he was forgetting to ask but it wouldn't come to him.

Thirty-Six

It had been Hugo's intention to catch up with Charlie Neuman and have him look at the photographs from the file to see if he recognized anyone other than Archie. When he called, Neuman's wife informed him that Charlie was on his regular run and wouldn't be home before midnight, that he usually slept late but would most likely be willing to speak with Hugo after ten the next morning.

He considered placing a call to Detective Durand but a glance at the clock squashed that thought. It was after hours in Paris and he had already inconvenienced the Frenchman once for no positive results. He hoped the neighbor really was as attractive as Durand's comment had implied. He would be more likely to respond quickly if the call came.

Kwanita's signed statement was on the top of the pile of paperwork stacked on his desk. He pulled it toward him and went over the high points again. Who had Tyrone left home that Saturday morning to straighten out? One of his dealers? The young Wyatt Earp he had left in charge of things while he was making the run to Chicago? They had tentatively identified Tyrone's lieutenant as Dab Rivers. But the current temperature of the city kept lips tight.

Had Tyrone even gone to Chicago?

He dialed information. It took some time to reach anyone who would give him the time of day at the Chicago Police Department. After forty-five minutes of being directed from precinct to precinct, he finally found a detective who vaguely remembered Tyrone. Hugo learned he had been a person of interest in a murder case but that it had gone cold. The detective agreed to put out some feelers and see if Tyrone had been in town around the middle of September. He didn't offer much encouragement as that had been nearly two months ago and Chicago police had more pressing issues on their hands.

Hugo swiveled his chair around and stared at the bits and pieces of the case. He rearranged the index cards to form different associations but nothing jumped out at him.

A young woman appeared in the entrance to the bull pen. She stopped and glanced around before approaching Hugo.

"Detective August?"

He nodded.

She handed him a manila envelope. "The phone records from your subpoena."

"Thanks."

He removed the dozen or so sheets of paper from the envelope and turned to the last couple of pages. These were the relevant calls that would aid them in establishing a timeline. He scanned down the numbers and the adjacent times. To his disappointment, there weren't any calls to or from the Camden number after four fifteen on the Friday before Ruth's death.

The phone on his desk rang.

"August."

"Detective."

He recognized the caller and sat forward. "Mrs. Shipley. I was just thinking of calling you with a few questions. Is everything all right?

"Yes. I mean. . .I was wondering. . .is there any news? I can't seem. . ."

Her voice broke.

"Are you alone, Mrs. Shipley?"

"I. . .yes, I. . ." Her voice was teary. "Oh, I don't know what's wrong with me!"

"Is there anyone I can call for you?"

She didn't answer immediately.

"Can you come? Would you. . ."

"Sure. I'll be on my way in a few minutes."

He was glad he'd hit Junior up for money at lunch. There had been something in Sharon Shipley's voice that told him she needed to talk. When people talk, they say things they don't intend to say. He couldn't let that moment slip away. At Argiro's he put three dollars of gas in the tank of the Thunderbird and practically flew to Point Clear.

The sun was riding low in the sky as he turned onto the driveway, the shadows around the house lengthening and darkening into dusky pools. The Jeep and old Mercedes were parked under the carport. As Hugo got out of his car, he looked across the long sweep of lawn toward the bay and saw her standing out at the end of the pier, outlined against the setting sun, her arms hugging her waist. A sense of melancholy swept over Hugo. She looked so alone. So totally alone. He had the irrational thought that nothing would ever be right again. For either of them.

He felt sure she had heard his car but she continued to stand where she was, silhouetted against the fading light playing on the water. But before he reached the pier, she turned and walked toward him.

As he waited for her to reach him, he tried to decide what he was feeling. But then she stepped off the end of the pier and raised her face to look into his eyes. She took his hand and they turned toward the Adirondack chairs and sat, her hand in his, as they watched the sun slowly sinking below the horizon.

It wasn't until the sky and water were a sea of rose and purple feathered with hints of gold that she spoke.

"Thank you for coming." She gave his hand a gentle squeeze and turned her face toward him. "I felt overwhelmed. I needed. . .someone. Someone who could understand." She shifted slightly in the chair so that she looked more directly at him. "You understand, don't you Detective?"

"Hugo."

"Hugo."

His name on her lips stirred something deep within so he looked away from the lovely oval of her face with the faint blue shadows beneath the eyes and the grief for something forever lost mirrored there. The image of the Pieta and the sense of great loneliness it evokes came to him and he closed his mind to it. He couldn't let himself become vulnerable to her pain, to her need.

And yet, when she stood and tugged gently at his hand, he followed her across the lawn in the deep dusk and into the house.

She didn't turn on any lights along the way as they trailed through the house and down the hallway. Neither of them hesitated at the threshold of her bedroom. It held the scent of her and when she stepped into his arms, he did not resist. He inhaled deeply of the cool autumn air and sun that was her and kissed the parted lips as her fingers tangled in his hair and she melded her body to his.

Her touch was a salve to his own loneliness, to his own loss, and, much later, when she stirred from the languid satiety of their love-making, she slipped her arm around his waist, turned her body into his and sighed, "Stay."

And he did.

⁂

HUGO WOKE TO the smell of brewing coffee. He was alone in the bed, the damp of steam from the shower still lingering on the air.

A clean towel rested on a little stool beside the huge cast iron tub. Large droplets still clung to the plastic curtain. He showered quickly, the pelting hot water kick starting his brain.

As he dressed, he saw the telephone on the bedside table. He called Junior and told him he was heading out for Ocean Springs to interview Charlie Neuman.

She didn't hear him when he walked into the kitchen. She wore a chenille robe belted at the waist. The tender flesh of the backs of her knees just below the hem of the robe struck Hugo as terribly erotic. Her hair was pulled haphazardly up on top of her head. A feathering of escaping curls teased the collar of the garment. Hugo's body responded to the image.

Sharon whipped a bowl of eggs and dropped two slices of bread into the toaster. When she turned from the stove, she saw him. She smiled. There was nothing shy or coy about the smile.

"I didn't know how you liked them so scrambled it is."

"Thanks. You shouldn't have bothered."

"You have to eat. So do I. I'm starving." She nodded toward the coffee pot on the back burner. "Coffee?"

"Sure."

She reached for a cup from the overhead cabinet, pulling the robe higher on her thigh as she did so. He told himself to look away. His lapse in judgment had already compromised his objectivity. But when she looked up at him again, she simply stood there, the cup in her hand.

"Hugo. . ."

The little catch in her voice was all it took. He crossed the room and removed the cup from her grasp. He placed it on the counter.

"Oh, Hugo."

Her words shattered the last shred of his self-control. He tugged the sash of her robe and as it fell open along the length of her body, she stepped into his arms. They surrendered to the lust fever that carried them back to the bedroom, chasing the loneliness into the shadows once again, desperately seeking that moment of forgetfulness.

An hour later Hugo hurriedly dressed as Sharon brewed a fresh pot of coffee. By the time he stepped into the kitchen she had a heavy mug ready for him and a peanut butter and jelly sandwich wrapped in a napkin.

"About all that—"

She shook her head and placed a finger on his lips to ward off a post mortem of the last fourteen hours. She pushed her hair back from her forehead. "Goodness, I'm a mess. The kids will be back from their grandparents soon." She smiled. "And you're off to Mobile?"

"Ocean Springs, actually."

Her brows shot up. "Really?"

"The bus driver. I'm going to see if anything else has occurred to him."

She lowered her gaze and adjusted the knot of his tie. When she looked back up at him, the sadness had returned. It looked out from her lovely eyes as she studied his face.

There was a haunting beauty to that sadness. He felt the pull of it.

"Goodbye, Hugo August."

Her softly spoken words sounded so final.

"I'll call you later."

She stepped back from the doorway. From there she watched him back the Thunderbird around and depart up the long driveway.

Hugo glanced at his watch and knew he would be hard pressed to make Ocean Springs by ten o'clock. Still, he didn't regret the turn the morning had taken.

Sharon's parting words had pricked the halcyon afterglow of their morning in bed. He felt it slipping from him and he wanted desperately to hold on to it.

They had used each other as a means of forgetfulness, a brief respite from a sadness too profound to bear. Hugo knew his demons, but what was Sharon trying to escape?

He hadn't asked her any of the questions ratcheting around in his mind. He still didn't know her views on Redman, the significance of the butter pats, and whether or not she had known about the gold. In that moment he realized his subconscious mind had been clouded by the desire for the occurrences of last night. From the moment Sharon walked into the house on Dauphin Street, bringing with her the cold fresh morning and a disheveled glamour, he had felt drawn to her.

He spent the long drive west along Highway 98 trying to focus on the task at hand but his mind kept circling back to Sharon.

⚜

CHARLIE NEUMAN PUSHED a lawn mower making neat rows across a small front lawn, the scent of fresh cut grass lingering in the air. He glanced at Hugo when he pulled to a stop in the sandy edge of the roadway but didn't stop until he had completed the current pass. He let the mower's engine die and took a handkerchief from his back pocket to wipe his brow and his balding head.

"You the detective from Mobile?"

"Hugo August." He followed Neuman onto the front porch and took the chair offered. As he sat back, he noticed the corner lot of Neuman's house took advantage of a nice slice of view of the Gulf of Mexico between the row of houses on the next street over.

The breeze off the water reached Hugo through the lightweight twill of his sports coat. The front door opened and Mrs. Neuman appeared with a tray with a pitcher of tea and two tall glasses of ice. After greeting Hugo, she disappeared back into the house.

Neuman eyed the file in Hugo's hand. "I hate you had to come all the way over here, young fella, 'cause I don't see how I can tell you anything you don't already know."

"I don't mind the drive. It's a pretty day for it." Hugo opened the file. "You're sure nothing else has come to mind about that day?"

"I've thought on it, seeing as how everyone is so hot and bothered to find the boy. But, I swan, I can't think of a thing."

"Do you mind looking at some photos?"

"I already picked him out for the Army guy."

"I have some others here. Maybe you'll recall seeing one of them."

Neuman ran the handkerchief across his bald dome again. "Sure, why not. But, that was two months ago, you know?"

Hugo had placed three photos of random people in with the shots of all the principals involved in the case. He handed them over to Neuman and watched the man's face as he leafed through them.

Neuman hesitated at the image of Bebe but moved on. He worked through to the last one then went back to Bebe.

Hugo closed his eyes briefly and exhaled a long, slow breath. But then Neuman thumbed back through to the last photo and said, "This one. She sat next to him on the bus."

It was the photo of Sharon.

For a moment, the words wouldn't register. Hugo shifted in his chair and took the close ups of the two women from Neuman. "This one?"

Neuman nodded.

"You're sure?"

He nodded again. "They look kinda alike. At first I thought it might be the first one." He pointed to Bebe's photograph. "But then when I saw this one, I knew it was her."

Hugo sat very still. The distant cries of seagulls and the faint surge of the surf the only sound to be heard. Why hadn't it occurred to him that the unknown passenger could have been Sharon? She fit the description but Hugo's thoughts had gone instantly to Bebe.

"Any of the others look familiar? Maybe you saw them somewhere along the route. At one of the other stops."

Neuman shook his head. "No. Just the woman. I'd know her anywhere.

Thirty-Seven

It had happened with no effort on his part. Even this morning, when logic would dictate that he get down to business, Hugo had been easily distracted. All it had taken was the whisper of his name and Sharon had forestalled the questions she didn't want to answer. So, why had she called him? What was to be gained by their little tryst?

She had known what he would discover from Charlie Neuman. That's what he saw in her eyes as he left her this morning, regret at being found out.

Hugo pushed the anger down, freed his mind of resentment and the bruise to his ego. There was something to be learned from Sharon's behavior. Something to do with the case. He would focus on that and only that.

Archie's decision to evade the draft happened on that bus ride. Hugo was certain of it. What had compelled him to jump ship at the last second? He had been willing to serve his time up until that two hour ride from Montgomery to Atlanta. A last minute appeal that had undermined his sense of duty?

There had to be more to it than that.

JUNIOR SPENT THE morning working his way through the list of calls to and from Ruth's phone from the first of August until the week after her death. He had identified a long list of people she regularly interacted with and was compiling a list of numbers he considered a one-off. These generally had to do with a repairman, the purchase of tickets for the opera, and an inquiry to her insurance carrier.

He found no calls to Abe's Bar-be-que so they could assume that all her negotiations with Tyrone had been through Viola. What did interest him were three calls to Sherbrooke, Canada. She had called *Liberté Partenariat* in early August and again the first week of October. He needed to find out who the other number belonged to.

At the moment, he was focusing on the calls in the days leading up to Archie's departure date and immediately after. Of note was an incoming call from Augusta, Georgia in the late evening of September 13th. When he dialed the number, he discovered it belonged to a Mrs. Richardson but was informed by the maid that she wasn't at home. He left a message for her to return his call.

The coffee in his cup was cold so he went in search of a fresh cup. The pot was down to the last dregs and he decided he really didn't have the stomach for it. When he returned to his desk he glanced at the notes on the murder wall. Someone had drawn a picture of a cat on the note card titled Beauregard with a noose around its neck.

Junior let his gaze travel around the detective squad and saw the half-hidden snickers from Finch and Hardman. "Very funny," he said to the room in general.

Hugo came through the doorway of the bull pen at that moment, his expression enough to quell the pranksters. "Something funny?"

Junior nodded toward the murder wall.

Hugo removed the card from the display, glanced at it before dropping it onto his desk along with the case file. He settled into his chair and pulled the phone toward him. He listened to the ringing on the other end of the line for a long time as the call he made went unanswered. Finally, he hung up and turned to Junior. "Any luck with the phone records?"

Junior tried to gauge his mood. Something had set Hugo's face in stone. The lack of a shave this morning only emphasized that hard expression. From experience, Junior knew that look meant trouble for someone. "A few interesting facts. How about the bus driver? Anything new?"

"He identified the blond with Archie." Hugo touched the knot of his tie.

Here it is, Junior thought.

"Sharon Shipley."

The answer caught Junior off guard. He studied Hugo's face. This should be a relief to him but it wasn't. "Anything else?"

"No." Hugo opened the file. "Tell me about the phone calls."

"Ruth made three calls to Sherbrooke. Two of them were to Moreau. At least I assume it was him she was calling. The first time was in August and they spoke for over ten minutes. The second time was in early October and much briefer."

Hugo considered this. "She and Bebe set things up before Archie received his draft notice. That explains the first call."

"And she was trying to find him with the second call would be my guess."

"Any calls to Paris?"

"No."

Hugo fell silent for a moment. "We need to get Bebe's phone records."

Such an invasion of her privacy would not go down well with Bebe but Junior conceded that it was necessary.

"The other interesting facts?"

"Only one, really. An incoming call from Augusta, Georgia late on the evening of the 13th. The day of Archie's departure."

Hugo leaned back in his chair. "The porter said he asked about the number nine bus to Augusta."

"Right."

"Who does Archie know in Augusta?"

"The number is for a Mrs. Richardson. Mrs. Thomas Richardson. She wasn't in when I called but the maid took a message."

Hugo sat studying the ceiling for a long time. He sat forward and stood. "Let's take a walk."

⚘

THEY ENDED UP at Bienville Square. A few of the downtown workers were still enjoying their sack lunches on the benches that surrounded the center of the little park in the heart of the city. There were enough patches of sunlight to counterbalance the nip in the air. Hugo and Junior found an empty bench and sat in silence watching the squirrels begging for bread crumbs and peanuts.

As the secretaries and sales clerks began to abandon the square and return to their jobs, Hugo spoke. "The motive is the nut we can't crack. So, let's forget about motive and list the people who could potentially want Ruth dead."

"Okay." Junior turned to a page at the back of his notebook and got out his pen. "Let's start with the people closest to her."

"Archie—"

"You don't really think he'd kill his grandmother?"

"I've discounted him from the beginning. That was a mistake. He didn't show up for basic. We have no idea where he is."

"But why? Everyone says he loved his grandmother."

"Stranger things have happened. We can't discount him if we can't find him."

Junior put Archie's name at the top of the list.

"Sharon."

Something in Hugo's voice caused Junior's protest to remain unspoken. He added her name to the page.

"The best friend. Aimeé Marlowe."

"For a necklace?"

"For the loss of a necklace, maybe."

"She's an odd one, that's for sure. She's hard to read."

"Bebe."

305

"You don't mean that, Hugo."

"These are the people closest to Ruth. The people who had access and opportunity. The two of them didn't get along in recent years but Bebe did take her to lunch a week before her death." He turned his face away from Junior, watching the water splashing in the fountain. "And she was there that Friday afternoon."

"But this is a list of murder suspects." When Hugo made no reply, Junior wrote down her name.

"Haywood Prescott."

Junior knew that was where Hugo wanted to place the guilt.

"Redman." Hugo's attention was now fixed on a squirrel that came up to the tip of his shoe. "And Tyrone Pritchett."

"Seven suspects."

"And not a damn clue to the guilty party."

They rehashed the known facts, noting the chinks in the timelines in the days leading up to Ruth's murder of the various people on the list. They would need to shore that up. Hugo decided it was time they laid out their case for the chief and asked for the manpower to nail down the activities of all of them.

Hugo ran his hand over his face. "I should probably shave."

"Look your best for the firing squad?"

"Something like that."

They stood and went their separate ways, Junior back to the station to attack the remaining numbers on Ruth's telephone list and to find a judge to issue a subpoena for both Bebe and Prescott's phones. *Good luck with that*, he thought.

Hugo turned toward home.

✺

HUGO FELT THE weight of his knowledge on the fifteen minute walk to his house. Had Bebe not been involved, this was the moment when he would let the excitement of the chase hold sway. That compelling moment when the vital pieces of the puzzle were jelling, that teasing at the forefront of his mind unrelentingly pushing him forward. That burning need to discover the truth that would not let him turn a blind eye. Even for Bebe.

He stood in front of the small mirror in his bathroom, his features slightly distorted by the mottling, his face lathered, and ran the razor down one cheek. The mundane act of shaving allowed his thoughts drifted. As he swished the razor in the warm water in the sink, Junior's words came back to him. There had been a third phone call to Sherbrooke. Who had Ruth called? He stood there, the razor suspended in midair. He thought he knew.

He wiped the remaining lather from his face and hurried to the phone. Junior was already at his desk and found the number. Hugo dialed it.

The voice that answered in French was female, and by the sound of it, Hugo assumed she was older. When he identified himself, she switched smoothly into a heavily accented English.

"Giselle Fournet?"

"*Oui.* Yes. How can I help you, Inspector?"

"Detective, ma'am. Hugo August."

"Detective August."

"Do you know about the death of Ruth Camden?"

"Yes. My grandson told me. It broke my heart to hear the sad news."

"Were you in frequent contact with Mrs. Camden?"

"Not for many years."

"When did you last speak with her?"

"It was some months ago. Toward the end of summer. I can't be precise."

"And before that?"

"Oh, dear. I can't remember. We wrote, of course. But only occasionally. You know how it is. Time slips away and before you know it a month has gone by, then a year. After a while it's only a birthday card with a note or Christmas greetings."

"When she called you this summer, what did you talk about?"

"We caught up on family news. She talked about Archie. It was very troubling to both of us. Another war. Another loved one facing danger. He had reassured her that he had nothing to worry about with the conscription."

"But in the end, he was drafted."

"Yes. I learned of these things from my grandson."

"Basile Moreau?"

"Yes. My eldest daughter's son."

"Did Mrs. Camden ask you to help her get Archie out of the country?"

"No. It seems the call was motivated by something else. It was the strangest thing. She wanted to know if I had a photograph of Aimeé."

"Her cousin?"

"Yes. Our cousin."

"And did you?"

"I told her I would look but I didn't recall having one. She left Paris many years ago. Before The War. My uncle was in desperate need of a husband for her. There was no money, you see. He thought to foist her off onto family connections in the states."

"When was the last time you saw Aimeé Marlowe?"

"I couldn't say exactly. They shipped her off so quickly with hardly time for anyone to realize what was happening. Sent her with only her governess as a chaperone. My mother was very upset about the way the whole thing was handled."

She tut-tutted. "I was angry with Aimeé. She had stolen my hair ribbon. It was my favorite. It matched my eyes. She denied it, of course. It hurt my feelings that she would take it. It wasn't like her at all." Giselle Fournet sighed. "The silly things you remember from childhood. We never got the chance to mend our grievance before she was gone."

"You came to visit Ruth in Mobile, didn't you, Mrs. Fournet?"

"Yes. Oh, my. That was so long ago. What a wonderful time we had. Of course, Ruth and Edward knew how to entertain. And the years after The War had been so hard on us. France was a shambles for years. Ruth knew just how to make my visit memorable. Such entertainments she thought up. Such great fun."

"Did you see Mrs. Marlowe on that visit?"

"No. The trip was planned weeks in advance but I arrived to learn that Aimeé had suddenly gone off somewhere. Can't remember exactly. Pity. I had been so looking forward to seeing her again. Ruth was very upset with her."

"And you haven't seen her in all the years since she left France?"

"No. But then, the cost of travel was prohibitive in my younger years. The War destroyed everything, you see, and then in the blink of an eye, we were caught up in it again. I should have listened to my son. He saw what was coming but I didn't want to leave my home and my family. Once I settled in Canada with him and his family afterwards, well, I just never got around to that return visit." She sighed. "Such a pity that we allowed ourselves to drift apart. But then Aimeé had basically severed all ties with us soon after she arrived in Mobile. She stopped writing. The only news we had of her was through Tia, my father's sister, and Ruth. We were all young then. Busy living our lives."

"Did you ever find that photograph of Mrs. Marlowe?"

"No. I did look but the only photograph I had was when we were small children. Me, Ruth, and Aimeé gathered at a family picnic under the trees in an orchard. The Haywoods would come every summer. I so looked forward to it. It was the highlight of the year. The photo was taken at the old family home outside Paris before The War." Hugo heard the nostalgia in her voice. "We had a large family then."

"Did you send the picture to Mrs. Marlowe?"

"I tried to call but kept missing her so I wrote and told her what I'd found. I knew she was looking for something from Aimeé's later years but I sent it anyway. You really couldn't tell who was who in that old photograph unless you knew. We were just three little girls. It must have been taken before 1910 by the look of us."

When Hugo hung up the phone, he went to stand over the scrap books spread out on his kitchen table and flipped through the pages. Ruth had been meticulous in her record keeping of the family history.

The evidence was there in the orderly placement by date, the event groupings, the neat lettering identifying various entries. He found no photographs of her cousin and best friend, Aimeé Marlowe. What would make this ardent keeper of the flame remove all evidence of her?

Hugo stood there, staring at the empty photo corners on a page. He cursed under his breath. His car was parked at the station. He slipped back into his shirt and tie, snatched up his coat, and took off on foot. He made it back to the station in under ten minutes, practically running the whole way.

He topped the stairs and burst into the detectives' bull pen, his hair windblown and breathing hard. Junior looked up from his desk and knew Hugo was onto something.

"What?"

Hugo made no reply as he pulled his chair out of the way and stood flipping through the case file. He found the envelope with the three photographs he and Sharon had discovered hidden among the silver.

He examined all three of the pictures trying to recognize either Ruth or her cousin in any of the faces. They had been young men and women with the exception of an older man. Nothing stood out that Hugo could determine on the single photograph that bore three names written on the back. It was a shot of three women and a man. One of the females stood slightly apart from the others.

Her hair color was light. Probably a blond. She was more petite than the other two women. Could this be Aimeé Marlowe? Her name wasn't one of those listed. The setting was outdoors under a tree.

Who would be able to identify these people? Not Sharon. Perhaps Haywood but he was nowhere to be found.

"Give me your magnifying glass."

Hugo took the offered glass and examined each face closely. The images were posed, unsmiling, sepia toned.

He handed the glass back to Junior, dropped the photo back into the file. In closing it, he revealed the note card with the drawing of a hanged Beauregard. He stared at it for a long minute.

"Damnit!" He snatched the card from his desk and headed for the door. "Come on!" he growled over his shoulder at Junior.

THEY ARRIVED AT the Camden house in record time. Hugo searched through the garage until he found a small spade. It only took a few minutes of digging to unearth the contents of the flower bed by Ruth's back door. Hugo wiped his brow with a dirty hand. "Damnit."

The only thing he had unearth was a dozen or so flower bulbs.

"If she poisoned the cat, why would she bury it here?"

Hugo had been so certain that he had figured it out. In truth, he still felt he was on the right track.

"She's our killer. I'm certain of it."

"But why? Because she was disinherited?"

"No. Something far more valuable in this town than an expensive bauble."

"Like what?"

Hugo made no reply. Instead, he took the key from his pocket and unlocked the back door of the house. The only sound was the ticking of the kitchen clock. There was something he needed to be sure of. Slowly he made his way through the house, ending in Ruth's bedroom.

He went straight to the collection of photographs on the dresser. There wasn't a single picture of Aimeé Marlowe among the people dearest to Ruth's heart.

For a minute Hugo debated calling the chief. He knew what his reaction would be. He decided not to risk it.

"Come on."

He and Junior walked down the alley to the back of Aimeé's house. The sun reflected on the gold fish drifting lazily in the fountain but nothing else stirred. They went around to the front door and rang the bell.

She answered the door. "You again."

Hugo studied her features. "Hello, Mila."

She dropped her gaze for an instant then looked up into his steady regard, her brows arched. No alarm, no surprise. "I beg your pardon?"

"Mila Bisset. Governess to Aimeé Jamet. Mila Bisset, presumed dead in a train derailment outside Boston in the spring of 1914."

She turned her profile to him, a shadow of a smile brushed her lips, then she preceded the two detectives into her living room. She sat in the chair to the left of the fireplace and gestured for them to take a seat.

Hugo sat across from her but Junior remained standing near the doorway into the hall.

"Mila Bisset did die on that fateful day, Detective August. I don't know what you're implying."

"You thought you removed all the photographs from Ruth's collection. With her dead, there was no one who could question your pretense. After all, you've gotten away with it for over fifty years."

There was fire in her blue eyes but Mila Bisset maintained the helpless, harmless countenance of Aimeé Marlowe as she glanced briefly at Junior, assessing and dismissing him from the skirmish, and focused on Hugo.

"You have quite an imagination, Detective."

"She was leaving you the precious family heirloom. The sapphire necklace that had been in the Jamet family for generations. After all, no one dressed like that anymore. And she thought, why not? You had always coveted it.

"Then, somehow, as she reminisced and mourned up in her attic over the deployment of Archie, she discovered you weren't entitled to this symbol of the family. You weren't even remotely related. That you were nothing more than a governess who had pushed herself into the heart of *her* family. The woman who stole her fiancé. A man who probably met the same fate as Ruth."

She turned her profile to Hugo once again and stared into the flames of the fake logs. "They were never engaged."

"It wouldn't have mattered if they had been, would it?"

She looked at him now and a slow smile lifted the corner of her mouth. "This makes an interesting story but really, it's all fiction. There's not a shred of proof to any of this nonsense and no one would believe me capable of murder."

Hugo picked up a little mother-of-pearl box from the table beside his chair. He had seen it before in Ruth's bedroom. "But I have proof. I have the photograph taken at the family home before your departure from France. I also have Giselle Jamet Fournet. She remembers her favorite cousin very well. In fact, she was terribly hurt that you skipped town on her one visit all those years ago. She wanted to make amends for the accusation she made about her hair ribbon."

Hugo smiled. "I have that, too."

Mila watched him for a moment then shrugged. "You're a clever man, Hugo August. I underestimated you. Still, you have no proof I poisoned her."

"We will, and before the day is out."

She glanced toward Junior as he stepped out into the hallway and found the telephone. They could hear him setting in motion the request for a search warrant for her house.

She dropped all pretense then and before Hugo's eyes, she became a different person, in her speech, and in her appearance. An aura of evil wafted off her. "Ruth was so goody, goody. It was tiring, really. I don't know why I didn't do it years ago." Her eyes were cold blue stones, much like the sapphires she coveted. "And as for Aimeé Jamet, she never made it off the ship. She was my ticket out of France and midway the voyage, she succumbed to a mysterious ailment. Very like a heart attack."

Her expression sent a chill down Hugo's spine.

"What was the plan?"

She lifted her shoulders in a slight shrug. "There was no plan, really. I was going to use the train ticket provided to make my way south. Once here, I would tell the family about poor Aimeé's death on the high seas. Shock and sympathy would give me time to find my feet. But then, the derailment happened and there were dead bodies all around me." Again, that slight shrug. "It came to me that no one would be the wiser. There wasn't much chance that anyone in the family would have the means to travel to the states for a visit anytime soon. They were all dead broke.

"The train accident gave me the opportunity to reinvent myself. No one ever questioned my story."

"And Marlowe?"

"Richard was a simpering bore. But, he served his purpose. I endured him for ten long years. Then, one morning, he kept going on about a bill from Hammel's and I decided I'd had enough."

"Poison, I assume."

"Dear, Detective August. Surely you don't expect me to hand feed you everything? You must earn your merit badges."

Hugo stood and with a sigh, Mila Bisset rose to her feet.

"Why plant the tulips?"

"Ruth wanted them for the spring." She smiled. "A little tribute to my dear, departed cousin. Pity she'll never see them."

Thirty-Eight

The herbal tea Mila Bisset used for her arthritis proved to be dried monkshood root. A sample rushed to the forensic lab in Auburn confirmed it. Giselle Fournet had been more than willing to fill in the blanks on her family history. She had agreed to fly down to Mobile to make an identification. Or, in this case, to declare that Mila Bisset was not her cousin Aimeé.

It was assumed that Mila learned of the poison while living in the Jamet household in France. Antoine Jamet, Aimeé's father, had spent some time in the foreign service where he discovered the beneficial qualities of monkshood while in Kurdistan. When used carefully it would ease pain. If steeped too long, it was a deadly poison mimicking a heart attack, effectively paralyzing the autonomic system and starving the body of oxygen.

Mila had been receiving the dried roots through the mail from a shop in Chinatown in San Francisco for years.

Hugo read the headline of the *Mobile Press-Register* where it sat on the corner of the chief's desk. For three days running there had been nothing else on the front page except the great scandal within the Haywood-Prescott family.

The chief finished reading the report and closed the file jacket. "You really think she killed Ruth Camden simply to keep her secret?"

"I do."

"I don't understand it. What difference would it make if people found out? So she lied. Her husband is dead and he's the only one who might have a grievance with that."

"She was a governess. She lived a life of poverty under the dominion of an aristocratic family. All that changed when she arrived in Mobile. Suddenly she had rich, eligible men competing for her attention. Her well-to-do relatives dressed her to the nines and touted her with all the regalia of royalty. Isn't that what Mardi Gras is, after all? Our own little imitation of European royalty?"

"She became 'Old Mobile.'"

"Exactly."

"But to kill someone to protect that image. I just don't understand it."

"Really? You've lived in Mobile all your life and you don't see it? Besides, she's a sociopath. She stole the butter pats. We found them in her silver chest. No attempt to hide them. There were other things that had disappeared from Ruth's house over the years. I think she knew because, according to Viola, she never made a fuss. There was a covetousness about her that Ruth recognized and tolerated."

"If she hadn't, maybe she would have been found out long before now."

"Maybe. Maybe not. That bit about the tulips shows how twisted her mind is. It was Mila's way of denying Ruth something that would have given her pleasure. She implied that she poisoned her husband, too. And Aimeé Jamet."

"Well, now that there's a lawyer in the mix, she's singing a different tune. We have a tight case on the Camden poisoning and that should put her away for life. That's good enough for me. We don't have the manpower to go digging up ghosts." He shook his head. "It's hard to imagine a little old lady like that killing three people."

"You didn't see her face when she confessed. I think she wanted an audience to her cleverness. The long years of holding on to her secrets must have been difficult for her."

The chief grunted. "So, what's with the Pritchett case? His death is unrelated after all."

"It would seem so."

"All in all, good work."

The compliment surprised Hugo. "We still don't know what happened to Archie."

"That's the Army's headache. Get back to the usual street scum on the Pritchett case. Whoever took over his drug trade would be my first guess."

"There's the question of how Tyrone came to be in possession of gold from the safe."

"We don't know that it came from the Camden's safe. Everyone in the family says there was nothing in it."

Hugo wasn't convinced but he knew the chief didn't want any more scrutiny of the Haywood-Prescott family. It had been a relief when the murderer turned out to be an imposter. No taint on any of the blue-bloods, just another titillating addition to the mystique of the family once the furor died down. In time a new scandal would grace the front page of the paper. The chief would breathe a little easier.

Hugo picked up the file and returned to his desk. He had two messages, one from Sharon and one from Judy Fohl. He threw the one from Sharon into the trash can.

Judy's whiskey voice sounded even huskier than the last time Hugo spoke with her. "What's up, Judy?"

"I'm feeling neglected."

"Sorry about that. Things have been a little hectic."

"So I see. The new rising star of the police department too busy polishing his ego to give an old friend a call."

"You know you're always at the top of my list."

"Umm. That line won't get you much from me. The photo in the paper was a good one, though. I'll bet the police department will be swamped with damsels in distress in the weeks ahead."

Hugo chuckled. "What's on your mind, Judy?"

"You owe me the inside scoop."

"That I do. How about lunch? Your choice."

"Well, then, it's the Sea Ranch. Pick me up at one o'clock. We'll miss the worst of the crowd and I want you all to myself."

Hugo gave a grunt of humor and hung up the phone. He glanced at the clock over the doorway of the detective squad. Only a little past nine and he still had loose ends to tie up.

⁂

TWIGGY APPEARED TO be her old self again. She had that determined look in her eyes as Hugo stepped off the elevator and approached her desk.

"He's busy."

"It's important."

She arched an eyebrow.

"Fine. Tell him we can discuss it now or the prosecutor can ask him about it on the stand at Mila Bisset's murder trial."

She gave him a look of loathing but popped up from her desk and marched over to the inner sanctum. A minute later he was ushered into Haywood Prescott's office.

Haywood did not rise in greeting this time, nor offer a handshake. Instead he leaned back in his chair and waited.

Hugo sat in one of the two chairs facing the desk and leaned back mimicking Haywood's attitude.

"How was France?"

"Very French."

"And the trip down to the coast?"

"You're well informed."

"That's my job. And I have a copy of Ruth's will."

Haywood made no comment.

"What took you to Fréjus?"

"Site seeing. Not that it's any business of yours."

Hugo returned Haywood's stare, dagger for dagger. "I'm the police. Everything's my business when I'm investigating a murder."

"And what? You thought I'd killed my aunt?"

"Yes."

Haywood stirred uneasily in his chair. "My trip to France had nothing to do with Ruth's murder. We might have clashed over business since Edward's death but she was family. No way would I allow any harm to come to her or any of my family."

"That's why you went there, isn't it? Family?"

"I told you—"

"It was during the war, I imagine. That's when you met the woman."

"There is no woman."

"There's always a woman."

"Speaking from experience?"

"So I've heard."

"You heard wrong."

"I've met him. Father Ambrose Enzo Caron. I interviewed him yesterday to see if I could discover if Ruth had confided in him about her suspicions. But you know the clergy. Tight lipped to the grave."

Haywood made no comment into the silence that followed this statement.

"Very handsome in a swarthy Mediterranean way, our Father Ambrose. But I've spent the better part of three weeks studying the faces of the Haywood-Prescott-Jemet clan. And, of course, he has the blue eyes."

"Is there a point to this?"

"The note. One hundred thousand dollars. It's one of those little loose ends that has to be woven into the pattern. I don't sleep well when there are loose ends. I have to be sure it had nothing to do with Ruth's death."

"That's ridiculous and you know it. Aimeé Marlowe—Mila Bisset—whatever the hell her name is, killed Ruth. You have her confession."

"Still, it would be unfortunate if the promissory note made its way into evidence."

"You bastard."

Hugo waited.

"I didn't know about the child."

"How did Ruth know?"

"When she went to France with Sharon. They were searching for family. I don't know how she came upon the boy and his mother but she did."

"And?"

"She wanted me to do the *right thing*." He swiveled his chair so that he was in profile to Hugo. "For Christ's sake! I was married with two children by then. She actually thought I'd tell Voncille, figure out a way to support them financially. Like I had that kind of money back then."

"Hence the note."

"Yes. She said she would take care of it. For now. But that there had to be a reckoning one day. That I had to bear the weight of my sin."

"She bought the house with the orchard in France."

"I didn't know at the time what she'd done. I didn't want to be involved. I didn't want to remember." He turned his head and looked at Hugo. "Ruth with her good old Catholic guilt. She bought the place in Fréjus as you say. After the war it didn't cost much. The rest of the money she put in an account for them to live on."

"Why did you go to France?"

"I wanted to see if she was still there."

"Father Ambrose's mother."

"Yes."

"Why?"

"I loved her. Even after all these years, I still do."

⁂

WHEN HUGO NEARED the corner of Dauphin and Royal, Redman's secretary came through the door of the Van Antwerp building, juggling a box loaded with files. He rushed forward to help her.

"Thank you." She released the box into his arms and pushed a lock of hair back from her forehead. "This is the last of them, thank goodness."

Hugo frowned. "Closing up shop?"

She laughed. "No, no. Just housekeeping." She opened the trunk of a Dodge Dart parked in a space a few feet away. "Mr. Redman wants to move these files into storage at his house. They all date back years ago."

"I imagine the files must be pretty empty by now since he only has a handful of clients."

"Yes. I keep all the active files in my office." She gave a nervous little laugh. "I worry that when he's done with Mrs. Camden's estate he'll decide to retire."

"He still has his other clients."

She nodded absently as she closed the trunk of the car. "Yes. Yes, I suppose that's true."

Hugo held the door of the building for her and watched as she hurried up the stairs to the second floor. Fear and worry, that's what he'd seen in her eyes.

Ruth's murder was the pebble in the stream that altered the course of many lives. Viola would be okay because of the inheritance. Redman would be able to allow his practice to slowly die away because of the hefty fees he would earn until the resolution of the estate. That could take years. Little things became big things with each alteration. Big things faded into obscurity. Not all bad and not all good. Such was life.

His musing caused him to smile as he made his way down Royal Street toward the station. Inspector Durand could take a new, pretty mistress if he played his cards right. Just another ripple in the stream.

⚜

JUDY WAS TRUE to form. Her martini appeared on the table in front of her before they could properly settle into their chairs. Her cigarettes and lighter were already out of her hand-bag.

"Do tell all, dear boy. And don't leave out any of the juicy bits." She sparked her lighter into flame and inhaled deeply on a cigarette.

"I'll tell you what I can. This is a murder case and I can't jeopardize a conviction."

She blew a plume of smoke over his head. "This is me you're talking to, handsome. My lips are sealed and I think I've earned the right to hear all."

She was right. Hugo knew he couldn't have pieced the puzzle together without her help. He smiled. "It's my job if you leak any of this."

"Heaven forbid. You're the most excitement I've had in years." She made a zipping motion across her lips.

By the time their waiter served them coffee, Judy was privy to the unraveling of the Gordian Knot of family intrigue of the Haywood-Prescott-Jamet clan with one exception. Hugo had held back the connection to Father Ambrose.

"How would Mila know that Ruth hadn't already spilled the beans?"

"The same reason Mila killed her. To protect the family name and status. Ruth was private and didn't want the taint of scandal. She was, after all, Old Mobile."

Judy studied him through the drift of smoke that rose from her cigarette. "And yet, you're not satisfied."

Hugo looked out across the bay. The wind was down and the surface of the water was as still as a mirror. "The money. The gold coins. They came from that safe. I know it in my bones. Tyrone knew who stole them and he had to be silenced. There's a rat still out there, hidden in plain sight, and the chief is telling me to let it go."

She continued to watch his profile for a long minute. "But you won't. You can't leave it unanswered."

He turned to look her in the eyes. "I'm the rat catcher."

"Then I guess you'd better find out who had the combination to the safe."

"No one, if I'm to believe all the players."

"When it comes to that kind of money, none of the players can be trusted." Judy smiled at him. "What was it you told me over our first lunch? The two most common causes of murder? Sex and money."

"That's the problem. They all have money. Lots of money."

"Well, as Wallis Simpson famously said, you can never be too rich or too thin. My money is on sex. The love interest. The one on the bus. Sharon?"

Hugo abruptly turned his profile to Judy.

"I see," Judy drawled.

To his surprise, Hugo felt the heat rising in his face.

"You old dog. First Bebe and now the other Barbie doll? I'm impressed." She ground out her cigarette in the ashtray. "It makes sense. She's was closer to Ruth than anyone else in the family other than Archie. If Ruth entrusted the combination to anyone, it would be her."

When Hugo made no reply, Judy leaned forward and placed her hand over his where it rested on the table. "You might want to take the chief's advice and let it go. If what you suspect is true, then the money is where it belongs anyway."

Hugo felt the reassurance in Judy's touch. She was telling him what he wanted to hear. He gave a small shake of his head. "Tyrone Pritchett is dead. Left as carrion for the rats and birds."

Judy sighed and sat back in her chair.

⁂

IT WAS HALF past two when Hugo returned to the station. The chief's office was empty. He would have to fly under the radar with his investigation. And he would keep Junior out of it as much as he could. The chief would not take kindly to anyone stirring the hornet's nest now that an arrest had been made.

He collected the case files for Ruth Camden and Tyrone Pritchett. As he turned to leave, his phone rang. He was tempted to ignore it but after the fourth ring, he answered.

"You're angry with me."

Hugo knew that he would have to confront Sharon to move the case forward. "Yes."

"It wasn't what you think."

"You don't know what I think."

She sighed. "Look, this isn't a conversation to have over the phone. Could we meet?"

"Sure. When?"

"Not today. I'm sending the kids to their grandparents tomorrow."

"Okay. Tomorrow."

"Around four? At Bucky's."

Neutral ground. "Four. At Bucky's." He hung up the phone.

Thirty-Nine

Junior rapped on the front door and whistled as he opened it.

"I'm in the kitchen." Hugo taped another sheet from the legal pad onto his wall.

Junior stood in the middle of the cramped space and let his gaze travel over the diagram of people and events that Hugo had created.

"I take it the chief doesn't know you're still at this."

"You would be right. It's best that you don't know either."

"Uh huh." The pages formed two patterns. A time line of events and a map of connections. "You're sure you want to do this?"

"Those coins came from Ruth's safe. Whoever took them killed Tyrone."

"And what about Archie?"

"Until a body turns up, that's a moot issue."

On the top sheet of paper Hugo had written two questions. Where's the money? Who knew the combination?

Junior took off his coat and draped it on the back of a chair. He loosened the knot of his tie. "Who would Ruth trust with the combination?"

"I doubt it would be Haywood, Voncile, or the phony cousin. Even before their falling out, Ruth knew Mila's covetous nature. I don't see it being Bebe but I could be wrong. They hadn't been close in a long time but, still, she might have entrusted it to her when they were on a better footing."

"That leaves Archie or Sharon."

"Or Redman. There's more to their history than simply a long association. Ruth's degree of loyalty to a disheveled, down-on-his-luck lawyer means something. He had some kind of power over her."

"Or maybe you're seeing villains under every rock. Maybe it was just as he said. They were friends. She felt sorry for him."

"The killer is taunting us, Junior. He knows he's gotten away with murder and a shit load of gold." Hugo clenched his jaw and relaxed it. "I won't stand for it."

Junior rocked back on his heels, his hands in his pockets, and studied the assembled facts. "It was a big safe. Assuming from the amount of coins Tyrone cashed in, there must have been a lot more of them. Where would you stash something that big, that heavy?"

"Someplace safe yet under your control. Under your watchful eye."

Hugo had been leafing through the file and suddenly his head snapped up.

Junior looked around at the same moment.

"It has to be."

Junior nodded. "Right there before our eyes all the time." He lifted his jacket from the chair and put it on. "We'll need a warrant."

Hugo shook his head. "The chief will shut us down. We have no proof and he wants all this to disappear from the headlines. Our thief has the coins stashed somewhere vulnerable right now. He'll want to move them to safety as soon as possible. The secretary was loading the last of the old files from his safe into her car this morning."

"Then he'll try to move them tonight."

"Let's hope he does. He'll wait until late when the patrol cars have found a quiet spot to pass the slow hours. We'll need to catch him in the act if we're going to convince the chief."

"A stake-out."

Hugo nodded. "You're sure about this?"

"Yes."

"Okay. Better take the unmarked car. He'd spot mine."

"We should get eyes on him. I'll check out his home address. Cruise by to see if there are any signs of life."

"Swing back here when you've done that. Bring a couple of radios so we can communicate. We can't know if he'll approach the office from Royal or Dauphin. You can park on the west side of the square so you can see the entrance to the building. The trees should give you enough coverage. I'll set up at the corner of the old Battle House Hotel. It's dark and deserted. No exterior lighting. I'll have a good view from there."

While Junior drove west to McDonald Avenue to check out Redman's house, Hugo opened the trunk containing his army fatigues. He found the heavy wool sweater, camo jacket, and sock cap. The day had been warm but the temperature would drop sharply as the night wore on. He started to close the trunk then took out his flak jacket. Mrs. K would never forgive him if anything happened to Junior.

Lastly, Hugo checked his revolver. He was ready.

⁂

THE WIND WHISTLED down Royal Street. Hugo turtled into the raised collar of his jacket. His feet felt like blocks of ice. He fingered the switch on the radio. "What's the time?"

"Quarter to two." Junior's voice crackled in his ear. "You want to swap places?"

"Let's give it a little longer."

"I don't think he's coming."

"Maybe. Maybe not."

Hugo bounced on his toes to stimulate the blood flow. He hadn't been this cold since San Francisco.

His radio chirped. "What?"

"Maybe we got it wrong."

"No. It's him."

The silence returned. The wind died down. Then Hugo saw movement. The car crept down Royal Street. No headlights.

He held the radio to his lips. "I've got him." In a crouched position, he eased toward the intersection at Dauphin. "Cut through the Square. Now. Try for the alcove at the book store next door."

The car came to a stop at the curb just before the intersection of Royal and Dauphin. Hugo hugged the wall of the building on the east side of Royal.

Redman sat in the car for a long time, assessing his surroundings. Finally, he got out and walked to the corner, checking down Dauphin Street. He had a gun in his hand.

He turned back to the car and opened the trunk. Hugo took advantage of the moment, sprinted through the intersection, and flattened himself against the bank building. The click of the trunk closing sounded loudly in the quiet street.

Redman hefted the small suitcase onto the curb and stepped around the corner with it to the entrance of the Van Antwerp Building. He was inserting the key into the lock when Hugo dashed across the street and came up behind him.

Redman heard the approach and reached for the gun in his belt as he turned. Junior was there before him. He stepped out of the entry way of the book store and held his revolver in a shooter's stance. Hugo reached around Redman and wrestled the gun from his hand.

"Getting an early start to your day, Redman?" Hugo pocketed the gun as Junior closed the gap between them. "Or going on a little trip?"

"What're you doing here?"

"Couldn't sleep. How about we get in out of the cold?"

Redman looked from Hugo to Junior. "Why all the cowboys and Indians, fellas?"

Junior swung the door open with his free hand and jerked his head at the opening. "Let's take this inside."

Redman hesitated and in that instant Hugo knew. His response was too late. The suitcase came up in a long arcing swipe, deflecting Junior's gun, the weight of it sending him backwards, and catching Hugo at the hips.

The heft of it did the work for Redman. He turned for his car as Hugo hit the sidewalk.

Hugo rolled and came to his feet. He caught Redman with three long strides and rode him to the pavement. He grabbed Redman by the hair and ground his face into the rough concrete. He leaned his body weight into him as he cuffed him. "Now you've gone and pissed me off," he said into Redman's ear.

He hauled Redman to his feet and marched him into the building and upstairs to his office. The huge wall safe stood open in readiness. Hugo shoved Redman into his chair.

"I don't know what you think you're doing but you're making a big mistake." Redman's breathing was still heavy but he had regained his composure. "What's this all about?"

Junior lifted the heavy suitcase onto the desktop and opened it. The glow from the coins shone like the rising sun.

Hugo whistled softly. "Where'd you get all those bright, shiny doubloons, Redman?" He picked up one of the coins and bounced it in his hand to check the heft. "Oh, wait. These aren't Mardi Gras throws. A little parting gift from Ruth Camden I'm thinking."

"They're mine. I've been collecting them for years."

"Uh huh. And out of the blue you decided to haul them downtown in the dead of night for what purpose?"

"Safety. I wanted to store them in my safe." He gave Hugo an assessing look. "It's the times, you know? Protests, rioting. I decided it wasn't safe to keep them at home under the circumstances."

"And your decision to take a swing at two police officers? What's that all about?"

"I thought you were trying to rob me."

"Two sworn officers of the law? Trying to rob you?"

"It's been known to happen."

"The problem with that story is that no one knew you had all this hidden wealth. Or that you'd be transporting it in the wee hours of the morning."

Redman gave a small shake of his head. "How do I know you didn't learn about it," he turned his gaze to Junior, "when eliciting information from my secretary."

"She knew about your stash? Is that why you paid her so handsomely? Because she kept your secrets?"

He said nothing.

Hugo let the silence play out. "I admit the question of who had the combination to the safe had me stumped. Of the people she might have confided in, I couldn't see any of them killing her." He scooped up a handful of coins and let them rain down through his fingers. "I guess I'm a little dense. Then it occurred to me. Who else but the person who would be in charge of the disposition of her estate? The long time friend she trusted. The man she championed and gave her undying loyalty to."

"I didn't kill Ruth."

"No. You simply took advantage of her death. You knew she had something of value in the safe. You knew because she entrusted the combination to you. In the event of her death, someone had to have access to the contents."

"I didn't even know about the safe. Gold is legal tender. Ownership untraceable. You have no proof of your cockamamie story."

"You made a mistake, Redman. You paid Tyrone Pritchett with your ill-gotten gains. He was a small-time dope dealer, didn't know the meaning of the word discretion."

"There's no connection between me and Pritchett."

Hugo took the revolver from his coat pocket and laid it on the desk. "Ballistics will say otherwise. I imagine the rifling on the bullet that blew a hole in Tyrone's skull will prove to be connection enough for any jury. We'll be able to trace the phone calls he made to you demanding something for his silence."

Hugo could sense the debate going on in Redman's mind.

"Call the station, Junior. Have them send a car to escort Mr. Redman to his new home. And the forensics team."

"It was my due!" Redman blurted out. "I had Edward in the palm of my hand. Then Haywood took over. He suspected I was up to something but he couldn't figure it out so he fired me."

The anger bubbled over. The color rose in his cheeks. Spittle formed in the corners of his mouth as he spoke.

"If she had married me I could have saved everything. But the high and mighty Queen of society was appalled by my proposal. I saw it in her eyes."

Hate radiated from his whole being. "So I lived on her charity disguised in the name of *friendship*. A mere pittance of what I lost."

"How did Tyrone know?"

"He saw me leaving the house. She had some documents from Haywood. Another expansion plan he wanted her to approve. I told her I'd drop by and pick them up Saturday morning to look them over.

"When I got there, she didn't answer the door. It was unlocked. So I went in. The cat flew past me. I knew she'd be upset that he'd gotten out. I called to her but got no response.

"I thought maybe she'd had a heart attack or had fallen so I searched the house. I would have never thought to check the attic but I felt a cool draft. The door was open. There she sat, looking like her true self for once.

"That's when I decided to get something of my own back. I went downstairs and found the safe. I'd memorized the combination years ago. When the door swung open I couldn't believe what I was seeing. I had to get it out of the house before her body was discovered."

"Weren't you afraid of being seen taking something from the house?"

"Yes. So I put it in a couple of old suitcases and took them out to the garage. I stored them in the trunk of her car until I could come back and get them. I didn't know who might have seen me arrive. I closed the door to the attic. If anyone saw me enter and leave the house, I could say I found it empty. That Ruth wasn't at home when I got there. I came back that night. Came down the alley and moved the suitcases to my car."

"When did Tyrone see you?"

"As I was leaving Saturday morning. When he brought his aunt to meet you the next day, he discovered that her body hadn't been reported until the afternoon. He called me first thing Monday."

"You didn't give him the song and dance that she wasn't at home when you got there?"

"I couldn't risk it. There was too much at stake." His voice turned more bitter. "I thought it was a heart attack. That they would put her in the ground with no one the wiser."

"Why did you pay him with the coins?"

"That was all I had. In case you haven't noticed, this isn't exactly a thriving practice."

"After the second demand, you knew you had a problem."

"I thought I'd keep him quiet for a while by giving him a large payment on the first demand. I needed time to move the money off-shore. I miscalculated. That only made him greedy for more."

"You should have paid him. You'd be planning your new life in the Bahamas right now." Hugo tossed Redman's keys to Junior. "Bring up the other suitcase."

As Junior hauled an even heavier suitcase up the stairs to Redman's office, Hugo called the station.

The sun brightened the sky with the approaching dawn as two patrolmen loaded Redman into the patrol car. Hugo and Junior stood on the sidewalk in front of the Van Antwerp Building watching. They had cleared out of the lawyer's offices to allow the forensics team to do their job.

"Ballistics on the bullet, huh?"

Hugo shrugged. "Semantics. Besides, they might find the bullet before the trial."

⁂

THE HUGE OAKS, with their trailing tendrils of Spanish moss, cast long shadows as Hugo drove the winding path from the gate keeper's hut to the entrance of the Grand Hotel. A young man hustled to open the driver's door for him. Hugo pressed a couple of dollars into his palm.

"Leave it. I won't be long."

He walked through the lobby that looked more like the great room of a posh but rustic family compound on the water than a commercial enterprise. At the entrance of the bar, Bucky stepped forward with a smile.

"Right this way, sir."

He led Hugo through the bar past a foursome of golfers enjoying their beer and the retelling of their match. An older couple sharing a sandwich with all the cutlery and crystal of a three star restaurant was seated near the doors leading onto the paved patio.

Bucky opened the patio door and ushered Hugo through.

Sharon was seated in an Adirondack chair gazing into the blazing firepit with the view of the bay beyond. She turned her head and smiled when Hugo approached.

"Thank you for coming. I wasn't sure you would."

Hugo took the chair beside her and as he did, Bucky stepped forward for his drink order. Hugo shook his head and Bucky, with a slight inclination of his upper body, disappeared into the bar.

"You wanted to talk to me?"

"Don't be angry."

Hugo turned his gaze from her and stared into the distance. "I'm not sure what you expect of me, Sharon. I've found Ruth's killer and the man who stole her money. You'll have to find someone else to locate your lover for you."

She was silent for a while, her eyes on the distant horizon. "He won't be found. I've known it for a long time but wouldn't accept it."

Hugo didn't want to express any curiosity. He didn't want to be drawn in by her sorrow. "You think he's dead? Why?"

"Tyrone was only gone two days. He lied to Aunt Ruth when he told her he had put Archie on a bus at a crossroad outside Sherbrooke. That's a six day round trip. Five days minimum."

"Why would he kill Archie?"

"I don't know. Maybe Archie regretted his decision and decided he could still make it to Fayetteville in time. Tyrone might have feared he would have to give back the car. An argument. A fight. An accident."

"Ruth didn't question him when there was no word from Archie?"

"Yes. He stuck to his story. He left Archie at the crossroads. I didn't discover that Tyrone was back in town within two days of his departure until after Ruth died."

"How did you find out?"

"A private detective."

"It was you in Paris in early October."

"Yes. I thought he might have gone there. That he was afraid to make contact. He knew the Army would be looking for him."

They sat in silence for a while. The light was fading and the boisterous laughter of the golfers reached them.

Sharon sighed. "It's all my fault. I should have let him go. But Aunt Ruth felt he needed to know."

"That you were pregnant."

"Yes. How did you know?"

"Nothing else had been able to dissuade him from his duty. He grew up without a father. And you gave him a reason that was strong enough to justify his actions."

"Poor fatherless boy. I should never have told him. He might have made it back to me."

"What will you do?"

"Nothing. I lost the baby. Two weeks before Ruth died."

"I'm sorry."

"That night— I needed something. Someone. You have that quality about you, Hugo August, that people turn to when life is too hard. When they need healing. Kindness, perhaps. The solace that only the touch of another can bring."

They sat in silence a while longer then Hugo stood. He took the 1933 Indian head gold eagle from his pocket and placed it in her hand. "This was in Ruth's safe. The rest is in evidence."

She caught his wrist and pressed the coin into his palm. "Keep it. Please."

Hugo shook his head. "I can't."

She folded his fingers over the coin. "For me. As a remembrance. Please."

Hugo looked into her lovely oval face and nodded. He slipped the coin into his pocket and turned toward the patio door to the bar. It opened for him and he stepped through. Bucky closed it quietly behind him.

Coming soon! Check out this teaser chapter of
the Hugo August Detective Series, Book Two:

SHE HAD TO DIE

One

T HE NEON PHOENIX stood out starkly against the night as
it rose above the horizon with wings spread wide. Hugo ran
his palm down his face and felt the stubble of a five o'clock shadow.
He angled his watch toward the dim light of the instrument panel
on the dashboard of the Thunderbird. A quarter past four in the
morning. "Christ."

The two-way radio on the seat next to him crackled with the
dispatcher's voice. "ETA to scene?"

He picked it up and adjusted the volume knob with his thumb.
"Arriving now."

"The forensic team's headed your way."

"Ten-four."

The flashing lights atop a patrol car formed a landmark in the
mist rising off the water that edged both sides of the seven mile long
narrow strip of land that bridged Mobile Bay and linked the city of
Mobile with the Eastern Shore. Hugo pulled onto the oyster shell
parking lot and surveyed the scene as he put the Thunderbird into
park and killed the engine.

Chief Goode was easily identifiable, the beginning of a paunch at
his midsection well defined by the back lighting of the motel entrance.
He stood with another man in civilian clothing. Behind and just to the
right of them, under the peaked portico over the glass double doors
leading into the building, two people stood in intimate conversation.
Smoke from the cigarette in the woman's hand drifted upward.

Hugo folded a stick of Juicy Fruit gum into his mouth and got out of the car.

The chief let his gaze travel over Hugo's tall frame. "You look like shit."

"It's four in the morning."

"You sober?"

"As a judge."

The chief studied Hugo a moment longer. "This is Chief Stanton. Spanish Fort Police."

Hugo shook the man's hand, waiting for an explanation as to why the Mobile Police Chief and, more particularly, *he* was standing outside a motel in the wee hours of the morning in what was clearly not their jurisdiction.

After another brief hesitation, the chief cleared his throat. "We have a murder in one of the rooms. The victim is Stanton's niece. Ruby."

Hugo looked from the chief to Stanton. "How?"

Stanton looked off across the highway into the mist dancing in the swamp grass along the far shore. "Single gunshot to the heart."

"What was she doing here?"

Neither Goode nor Stanton replied.

The female smoker caught Hugo's eye as she ground out her cigarette with the toe of her shoe. One corner of her mouth lifted in a knowing half smile as she touched her companion on the arm and the two of them went through the double doors into the motel lobby.

"Okay," Hugo said. "The forensics team is on the way. Anything I need to know before they get here? Like why we're here and not the state police? Or the county?"

"Ruby was engaged to Arnie Hollingsworth. He's one of the highway patrol officers for Baldwin County. She broke it off about a year and a half ago." Stanton rubbed the back of his neck and exhaled a weary sigh. "And I don't want the new sheriff all up in my business, if you want to know the truth of it."

Chief Goode gave Stanton a slap of consolation on his upper arm. "Buzz and I go way back, don't we?"

Stanton nodded, studied the ground at his feet, and blinked rapidly. "God Almighty," he said in a soft voice. "How am I going to tell Nora?"

Goode cleared his throat. "Look, Buzz, you pull your guy and high tail it out of here before anyone shows up. We'll do what we can to keep everything as low key as possible. Won't mention the family connection but you know it'll get out. Be sure Nora's prepared. And Ruby's mama."

Hugo and the chief watched as Stanton walked toward the motel entrance. Just before he reached the door, he swayed a couple of steps, a small drunken dance of grief, or perhaps it was simply a trick of the flashing light of the neon sign. The weight of the door almost defeated him as he went inside to collect the patrolman guarding the room. As soon as it closed behind him, Goode turned to Hugo, his voice a fierce, low growl.

"Keep a lid on this, August. Not one word to the press about it. Not one, you hear me? Make sure everyone else gets the message." He opened the door of his car and as he slid onto the seat he looked up at Hugo. "I want a detailed report of the initial findings and progress reports on every little detail. I don't want to be blindsided. This is going to be one hell of a mess."

The chief sped away as Stanton and a uniformed patrolman came out of the entrance of the motel. Both of them looked shell shocked. Neither of them spoke to Hugo as they got into the patrol car. As they pulled away, the driver killed the flashing lights and turned east toward Spanish Fort.

The smoker was behind the registration counter when Hugo entered the motel. She was already lighting another cigarette. With a flick of her head she sent blond curls cascading behind her shoulder. She appraised him from head to toe as he crossed the small lobby.

"What's your name?" Hugo asked.

"Dixie."

"You the night manager?"

She nodded.

"Who found the body?"

"Me."

"What time?"

"Two forty-five or there about."

"You randomly check the rooms at two forty-five every morning?"

That garnered him a hint of a smile.

"Not usually. She wanted a wake-up call for two. No one answered so after a couple more calls, I decided she had left already and I went around to check the room."

"Was anyone else in the room?"

"Not when I got there."

"Anyone come and go before you checked the room at two forty-five?"

"Not that I saw."

"How'd you get in?"

"Pass key."

"Anyone else have a key?"

"There are generally two keys for each room. The guest gets one. Sometimes two if the circumstances call for it."

"And what might those circumstances be?"

"Oh, shuga, you know what circumstances. This ain't the Ritz."

"By that you mean The Thunderbird Inn is a rendezvous establishment."

"You didn't hear it from me."

"Were you here when she checked in?"

Dixie nodded.

"When was that?"

"About ten, I think. Something like that."

"Was anyone with her?"

"No."

"Anyone show up looking for her?"

"Not that I know of."

Hugo looked past Dixie into the open office where a pegboard mounted to the wall held keys under their allotted numbers. "Which room is it?"

"Lucky number seven."

"You think it's lucky?"

"She did."

"Yeah?"

"Always the same room. Lucky number seven."

"She asked for it specifically. On a number of occasions."

"You are a bright boy."

Hugo let his gaze travel around the lobby. Off to his right a glass door led into a darkened room that appeared to be the restaurant. To his left a long hallway was the conduit to the rooms. There were only two dimly lit fixtures spaced far apart along the whole length. At the far end he could barely make out what appeared to be a door to the outside.

"Is the door at the end of the hallway locked at night?"

"It's supposed to be."

"Was it tonight?"

"I haven't checked."

"Did the police officer who was here earlier check it?"

"I don't know."

Hugo walked around the counter and into the office. Hanging under number seven was a single key. "Is this the key you used?"

"No." Dixie opened a drawer of the registration counter and pulled out a ring of keys. "People are always walking off with the keys so we keep a back-up on a master ring." She handed them to Hugo then leaned against the doorframe of the office, the smoke from her cigarette spiraling upward. "They're all marked with the room numbers."

"Is the desk always manned?"

"Mostly."

Hugo looked around the office at the recliner with a blanket over the arm rest, the empty coffee cup with Dixie's hot pink lipstick smudging the rim, and a plate with the remains of a sandwich on it.

"Did you use the master key to let the police into the room?"

"Yes."

He nodded at the single key still on the pegboard. "Has anyone touched this one?"

She shrugged. "Not since it was placed there after the last occupant, I guess."

Hugo opened drawers on the office desk until he found a stack of envelopes. He took a tissue from the box of Kleenex on the desk and used it to remove the key from the pegboard and drop it into the envelope. Dixie watched without comment.

"Did anyone go into the room after you found the body?"

He saw the flicker of indecision before she could control her reaction.

"Who?"

"I didn't know what to do. So, I told Harry."

"The guy you were standing with outside?"

She nodded.

"Did he go in alone?"

"No, I was with him."

"Did either of you touch anything?"

She thought a second and shook her head. "No. Except the light switch. When I opened the door, I flipped the switch. That's when I saw her."

"How did you know she was dead?"

"The bullet hole in her chest. And the blood."

"You didn't touch her? Check for a pulse?"

Dixie shook her head and looked away from his steady regard as she rubbed her hands up and down her upper arms.

Hugo jangled the master keys in his hand then walked the length of the hallway to the emergency escape door. There was a deadbolt lock mounted above the door handle which had a thumb lock. When Hugo turned it, the door opened onto the pre-dawn light and the smell of damp and decay.

He retraced his steps to room number seven. It was locked. He used the master key and stepped inside, closing the door behind him.

The room lay in darkness, broken only by pulsing flashes of neon light slanting intermittently through the partially open venetian blinds.

Ruby lay on her back on the floor at the foot of the bed. Her face was turned slightly toward the window, her lips parted as if in a sigh, her eyes open as if watching the strobing light of the motel sign. One hand lay on the floor, palm up, in the tangle of long red curls that framed her face, the other lay across her abdomen. Her legs were pulled up slightly as one does in sleep. A short, sheer robe was tied at the waist. A single dark ribbon of red trailed from an entry wound on the inside rise of her left breast. Her face and limbs were the white of a delicately sculpted marble statue. She was beautiful, and she was dead.

Acknowledgements

THROUGHOUT MY WRITING career many generous people have helped me along the way. For *The Rat Catcher*, Jeff Johnston deserves my undying gratitude in helping me discover the true image of Hugo August. Jeff's talent as a photographer is phenomenal and his ability to manipulate images to evoke a sense of time and place is extraordinary. I can't thank him enough.

I wish I had Ginger Davis McSween's ability to retain information, attract lifelong friends, and inspire confidences. Her many friends throughout the years have given her a wealth of knowledge about the Vietnam era and she has helped me bring life and authenticity to Hugo's story.

This book is, of course, a work of fiction. There are instances where poetic license was necessary for the purpose of story. That said, without the fundamental facts of how the Mobile Police Department operated in the sixties and seventies, this story would have no legs. For that I'm grateful for Joseph (Joe) V. Connick III, a former sergeant with the Mobile Police force, and currently a gaming enforcement officer for the Mobile County Sheriff's Department. His generosity and engaging stories of law enforcement have been a gold mine of information.

Lastly, I want to thank Rebecca Bayne of *Becky's Graphic Design LLC*. She is many things: techno savvy, a talented graphic designer, knowledgeable not only in formatting and design to bring your book to a finished product, but a whiz at social media, web design and function, marketing and promotion.

The creative process if often a tough slog but these talented people and many others have helped me bring my vision to life. Thanks to you all.

About the Author

REBECCA BARRETT WRITES historical fiction, short stories of the South, children's stories, cozy mysteries, and post-apocalyptic fiction (writing as Campbell O'Neal), in addition to the *Hugo August Detective Series*. An avid reader all her life and a product of "front porch" socializing, she became a story-teller at an early age. Her publishing imprint—Witch Creek Publishing—is inspired by a humorously paradoxical sign welcoming visitors to her hometown: The Churches of Witch Creek Welcome You!

Her cozy *Familiar Legacy* mysteries feature Trouble—a handsome, sleek, black cat detective—in *Trouble in Paradise* and *Trouble in Dixie*. Rebecca has written two books in this series written by multiple authors (The Mad Catters) who follow the antics of super-sleuth Trouble as he lands in first one crime scene then another. Of course, the humans help a little. These mysteries are fun and light-hearted and just perfect for a beach read or a rainy day.

Rebecca Barrett resides in the lovely artist colony of Fairhope, AL, on the shores of Mobile Bay where she draws inspiration and joy.

Visit the author's website **rebeccabarrett.com** to enjoy some of her short stories.

Leave a Review!

FOR A SELF-PUBLISHED author like myself, reviews mean the world! Please leave an honest review—don't worry, you won't hurt my feelings—and tell me what you truly thought. I read each and every one!

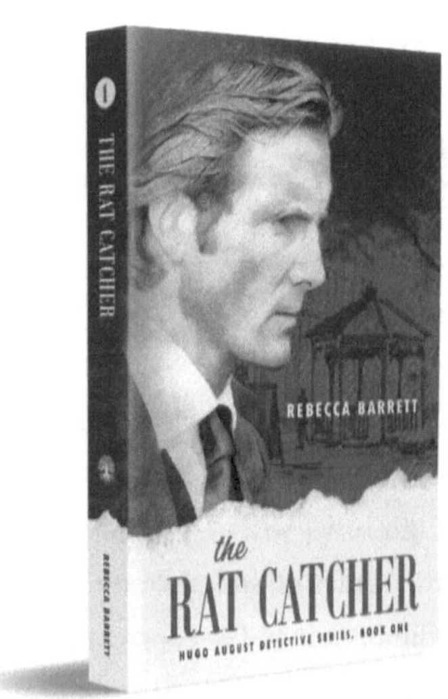

REVIEW ON

amazon

goodreads

AND OTHER
ONLINE RETAILERS